LINES OF INQUIRY

A DCI EVAN WARLOW THRILLER

RHYS DYLAN

WYRMWOOD
BOOKS

COPYRIGHT

eBook ISBN - 978-1-915185-16-7
Print ISBN - 978-1-915185-17-4

Published by Wyrmwood Books.
An imprint of Wyrmwood Media.

EXCLUSIVE OFFER

Please look out for the link near the end of the book for your chance to sign up to the no-spam guaranteed VIP Reader's Club and receive a FREE DCI Warlow novella as well as news of upcoming releases.

Or you can go direct to my website: https://rhysdylan.com and sign up now.

Remember, you can unsubscribe at any time and I promise won't send you any spam. Ever.

OTHER DCI WARLOW NOVELS

THE ENGINE HOUSE
CAUTION DEATH AT WORK
ICE COLD MALICE
SUFFER THE DEAD
GRAVELY CONCERNED
A MARK OF IMPERFECTION
BURNT ECHO
A BODY OF WATER

CHAPTER ONE

MORFYDD DAVIDSON WAS the first out of the water on Telpyn Beach that morning. She wore a Zone 3 medium – just – wetsuit designed to keep her body warm in the cold waters of the ocean. Despite the promise, and though the Bristol Channel water temperature wasn't anywhere near arctic in West Wales in October, the Indian Ocean it was not. She stood, hands on knees, sucking in air after a thirty-minute swim in the open sea. Two minutes later, her training partner, Nerys Mears, joined her after putting in an extra few yards of freestyle.

'Please tell me,' Morfydd said between gasps, 'that this gets flippin' easier.'

Nerys grinned. 'It's what, week three?'

Morfydd nodded. 'With all of winter…' she heaved in a couple of deep breaths before finishing the sentence, '… to go.'

'And the summer after,' Nerys reminded her in an attempt at reassurance.

Morfydd tried not to be too miffed that Nerys, whose wetsuit was a definite small, seemed to be puffing far less than she was. 'We'll either be dolphins by the time next

September comes around, or dead from hypothermia. And this isn't a beach that has one of those disgusting sewage pipes emptying into the waters, is it?' Despite her best efforts, she'd swallowed a good cupful of seawater, with all the biological cornucopia it contained.

Nerys grinned and stroked stringy, sea-slicked hair out of her face to reveal a grin behind mauve-tinged lips. 'No way back, Mor. You signed up.'

'I know. But only after half a dozen tequila shots. Sam says he can feel a fin growing out of my back.'

'Tell him to keep his grubby paws to himself. Come on, let's run. That'll warm you up.'

Morfydd groaned but followed Nerys in a jog up towards the northeast corner of the beach and the trail that would take them to the cliff-top path. This being the last Sunday in October and, thanks to daylight saving, it was light at 7am. It had not been this time last week or the week before and wouldn't be in a month's time. But at least their early morning sessions would still work for a while longer.

Fitness and charity had a lot to answer for.

The girls had been in Tenby for the weekend of the Iron Man triathlon and been inspired. As one well might, watching it unfold on a beautiful September late-summer day from a packed pub and a Sunday lunch with partners. It had been Sam, Morfydd's significant other, who'd said it. Looking out of the pub window and seeing the crowds, and the cyclists still dripping from their swim, zip past, he uttered the fateful words. 'Anyone fancy actually doing that?'

It had snowballed from there. Neither of the men had taken the bait. But the girls, both fit in their own neat way, thanks to regular leisure centre swimming and gym – well regular-ish in Morfydd's case – read the derision in both Sam and Jared's faces when Nerys had not immediately dismissed the idea. The girls took up the challenge there and then in a fit of Prosecco-fuelled bravado. And Nerys, being Nerys, had drawn up a twelve-month training programme, which included open water swimming. Or, as Sam had described it, open water avoiding the turds and jellyfish. The schedule began the month after the last Iron Man, or woman, had crossed the line. This was the third Sunday they'd pitched up after a ten-mile bike ride to an almost deserted beach for their swim. Telpyn was far enough from habitation to deter the casual visitor. You had to drive here, for one thing. And the early start was even more of a deterrent for ordinary ramblers.

Still, the rain held off, and the clouds hung sparse and pink-edged as the women ran up the beach and across the pebbles to the track. Some runners appeared on the path above, and they'd seen a few dog walkers on the beach itself. But no one else had swum.

No one else was mad enough.

They'd locked their bikes together on the field side of the hedge bordering the road, out of sight of casual thieves, they hoped. The cycle back home made up the final part of their regimen.

As the women crested the cliff-top track, they were met by an offshore breeze. A mild one this morning, but that, too, would get worse as winter and the Atlantic gales that came with it started howling in. Still, in the race, there would be no puffy anoraks or sweatshirts to slip on thanks to it always being held in late summer. But that seemed, this brisk autumn morning, a very long way off.

Morfydd heard Sam's sleepy groan echo in her head. The one he'd uttered as she'd slid out of bed an hour and a half ago in the darkness.

'You must be bloody mad.'

She gritted her teeth against the cold. He was probably right. But once Nerys got the bug, there was no stopping her. And in all honesty, Morfydd had become fed up with turning dutifully up to watch Sam and Jared play football on a Saturday. Tenby loitered in Division Two of the county soccer leagues. That meant twenty-four games in the season and cup matches. She and Nerys didn't go to all the games; they did not consider themselves pathetic WAGS. When they did go, it was only to home fixtures. But one thing they'd bonded over, having met through their partners' friendship, was the competitive streak that ran through both. A streak that remained unsatisfied as supporters of Sam and Jared. And although neither man was stupid enough to say it – they wouldn't dare – both boys would be silently waiting for them to fail in this Iron Man endeavour. They still might fail, of course. But it hadn't happened yet. And secretly, Morfydd couldn't wait to see that look of surprise and, dare she imagine it, admiration on Sam's face when she and Nerys crossed the finish line. More than enough motivation there for a little girl power.

They were halfway between the turnoff to the beach and the bikes when the staccato cracks of gunshots erupted. Five, in rapid succession. Neither woman stopped, but Nerys said, 'They've started early today.'

"They" referenced the clay pigeon shooting range over the hill to the north. Gunshots were not an unusual noise to anyone visiting Telpyn Beach. Morfydd didn't bother responding to Nerys's comment, but she noted the sudden flurry of crows that took off ahead of them. Spooked by the noise, no doubt.

They got to the bikes and unlocked them. Morfydd steeled herself for the cycle back to the basement apartment on Victoria Street in Tenby she shared with Sam. It would be a little further for Nerys, where she and Jared were renting up in Oakridge. It was only once Morfydd wheeled her bike through the steel gate guarding the path she noticed the marked police vehicle parked on the other side of the road with one of its doors open. Parked and blocking the entrance to a water treatment works a quarter of a mile further in.

She turned with eyebrows raised to Nerys, who grinned. 'They finally caught up with you, Mor?'

'Hilarious.' But then Morfydd frowned as the memory of the shots and the crows nudged its way back into her mind.

Surely not.

The coast road was empty. No sign of traffic. To the right of the police car, another car was parked, tucked in behind the hedge on the opposite side of the road, much like the girls had placed their bikes. Morfydd didn't think you could park there. Maybe that's why the police turned up.

The groan, from the other side of the hedge, put an end to all her wonderings.

She turned her face to Nerys once more. 'Hear that?'

'I did.'

The women pushed their cycles over the road and leant them against a steel farm gate next to where the police car had parked over a cattle grid. They stood behind the vehicle, trying to see over the hedge into the field to the second car.

'Hello?' Morfydd asked. 'Are you okay?'

Nothing for several seconds, and then, again, a croaked and harrowing, 'Help.'

Morfydd wriggled around the side of the parked car. The gap between it and the gatepost was narrow and her wet suit squelched against the paintwork. She squeezed through far enough to get a view into the field. When she did, the breath seized in her throat.

Three people lay on the ground.

One face down, one on his side, another, the groaner, on her back.

The one on his side and the groaner were in uniform.

The third, an unmoving man, was not.

Every one of them had blood either on their bodies or pooling around them.

'Please …' Another plea from the female police officer. She raised a weak hand.

Morfydd turned to Nerys and shouted in a quavering voice.

'Nine, nine, nine, Nerys. Phone nine, nine, nine. These people… they're police… I think they've been shot.'

CHAPTER TWO

DCI Evan Warlow of the Dyfed Powys Police watched his toddler grandson, Leo, ignore the animal picture book his father, Alun, was attempting to show him.

'Leo, what's this? What's this, Leo?' Alun's repeated attempt at engaging the child for the purpose of demonstrating his development was meeting with a distinct lack of cooperation as Leo squirmed away from Alun's restraining hands.

Next to them on the settee, Leo's mother, Reba, looked on with a mixture of amusement and exasperation.

'Oh, come on, Leo. Show your *Tadcu* how clever you are, mate.' Alun's persistent cajoling was getting nowhere.

No, that wasn't strictly true. It was getting somewhere. That somewhere being a point where Leo was going to throw a toddler wobbly.

'He's not going to cooperate, Al,' Reba said, wearing a resigned smile.

With a final desperate wriggle, Leo slid off his father's lap and tottered out of view of the phone's camera. Off stage, the word 'Oppa' could clearly be heard.

Alun growled in frustration and looked up into the

camera. 'I swear to God, he was saying horse all morning. He learned that today. He can say mama, dada, dog, and car. If he sees a baby, he says baba and he's repeating stuff. If Reebs says bath time, he sings it back at her.'

'Wow, another half a dozen words and he'll have the same vocab as you, then, Al.' The insult, delivered from Warlow's living room in Nevern, Pembrokeshire, and travelling the almost fifteen thousand miles to Perth in Western Australia, contained no malice. It was exactly the sort of insult you'd expect from a younger brother, and Tom Warlow wore a broad grin as he delivered it.

'Very funny, Tom.' Alun sent back a faux smile that made Tom's grin broader.

'Oppa,' Leo's voice wailed off camera.

'Okay, Leo, okay.' Reba eased herself up off the sofa. Not an easy feat given her thirty-nine-weeks pregnant condition. She leaned forward towards the phone. 'Let me set up my child with his Hopper Hog fix on the TV and I'll be back in a jiffy.'

When she'd left, Alun gave a little shake of his head. 'Honestly, that cartoon is like crystal meth, only a lot cheaper. Leo's addicted.'

Warlow had never seen an episode, but he'd heard much the same about the purple pig's attraction from Detective Sergeant Gil Jones. His colleague had grandchildren of his own and had seen more episodes, often the same repeated episodes, than he could shake a 'two-by-four at', in his own words. Warlow, aka *Tadcu*, the Welsh word for grandfather, being on the other side of the world to his only grandchild, had so far escaped that porcine pleasure. Though he suspected it might be a temporary respite.

They'd set up the morning call because there was a lot to discuss. Tom and Jodie, his partner of two years, rang mid-week to say they were coming down for the weekend. Or at least, part of the weekend since today was Sunday.

They'd driven down from London on Friday night but then gone off to hike and spend a romantic night away in an Airbnb on the coast. At least, that had been the plan as announced by Tom. What actually happened was that Tom took Jodie to a Michelin-starred restaurant in Aberystwyth, walked her along the seafront on a cold and starry night, got down on one knee, and proposed.

A proposal that Jodie accepted.

And so, here they were, the following morning in Warlow's living room at Ffau'r Blaidd in Nevern enjoying a brunch of scrambled egg and smoked salmon and sharing this auspicious occasion with the rest of the Warlow diaspora via the wonders of modern technology. Warlow had splashed out on a video camera microphone system that allowed the whole of his living room to be beamed through the stratosphere, or whatever sphere such things travelled in. Alun always complained about the poor quality of the image on Warlow's phone when they video-called that way. A phone which, Warlow admitted, was not exactly the latest model. But then Alun was always complaining about something. Tom, the doctor, inherited Warlow's calmer, analytical genes. Whereas Alun had most of his feisty mother's.

Reba arrived back in a shot. 'Right, I'm back.' She held on to her bump and folded one knee under her as she sat. 'Come on, let's see it up close, Jodie.'

The woman who was going to be Warlow's second daughter-in-law held up her hand and advanced across the room towards the camera perched on top of the TV. A magnified image of a sparkly engagement ring filled the screen.

'OMG,' Reba said. 'It's gorgeous.'

'How many goes on the claw grabber at the funfair did it take to snaffle that, then, Tom?'

Tom snorted. Alun's banter always had that slightly

acerbic, older-brother edge to it. After rotating her hand for a three-sixty view, Jodie, hippy-ish in stripy socks and a corduroy pinafore dress, rejoined Tom on the sofa.

'So, when is the big day?' Reba asked.

'Hold your horses,' Tom said. 'Sometime next year, but there's no actual save the date.'

'Are you going abroad? Large or small? Church or registry?' Alun wasn't letting them off the hook.

Jodie remained in a copacetic post-engagement haze. 'Small-ish. My sister had the whole nine yards—'

'Was that the length of her train?' Tom quipped.

'Yeah.' Jodie nodded. 'But that isn't me. I mean, what about yours and Al's, Reba? How many guests?'

Jodie'd missed it because she and Tom had not been an item then, but Warlow remembered the numbers down to the last cousin. A hundred and twenty. Not huge, but not small at his ex-wife's request. She'd wanted a big splash and convinced Reba to invite the hordes. Warlow hadn't enjoyed it. Not all of it anyway. Mainly because of trying to limit the damage his wife might inflict on the proceedings. He'd even topped up the wine bottle she kept guzzling from with water. It worked to a degree in that it delayed the inevitable alcohol fuelled melt-down for a good hour. By the time she got to the stage when she couldn't stand up, he'd already taken her to their room at the hotel where the reception was being held and let her pass out, placed safely in the recovery position. Just as he had so many times before. By then it was 11.30pm. The band played until midnight. The last half hour of the wedding, that thirty minutes without Jeez Denise, was the half hour Warlow enjoyed the most.

'What do you think, Dad?'

Tom's question brought Warlow back to the present from the unhappy mental jaunt thoughts of Denise unfailingly took him on.

'Your day. You need to choose,' he said.

'That's what people always say,' Reba agreed. 'But often you end up trying to please everyone. Relatives, I mean. My advice is not to; try and please everyone, I mean.'

Alun's lips stayed zipped shut. Though Warlow had tried his absolute best to keep Denise on a tight leash and not let her brash drunkenness impinge too much, there'd inevitably been one or two car-crash incidents. Her slurring attempt at trying to sing one of the band's songs having snatched the microphone from the singer was a prime example. As was her insistence on engaging Reba's dad in a bump-and-grind dance while whooping like a Howler monkey. Luckily, most of the guests had been wedding-oiled by that stage and bought into the episodes as Alun's up-for-it mum having a good time.

If only they knew.

But this time, Tom and Jodie's marriage would be Denise-free. Bittersweet, no doubt. Unless the harridan could come back from the dead for one last excruciating zombie spectacle. Now that was an image to conjure with.

'Well, you'll have a while to think it through.' Warlow dragged his thoughts away from the troubling image of Denise as one of the living dead. 'What's the average time from engagement to marriage these days?'

'I read in Harper's it was twenty months,' Reba said.

'Plenty of time, then,' Warlow added, and shut up because he realised that could be interpreted in several ways. Plenty of time to plan on the one hand, or plenty of time for things to go mammaries up on the other.

Tom and Jodie exchanged a knowing glance. If they'd talked about it, they were not prepared to share.

At his knee, Warlow's black Lab Cadi nudged her snout into his hand, and he fondled her head and ears in response. He wondered, not for the first time, how she sensed when he needed that little bit of contact. That reassurance and succour. Of course, on one level, he knew it was she who craved it. But then again, it was uncanny when, in moments of stress or turmoil, she'd simply come over and touch him. Let him know she was there.

Dogs really were a bloody miracle.

'What about you, Reba? How are you feeling?' Warlow asked.

'Yes,' Jodie chipped in. 'What is it, four more days?'

'If she gets any bigger, we'll have to get her airlifted,' Alun said with a grin that faded into a sickly thing in the glare of Reba's glower. 'Just a joke, Reebs,' he added weakly.

'Yeah, well, next time you carry an alien in your womb for nine months. Let's see who's laughing at the end of that.' Reba, blonde and pale, despite, or perhaps because of, the Western Australian sun, still bloomed in the late stages of her pregnancy as she tilted her head in challenge. Alun didn't respond. Very wisely, thought Warlow, not bothering to hide his grin. Reba had lost none of her Yorkshire accent, or her no-nonsense attitude. He liked her a lot.

'Were you late with Leo?' Jodie asked.

'A bit. But I don't want to faff about like last time.'

'Fourteen hours of labour isn't funny,' Alun said.

'No.' Reba nodded. 'I'm not having any of that. We're staying here until we see the head.'

'Don't say that.' Alun winced.

'Don't be such a wimp,' Reba teased.

'So long as the taxi driver's a midwife, right?' Warlow said.

Alun frowned. 'Dad, there's a terrible echo on the sound here. Where did you get this system from? The pound shop?'

Warlow said nothing, but he saw Tom drop his head

and smile. Alun's short fuse was never too far away. So, never mind the technological miracle of being able to talk to everyone live. That little echo would irritate and grow in Alun's brain like a parasitic worm. But, Warlow surmised, if that was the only negative trait Denise passed on, he'd take that in a heartbeat.

Warlow's phone buzzed in his pocket. He'd had the sense to put the thing on silent so as not to invoke Alun's ire should it ring during their call. But the name filling the display when he glanced at the screen had his radar bleeping.

Detective Superintendent Buchannan.

A call from his boss that he ought to take. He waved the phone at the TV with an apologetic grimace.

'What, on a Sunday?' Alun registered his objection to Warlow's work impinging on family time yet again.

Warlow didn't bother responding to that. But Alun's objections followed him to the door. 'We still haven't talked about your trip,' he said through the screen.

Warlow half turned. 'January, we said, wasn't it?'

'Yes. That's only three months away, Dad.'

'Gives me a chance to tie some corks onto my bush hat, then.'

Very lame as banter went. But Warlow didn't give his eldest son any more of a chance to complain. He'd heard it all before. Alun's resentment about missed attendances at rugby matches and late pickups from friends' houses during his teen years had been well documented on more than one occasion. Some of that was down to his mother's descent into alcoholism. Some of it was down to Warlow's desire to escape from her through his work. Alun had cause to grumble, and even as a grown-up, he could be unforgiving and petulant when it came to family.

'Besides, Tom is doing all the research for flights.' Warlow threw his youngest a glance.

'Am I?' Tom looked surprised.

'I thought—'

'Take no notice, Evan. I'm on the case.' Jodie smiled at him.

'See, we're on the case.' Warlow beamed at the camera on top of the TV. 'I'll be two minutes.' He nodded at Reba and turned, with Cadi on his heels, towards his sunroom to take the call from Buchannan, leaving everyone to wonder if their cosy Sunday chat was over.

When Warlow returned to their presence a few moments later, the look on his face told them it was. DCI Warlow had work to do.

Crime had no respect for the Sabbath, that was clear. And this one, from the details he'd just been given, sounded like a real horror show.

CHAPTER THREE

UNIFORMS HAD SHUT the road at Telpyn Beach by the time Warlow got there. Vehicles were getting through slowly and only after their occupants had been quizzed. Warlow knew the road. Not popular or busy, but still the scenic route between the beaches of Pendine and Amroth. A nice spin on a Sunday afternoon under normal circumstances.

But circumstances were far from normal today.

The theory behind the checkpoint centred around the hope that some drivers might be local. It was the end of October, and half term was over. Most people using this stretch today were regular users, not tourists. Either going somewhere, or returning from wherever they had been earlier, and so had used the road already. If they'd seen anything unusual, the police wanted to know.

As laser-focused detection work went, it was about as sharp a tool as an elephant's rear end. And since that was situated diametrically opposite the pointy tusks, it wasn't sharp in the slightest. But then, if an elephant sat on you, it would be just as effective as spearing you with its tusk.

Wouldn't it?

Warlow, sitting in the crawling traffic, shook his head as

he tried to analyse the elephant metaphor that had wormed its way into his head. What had elephants' arses to do with anything? But then, up ahead, the shape of a man dressed in some kind of voluminous cape came into focus and the elephant reference crystallised. The shape, accompanied by a uniformed officer, was walking towards the point in the tailback where Warlow sat. After a double take or two, Warlow realised that the voluminous shape was, in fact, DS Gil Jones, his colleague in the Response Team that Warlow ran whenever a serious crime, especially one involving murder or potential murder, arose on the patch.

Gil was a bigger man than Warlow, taller, but more than a bit heavier and rounder. Warlow, through walks with Cadi, had been attempting to affect two out of the three separating features. Not enough, by any means. Both men agreed Gil was a work in progress. Warlow's mental acrobatics in linking an elephant's backside with the sight of the oncoming sergeant felt uncharitable, to say the least, but it must have had something to do with the small, dark tent Gil seemed to be wearing.

The officers progressed until, sure enough, they arrived opposite the passenger-side window and leaned over. Warlow wound the window down.

'Morning,' Gil said, a serious edge to his normally jovial demeanour. And what were those traces of white stuff on his neck? 'I've brought DC Chalmers with me, sir.' Gil's use of the formal address was unusual between the two men. Gil was older, but the relationship they'd developed over the months had put them on first-name terms, unless other officers, especially junior officers, were in earshot. 'He's volunteered to sit in the driving seat and take your car to the field we've designated as parking. Free you up to get to the scene on foot if you're happy?'

Warlow nodded. It made sense. He put the car in

neutral but left the engine running, grabbed a jacket, and exited with a nod to Chalmers.

'I'll look after her, sir,' said the young officer, who looked to be about sixteen years old but who was probably a good decade older.

'You'll bring me my keys?'

Chalmers's turn to nod. 'I'll find you, sir.'

Warlow slid on his jacket. The blustery on-shore breeze nipped at his torso through his buttoned-up suit. He'd not bothered with a tie. It was Sunday, after all. As he zipped up the waxed Barbour, he took a moment to assess Gil's unusual apparel. Close up, it was more poncho than cape in a dark nylon material. They started walking, but Warlow couldn't prevent his gaze drifting up over Gil's neck.

'There's a bit of something there on you.' Warlow pointed at his own neck to show. 'Shaving soap?'

Gil frowned and rubbed at his neck. 'Flour. Thought I'd washed it off.'

Warlow nodded. 'Flour. Of course. And the poncho?'

Gil's expression darkened, and he put both hands up. '*Er mwyn yr Arglwydd,* I've already been asked how many weeks pregnant I am.'

'It's an unusual fashion choice, you must admit.'

'Given to me as a present by a colleague abroad. It's a US police surplus SWAT rain poncho.'

'Naturally. And are we expecting a typhoon?'

Gil provided the effigy of a smile. 'No, but tomorrow is Halloween. My daughter had the bright idea of making a scary video for her kids. And guess who was given the role of Uncle Fester?'

'Does he wear a poncho?'

'This is what the wardrobe department, i.e., the Lady Anwen, came up with. It's the only voluminous black thing that fitted.'

'I thought it was made to measure,' Warlow said, his face straight.

'Side splitting. I put flour on my face and the girls, my granddaughters, had a whale of a time putting dark makeup around my eyes. Took a bloody age to get that stuff off, I can tell you. Worst of all, we were out in the park when I got the call. My daughter's idea as there are some old ruins there. They wanted atmosphere. I didn't have time to change. Scrubbed my face with sterile wipes as I drove here. I think I've taken most of my eyelid skin off.'

'Uncle Fester, eh? We'll be fine if we need a torch. All you'd need to do is stick a light bulb in your mouth.'

Gil glanced down at himself. 'I will get rid of this… garment as soon as possible. Unfortunately, being nylon, it retains the heat.'

'The sweat, you mean?'

'I only have a T-shirt on underneath.'

'What does it say? Available for kids' parties?'

'I'm not answering any more clothing-related questions without a solicitor.'

They walked on towards the police tape cordoning off the road and the entrance into the fields where the response vehicle was still parked.

'Who's here?' Warlow asked, switching to professional mode.

'Catrin and Rhys.'

'The people who found the mess?'

Gil nodded. 'They're warming up in one of the vehicles. Catrin and Rhys are over there. DI Allanby has gone to talk to one of the shot officers.'

Warlow ground his teeth together. Those were not the words he wanted to hear at any point in his career. He reached the tape and nodded to the crime scene officer who proffered a sheet stuck to a clipboard for him to sign in. He did so and walked past, all thoughts of Gil's amusing poncho evaporating as he got down to the business he was paid to do.

———

DS CATRIN RICHARDS sat in the front of a marked response vehicle, with DC Rhys Harries in the seat behind. The women who'd called in the horrifying discovery were sitting in the back seat of a different vehicle with its heater on, awaiting their return. Morfydd and Nerys had become seriously cold waiting around for the emergency services to arrive. Not surprising since they'd been in wet suits fresh from the ocean. The paramedics who'd dealt with them had wrapped them in space blankets. But by the time Rhys and Catrin had arrived half an hour ago, both the women were in shock. Traumatised by what they'd seen. A state not helped by being almost hypothermic. Catrin got them out of the wind, into the car and suggested hot drinks. The detectives left the women to warm up and commandeered a driver and a marked car to drive them to Amroth in search of a café. They'd used farm tracks to bypass the congested road.

Job done, they were on the way back with two cups of hot tea for the witnesses and a coffee each for themselves.

'Do you do Halloween, sarge?' Rhys asked. The café in Amroth had been all guns blazing with pumpkins, bats suspended from the ceiling on string, and a skeleton at one end of the counter.

'Oh, yes,' Catrin said. 'Me and Craig do the full Monty. He goes zombie and I dress as an axe murderer. That's how we open the door to the trick-or-treaters.'

'Really?' Rhys grinned.

Catrin turned in her seat, scorn etched into her features. 'No. Not really. I honestly do not know when, or why, it became such a… *Thing*. You haven't been able to move in the shops for fake blood and plastic tarantulas for weeks.'

'Trick or treat is good, mind. I loved it as a kid. I carried a bag to keep my scoff in.'

'No surprises there.' She glanced at the half-eaten carrot cake on his lap. 'I mean, some of it is interesting, admittedly. It's a pagan festival, after all.'

'I thought it was American.'

'No. European. But the Americans have taken it over. Now it's all plastic pumpkins, scary masks, and overindulging in cheap sweets.'

'Don't forget the vampire bats.'

Catrin, irritated in part by Rhys's ignorance, and by the light-hearted nature of this conversation, realised that it was his way of dealing with a harrowing situation. A coping mechanism. On the one hand, it seemed wrong to be joking about Halloween with two of their colleagues in hospital. But if there was one thing she'd learnt working in this team, it was that being dour and indulging in catastrophic thinking got you nowhere. It certainly got you nowhere with DS Gil Jones. And as for Warlow, he'd be seething at what had happened. But if Rhys came out with one of his classic non sequiturs, he'd crack a smile or a chortle. Being miserable on their colleagues' behalf would not help them catch whoever did this. Being determined would. Warlow had said that on more than one occasion.

So, Catrin thought about explaining that the bat side of Halloween came from an old tradition of lighting bonfires to attract insects, which would attract bats. Just a kid's game. Nothing more than that. The vampire bit was pure Hollywood. But she reined that little biting comment in and went for placation instead. 'Well, I'm not a pagan and we don't do trick or treat in our house.'

'Shame,' Rhys said through a mouthful of carrot cake. 'I can just see you as an axe woman.'

'Thanks.'

'And Craig is halfway to being a zombie at the best of times.'

Catrin threw him a look that would cut glass. 'I'll be sure to tell him you said that.'

Rhys grinned.

They reached the field where the ambulances, crime scene investigation vehicles, and a cluster of police cars, both marked and unmarked, were parked.

'Right, we'll take one witness each. You stay in this car; I'll go to the one they're in and send one back to you.' She picked up a tea via its cardboard sleeve. 'You take Morfydd Davidson, I'll do Nerys Mears. And make sure you brush those crumbs off your trousers. Let's at least try to be professional about this, even if circumstances aren't ideal.'

The smile slipped from Rhys's face. 'I haven't forgotten, sarge.' His gaze flicked to the left. 'Isn't that DCI Warlow's Jeep?'

'It is. So, we'd better get a move on or there'll be uncomfortable questions to answer. And they won't be about Halloween.'

CHAPTER FOUR

THE CRIME SCENE INVESTIGATORS, squeaky clean in white Tyvek coveralls, had erected a screen between the second vehicle, a Porsche SUV, and the road. Primarily to preserve the scene, but also to prevent rubberneckers from seeing things they had no need to.

Both injured officers had been rushed to hospital. But the murder victim's body was still where it had been found. Warlow approached from the rear after entering the scene through a side farm gate. The same one that Morfydd and Nerys had leant their bikes against a few hours before. Someone was hunched over the body. Warlow recognised Tiernon, the HOP, or Home Office Pathologist to pedants, based in Cardiff. Next to him stood the white-suited figure of Alison Povey, the senior crime scene tech, only her eyes showing above the mask she wore in order not to contaminate the scene. She raised a hand to Warlow but said nothing, merely widening her eyes as an unspoken signal.

Both detectives knew what that exaggerated stare implied. Tiernon was working. And the sour sod insisted on quiet when he did. Even out here in the field. Alison's glare was a reminder of all that affectation and that she was playing dumb for a reason. Warlow hoped to God that the sheep nearby would have the sense to keep quiet. He'd seen Tiernon shout at a passing motorbike before now.

The two detectives found protective gear and suited up. Unfortunately, that led to a reveal of Gil's T-shirt once he'd removed his poncho. The logo read SANDAD: Coarse, irritating, only good for castles.

Warlow raised one eyebrow.

Gil obliged. 'Comedy T-shirt present from the grand-daughters. It's ironic, obviously. Apparently, I'm always suggesting going to castles, Dryslwyn, Carreg Cennin, Dinefwr. Of course, the Lady Anwen decided that the other adjectives were too funny to ignore.'

Warlow declined to comment.

Back outside, both men approached the spot where Tiernon squatted, along a demarcated path to where the body lay.

'Alison,' Warlow said, deciding to take the Tiernon irritation bull by the horns. 'Not exactly the Sunday any of us had planned.'

From where he was peering at the body, hunched down on his haunches, Tiernon looked up, miffed by this intrusion. But Warlow was having none of it. They both needed to be there and Warlow didn't do eggshells, no matter who it was. Tiernon was a good pathologist, but a bit of a diva and a miserable sod into the bargain. You could forgive that developmental trait in someone who spent his days tearing apart the dead looking for evidence, both criminal and otherwise, of what caused a person's demise. And no matter how much jaunty music, or, as in Tiernon's case, dreary classical stuff, one played in the background, you were, to all intents and purposes, a ghoul. Since their own Rhys Harries had shown an interest in forensic pathology, he'd earned the same label. And though they'd both deny it, the dictionary definition of a person morbidly interested in death or disaster had to be the tongue-in-cheek label applied to both the DC and to the HOP.

'What have we got?' Warlow asked.

Alison could have answered, but she deferred to the expert. Tiernon didn't reply immediately and turned his face back to the corpse lying face down on the ground, its face grey, its mouth distorted and open in death. When Tiernon finally answered, he did so without turning his head away from the body.

'Two shots, both to the chest. We have exit wounds here and here.' He pointed to dark spots on the wind-cheater the corpse wore. 'Enough as a cause of death until I have a proper look.'

'Have we identified?' Warlow sent a glance towards Povey.

She answered with a shrug. 'The car is unlocked. Wallet with a driver's licence on the front seat along with a water bottle. Lee Barret, aged thirty-seven. There was a dog's lead also on the seat and we found an animal in the corner of the field. A Staffie.'

Warlow nodded. He knew a few Staffie owners and a few Staffies. On the walks he did with Cadi, along country lanes and on beaches, the Staffies he'd met were strong, ebullient, family dogs. On the streets of the city, they still had the reputation of being the mean-looking status symbols of young males with too much testosterone and not the highest of educations. Unfair on the dog, but clichés seldom lied.

'Where is it now?' Warlow asked.

'One of the Uniforms has it in their car until we contact next of kin.'

Warlow nodded. The dog would be scared and confused.

'Glad to see you have your priorities in order, Evan,' Tiernon muttered.

'None of this is the dog's fault.' Warlow's reply was terse. As planned.

Tiernon, still peering at the corpse, shook his head.

Not a dog person, then, Warlow surmised and added that to his list of reasons not to spend any time, other than professionally, with the pathologist. Tiernon stood up, his knees popping. Warlow noted the flinching grimace flutter over the man's face. When he spoke, he avoided eye contact with the DCI. 'Difficult to say with any certainty yet, but from the position of the left exit wound, there's a possibility that the entry was close to the heart. Blood loss and pooling also suggest he died where he fell.' He turned to Alison. 'I'm happy to move him. I'll get to him first thing in the morning once he's up in Cardiff.' Only then did he flick his gaze towards Warlow. 'Look forward to your company then, Evan.'

'It'll be me or Jess Allanby,' Warlow said.

'DI Allanby was here on time. She was the one who briefed me. If I had a choice, I know which one I'd pick.' Tiernon's attempt at a smile was unpalatable.

'Hah,' Warlow replied with an exaggerated chortle. 'I'll make sure it's me, then.'

The pathologist's smile froze. 'That's not…' He didn't finish the sentence, suddenly aware of the little hole he'd dug for himself. He turned with a brusque, 'Quick as you can,' to Alison, before walking off, unbuttoning the disposable suit as he went.

'Does he have a middle name?' Gil asked.

'Not sure,' Povey replied. 'Why?'

'Dick just sprang to mind, that's all.'

'What about our lot?' Warlow asked, flicking his gaze to the empty response vehicle.

Povey's grin hardened into a razor-thin line. 'Both PCs in the response car were shot. Daniel Clark was hit in the head and shoulder. Leanne Abbot in the arm. That was a through-and-through injury. Abbot's gone to Glangwili, Clark's gone straight to neurosurgery at UHW.'

The University Hospital of Wales in Cardiff. The same hospital where Tiernon would perform a post-mortem on Barret tomorrow morning.

'So, how do you see this, Alison?' Warlow looked around at the scene, trying to piece together what could have happened.

'Not much to say yet. The injuries are from a handgun, that's according to Tiernon. My guess is that someone targeted Barret and the Uniforms got in the way. Though not all of it fits. Why was Barret parked here, of all places? Why was the response vehicle here?'

'We've got something on that,' Gil said. 'There's a logged call. Anonymous, at around 7am, claiming that Barret had been a nuisance on the beach that morning and had used his dog to threaten some walkers. He'd been abusive, and the caller thought he might be drunk. The response vehicle was in the area. On the way back to HQ.'

'Oh, God,' Alison said. 'Wrong place, wrong time.'

Warlow didn't like it. People did not get shot in this part of the world. They simply didn't. And yet, three people had been involved in this incident. Gil had turned away and was on the phone, getting information about the victim. Alison had stepped away to talk to some of her techs, arranging for a body bag, and preparing to examine the ground and take more samples once Barret was removed.

Warlow glanced up at the sky. No rain yet. There'd be a chance they might get this done in the dry. He murmured a thank you to the gods for small mercies.

———

RHYS, because of his long levers, opted for the passenger seat in the "borrowed" response vehicle, with the seat slid fully back. Morfydd Davidson sat in the back looking a lot better than she had forty minutes before when Rhys had arrived at the scene. Not an ideal situation to take a statement. In fact, a bloody uncomfortable situation since Rhys had to twist his body and his neck. At least he'd had the sense to position Morfydd behind the driver's seat, so his head didn't have to go all the way around. He wasn't a sodding owl.

But needs must.

'We'll get you home to change out of that wet suit as soon as possible. But I need to run through a few things with you.'

Morfydd, the silver space blanket wrapped around her shoulders, clutching the tea without its cardboard sleeve to get maximum warmth from the cup, nodded. 'Sooner, the better. But your colleagues, are they okay?' The words came out heartfelt, and she looked on the verge of tears.

'They're in hospital, so they're getting treatment. It's as much as I know now.'

Morfydd nodded and took a sip.

'Could you tell me what happened? How did you come to be here?' Rhys asked, notebook at the ready.

She did, concisely, while he wrote it all down, pausing only to interrupt her words with the odd question. 'And you say this is the third time you've been on the beach this month?'

'Third time, yes. Nerys doesn't do things by halves.' The little smile that shaped her mouth was fleeting.

'Do you remember seeing the man that you saw on the ground earlier, on the beach? The man in the blue windcheater?' He could have said dead man but thought better of it.

Morfydd's hair had dried into a windblown mess that

framed her pale, freckled features and lent her a slightly wild look. 'He might have been, but I wasn't aware. We're both focused when we get there. To the beach, I mean. I'm nowhere near as fit as Nerys. Once I'm in the water, all my attention goes on not swallowing half the Bristol Channel and keeping going. I mean, there were some people walking dogs, but I can't remember any of them well enough to describe one to you.'

Rhys persisted. 'What about last week, or the week before?'

Morfydd shook her head. 'Sorry.'

'The dog, it's a Staffordshire Bull Terrier. Big light-brown thing. Square head.'

She stared back at Rhys unhappily.

'Don't worry. Let's go to where you walked back up from the beach.'

'Jogged back.'

'Right. See anyone then?'

'Some runners further up on the coastal path, but no dog walkers. We were, or at least I was, concentrating on the cycle home. Cycling is probably my strongest discipline out of the three.'

'Three?' Rhys's eyebrows went up.

'Swim, run, cycle. The Iron Man. We're training for that. In Tenby next September.'

Rhys nodded, impressed. 'You saw no one as you jogged along the field to where your bikes were?'

'Correct. As we wheeled the bikes out through the field gate onto the road, that's when I saw it. The police car. It had one door open.'

'Is that what made you cross the road?'

'The open door, yes. I was curious. Someone might have needed help. But I suppose that's when I realised the noises might have had something to do with what we were seeing.'

'Noises?'

Morfydd frowned. 'We heard shots as we ran up from the beach. Five of them. We assumed it was the firing range. Though Nerys did say she thought it was a bit early for it to be open. But when I saw the police car and heard someone groan...' She shivered again.

'Take your time,' Rhys urged. 'When you crossed the road, there was no traffic?'

'Empty. We put the bikes up against the farm gate next to where the police car had parked. We heard groaning. I walked around the side of the car. I had to squeeze through until I could investigate the field...' She clamped her eyes shut, remembering it, seeing it again.

'Let me know if you want to stop.'

Morfydd looked up into Rhys's face and he read determination there. The sort of look that got you up out of bed at 6am on a Sunday to swim in the cold, cold sea. 'No. Those poor police officers. That poor man. I want to help.

CHAPTER FIVE

IN A DIFFERENT VEHICLE twenty yards away, DS Catrin Richards had adopted the same front seat/back seat arrangement to talk to Nerys Mears. Catrin had already established that both she and her friend Morfydd were teachers and that they'd been on the beach as part of their training programme. Nerys came across as a straightforward type, observant and calm. Just the sort of witness you needed. She was an attractive woman with high colour in her cheeks from the tea and the heat of the car. Her hair, salty stiff from the swimming, hung in bangs framing her face.

'What happened when you came around the car?'

'Morfydd yelled at me to phone 999. I did that. But poor Mor, she just stood there while I did it.'

'So, you called it in. Then what?'

'I said we ought to check on them. The female officer, she was awake and in shock. Morfydd went to her, asked if she was alright. Then she contacted someone on her radio. But I went to the man lying face down. I couldn't feel a pulse. And the other police officer… he had a pulse, though it wasn't strong. His head… I could see… it looked bad.' She dropped her gaze down into her empty cup and swallowed loudly.

'You're doing great,' Catrin said, looking up from her note taking. 'This must be hard for you.'

A smile quivered on her lips. 'Last thing we expected to find on a Sunday morning. The worst we've ever come across before is a jellyfish.' The smile faltered and failed. 'Hard to believe that there is so much blood inside someone, isn't it? All over the grass, seeping into the soil. It looked more black than red.'

'Yes, it can do once it's outside the body.'

Nerys sucked in a big lungful of air and huffed it out.

'But it's important we go through this. You've done all the right things,' Catrin said. 'You've gone to help. But it means your DNA and fingerprints will be all over the crime scene. We need to know that.'

Nerys nodded.

'Did you move the body at all?'

'No, I touched his neck for a pulse. The man lying face down, I mean. He was still warm. But there was no pulse.'

'Okay. Did you touch either of the vehicles?'

'Morfydd went to the police car to see if there was anything we might cover the officers with. The wind was quite fierce. It took about ten minutes for the first ambulance to arrive. We got cold. Freezing. Or maybe it was the shock. Hard to tell. I've never been so relieved to hear a siren in my life.' She sat back, as if spent.

Catrin read the signs. 'Okay. I've got all your details. Phone number, etc. We'll get someone to run you home.'

'What about our bikes?'

'We'll sort all that out. It's likely we'll want to speak to you again at some point. Perhaps you could come into the station to make a more formal statement?'

Nerys nodded slowly. 'I don't know how you do it. How do you cope? You must see this sort of thing all the time.'

Not all the time, thank God, thought Catrin. But enough times that it allowed you to compartmentalise the worst bits so that you could get on with what you were paid to do.

'More than our fair share,' Catrin said. 'But it's not the sort of thing you ever get used to. Especially not when some of your own are involved.'

'I hope you catch whoever did this,' Nerys said in a ragged murmur.

'We'll do our best,' Catrin replied, surprised at the quiet anger those words spurred in her.

———

WARLOW AND GIL crossed the road to the lay-by and the two gates that led to the track down to the beach. A green walking-man sign showed direction, but their attention was drawn to a large red and white sign warning against the dangers, in both Welsh and English, to anyone venturing in this direction.

Gil, back in the poncho, stood underneath the sign and read out loud. 'No swimming near the rocks, danger cliff edges, beware of the tides.' He grimaced. '*Mam fach*, not exactly a welcome mat, is it?'

'Off-putting to the average punter, I agree. Probably why people choose it. Bit of peace and quiet.'

Warlow led the way, looking at his watch to time the walk to the beach itself. Neither man spoke. They simply needed to get a feel for the place. And, as spots where crimes had been committed, this one was incongruous. It wasn't the most accessible of Pembrokeshire's beaches. And it was only in Pembrokeshire by the skin of its teeth since the welcome to Carmarthenshire sign was but a few yards up the road. But then again, it wasn't exactly isolated, like some places he and Cadi frequented further north on the Cardiganshire coast. Warlow now remembered he'd visited Telpyn with the kids and Denise once. From what he remembered, at low tide you could walk to and from Marros Beach to the east and from Amroth in the west. But not when the tide was in, which lent it a degree of seclusion at certain times of the day.

Especially out of season. Like now.

Initially, the path tracked across an open field. There was one property on a ridge a couple of hundred yards away, but the hedges and low trees prevented any line of sight to the road behind. And within thirty yards, the path to the beach sank into an avenue of beech and hazel as it wound ever downwards.

When it finally opened out, the view was spectacular. Warlow breathed in the sulphurous tang of sea air. To the right, a separate path led down to the beach. The tide was in, the beach empty thanks to the Uniforms shutting off access.

'Any point going down?' Gil asked.

'No. We'll get Uniforms to come back early mornings to check on regular walkers. And I don't fancy getting wet feet.'

Warlow turned to study the view towards Marros. The coastal path climbed and fell away again. But behind them, a landslip had closed the way back to Amroth. 'Thoughts?' he asked Gil.

The DS let out a sigh. 'Not many, I have to say. We need to know more about Barret. But whoever he is, he's the target here. He's the dead man. If we discount the possibility that this is just some random shooter on a spree, that is.'

Warlow shifted his feet. 'Can we discount that?'

'Christ, I hope so, Evan.'

They couldn't, of course. Not yet anyway. If another report came in, another incident, then they really would be staring down the barrel of a different operational gun. Now was a question of hoping for the least bad scenario. And bad though it was, so long as no one else got shot, Warlow would take Barret as the only victim, and the injured police as collateral damage. Just as Gil suggested.

Christ, what sort of world was it when you'd accepted a dead man and two people shot as a best option?

Warlow glanced at his watch. 'How are Rhys and Catrin getting on?'

'Catrin's texted. She says they've talked to both of the witnesses, and they've packed them off home.'

'Good. Right, let's get back to HQ and set things up. I want to hit the road running on this one. As soon as the press gets wind, they'll be like piranhas around a dead sloth.'

Gil sent Warlow a pained look. 'As imagery goes, that one is… different. I must admit.'

'Blame that Attenborough bloke and his wildlife photography team.' Warlow shuddered from head to foot. 'Some things you can't un-see. Had the poor bugger stripped to the bone in minutes, did the sharp-toothed little bastards.'

'Good analogy for the press, then.'

'Exactly. The only saving grace was that the sloth was dead before being washed into the water. It turned out neat and tidy if a bit gruesome. Recycling in nature and all that. Now, we need to get off this beach before Attenborough turns up.'

'Why?'

'Never mind, Uncle Fester. That thing you're wearing, from a distance, makes you look like the biggest penguin on Earth. You can bet someone will have phoned in a rare sighting.'

Gil took umbrage. 'There's no one within four hundred yards of us.'

'No, but there is a jet passing overhead. I expect all the passengers will be craning their necks to stare, because I have no doubt, you'll be highly visible even to them. And they have internet on planes now, I'll have you know.'

Back at the scene, Barret's body had gone, and Uniforms were moving both vehicles to the garage where Povey and her team would peer into every crack and crevice, find every hair and fibre, and subject them to tests Warlow could only wonder at. The officer that had parked his Jeep was hovering anxiously in the field when Gil and Warlow arrived back.

'Thought I'd lost you, sarge, sir.' He nodded to both and held out the keys.

Warlow took them and then glanced at Gil. 'I don't think there'd be much chance of losing DS Jones today in that getup, do you? You're more likely to misplace the moon.'

Chalmers laughed. A bit too enthusiastically for Gil's liking. Warlow's quip would now spread through the gathered officers like wildfire. 'At least I've got a sweatshirt stashed away at work,' the DS muttered as he and Warlow walked to their cars.

'That thing you wore with a reindeer's face on it last Christmas?'

'It's either that or sit about in the poncho. Lesser of two evils.'

Warlow frowned.

'You don't approve?'

'Not a question of approval,' Warlow said. 'But it's going to confuse Rhys to no end to see you in festive attire.'

CHAPTER SIX

JESS ALLANBY SAT in the soulless waiting area at the A&E department of Glangwili Hospital trying, and failing, to not look at her watch for the umpteenth time. She'd been there, what, an hour and a half already? The room was relatively quiet this early on a Sunday morning. Last night's drunks had come and gone, either thrown up or on a drip somewhere, earning zero points for their performances from the harried staff. A few chairs away sat a man and a boy, the latter perhaps ten years old, a mini version of his father and obviously not the wiry sprinter of the team he'd been playing for, judging by his rugby shirt's snug fit. He still wore a blue scrum cap and muddy boots on his dangling feet, looking forlorn with his arm in a makeshift sling. Further back, an older woman coughed gently into a sodden handkerchief.

A couple of Uniforms hovered outside. Standard practice with one of their own involved in a shooting. They weren't armed, but they'd been told to make their presence felt on the off chance that whoever had done this to Leanne Abbot might want to come back and finish the job.

Jess knew it was an emotional reaction on the Force's part. If they truly wanted to prevent someone with a gun coming back and killing Leanne Abbot, they'd need armed officers. Not that Leanne was thought to be a target. Not in Jess's way of thinking, anyway.

She'd had a few texts from Catrin. They'd identified the dead man. In Jess's opinion, and unless this was the beginning of some insane random act of monstrousness by a deranged shooter, Barret was the key here.

She exchanged a few pleasantries with the Uniforms wandering in and out, but what she desperately wanted to do was talk with the injured PC. By way of distraction, she'd started bouncing her bent leg up and down, balanced on the ball of her foot. Ridiculous. But it seemed to help.

Her phone buzzed. She read the caller ID. Her daughter, Molly.

Jess got up from the uncomfortable plastic seat and walked outside to take the call.

'Hi, Mum. You okay?'

'Fine, Mol. You eaten breakfast?'

'Marmite on toast. That seeded bread you got is so good.'

'It is, isn't it? I got it from that shop in Narberth that you like.'

A beat. Molly was building up to the reason for her call. 'Mum, there's stuff on the radio. They're calling it a serious incident. Someone has even mentioned a terrorist incident.'

They would. Of course, they would. Conjecture always stoked the fires.

'It's not,' Jess said. 'I mean, it is serious. Very serious, but I don't think it's a terrorist thing. Don't worry about that.'

'They said someone's been shot.'

Jess sighed. 'That bit is true.'

'Oh my God, Mum.'

'It's fine, Mol. We're looking into it.'

'Oh, good. That's alright, then.'

Jess smiled, imagining the dramatic look of wide-eyed, open-mouthed horror on her seventeen-year-old's face. This was her way of showing concern, and there was something quite touching about it, even if it was covered up in caustic wrapping paper. Time to calm the troubled waters with laundry talk. 'I've got a wash in the machine ready to go. Make sure you put your jeans and that sweatshirt you've been wearing for a week in there and put the thing on express. You'll want it by next weekend, I take it?'

'Yeah, probably.'

'Might be a good idea if you put what you want to pack out on your bed.'

'I'm only going for a long weekend in London, Mum, not for a month to Kilimanjaro.'

'I don't want to be running around trying to get things washed and ready when you have all the time in the world today.'

Another beat while Molly considered arguing. But all that emerged was a resigned, 'Fine.'

Molly's big trip to London to see her boyfriend Bryn had been a long time in coming. It was late October already. Bryn had been at university since late September and plans for Molly to spend the weekend with him had been deferred for a variety of reasons. Firstly, there'd been fresher's week, then Bryn came home for his mum's birthday. Following that, the poor chap caught Covid. Molly had weathered these obstacles stoically. But for the last week, all she could talk about was the London trip. Bryn had permission for her to stay with him in his halls of residence and Molly had two days of no college thanks to an inset day and an agreed holiday that Jess had fixed up. She'd go up on a Friday and come back on the Tuesday. When her mother asked about sleeping arrangements, Molly had an answer ready.

'They provide blow-up mattresses. Bryn can have that.'

Both Jess and Molly knew full well it was unlikely that the mattress would be used at all. But it remained unsaid. Jess trusted her daughter enough to be careful. She'd been on the pill for six months, would be eighteen in a few weeks, and Bryn was a nice boy. But even nice eighteen-year-old boys possessed testosterone levels off the scale and Molly was a very pretty girl. Jess pushed these thoughts away. Not because she was uncomfortable with them, but she'd treaded these mental paths many times before and now she was at work and time was passing.

'You've got that essay to do, right?' Jess changed tack.

'Yep. Just need to go through it. I did most of it yesterday.'

'Okay, if you need me to proof it, send it over.'

'Does that mean you won't be home until late?'

'Probably.'

'But there's no crazy shooter out there now, is there?'

'Whoever did this isn't lurking in the bushes, Mol. Besides, I have the very glamorous job of talking to an injured colleague at Glangwili.'

'Okay. I'll have yesterday's lasagne for lunch. Shall I keep you some?'

'No, I'll grab something on the run. But I'll text you when I know a bit more about how things go. When I'm likely to be back.'

'Take care, Mum.'

'I will.'

When the call ended, Jess looked at her phone for a few seconds, not fighting the wry smile that appeared on her face. Molly was maturing. Old enough to start expressing her concern about her mother and her job. Old enough to go to London to visit her boyfriend. Some people might have baulked at that, but Jess was a pragmatist. And she remembered well what being told you couldn't do things at seventeen felt like. The spats with her own parents. The sulks. The abject misery over meaningless slights. That would not happen to her and Molly. Neither of them was perfect, but they'd gone through enough together to earn each other's trust.

Jess walked back into reception. The clerk behind the glass of the desk saw her and waved. Next to her stood a nurse in light-blue scrubs. She looked to be only a year or two older than Molly.

'Detective Inspector Allanby?'

Jess showed her warrant card.

'The consultant says you can come in now. I'll take you to Leanne.'

A door buzzed open, and Jess walked through into the busy clinical area and over to a curtained-off bay. Leanne Abbot was in a patterned gown, pale, her arm bandaged, a plastic line leading from a bag full of claret-coloured blood running into her arm.

Jess smiled. 'Leanne. How are you?'

'Okay, ma'am. They've given me something for the pain.'

'Do you feel up to talking?'

Leanne frowned. 'Daniel… is he—'

'At the Heath. He's in surgery.'

This time, Leanne nodded as if she'd been expecting Jess to say exactly that. Relieved that she had said nothing else.

'There will not be a good time to do this,' Jess said.

'This is the time. The sooner, the better. He's still out there.'

Jesse's turn to nod. 'Okay if I record it?'

'Of course.'

'Good girl.' Jess moved closer and put her phone on the bed, pressed a few buttons and then looked up at her injured colleague 'Start when you can and stop whenever you want to.'

CHAPTER SEVEN

THE MAIN INCIDENT Room at Dyfed Powys's Police HQ
was buzzing by the time Warlow and Gil got there. Catrin
and Rhys were busy. The boards were already filling up
with photographs and information. Warlow knew where all
this was coming from. One of their own had been injured.
Correction, two of their own. That always added an extra
layer of horrified urgency and determination. And there
was no hiding the fact that serious crimes, assaults, and
murders were always abhorrent. But when an officer paid
to uphold the law and protect the public got embroiled in
actual violence, it injected a unique element to
proceedings.

And, as if the atmosphere wasn't tense enough, it
ramped up another notch or two when the Incident Room
door swung open and two Police Superintendents walked
into the room. Sion Buchannan in plain clothes, six-four
and imposing as always, held the door open for a significantly shorter officer in uniform. But then, who wasn't
significantly shorter than the Buccaneer? Pamela Goodey,
aka Goodey Two-Shoes, or Two-Shoes to the majority of
HQ, wore a crisp white shirt and no tie. Devoid of

makeup, she eschewed any attempt at being fashionable in the hair stakes, and kept it short, as in back and sides. No fleck of grey was visible as she stood in front of Buchannan, her barnet as dark as Gil's poncho.

And just about as natural.

'How goes it, Evan?' Buchannan asked.

'Prelim stage. Fact finding. You know the drill. We have an ID on the victim, so that's a start.'

Goodey gave a little irritated clearing of her throat. 'I would hope that knowing two of our own have been attacked in the course of their duty would have you pulling out all the stops here. Not calling it a drill.'

Silence fell over the team and the other people in the room close enough to hear Goodey's carping tone. Mostly, they were waiting for Warlow's reaction. When it came, it emerged calm and collected, but dripping with sarcasm. 'Because, of course, we only pull half the stops out in our everyday murder enquiries.' The grin on the DCI's face was a terrifying thing to behold.

Goodey's expression gave nothing away, but her eyes widened like a cat realising her miaow had just alerted a very large Alsatian. 'What I'm saying is that we'll be under the microscope on this one. We've already had the press hounding us for a statement.' And then, as if having planted one of her size fives in it wasn't enough, she proceeded to tread the other one into the same steaming mire as she dropped her voice down into hiss mode. 'Though how on earth they find out about these things so quickly is beyond me.' She sent a leery glare around the room.

No names and no pack drill in that glare. But the implication was as clear as the beaky nose on Goodey's sharp-featured face. Of course, it wasn't beyond reason to think that a poorly paid copper, or even someone co-opted from the civilian population to work on a case such as this, might find a swift £200 backhander from a nosy reporter very welcome in these times of inflation and strikes. But to suggest someone in his team might be so tempted stuck in Warlow's gizzard.

'You don't think it might have something to do with the fact that we've had two dozen blue-light vehicles descending on a beach next to a sleepy seaside town on a quiet Sunday morning? A morning which meant the sirens would be audible for miles around. Any one of the dozens of motorists we stopped and quizzed today could have uploaded a video of the circus. The press would need a severe case of "Tommy" not to have noticed.'

Rhys, looking perplexed, mouthed the word to Gil. 'Tommy?'

Gil leaned over to whisper, 'The Who. '69 or '70, I think. Rock opera album about a sensorially challenged pinball player. No see, no speak, no hear. Very last century. You had to be there.'

Two-Shoes blinked and frowned, but the wind had left her sails. 'Whoever or whatever the source, the floodgates have opened. And it is me who will need to deal with the press. I would like to have something concrete to give them as soon as possible.'

Warlow held her gaze. 'And you will, ma'am. As always. As soon as something appears.' She turned on her heels and clip clopped out into the corridor.

Buchannan waited, the look on his face like that of a child knowing that the stain on the front of his trousers could only mean one thing. An expression of apology and misery all mangled together. For a moment, Warlow stood confused. And then he remembered and squeezed his eyes shut, his body as stiff as a statue.

'The cruise,' he said and then opened his eyes again.

Buchannan nodded. 'I can't get out of it. Mrs Buchannan would divorce me on the spot. It's been planned for three years. Mumbai to Singapore via Sri Lanka. It's our thirtieth anniversary. Pearl treasures of the Orient. Get it?'

'You're abandoning us, sir?' Gil said, twisting the knife.

'I'm sorry. It's for two weeks. Seventeen days, in fact. I'll be back then.'

'And Superintendent Goodey is deputising for you, sir?' Rhys asked, his voice a little higher than normal.

Buchannan nodded. 'Pamela is very thorough, as you all know.'

She was that alright. Along with being a shouty, micro-managing gobshite, an irritating stater-of-the-obvious par excellence, and a dyer of hair poncho-black. Warlow could never be sure which of these traits irritated him the most. She and Warlow had history. And not the good type, like glasnost. Theirs was more War of the Roses. Bloody and unremitting, waged as part of her never-ending quest to find a new feather for her bloody cap.

Warlow grinned and held out his hand. Buchannan took it.

'Enjoy it, Sion,' were the words that came out of Warlow's mouth.

But his eyes said, '*You utter bastard.*'

CHAPTER EIGHT

WARLOW MADE a quick phone call to Tom and Jodie, still at Ffau'r Blaidd.

'Sounds awful, Dad,' Tom said when Warlow explained the gist of the case to him. 'We can hang on a while if you think you'll make it back?'

'No, I won't. You were planning to leave mid-afternoon, right?'

'Yes. But we'll probably go earlier now. Since you're tied up.'

'I am sorry. And I was joking when I said I was waiting for you guys to organise the trip to Australia.'

'Were you? Why? Jodie bloody loves doing that kind of stuff.'

Warlow recalled the detailed and unusual trips Tom and Jodie had been on as a couple. The salt flats of Lake Minchin in the Altiplano of Bolivia. Trekking in the Indian Himalayas. Jodie seemed to have a knack. Or was simply organised as hell, which was Tom's explanation for it.

'Sounds good. January, you said?'

'Yes, we'll get Christmas over and done. By that time, Leo's sister will be into some kind of sleeping pattern.'

Sister.

Warlow smiled. He kept forgetting there was going to be a little girl in the family. Denise, the old Denise, would have done a cartwheel.

'Dad?'

'I'd better go. I'll fall in with whatever you two want to do. There may be a vineyard or two in Margaret River I'd like to visit when we're out there. But otherwise…'

'Don't worry, that's on my list, too.'

'Let Cadi out for a quick toilet break before you go. And congratulations once again.' Warlow paused as a new thought struck him such that he let out an unforced groan. 'Oh, God.'

Tom heard the pain in Warlow's voice. 'What's wrong, Dad?'

'You two getting married.'

'Is the idea that bad?'

'No, it's fantastic. But it means I'm going to have to buy a new suit. And you know how much I love shopping.' He hung up and regarded the room. Information was coming in fast from many sources and it would need filtering. But at that precise moment, the most welcome source breezed through the door carrying a big tray of coffees and a weighed-down paper bag.

DI Jess Allanby, unlike the rest of them, had come to work dressed as she usually did. And though her clothes were practical – a dark roll-neck sweater and a sage jacket – she wore them elegantly.

Rhys picked up on the aroma immediately and went into excited puppy mode. 'Are those rolls I can smell, ma'am?'

'They are. Golden Arches brekkie rolls. Only thing open on a Sunday.' She leant down to ease the tray onto the table and plonked the bag after it.

'Are you related to Florence Nightingale, ma'am?' Gil

asked. He'd shed the poncho and was now wearing his Christmas jumper. So far, no one had commented. This was Gil, after all.

'Might as well be, the amount of time I've just spent in the hospital.'

'Any joy?' Warlow asked.

'Some. Shall we eat first? I am starving.'

They dived in. Even Catrin, who could be finicky when it came to food, bit into a roll but chose not to adorn it with either brown or red sauce.

'You are so missing out,' Rhys said through a mouth full of food, proving his point by getting a dollop of the red variety on his chin. For all of five minutes, only one question was posed as they refuelled, addressed to Gil from Jess.

'Is the jumper a bet?'

'No, ma'am. But it is the least offensive of the choices open to me. Won't happen again, ma'am. At least, not until December 18th. A week before Christmas is the Jones's rule.'

Rhys finished first. A feat that surprised no one. 'Don't suppose there are biscuits for dessert, are there, sarge?'

Gil tutted. 'Greed is such an ugly vice, Rhys.'

Crestfallen, the DC folded his arms.

'Since you've wolfed down that bap before the rest of us are even halfway through ours, you can start us off with what the witnesses had to say.' Warlow nodded to the whiteboard, commonly known as the Job Centre where Morfydd Davidson's name had been written up next to Nerys Mears's in Catrin's neat hand.

Rhys stood up, flipped open his notebook, and ran through the conversation he'd had with the woman in the response vehicle.

'You told her we'll need swabs and fingerprints for elimination?' Jess asked when he'd finished.

'Yes, ma'am. I could ask her to come in today. It's just that she wasn't exactly dressed for it. She'd been in the sea.'

Catrin echoed Rhys's statement. Nerys Mears gave an identical account. 'I've asked her to come in first thing tomorrow, ma'am. Rhys, why don't you ask Morfydd Davidson to do the same?'

'And both women heard the shots?' Jess asked.

'They did.'

'Where were they when they heard those shots?' Warlow sat up.

Catrin got to her feet, the uneaten third of her roll on a napkin on her desk. Rhys's eyes flicked towards it. 'Don't even think about it,' the DS warned without even glancing at him. She walked over to a blown-up Ordnance Survey map of the crime scene. 'They were still under the trees at the start of the ascent from the cliff above the beach. They heard the shots at 07.35. Nerys remembers looking at her watch and commenting that it was early for the firing range.'

Warlow followed Catrin's finger. 'No more than a couple of minutes away from the scene as they were jogging. Add on another couple for them to fiddle with their bikes, cross the road and call it in.'

'That's about right, sir.' She wrote another time up. 'The call from Nerys to emergency services came in at 07.41.'

Jess nodded. It came as a grim realisation. They'd missed the shooting by less than five minutes. Missed the shooter, too. On the one hand, their appearance might have spooked him or her. On the other, they might have ended up as victims. Hobson's choice on that one. 'Have we checked that the firing range wasn't open?'

'Doesn't open until eleven on Sundays.' Catrin returned to the desk and took another bite. Rhys turned away.

Warlow wiped his fingers with the napkin and swallowed the last of his brunch, washing it down with a mouthful of coffee, surprised at how acceptable it was, considering. 'Gil and I walked the path down to the overlook. It's quiet but gives access to the coastal path.' He knew once he spoke those words, he'd get a reaction. This team had been formed after a cold case they'd investigated on that same coastal path, albeit a section many miles away. Still, the path had taken on a different connotation because of that case. It triggered unpleasant memories in all of them. He waited for Gil to murmur, 'Bloody coastal path', but the DS stayed silent and so Warlow continued, 'There is no access on the path from the west as the result of a landslip. But it is open to the east.'

'Someone could have got to that point by road or via the path?' Rhys asked.

Warlow agreed, evaluating the map as he spoke. 'The road would be riskier in terms of visibility. The path would be less obtrusive. Especially if you took the closed section.'

'Dangerous,' Jess suggested.

'But a guarantee of not being seen. If you were the killer.'

Gil and Catrin both nodded.

'What about the officers, ma'am?' Catrin asked.

The DI had one bite of roll left. She left it, took a sip of coffee, and stood up. 'As you all know by now, Leanne Abbot's injuries are not life threatening. The same is not true of Daniel Clark. We sent someone up to Cardiff with him. His family is there now, too. He's in surgery. One shot to the torso, one to the head. No prospect of speaking with him. But I managed to speak to Leanne. It's a nasty wound, but it missed the bone. She lost some blood and will be kept in, but she's a fighter.'

Warlow asked the questions they all wanted an answer to. 'Did she or Clark have their body cams activated?'

Jess sighed. 'No. They saw no need.'

'Shit,' Warlow whispered.

Dyfed Powys Uniformed Officers wore body cams. But their use was discretionary. The rule of thumb was that any encounter where a written record might have been needed justified their use and the public should be made aware that they were being used. But Clark and Abbot had barely encountered Barret and so why would they have had them on? But how much easier would it have been if they had?

'She said they saw the car parked off the road on private property. They spoke to Barret for only a minute or two before shots were fired. Barret was genuinely surprised when they said they'd taken a call from someone who'd said he'd threatened them with his dog on the beach. Abbot said he had the dog with him on a lead and it did not appear to be aggressive. They asked for his name, but he refused to give it. In fact, Barret's attitude was one of shock and anger. When they asked him if where he'd parked was his land, he said no, but that he always parked there when he came to the beach so that his car was off the road. When they asked him why, he said he didn't trust parking on the lay-by because of the risk someone might hit his car and the grass verge was too wet. At that point, Barret suddenly looked surprised at seeing something. Shots were fired from behind where Clark and Abbot were standing. Barret fell to the ground immediately. They turned and ducked, but two more shots hit Clark and the last shot hit Leanne. She only saw a figure dressed in dark clothing and wearing a balaclava. He, or she, ran back through the gate to the road. By that time, Leanne was on her back.'

No one spoke for a long time. Jess had been matter-of-fact in her delivery. Even so, the stark horror and implication of what sounded like a cold-blooded attack left them all reeling.

'She heard no other vehicle?' Warlow asked.

'No.'

'Then it sounds like the shooter was on foot.'

'Or a bike, sir?' Rhys asked.

'Maybe.' Warlow didn't think so. A bike would need the road again and travelling slower than a car meant it would have been seen by someone. But the DC had made a valid point. 'We have a timeline, so let's make sure the right questions are asked. We're looking for any cyclists at that time, and walkers and runners in dark clothing.'

Warlow stood and went over to the map. The road over a cattle grid where Clark and Abbot had parked the response vehicle led to a water treatment plant. To the west, tracks led to a farm, to the east, a flattened area where the farmer offered summer camping to caravans which, at this time of year, remained completely empty. The shooter could, of course, have come from any of those areas. But it sounded like he'd got away via a different route.

'So, that brings us to why any of this has happened. Are we looking at a random shooting? A spree killer? Or is there a reason Barret was killed?'

Gil brushed crumbs off the reindeer's face covering his ample chest, and stood up. 'And that's where things get a bit murky.'

CHAPTER NINE

'LEE BARRET,' Gil said. 'Thirty-seven years old. Current address is in St David's Close, Tenby. That's up near the schools. Partner in L&M Jet-Ski Hire. Listed in Companies House as a jet-ski rental company.'

'Known to us?' Warlow asked.

Gil swung around to his desktop and clicked the mouse. 'Not much on the PNC, but there is an arrest record. Tenby born and bred. DUI as a twenty-year-old. Speeding and a fine for possession of cannabis.'

'Jet-ski hire,' muttered Warlow, his head filling with images of futuristic-looking toilet seats fizzing about the water. 'Is that a big business?'

'It is in the summer, sir, yes,' Rhys piped up. 'I know people who go down there on a weekend.'

'So, it's seasonal?'

Gil answered, 'Mainly. Though you get a few nutters who do it all year round. Buzz addicts, I call them. Can't stand the sodding things myself. *Diawledig* bloody things.'

This was a new one on Jess who raised one eyebrow at Catrin. '*Diawl* I know,' she said. 'Devil?'

'Exactly, ma'am. Sergeant Jones just said diabolical.'

Warlow joined Gil at his desk and studied the record. The photograph that appeared was of a man in his early twenties. Defiant, good looking, and devoid of the stubble that had become so popular over the last decade. 'Have we got a more recent photograph?'

'There's a Facebook page for Tenby Ski. He's on the About page.'

Warlow took a few steps in as Catrin blew up the image. The same man, fifteen years older. Tanned, smiling in the sunshine in a wet suit astride a jet-ski.

Warlow stood back and arched his back. 'Anyone been to his property yet? Is there a partner, a wife or a husband?'

No one answered.

'Okay, then that'll be our first port of call. If there is, we'll need a family liaison.' Warlow sent Rhys a quizzical glance. The DC responded. 'Not Gina, sir. Not on duty. She's at home. Probably still in—' There was no doubting the wistfulness in the DC's reply, but he had the sense to catch himself before saying 'bed'.

But Gil swooped down, osprey-like. 'Never easy getting out of a warm bed, is it?'

'It was very hard, sarge.'

'Must have been a nightmare trying to get your trousers on, then.' He paused, waiting for Rhys to flush a bright red, before qualifying his statement with, 'In the dark, I mean.'

Warlow groaned. 'Is this a bloody Benny Hill sketch?'

Catrin tilted her chin down. 'If that's the level of humour we're stooping to, I'm buying ear plugs.'

'Who's Benny Hill?' Rhys asked.

Jess threw him a glance. 'Don't bother. Trust me.'

'Pity about Gina not working today, though.' Warlow liked Rhys's partner a lot. She was a bloody good FLO.

'Because Tenby is my first port of call and Gina knows what kind of tea I like. Saves the bother of explaining.'

'Milk and one sugar is such a laborious sentence,' Gil said with a bewildered stare at Warlow.

The DCI reached for his coat. 'Catrin, you're with me.'

Rhys made a face, to which Warlow responded, 'Don't look so disappointed. There's a ton of work to do here. Get on to dispatch. I want a copy of the call that led to Abbot and Clark going out to Telpyn. Besides, I will not be stopping for snacks on the way to Tenby.'

'Won't need to stop. I've already stocked up, sir. In anticipation.' Rhys picked up a plastic NISA bag.

'I should have known. But I'd prefer to have a female officer along.'

Rhys raised his eyebrows.

'What?' Warlow demanded. 'We can't say that now? Female officer?'

'It's a bit—' Rhys began but was shut down by Gil.

'Never mind the jiggery-wokery, Rhys. What if Barret has a partner, and she is female and demands to speak to a female officer? What then?'

'Never thought of that, sarge.'

'No, well, think on, detective constable,' Gil said. 'Every day is a school day.'

'You can finish my roll if you like.' Catrin stood up from her desk and handed over the remains of her food.

'Sure?' Rhys asked.

'But it hasn't got any ketchup.'

Rhys shrugged. 'I'll survive.'

'Sometimes,' Warlow muttered as he made for the door, 'I think it'd be easier if we substituted Rhys with Cadi. She's obedient and less demanding.'

'What about cleaning up her mess, sir? At least Rhys uses a toilet.' Catrin did not have a dog. And, like most non-dog owners, viewed the practice of using a hand inside an inverted plastic bag to scoop up the recently deposited contents of a dog's bowel, repulsive.

Warlow tilted his head. 'Have you looked under his desk? Who knows what's in all that debris?'

Catrin took a moment to consider this. 'Fair point,' she said eventually and with a very troubled expression. At the door, she hesitated for a moment and her gaze rested on Jess, who had already begun writing up her report on her interview with Leanne Abbot.

'Would it be okay if I had a quick word with DI Allanby, sir? Personal matter. I'll be two minutes. I can meet you downstairs.'

'Fine,' Warlow replied. 'I'll pull the car up to the main entrance.'

She hurried away. With her back to Warlow, she spoke to Jess who looked up, interested, before nodding. Warlow read understanding in that nod. But Jess stood, put a hand on Catrin's arm and they both moved quickly through the room to the cubicle laughingly known as the SIO's office. Whatever it was they were discussing demanded a tad more privacy than whispering at a desk could get them.

By the time Warlow got to his car, he'd filed it away. Personal business, she'd said. Therefore, by definition, none of his. Even so, it had registered in his mental filing system. That was the trouble with being a detective. Everything was significant until it wasn't.

CHAPTER TEN

RHYS'S PHONE BUZZED, and he read a message from Gina. *How bad is it?*

He left the Incident Room and found a quiet area in a stairwell that had become the default spot where people often took calls or made them. As Gil had quipped, GCHQ must be having a bloody field day monitoring the gossip.

Rhys pressed the little phone icon on the WhatsApp page. Gina answered after three rings.

'Hey,' she said, her voice soft with sympathy.

'Bad enough, to answer your question. Leanne Abbot is in Glangwili, but Dan Clark is in surgery in the Heath.'

'Oh, my God. I know them both. The news said one dead?'

'There is. But he isn't one of ours. We think the dead bloke is probably the target. Daniel and Leanne...' he hesitated before answering, 'wrong place, wrong time.'

Gina's expelled breath sounded ragged. 'But how can that happen?'

'No idea, yet. Warlow was disappointed that you weren't the FLO involved.'

'Really?' She sounded sceptical. But Rhys knew she'd be pleased. 'That might be Rob today. He's good.'

'The Wolf and Catrin are on the way to see the dead man's partner now.'

She sighed. 'Any idea when you'll be home? I could—' She broke off. 'Hang on Rhys, there's another call.'

Rhys sat on the stairs while Gina answered whoever was the other caller. She came back to him forty seconds later. 'Right, well, looks like it's all hands on deck.'

'They calling you in?'

'Not quite, but they want me to be the support officer for Daniel's family starting first thing tomorrow.'

'Oh, God.'

Gina groaned. 'It's fine. I know Daniel, but not his wife. Siwan, is it?'

'She's the actress, right?'

'Yeah. She's been in one of the Welsh soaps. Or is that her sister?'

'Bet Warlow will be pleased that you're involved. He's a fan.'

'Nice to have one,' Gina said.

'You've got tons. But I'm number one.'

'Really? Didn't seem like it this morning. You didn't even make me a cup of tea.'

'I did ask,' Rhys protested. 'All you did was moan. No words, just a moan. I couldn't tell if it was a yes or no.'

'Well, you'd better learn. That was a yes moan.'

'Sorry.'

Gina laughed. 'I'm only kidding. Right, any idea what time you'll be back?'

'No.'

'Okay. I'll ring your mum. We were meant to be at hers for lunch, but I'm sure she'll plate something up for later. I'll fetch it and we can eat when you get home.'

'Sounds like a plan. Brilliant plan, in fact. Something to

look forward to. Getting back to our own place with you and Sunday lunch.'

Gina laughed. 'Which part of that plan is the best bit?'

'I'd say fifty-fifty.'

'Wow, I'm up there with your mum's Sunday roast. I'll take that.'

Rhys shifted to a pout. 'I was looking forward to a lazy morning in bed.'

'Well, depends on what time you're home, but there is always the possibility of an early night.'

'That could be our pudding.'

'I love it when you talk dirty.'

A door opened in the stairwell before Rhys could say anything else, though Gina had a way of easily rendering him speechless with the simplest of glances or throwaway remarks. He said his goodbyes and pocketed his phone and made his way back to the Incident Room, turning his mind, with difficulty, away from this evening's pudding and towards speaking to the call-handlers as per Warlow's instructions.

CHAPTER ELEVEN

TENBY. It had another name. A Welsh name. *Dinbych y Pysgod*. More descriptive as the "fortlet of the fish", hinting at its roots both as a fishing hub and a strategic stronghold. Some people called it the perfect seaside town. If you looked it up on Tripadvisor, the words "Picture Perfect" often came up. And why not? A walled harbour with cobbled lanes, yellow sandy beaches, boats moored in the sheltered waters. Norsemen had been here, then the Normans. More recently, different invaders had come: the hens and the stags, though the town was fighting back. These days, most of the pubs refused entry to groups dressed like wand-toting fairies or nappy-wearing pink babies. The town wanted the families back. So, they kept the Georgian houses rising in an elegant arc around the town, freshly painted in pastel hues. Kept the two picturesque beaches clean. Pushed the boat rides out to Caldey Island and clamped down on anti-social behaviour.

Warlow's earliest last-century Tenby memories from the seventies were of Sunday-school trips, either sweltering in the heat getting sunburnt as he queued for the trampolines and ice cream, or huddled inside an anorak and a windbreak on the drizzly beach. Such trips were planned months in advance, and they'd all go, rain or shine. But he'd never complained. Not when the Lord was providing, or at least subsidising, the charabanc and chips.

'How about you, Catrin? Tenby one of your summer haunts?' Warlow asked as they hit the traffic.

Catrin guffawed. 'Not really. First, it's mayhem in the summer. Second, look at me, sir. Thirty minutes in the sun and I go from milky to beetroot without passing go.'

Warlow hadn't factored in Catrin's Celtic colouring. 'Not even under a parasol with a good book?'

'Parasol?' Catrin fought a smile.

'Beach umbrella, then. Though I thought parasol added a certain old-world sophistication to the conversation.'

'No. Not even under a parasol with a good book. Now Craig, he's half-lizard. As soon as it's warm enough, he's out in the garden on a deck chair.'

'Does that make holidays difficult?'

'Not really since we can't afford to go on any. Other priorities.'

They'd reached the B & Q roundabout. A blow-up inflatable Halloween ghost riding a motorbike shook and shivered in the breeze on the grassy verge outside the store. Both officers stared while they waited for traffic to move.

'Is that a skeleton chained to the fence there, too?' Catrin asked.

'Yes, it is. I swear, it gets worse every year. Bloody Halloween. Is this something you and Craig celebrate, Catrin? Though I can't see him bobbing for apples.'

'Not for me, sir. Craig may coax me into a scary film and popcorn, though I am not good with that sort of thing. Scary, I mean, not the popcorn. Blood and gore I'm fine with, but the paranormal stuff, no, thanks. I realise it's all camera trickery, but I've seen enough strangeness in the job to last me a lifetime.'

'Well, every other bugger seems to be carving a pumpkin or dressing up like they're half dead. Did I tell you that Gil was being Uncle Fester when he got the call this morning?'

Catrin turned a delighted face towards him. 'No, sir, you did not. But that's now been stored away in the ammunition box. How about you, sir? You into pagan rituals?'

'No one comes near my place. If someone dressed as a vampire or a ghost tried it, I'd set the dog on them.'

Catrin's expression adopted a suitable level of scepticism. 'Cadi's hardly a deterrent, sir. Unless you've trained her to lick someone to death.'

'You're right, there. She'd probably ask the buggers in. We need to work on her attack mode.'

'No, you don't. That dog doesn't have a nasty bone in her body.'

Warlow threw her a glance. 'I didn't think you liked dogs, sergeant.'

'There are dogs and then there is Cadi, sir.'

Warlow snorted. They drove on for a while in silence until Warlow finally scratched the itch that had been irritating him.

'Everything alright otherwise? In the job, I mean?'

'Yes, sir.' She dug for a little context. 'Why do you ask?'

Warlow considered his response. A couple of cases ago, they'd unearthed a very nasty criminal working from the inside. A rogue DI who'd gone over to the dark side and who'd coerced Catrin into acting against the team. 'That business with Caldwell when he asked you to play spy. That put you in a difficult position. I wonder if it left too much of a nasty taste.'

'I have mouthwash, sir.'

Warlow grunted. Classic Catrin Richards answer. But,

as expected, his probing was getting him nowhere through her pachyderm skin. The quiet word which he'd seen her have with Jess might have been nothing at all. Certainly, none of his business. He put it to one side.

The traffic moved, and they exited the roundabout onto the dual carriageway. 'Right. Do we have an actual address?'

———

LEE BARRET LIVED in a house on a plot that looked like it might have had two properties on it at one stage, seeing as it was twice as big as any of the other houses. And unlike them, this was a new build. Rendered all white with a grey-set driveway. The place was very modern.

'Blimey,' Catrin said. 'The business must have been doing well.'

She was right. Warlow was no expert, but even though it was on an estate, his best guess was that there'd not be much change out of a million quid here for a prospective buyer. It was Tenby after all. Warlow parked in front of the garage. The driveway stood empty. And when they knocked on the grey front door, no one answered. Not even after three loud goes.

He walked around a path at the side next to a white-washed wall into an enclosed garden. A covered hot tub took up half a patio. The rest was a plain bit of shrub-less lawn. Its stark utilitarianism yelled back "low maintenance".

Through the large bifold doors next to the barbecue area, Warlow cupped his hands on the glass to peer into a TV room with red leather furniture. Further along the patio, Catrin did the same through another set of bifold doors.

'That's probably the biggest kitchen I've ever seen,' she

said with an awe that made Warlow look himself. He joined her and immediately agreed. Grey marble flooring, white breakfast barstools, a table with grey seats and a glass top.

'You sure Lee Barret isn't a footballer, sir?'

He knew what she meant. Everything was nice and spotless, but all a bit too shiny and new. As if someone had said to the builder, 'Here is a lorry-load of cash, now make it like a show home.'

No photographs adorned the walls other than an irregular line of four action snaps of various sizes, all showing a man in the throes of riding a jet-ski, complete with bursting waves and bright sunshine. It might have been Tenby, then again it could just as well have been Mykonos.

'Don't see any sign of kids' stuff, sir.' Catrin walked around to each window and peered in.

'No. Everything looks tidied away.'

When they got back to the front of the house, a woman stood on the pavement opposite. Mid-forties, arms folded across her chest, dressed in a puffer jacket, leggings, and fluffy slippers. She was what Gil might call a bit 'top-heavy'; a term that Warlow sincerely doubted would appear on any type of politically correct list of terms these days, no matter how descriptively accurate it might be. But she had the same shape as Warlow's ex-wife, Denise. A shape exaggerated, in Denise's case, by the alcoholism that piled the weight on above the waist and made her legs thinner as the years rolled by.

'You looking for Lee?' the woman asked, with no belligerence.

'We are.'

'Left early and hasn't come back yet.'

'Any idea where?'

'None. Comes and goes, does Lee.'

'Are you a friend?'

'A neighbour, that's all.'

Catrin held out her warrant card. 'DS Catrin Richards.'

The woman looked at the card and then at Catrin. 'What's happened?'

'We are not at liberty to discuss that, madam.'

The woman didn't look as if she believed them.

'What time were you up, Miss…?' Catrin let the question hang.

'Mrs. Around eight.'

'And his car definitely wasn't here?'

'No.'

Warlow stepped forward. 'When did you last see Mr Barret, Mrs…'

The woman took the bait. 'It's April. April Slater. We always say hello. He throws brilliant parties, does Lee. Invites the whole close sometimes. But I heard the car go while it was still dark. Sometimes I see him with Mitch, his dog. He often leaves early, though.'

'And he lives here alone, does he, April?' Warlow asked.

She nodded. 'Lots of girlfriends. But no one steady.'

'Do you have his phone number, by any chance?'

'I do.' She hesitated, anxious about giving away a secret. 'He isn't in any trouble, is he?'

'We can't answer that question,' Warlow said and knew she'd draw her own conclusion.

'Not that thing over near Amroth, is it?' She looked suddenly horrified. 'It's all over the news. A major incident. They say someone's been shot.'

Neither Warlow nor Catrin answered. April took up her arms-folded position again. 'Has someone really been shot?'

Warlow saw no point in denying what the press had already told the world. 'Yes. So, you appreciate how serious this is.'

April nodded, her eyes wide now.

'You don't have a key to the property or know who does?' Catrin asked.

'No. Lee keeps himself to himself most of the time.'

'If we could have that phone number, it would be a great help,' Warlow said.

April took out her phone and read out the number. Catrin wrote it down and double-checked before adding, 'If you see anything, or remember anything out of the ordinary, give me a ring.' For the second time that morning, the DS handed over a card.

Back in the car, Warlow watched Catrin texting. 'Craig?' he asked, teasing.

'No, sir. Rhys, to organise a locksmith and to get the warrant started for us to gain access. Not that Barret would object to us getting in there now, but you never know.'

'You never do, sergeant. You never do.'

CHAPTER TWELVE

AWAY FROM THE buzz of the Incident Room, Jess, Gil, and Rhys sat in the SIO office with freshly made cups of tea to listen to the audio file. They were on the slippery slope to lunchtime and so the Human Tissue For Transplant box had not been opened. Gil's clever ploy to hide the team's biscuits in a large Styrofoam container that had once transported organs continued to work well in that the average biscuit pilferer generally avoided boxes with labels such as that. Though no one had quite worked out what bit of human tissue could remain in a box for months on end without causing the room it was in to reek to high heaven, the ploy remained effective. The Box came out only when the entire team was present. But Gil's rules regarding the *biscuits* – he preferred the French pronunciation when referring to hard-baked unleavened flour-based cakes – would have made Alexander Dumas proud.

'One for all and all for one,' he'd explained to Rhys once.

To which the DC had replied, 'But I only want one, sarge.'

And so, biscuit-less, they sat in the cramped room and

listened while the imported call-handler's file that had appeared in Rhys's inbox and which he'd circulated to the team, played.

06.59

'Police, what's your emergency?'

'There's a man on the beach. He has this dog, a big dog.'

'He has a big dog?'

'Looks like a Rottweiler or a pit bull. One of those dangerous things. It went for my dog.'

'Where are you, madam?'

'Telpyn Beach.'

'Telpyn Beach. That's near Amroth, is it?'

'Yes, I was walking my dog and this man… his dog, it went for my dog and then he threatened me.'

'How did he threaten you, madam?'

'He said he'd set his dog on me. He sounded a bit drunk. He said my dog was nothing more than a rat and that his dog would kill it with a couple of shakes. I had to pick Pickles up.'

'Were you hurt, ma'am?'

'No, but he had his dog on a lead and it went for me. He could only just hold it back. It would have killed my dog if I hadn't picked Pickles up… I've never been more scared in my life.'

Jess paused the recording and looked at her colleagues.

'Sounds genuine, ma'am,' Rhys said. 'She sounds scared.'

Gil nodded.

'She's young, the caller. How old would you say?' Jess asked.

Gil answered, 'Under thirty, definitely.'

Rhys's eyebrows shot up.

Gil remonstrated, 'I realise it's hard for you to contemplate anyone over twenty-five as being young, but believe me, it is all relative. And I'd say not a local accent. Sounds like she's moving fast, too.'

'Definitely an English accent, ma'am,' Rhys added. 'Any more details?'

Jess pressed the play button. The call-handler came back with a question.

'Where are you now?'

'I'm getting to the road. To my car...' Her breathing sped up until she was gasping.

'Are you alright? Are you hurt?'

'No, but I'm scared. I think I'm having a panic attack. He was behind me... I'm going to my car.'

'Okay, okay, get to your car. But stay on the line.'

Sounds of a car door opening followed by some whimpering. The call-handler asked again. *'Are you hurt?'*

'No, no, I'm not. But this man... I've seen him before. He parks in a field on the other side of the cattle grid.'

'Where exactly are you, madam?'

'I'm on the grass verge. Opposite the gate that leads to the beach. I've seen him and his car before. But that dog, it's... I have to go. I can't breathe.'

'Madam, stay calm. I can get you an ambulance.'

'No, I have to go.'

'Stay on the line. Madam. What's your name? Can you tell me your name?'

A car engine fired and moved off. Then the call ended.

Gil sighed. 'Did we get a number for the caller?'

'A pay as you go. Not registered.'

'Someone will have seen her. There weren't that many people on the beach on a Sunday at 7am, surely?' Rhys said.

Jess shrugged. 'We'll have to wait for that.'

'So, the call-handler contacted Clark and Abbott?' Rhys asked.

'They'd been in Amroth. Reports of a domestic disturbance, which turned out to be nothing. They were only a couple of miles away.'

'*Arglwydd,* talk about bad bloody luck.'

'Do you think this caller might have had anything to do with it, ma'am?'

'In what way, Rhys?'

'She sounded pretty upset. If Barret's dog had attacked her dog, I mean. People get very upset about animals.'

'Right,' Gil said slowly. 'And she conveniently has dark clothes, a balaclava, and a handgun in the glove compartment. Is that what you're saying?'

Rhys pondered the idea before shaking his head. 'Bit unlikely, sarge.'

'Yes,' Gil said. 'You've been watching too much of that Killing Leaves stuff. Not every young woman is a potential assassin.'

'It's Eve, sarge. And, yes, not every young woman is a potential assassin, but I know a few who could be.'

Gil narrowed his eyes. 'You're right. Who was it that said anyone was capable of murder? All it takes are the right circumstances.'

'Like leaving the toilet seat up… again,' Rhys said with a hollow look and a shiver.

'Or not emptying the dishwasher,' Gil added, wincing.

'Both grounds for justifiable homicide,' Jess said drily. 'But Gil's right. I can't see this caller turning into a killer.'

'What about the dog? What kind is it?'

'Staffordshire bull terrier.'

'Ah,' Rhys added a loaded grimace to his acknowledgement.

'Goes by the name of Mitch and is as nice as pie, apparently.' Gil smiled.

'But we don't know what it was like when goaded,' Rhys observed.

'No, we don't. Not yet. DCI Warlow is our dog expert. We'll need to ask him. Meanwhile, we add this caller to our list of people we'd like to talk to. Who knows, if she was parked on the verge, someone might have seen her. Get the word over to the crime scene manager, Rhys.'

'Will do, ma'am. And DS Richards wants the address of Barret's business partner, Michael Dunbar.'

'Tidy. See, you have no time for biscuits,' Gil said.

'There's always time for biscuits, sarge.' Rhys had meant it as a quip, but it emerged with such a depth of feeling that Gil could do nothing but glance at Jess and shake his head in sad disbelief.

———

L&M Jet-Ski had a booking office – a glorified booth – on Bridge Street in Tenby, amongst a mishmash of other companies offering boat trips and sea safaris. The booth wasn't open, but a couple of questions aimed at the lugubrious man in an adjacent booth advertising a "Caldey Island dolphin experience" quickly led them to the North Beach, where L&M Jet-Ski launched their skis and boards from. They parked high on the Croft and walked down the winding concrete steps to the glorious stretch of sand and sea below, and the lockup at the far end, where a low wooden hangar housed what was for hire. The doors to the hangar hung open and a man and a woman, mid-twenties, stood outside, both in wet suits and both hosing down paddle boards. Neither of them doing it with much gusto.

Once again, Catrin made the introductions. The man, name of Toby, frowned when Catrin asked if they knew where Michael Dunbar was, but then grinned broadly as if she'd just told the best joke ever.

'What's he done now, then?' Toby asked, laughing.

'Nothing. We wondered where he was, that's all.'

The woman, Sienna, sent Toby a quick side-eyed glance meant, Warlow suspected, to imply to the two officers she was as bemused by his attitude as they were. 'We don't see him on weekends,' she explained. 'Besides, it's the end of the season. We probably won't see him until next April.' Sienna was rangy with long arms and hair damp from spray, barefooted, and fit-looking in the figure-hugging rubber.

'When did you last see him?' Catrin asked.

Toby discharged a derisory huff through pursed lips. Clearly, he found the question ridiculous. 'About a month ago. We had an end of season party.' Toby jutted his chin out and gave them a thumbs up.

Again, Sienna offered more explanation, keen to shut Toby up by the look of it. 'We say end of season, though we've kept going on weekends because of popular demand and good-ish weather.'

'And what about Lee Barret?'

This time, Sienna cocked her head and gave them a rueful smile. 'Funny you should ask. We've been expecting him since eight.' She shot Warlow a wary glance. 'But he's not answering his phone. Is that why you're here? Has something happened?'

Warlow nodded. 'We're investigating a serious incident and we need to establish what Mr Barret's movements were.'

Toby's grin did not slip. 'Beats me, officer. Well, he doesn't but—'

Sienna stepped in again, raising her voice to quash Toby's. 'He always takes one ski out on a Sunday. Especially if one has been serviced or had maintenance.'

'Out there?' Warlow pointed into the bay.

Sienna shook her ringlets. 'We have a van, specially adapted. He comes and winches one in. Takes it off somewhere. Says he likes a change from North Beach. Usually, that is. Now and again, he'll stay here. Or get one of us to ride it.' She gave Toby a knowing glance. 'When the weather is too shit.'

Catrin wanted more detail. 'You say you were expecting him this morning?'

Toby nodded, deeply and slowly. 'We were.'

'Did he say where he was heading?'

Toby huffed out some air. 'Nah. Never does. He's the boss. He can do what he wants.'

'And your shifts? What time do you start?'

'Seven today. Now that the hour's gone back,' Sienna said.

'How long have you worked for them?' Catrin asked.

'Ooo,' Toby said, both hands held up.

'My first season,' Sienna clarified. 'Toby's been here a couple of years.'

'And how is it, the business?'

'We've had a busy season,' Sienna replied.

Warlow glanced in through the open doorway. A dozen sleek machines were neatly parked on wheeled trailers. Every one had been painted light-blue and green and bore the L&M logo on the prow.

'We thought maybe you were coming to do some peddleboarding… paddleboarding,' Toby corrected himself and turned his mouth down in exaggerated apology.

'You get many asking this time of year?' Warlow asked.

'A few walk-ins,' Sienna said. 'But we had a bet about who you might be. I said police. Toby said Martians.'

Toby giggled.

Warlow took a couple of steps towards the building, stuck his head forward and sniffed. A faint sweetness hung in the air. He turned back and studied the sand around Toby's feet before letting his eyes stray half a dozen yards further away to a point where more sand had been scuffed up.

'Must be very boring out here, hosing down peddle boards,' Warlow muttered.

'Paddle boards,' Toby said, holding up a finger in remonstration.

'I know,' Warlow nodded. 'And I have no problem with you smoking a little dope when there are no customers around. But only one of you is driving home, right?'

Sienna squeezed her eyes shut and put up an index finger, accompanied by a nod.

'Good. Toby, you will be a passenger, both in the car and for the rest of these questions, understand?' Warlow gave Toby a little chin down look by way of a warning.

Toby replied by wiping an extended index finger over his lips in a zipping motion.

'Okay, Sienna.' Warlow turned to the woman. 'Where does Mr Barret keep the van?'

'We have two vans. They rent a spot up near the campsite on Mallam's farm.'

Catrin wrote down the directions. Toby looked on, still amused by events.

'And you've experienced nothing odd going on here?'

'You mean, apart from that big seagull over there who I swear has been trying to crap on me for like, the entire morning? He's—' Frosty glares from both Sienna and Catrin dried up Toby's unwelcome contribution.

'What do you mean, odd?' Sienna asked.

'Strange people. Anything different. Animosity between Mr Dunbar and Mr Barret?'

'Animosity? No, nothing like that. When they're together here, which is rare, they're like two school kids. Always messing about.'

Warlow turned to look out at the grey sea and the view south to the harbour that had adorned a million picture postcards. Tenby was often quoted as being a jewel in the crown of the coastal resorts. Maybe not the sea-shanty charm of some of the tiny old Cornish fishing villages, but it had everything else going for it. Craggy cliffs,

Napoleonic fortresses, even a walrus on the harbour. But where there were people, especially people willing to spend money, there was inevitably someone looking for an edge. A way to take that money. L&M Jet-Ski looked like they had a nice little business going here. But people didn't get murdered because a paddleboard experience didn't live up to the hype. Something else was going on. Something bad.

'Is that it, then? What do we tell Lee when he turns up?' Toby asked when the silence got to almost a minute.

'Mr Barret won't be turning up today, Toby,' Catrin said.

'Ooh,' Toby said. 'Mysterious.'

But Sienna was clueing in to the seriousness of what wasn't being said by the officers. 'He's okay, isn't he? Lee… Mr Barret?'

'Does Mr Barret have a partner?'

'God, no,' Toby said. 'Free agent, is Lee.'

'What about Mr Dunbar?'

'Yes, he does. That'll be Stacey. They have a kid, too.'

'We'll need both their contact details, Mr Dunbar's and his partner's,' Warlow said. 'Then I suggest you lock up and go home. But it's likely one of our officers will be in touch soon. We'll need statements of when you last spoke to Mr Barret.'

'Something has happened, hasn't it?' Sienna asked with a little quiver in her voice.

Catrin sighed. 'We can't discuss the case with you. But yes, something bad has happened.'

'To Lee?'

Once again, Catrin's silence answered the woman's question.

'Oh my God, has he been shot?' Sienna took a step back and dropped the hose.

'Shit, man,' Toby said, his smiley face contorting into something else.

'Shit, man, indeed,' echoed Warlow. He let his eyes drift to the scuffed sand again. 'Next time, bury your spliffs a little deeper, Toby. And we cannot discuss Mr Barret's situation any further. But this is a very serious matter, so your cooperation would be appreciated.'

Catrin took Michael Dunbar's details and those of his partner. The walk back up the winding staircase to the Croft and their car was no joke. By the time they reached the road, Warlow was out of breath.

'Christ, you'd think they'd have put in a bloody lift.'

'Think of it as part of your ten thousand, sir.'

'I'd rather not think of it at all. Impression?'

Two red spots glowed on Catrin's cheeks, the only outwards sign of exertion she showed. 'Just kids. They wouldn't know anything, sir.'

Warlow resisted the urge to point out that they were probably only a few – perhaps half a dozen – years younger than she was, but he had the sense to keep shtum.

'Genuine enough,' Catrin added. 'Though Toby was pushing it.'

Warlow nodded. 'Well, it is off-season. I'll give him that. Nothing to be gained by hauling him over the coals for a bit of weed. Too much paperwork.'

'Agreed, sir.'

The noise of wheeling gulls above drew Warlow's attention. 'Besides, even though he might have been high as a kite, I think he has a point about these shifty buggers. I'm sure one of them has his beady eye on me as a target.'

'Lucky you're not eating chips, sir.'

'Did you have to mention food, Sergeant?'

'Sorry, sir.'

Warlow arched his back. 'Right, let's check out these vans.'

They weren't difficult to spot, bearing the same logo as the jet-skis and the paddleboards that Toby and Sienna had been hosing down, and parked up in a space outside a reception area of a caravan and camping site, just half a mile further north. 'We'll get Povey's team to give them the once over. But obviously, neither Barret nor Dunbar have used them today.'

'Where does that leave us, sir?'

'None the wiser, Sergeant. But a little hungrier. Still, there is one more call I'd like to make before heading back to HQ.'

CHAPTER THIRTEEN

MICHAEL DUNBAR DID NOT ANSWER his phone when Catrin tried it. But his partner, Stacey Campbell, answered hers. After only three rings. Suggesting to Catrin that she was expecting a call. Once the brief conversation ended, Catrin turned to Warlow. 'She's staying with a friend, sir. Up near Knowling Mead. And, as you heard, I suggested that we complete the conversation face-to-face.'

The development sat on the western fringes of the town. Convenient for the schools, and the leisure centre, but a long way from the beach.

Warlow had to park quite a way from the address that Catrin had up on her Google Maps app. They walked back along a street lined with semi-detached houses. Most looked well kept. One or two had the tell-tale signs of abandoned furniture in the front garden. Having a damp and rotting sofa on your lawn was, in Warlow's experience, a good indicator of the state of play inside. But the house Catrin stopped in front of had no furniture on its lawn and had been recently painted in grey with a vertical line demarcating the join between it and the bile-yellow property next door. Some inflatable pumpkins and a spooky tree sat at the side of the front door.

Kids, then.

The woman who answered Catrin's knock wore no makeup, but her lips had gone the way of misguided fashion and been filled out to appear thick and pouty. Warlow always thought all it did was make people look like they'd been stung by bees and had said as much to both Catrin and Jess. Not that either of them was in danger of following the herd. Stacey Campbell, however, was a slave to fashion. She'd piled her bright-blonde hair on her head and looked back at him through long black lashes and a mouth with lips that looked like they'd recently been... stung by bees.

Catrin made the introductions, but Campbell did not invite them in.

'What's the problem?'

'Any chance we can come in, Miss Campbell?' Warlow asked.

'No, you can say what you've got to say out here.'

There were people in the street going about their own business and Stacey Campbell wore a wary expression which, from her appearance and the whiff of stale alcohol on her breath, came courtesy of a hangover.

'You know Lee Barret?'

'Yeah, of course, I do.'

'Then what we have to say definitely should not be heard on a doorstep.'

Stacey's painted brow-lines morphed into a full-blown frown. With a shake of her head, she stepped aside and let the officers in.

'On the right,' she said, waving at a door in the semi's hallway that led into a sitting room where another woman in a loose-fitting T-shirt and jeans sat on a dark-navy, L-shaped settee. Two small children sat on the floor playing a matching card game. They looked up as Warlow and Catrin entered, but almost immediately went back to their play.

'This is Alex, my friend,' Stacey said. 'Sorry, I forgot your name. Rough night.'

'Detective Sergeant Catrin Richards,' Catrin explained. 'And this is DCI Evan Warlow.'

One of the kids squealed as the boy yelled, 'Bagsie.'

'These are Dion and Star. Dion's mine, Star's Alex's.'

Warlow stepped forward. 'Alex, could you do me a big favour and take the children somewhere for a minute?'

Alex looked a little taken aback, but stood up without comment and ushered the children out with a tempting, 'Who wants juice?'

A chorus of 'Me, me' rang up from the kids.

Stacey sat heavily on the settee, as if the effort of standing was proving too much for her. 'Can you tell me what the hell this is about? I'm not feeling brilliant—'

'It's about Lee Barret, Stacey. I'm afraid he was found dead earlier today.'

Stacey didn't move. She remained seated, her mouth open with the lost expression of someone who'd plunged into a nightmare with no handholds to slow her descent.

'What?' she whispered, her lower lip wobbling.

'I realise this is a shock—'

'Oh my God.' She thrust herself forward on the settee. 'What about Mike? Has anything happened to Mike—'

'Are you referring to Mr Dunbar?'

Stacey nodded.

'Not as far as we know,' Catrin said.

'But how… what …?'

'I can't tell you any details yet, Stacey. Only that we do not think it was accidental or natural.'

Stacey had a hand over her mouth when she whispered, 'Jesus. No… no… how do you know it's him?'

'You mean, Mr Barret?' Catrin asked.

'Lee, yeah. It could be a mistake.' She took in the officers' frowns but persisted. 'It could, though. I've seen stuff on TV. It might be the wrong bloke.'

'No,' Catrin said. 'There's no mistake. We have his driver's licence and photographs. We're satisfied.'

'But it might be someone who looked like him. Do you want me to—?' Her lip had stopped quivering and anger flushed in her face. It wasn't an unattractive face once you got beyond the ridiculous lips and the ice-white teeth. She wore a light-beige tracksuit with a red stripe down the sides and white trainers. An inch of tanned abdomen showed beneath the cream T-shirt under the leisurewear. The flesh on show wasn't taut.

Warlow provided the answer to Stacey's question. 'In cases of violent death, Stacey, it's important we proceed quickly if we want to find out who did this. Unless there is any doubt, we wouldn't let anyone see the victim because of wanting to get on with what we need to do. But what we really want to ascertain is if you've seen Mr Dunbar.'

'Mike? Not since yesterday. Why?'

'He isn't answering his phone.'

She nodded. 'Maybe he's out somewhere. At sea, I mean. He doesn't answer when he's at sea. Sometimes, he goes fishing on a boat.'

'So, he hasn't contacted you this morning?'

Stacey shook her head.

'We need to ask you some questions,' Catrin said. 'Important questions, so that we can find out what happened to Mr Barret.'

Stacey stared at the floor, but Warlow doubted she was checking out the pattern on the carpet. In her hand, she clutched a mobile phone wrapped in a pink protective sleeve. Her knuckles looked white around it. Warlow let his gaze drift across the room. A few framed photographs.

Mostly of the other woman, Alex, and the little girl, Star, with curly hair. But then he noticed a few more containing the two women and their two children. Alex and Stacey were old friends. That was obvious.

'Is there anyone that might have wanted to do anything violent to Mr Barret?' Catrin asked.

'What do you mean, violent?' Her voice became high pitched, close to hysteria.

Warlow waited.

'No.'

'Were you with Mr Dunbar last night, Stacey?' Catrin kept her voice low but firm.

'No, me and Alex… we went out. We got a sitter and I stayed here. It was her mate's birthday, so we had a big night. Last time I saw Mike was Saturday lunchtime. He drove me over here. He kissed Dion and told him to be a good boy.'

'Dion, he's your son?' Catrin led the questioning.

She sucked in a great breath then. As if the mention of the boy's name had almost made her drown. 'Our son. Mike is Dion's dad.'

'But normally you'd be at Mr Dunbar's house?'

Stacey nodded. Trying her best to keep it together.

'And you knew Mr Barret through Michael, your partner?'

'I've known Lee for years. But yes, through the business and Mike.'

'And that was going well? No troubles at work?'

'Mike never talks about work. But they love it, they both love it.'

'And business is good?'

'Yes.'

'You don't work for them in the business?' Warlow asked.

She offered a rueful waggle of her head. 'Dion was my

job. *Is* my job. Mike wants it that way.' At this last mention
of Dunbar's first name, the well-head exploded. Tears
came, big ones, coursing down her cheeks and redirecting
to run around her mouth when they reached the thick
barrier caused by her exaggerated lips. She gulped big
shuddering sobs, bent forward on the settee, clutching
herself, that big, pink phone still in her hand. The lifeline
she couldn't give up. Warlow wondered if she was hoping
perhaps that it might ring, and she'd glance down to read
Mike Dunbar's name.

Next to her, Catrin's arm got tighter, cupping her palm
over the woman's shoulder. Stacey didn't object.

'No arguments recently? Mr Dunbar hasn't confided
anything to you?'

'What?' Stacey screwed up her face in bewilderment.

'Stacey, it's important that we find Michael, you understand?' Warlow asked.

She nodded but didn't answer.

'Did Lee Barret have anyone? What about his parents?'

She managed to breathe out some words. 'His mum
died of breast cancer five years ago. He had no idea where
his dad was. Dion and me and Mike… we were his family.'

Warlow took out a card from an inside pocket. 'I'm
going to leave my contact details here, Stacey. Anytime you
want to speak to me, my mobile number's on there. DS
Richards will do the same. If you think of anything, if
Michael contacts you, please let us know. It's vital we talk
to him as soon as possible. I can see you're shaken and
you're not well. But if we can't contact Mr Dunbar, then at
some stage, we'll want to visit your home. The house you
share with him. Would that be okay?'

She didn't look up, lost in her grief, but Warlow was
pleased to see a brief nod.

Catrin stood up and both officers left the house and
took in a deep draft of air once they were outside.

'Never gets any easier, Sergeant,' Warlow muttered.

'No, sir,' Catrin answered without looking at him, keeping her eyes straight ahead and blinking rapidly. 'It doesn't.'

———

'AHA, THE WANDERERS RETURN,' Gil looked up from his desk as Warlow and Catrin walked through the Incident Room door.

'Got that tea ready, Rhys?' Warlow asked, gazing about but not seeing any mugs. 'And we can break out that Transplant box of yours, Gil. We're into emergency rations here. My blood sugar is somewhere around my laces.'

Rhys looked up with his pasted-on smile full of apology. 'About the tea, sir. Someone thought it might be best if we waited a bit.'

Warlow frowned. 'Did you not see our text message? Which part of "get the kettle on" was difficult to interpret?' He rounded on Catrin. 'You haven't got a Sanskrit app on your phone, have you, Sergeant? One that transforms plain English into indecipherable squiggles.'

Gil, beaming, let out a meagre Muttley giggle. 'I love it when you're hangry.'

Warlow glanced at the board. Crime scene photos had appeared, but not much else yet. 'I see you two have been busy.' But then his irritation spiked a little higher as he remembered the words that Rhys had used to explain the lack of a brew. 'And who is this mysterious "someone" who thinks it best we wait a bit for a cup of bloody tea?'

Warlow had his back to the SIO's office as he berated his colleagues over the lack of refreshments following a direct, texted request. He didn't see the door to that office open and a figure emerge. But he heard the voice.

'Ah, Evan, you're back.'

Warlow winced in much the same way ultra-sensitive people did when nails were scraped across a blackboard. He threw first Rhys, and then a grinning Gil, a narrow-eyed squint that promised swift and merciless revenge for the lack of warning before turning, with his own version of a composed smile – one that left a lot to be desired – to address the owner of the voice that had called to him.

'Superintendent Goodey. Checking on progress?'

'Hopefully, not just checking, Evan.' She dropped her voice and added a self-satisfied smirk. 'I hope I may have some material and practical help. I have DI Allanby in here, but we wanted to wait until you were back so that I could brief you both.'

From behind Two-Shoes, Jess popped her head up and promptly brought two hands together as if in prayer as she mouthed words to Warlow.

'*Please help me. Please.*'

Catrin turned away to cough. Though Warlow suspected it was more a triggered giggle, she managed somehow to just about disguise it.

'I asked your DC to hold off on the refreshments until we're finished. That okay?' Two-Shoes smiled.

'Tidy, ma'am, as Sergeant Jones would say. No problem at all.'

But no one in that room, apart from Goodey, believed for a moment that he meant it.

CHAPTER FOURTEEN

'THERE HAVE BEEN SOME DEVELOPMENTS,' Two-Shoes said, fingers intertwined on the desk like a teacher about to give the class an announcement about their exams. An affectation that made Warlow's toes curl.

'How, ma'am?' Jess asked. She and Warlow sat on the non-SIO side of the desk while Two-Shoes held court on the other, eking out whatever the hell it was she had to say to maximise the importance of it. Christ, she was a drama queen. Warlow contented himself by inhaling some of Jess's aroma. Subtle, but very pleasant.

'This morning, a walker reported something washed up on a beach at Abermawr.'

'Not another body, is it?' Warlow asked, his face falling.

'No. Not a body.'

'Abermawr is a new one on me,' Jess said.

Warlow tilted his head, recalling the coast he was so familiar with. 'That's far west. On the way to Strumble Head.'

'Very good, Evan,' Two-Shoes said.

Warlow half expected her to hand over a gold star for

him to pin on his lapel. Instead, she continued, 'It's the beach where there's a petrified forest at low tide.'

'Just spongey blobs now, ma'am. Nothing like trees. My dog enjoys sniffing them.'

'Lovely image, Evan. But let's allow DS Hopper to explain.'

'Hopper?'

'One of our SOC team. He's awaiting my call.'

Acronyms came and went in the Force. At one time SOC meant Scene of Crime. But Warlow knew Two-Shoes was referring to Serious and Organised Crime. Povey's lot, always present at scenes, preferred being known as Crime Scene Investigators these days. Though SOCO, Scene of Crime Officers still functioned in some forces' lexicons.

Two-Shoes placed her phone flat on the desk and pressed some buttons. A moment later, the call she'd placed was answered.

'Hopper,' said a voice.

'DS Hopper, this is Detective Superintendent Goodey. I now have DCI Warlow and DI Allanby with me. They are leading the investigation into the shooting that took place this morning. Are you still at Abermawr?'

'Yes, ma'am. We're extending the search to adjacent beaches.'

'Glad to hear it. But, for completeness's sake, can you tell Evan and Jess what's happened?'

'No problem, ma'am.' Hopper launched right into it. 'Early this morning, a dog walker spotted something washed up on the beach here. Tide was on the turn. Long story short, what they'd seen was a twenty-foot-long snake of black bags attached to empty twenty-five-litre plastic jerry cans. The cans were empty because they were used as buoyancy aids. The bags were wrapped to be watertight in plastic bags with bungees and nylon rope. The lot held together with more nylon rope. We've tested two and they are full of cocaine. I've sent some photos, ma'am.'

Two-Shoes had already shifted the monitor to a point where all of them could view it. She clicked the mouse, and an image appeared. Much as described, there, lying on a pebble beach was a trail of black plastic-wrapped oblong parcels sealed with tape and secured by ropes, tied to white plastic jerry cans along a length of thicker, three-stranded rope.

'Each parcel is about five kilos,' Hopper explained.

Warlow let out a low whistle. 'Street value?'

'A rough estimate would be between thirty and forty million.'

Jess's neat eyebrows shot up. 'Congratulations. If that is the right word.'

'Oh, it is,' Warlow said. 'You're buying the next round, Sergeant.'

'"This is a hole in one if ever I saw one,' Jess said.

'A stroke of luck, I'd say.' Two-Shoes beamed. 'For both the Serious and Organised Crime team and for you, Evan.'

'I haven't lost any cocaine, ma'am. At least I hadn't last time I looked. But thanks for asking.'

His joke fell on hard and stony ground, which just about summed up Two-Shoes' expression. 'Sergeant Hopper will elaborate.'

'Word of the shooting got to us first thing,' Hopper continued. 'Once we knew who it was, it sent up a red flag.'

'Why?'

Hopper sighed. 'None of this is a hundred percent, and it is part of an ongoing multi-team investigation into drug smuggling and county lines, but we've known for a while that big hauls were coming in. From Ireland, we suspected. So, by sea. Your victim, Barret, has a partner called Michael Dunbar. He's been on our radar for a while.

Money laundering and supplying. They've both been splashing the cash for years now, but we were never sure quite what Barret's role in the distribution network was.'

'Of drugs like you found today, I assume?' Warlow asked.

'Exactly, sir. This find, brilliant though it is, has thrown a spanner into the works. We've been monitoring harbours, looking for boats that come in for short periods into berths. But this find… it means we've been looking in the wrong places.'

'You don't think it's simply fallen off a ship, your cocaine?' Jess asked.

'No. The buoyancy aids are a give-away. What we suspect is happening is that a boat will stay offshore and dump the drugs into the water. Then someone, probably not in a boat, to keep a low profile, harvests the floating product and brings it ashore at some quiet beach or inlet.'

'Wouldn't you still need a boat for that, too, no matter how small?' Jess asked.

'Not necessarily, ma'am. You'd need something quick and manoeuvrable.'

'Like a jet-ski,' Warlow muttered.

'Exactly. I mean, who pays attention to a jet-ski zooming up and down the coast these days?'

Two-Shoes beamed, but no one spoke for half a long minute. Finally, Jess broke the impasse.

'And you assume the two things might be related?'

'It's a coincidence at least; a direct link if it all adds up,' Hopper said.

Warlow didn't need it spelled out. Anything was possible where drugs were concerned. And it did not take a genius to follow Hopper's and consequently Two-Shoes' trail of thought. And it was a fiery trail, he had to admit. Time to fan the flames.

'According to his employees,' Warlow said. 'Barret was

in the habit of taking jet skis out for test runs of a Sunday morning. They'd been expecting him to do exactly that this morning. But he didn't.'

'That might explain how the drugs washed up, then, wouldn't it?' Two-Shoes asked, animatedly. 'If he didn't make the pickup, the tide might have done the rest.'

As theories went, Warlow had to admit it was a good one. Though he was loath to add two and two together quite as quickly as the superintendent. He'd got his sums wrong too many times before.

'Right, that settles it.' Two-Shoes got up. 'I've spoken to the Super running the SOC operation, and he's agreed that Sergeant Hopper can join your team from tomorrow. His expertise in this will be invaluable.'

Warlow and Jess exchanged glances. In principle, Warlow did not like outside "help" other than what was necessary. But if this was a drug-related killing, they would need intelligence from someone with his or her finger on the pulse.

'Evan?' Two-Shoes expected validation.

'Sounds like a good idea, ma'am.'

Next to him, Jess agreed.

'Good. Sergeant Hopper, we'll expect you bright and early in the Incident Room. DCI Warlow will be waiting.'

'I won't be,' Warlow said. 'I'm up at the post-mortem, but we'll have a catch-up at lunchtime. Why don't you try and make that?'

'I'll see you both tomorrow, then.' Hopper rang off.

Two-Shoes picked up her phone, her expression now more a smirk than ever. 'How about that for joined-up police work?'

'Commendable, ma'am,' Warlow said, using one of Two-Shoes' magic words as embellishment.

'All in a day's, as they say.' The smiling superintendent moved the monitor back to its original position on the desk. Neat and tidy as always. 'Right, I will leave you to it. I've rearranged my Sunday lunch for an early evening supper. Until tomorrow.'

She left. Warlow half expected her to whistle. She didn't. But by the time she got to the Incident Room door, she'd started humming. Later, when they quizzed Gil, he thought the tune was "My Way". Warlow suspected Gil had made that bit up.

'You going to look him up, or will I?' Warlow asked.

'Hopper?' Jess posed the question rhetorically. 'Rhys already has. Two-Shoes told me most of this while we were waiting for you. The repeat was all for dramatic effect.' She got up and stuck her head out of the door. 'Rhys?'

The DC joined them. Warlow took up his usual position, leaving just about enough room for the young officer inside the door.

'Cosy in here, sir, ma'am.'

'It's a bloody cupboard and you know it,' Warlow said.

'Right. DS Hopper, what can you tell us about him?' Jess asked.

'I don't know him myself,' Rhys replied, 'but he started off down here and moved to Mid-Wales with Serious Crimes. There was a Task Force set up with North Wales and Merseyside police. Lots of arrests last year on our patch and in Chester and Liverpool.'

'I remember that. Wasn't someone shot?' Jess asked.

'Two informants,' Rhys explained. 'The Chief Super in charge got hauled over the coals for what happened. But the shootings were in Liverpool. Wil… DS Hopper… Only just got out intact. He was eight months undercover, ma'am. There isn't much I could find out about all that. I think there's an internal investigation pending. Not involving him, though.'

'Drugs,' Warlow muttered darkly.

'But,' Rhys added, 'seems like he's a top bloke. Catrin said Craig might have worked with him.'

'Good. He'll be working with us on this case.'

'Will he, ma'am?' Rhys brightened.

'He will.'

'That kettle on yet?' Warlow barked.

Rhys flinched. 'I thought you wanted this report first, sir?'

'We did,' Jess said.

'And now we need promised refreshments and a run through of where we are.' Warlow murmured with feeling.

Once the Human Tissue For Transplant box was opened and tea provided, Jess led the charge. They listened to the 999 call once more, for Warlow and Catrin's sake, and Catrin posted up images of L&M's lockup on Tenby's North Beach, regurgitating a cut-down version of their interviews with both the jet-ski-hire company's weed smoking employees, and Stacey Campbell. But by the time questions were asked, it was nearing five.

There wasn't much more they could do that day, except that Warlow wanted to hang on for Povey's preliminary report in case they'd found something useful. And there was paperwork to finish on his first look at the crime scene. But then there was always paperwork to finish.

Jess stuck her head around the SIO office door at five-thirty.

'I've let the troops go.'

'Anyone got word of Clark? How's he doing?'

'In ITU. But stable,' Jess answered.

Stable always sounded ominous to Warlow. It somehow hovered between improving and unstable. A limbo status. 'You get off, Jess. That daughter of yours will no doubt need chivvying.'

Jess laughed, but then gave him one of her appraising looks. 'You okay?'

'Yeah, fine. Cadi'll think I've abandoned her, but otherwise—'

His phone buzzed, still on vibrate from the meeting with Two-Shoes. Warlow squinted at the caller ID, sent Jess a quizzical glance, and answered the call.

'Molly? What can I do for you? Is it your mum you want? If so, she's standing right here.'

'I am capable of ringing my mother's number, Evan,' Molly answered. Her sharp delivery brought a much-needed smile to Warlow's lips. 'I'm ringing to tell you I've been over to yours and walked your dog before the sunset. You don't need to worry. Though she was looking very sorry for herself.'

'Molly, you are a star,' Warlow said with genuine relief. But then he had a thought. 'How did you get in?'

'Let's not pretend you've changed the secret location of your front door key from under the loose coping stone on your wall to somewhere else.'

'Ah.'

'I stayed with you for a week, if you remember?'

'How could I forget?' Warlow went for pithy. Whilst Jess had been on a mandatory training course, he'd hosted her daughter at Ffau'r Blaidd, the house he'd converted in Nevern. He and Molly and Cadi had got on well. 'All my secrets and passwords are now useless, then.'

'They are. Oh, and by the way, it was Mum's idea. She texted me to say you'd be stuck, and it would be a nice thing if I could do it.'

'Thank you,' Warlow said.

'Bye,' Molly sang out her farewell.

Warlow looked up at Jess. 'That was a random act of kindness, DI Allanby.'

'We both owe you a lot, Evan. It's a small thing.'

'I appreciate it.'

'Right, I'll be off.' Jess turned away.

For one fraction of a second, Warlow felt an urge to say something else. To tell her she'd smelled nice when they'd met with Two-Shoes. But he held back, as he always did. There might be a time, but it wasn't now.

When then, Evan?

'Bye, Jess, and thanks again,' he shouted after her as she walked up through the Incident Room. She held up a hand without turning around to wave.

Sighing, Warlow flicked his gaze back to the screen and started typing. Once he'd finished the report, he'd ring Daniel Clark's parents. It was the least he could do.

CHAPTER FIFTEEN

SUNDAY REMAINED PRETTY traditional for many families. Sunday papers, Sunday lunch, a relaxed Sunday evening in front of the TV. Later, a film and a glass of wine, perhaps, to wash down a cheeky sandwich made from cold cuts left over from the lunchtime roast.

But the Menzies were not your typical Pembrokeshire family. Though they were creatures of habit. Or rather, creatures intent on stimulating and then feeding habits in those unfortunate enough to cross their path. But there remained an element of tradition to this particular Sunday, being the last of the month.

This was delivery day.

On this day, the Menzies went to church. Never all the family. Usually just two. Sometimes Paul Menzies, the patriarch, took one of his sons. Sometimes, like today, the boys, Luke, twenty-four, or Zac, seventeen, drove across together in Luke's wheels, with the music on loud as they belted down the A477 until they got to Carew, where the church was. Then they'd turn the music off. Show a little respect and not disturb the walkers and tourists intent on visiting Carew Castle. Not that either of them respected much of anything or anyone. But they did respect Paul, their father, whose quick hands, and sharp tongue had instilled unquestioning respect based on swift punishment with those quick hands over the years. And he'd told them to always turn the "fucking music down" or suffer the consequences.

The Menzies weren't interested in the two-thousand-year-old castle and its tidal mill, either. Or the underlying Iron Age fort that had guarded the inlet from the Milford Haven waterway millennia before. In fact, had they been asked anything about its history, which encompassed treachery and horror in the form of the Black Death, their reply would have been, 'Who gives a shit about crumbling castles? 'S'not exactly Game of Thrones, is it?'

Their interests lay half a mile south of the castle at Carew Cheriton where the 14th century Church of St Mary with its Old Mortuary Chapel was situated. One Sunday a month, regular as clockwork, at around 2pm, the Menzies would arrive at Carew Cheriton. Of course, there were no services in the church at that time of day. In fact, they went nowhere near St Mary's. What they did was visit the little cemetery just off the A477 roundabout a hundred yards from the church itself. They'd park in a lay-by on the road to the market and the old RAF control tower and walk back. By then the car boot sale and airfield market would have wound down. But since the church sat halfway between Tenby and Johnston in Haverfordwest, this spot was convenient for the parties involved. Ideal for collection and delivery of the product necessary for their operation.

The way it worked was that one of the Menzies would sit in the car – a new souped-up Hyundai N i30 in Ultimate Red. The other, whoever it might be, would take a plastic bag containing flowers and walk up to the little church graveyard, through the iron gates, along the path and then left, towards the very end, to a spot hidden from the road by the hedge and a grave marked by a carved stone cross. Letters etched into that cross were now so weathered as to be illegible. But it would be on this grave that flowers would be laid by whoever's turn it was. And the old bunch, a month old by then, desiccated or rotting, would be removed. While all that was going on, a parcel, wrapped in black plastic against the weather, twelve inches by twelve inches and six inches thick, well hidden under the hedge and placed there a little while before, would be retrieved when no one was looking and placed in the convenient, nondescript plastic bag with the dead flowers on top.

But today, there was no black parcel.

Zac had been back three times. Luke twice. They'd even driven to Pembroke Dock for a late KFC lunch and gone back again. But now it was getting dark, and the funk of stale food filled the interior of the car.

'What the fuck is going on?' Luke said for the tenth time since they'd arrived back.

Zac, wise enough to realise that suggesting something would only irritate his brother, shrugged.

'I mean, shit, what is Dad going to say?'

'We should tell him,' Zac said.

'Right.' Luke kept tapping the steering wheel. 'Right.' Always a little antsy, Luke was getting more wound up by the minute. 'I never trusted that Barret. He's always so full of it.'

'He wouldn't mess us about, would he? I mean, he wouldn't mess Dad about, right?' Zac said.

'Barret is a complete twat. I wouldn't be surprised if he nicked our stuff.' He threw Zac a desperate glance. 'Text Dad, tell him what's happened.'

Zac shook his head. '*You* do it.'

'You're better at explaining it than me,' Luke said.

Zac let out a long-suffering sigh and began composing

a message to his father. He was already not looking forward to getting home.

———

WHEN WARLOW MADE it out to the Jeep, he was surprised to see Catrin walking ahead of him towards the main entrance of HQ.

'Don't you have a home to go to?' Warlow called to her.

She turned and smiled. 'Craig came off shift ten minutes ago. I brought the car this morning, so I am driving him home. He got a lift in.'

'So, no Sunday lunch waiting for you with all the trimmings?'

'There's a pub near us that does Sunday night pizzas.'

Warlow caught up with her, and they walked together. 'Sounds like a plan. Craig okay?'

'Fine, sir.'

'Rhys told you about Wil Hopper?'

Catrin nodded. 'Yes. I don't know him well, but Craig worked with him back in the day. Ambitious, he called him.'

'His CV certainly looks impressive.'

Outside the doors, the cool October air smelled damp. Catrin hesitated and turned to Warlow. 'I've been meaning to ask you, sir, about your… illness.'

'My HIV, you mean?'

'Yes.' She gave a little nervous laugh. 'Difficult to believe you have it. I mean, you look so well.'

'It's under control, so they tell me. What do you want to know?'

'It's been bugging me, sir. The way you got it. You've never talked about it much, but am I right in thinking it was that junkie we dealt with? When you offered to come with me that very first day I worked as a DC.'

Warlow saw no point in soft soap. 'Difficult to prove, of course, but the chances are very good that the charming Cerys McLean was indeed the person kind enough to place dirty needles in her hair, one of which transmitted the virus.'

Catrin gave an involuntary shudder. 'I'd kind of worked it out, sir.'

'That's why you're a detective, Catrin.'

She didn't laugh and her smile was a half-baked affair. 'I can't help thinking that if you hadn't been with me, if you hadn't taken her on that day, it would have been me.'

'Ideas like that will get you nowhere.'

'Even so. I haven't said thank you, or that I'm sorry.'

Warlow cocked an eyebrow. 'Sorry that it wasn't you instead of me?'

'No, but… you know what I mean.'

He eased her discomfort with a wry smile. 'I do. But playing the blame game is unrewarding, in my experience.'

'It's why I haven't said anything up to now. It's weird. I mean, I'm grateful, but guilty for feeling that way. And then I think, what if it had been me? I wouldn't be with Craig and—'

'That's a dark and deep rabbit hole, Catrin. You are doing yourself no favours scrabbling about down there. Besides, I am well. Or as well as might be expected for a man of my age.'

His weak attempt at humour fell way short of its mark, and to his consternations, he saw Catrin's lower lip wobble. 'You are bloody hopeless, sir.' Before he could move, she stepped forward and grabbed him into a tight hug, whispering into his chest as she did so. 'You act as if it doesn't matter, but it must play on your mind. Something like that has consequences. It would for me, even if I was okay on treatment.'

'What's up, Catrin?' Warlow asked. He couldn't quite work out where the question had come from. But she pulled back, head down, dragging a tissue out from her coat pocket and blowing her nose.

'Just me being silly, sir.'

That made him ponder. Being silly and Catrin Richards were chalk-and-cheese concepts.

Away to their left, a couple of men were walking over to the car park. Catrin glanced across. 'There's Craig. I'd better go.' She regarded him once more and dropped her voice. 'Sorry about that. It's been bugging me lately.'

'No need to apologise, Catrin. It is what it is.'

She nodded and turned towards the men.

'See you tomorrow,' he said as she trotted off.

Fifty yards away, Craig Peters raised his hand in greeting. Warlow reciprocated and unlocked the Jeep with a couple of chirps from the alarm. But on the way home, his thoughts went back to Catrin's words. Of course, she was right. Despite the retrovirals that kept the disease at bay and his viral load virtually undetectable, its presence coloured his thinking when it came to other people. Especially other people to whom he might be attracted. He'd parked all that for many, many months. But increasingly of late, he'd wondered what it might be like to get a little companionship. Not so much lust as consensual enjoyment.

Today's youngsters had a hard line to tread, and he didn't envy them that minefield with all the right and left swiping traps laid by social media for the unwary. But as a fifty-something-year-old, his own way was equally poorly lit and meandered down some very dark alleys. There were things he could do to light that path. Places he could go to socialise, apps he could download, but the idea of it filled him with trepidation. He'd much prefer serendipity to step in. But she was a fickle, impossible to pin down, little minx. Worst of all, she was hardly likely to give him any warning. Better he kept his head down and got on with the work at hand. That way, he could keep all these uncomfortable thoughts of "other people" at bay. Something he usually succeeded extremely well in doing. Catrin Richard's outburst this evening, though, had brought them out into the light, warts and all.

The sergeant's words came back to him now.

Something like that has consequences.

Of course, it did. And he'd fought shy of them ever since he'd been diagnosed. Truth was, he hated being reminded of that fact. And work, his kind of work, was a bloody good distraction. Yet, when his well-buried HIV bubbled to the surface, as with Catrin asking him, it was a difficult thing to shake off. Compartmentalising life's unpleasantries was his way of coping. Vile people. Vile acts, death, and horror. Those were the labels of the drawers in his head where he stored the images and inter-actions of his professional life. The one underneath marked "Warlow-personal", he kept locked. But Catrin had made him open it this evening, and inside was a clut-tered mess. He gave a little shake of his head; his go-to sticking plaster for unhelpful mentation. He had enough to think about, what with the shooting and the prospect of what tomorrow might hold.

Later, as he sat in his green oak extension, staring out at the lights glinting across the estuary, Cadi came and sat at his side and put her head on his knee. Warlow murmured, 'Good girl.' He hoped that Daniel Clark's wife and his mother and father had a dog. One that might bring a little comfort to them as they worried about their son. Thinking of them made him wince and he glanced at his watch. He hadn't phoned the Clarks even though he'd meant to. Too late now. They wouldn't be sleeping, but perhaps a kind GP might have given one of them something to ease the pain and get some rest. He'd also meant to speak to the crime scene manager to make sure Barret's dog had been taken back to Stacey Campbell, too. He sent off a text and got an OK by return.

'Not the best of Sundays, eh, girl?'

Cadi put a paw on his leg. She was asking to be let out. Warlow did the needful and waited at the back door for her to relieve herself. The night air cooled his face. Soon, there'd be frosts. And tomorrow night was Halloween. Samhain. The official end of summer when the darkness ruled sway for the next few months. Christ, he was getting maudlin in his old age.

He needed something to break out of this funk. He called to Cadi and turned back inside. A glass of red was called for. Something Sicilian, with a promise of summer, and a hint of dark cherries and vanilla in its tail. The best antidote, taken in moderation, for banishing the ghosts of the past and the horrors of the future.

CHAPTER SIXTEEN

Warlow learned all he needed to know about Lee Barret's death within fifteen minutes of the post-mortem. Tiernon already had the chest open when they arrived. Late, courtesy of a holdup on the M4, he and Rhys had endured Tiernon's terse silence as they'd apologised, but frankly, Warlow didn't think they'd missed anything. In fact, it looked like they'd timed it just right. Within five minutes of getting gowned up, they listened and watched as Tiernon showed them the ragged tear in the big vessels above the heart that would have resulted in massive internal bleeding. The second shot entered more to the right and would not have been fatal. But the two shots were close together.

'Double tap, sir?' Rhys asked.

Tiernon looked up, but it was Warlow who answered the DC. 'Could be. Care to elaborate?'

'I don't think it's taught to armed officers now, but it's still a technique I've read about. One of my mates is being firearms trained, and it came up as a question. Probably because he plays a lot of Call of Duty. But I read that two shots fired in rapid succession is a technique developed by the British Police in Shanghai before that city became what it is today. Two quick shots to ensure sufficient damage.'

'Very good. Dr Tiernon, what's your opinion?'

Tiernon had a look in his eyes above the mask, suggesting a great deal of impatience brewing behind whatever opinion he was harbouring. But Warlow was having none of it. Even though Tiernon liked to believe he ruled his little empire, he was here acting on behalf of the Home Office as a designated forensic pathologist. And Warlow was the Senior Investigating Officer. Tiernon might not like it, but the DCI called the shots. And in this instance, he called them double taps.

'The position of the wounds suggests rapid firing,' Tiernon admitted.

'No sign of the bullets, then?'

'No. We'll have to hope Povey finds them.'

Warlow nodded.

Tiernon remained unmoving.

'Have we finished?' Warlow asked, knowing full well that they hadn't. Many organs had yet to be removed, weighed, cut open, and then returned from whence they'd come.

'Oh,' Tiernon said, feigning surprise. 'Does that mean I have your permission to carry on, Detective Chief Inspector?'

At the rear of the mortuary, two technicians, busy doing whatever mortuary technicians did, looked up at hearing the heavy sarcasm in Tiernon's voice, aware that he was baiting.

'Tell you what,' Warlow replied. 'Next time I'm up, I'll bring some flags and we can adopt a semaphore system. That way, we can minimise the talking. When I wave a red flag, you stop while I discuss relevant to the investigation points with my colleague. Then, when I'm done, I'll wave a green flag and you can carry on, devoid of any kind of attitude.'

Tiernon snorted. 'While I appreciate your desire to indulge your junior colleague, you also need to appreciate that we are backed up with cases and extremely busy. There isn't time for you—'

Warlow raised his hand and pretended to wave something. 'Just imagine it's green,' he said.

The technicians, both fighting giggles, turned back to their work. Tiernon muttered the words, 'Childish rubbish.' Then leaned forward to examine another part of Barret's internal workings, dictating his finding as he went.

Warlow took out his phone and typed a text message. Next to him, Rhys's phone vibrated. The DC read Warlow's text:

> Off to visit Daniel Clark. Stay here and ask more questions. As many as you like. Tiernon loves you.

RHYS, whose interest and enjoyment in post-mortem had become the stuff of legend within the team, fought back a smile and nodded.

Warlow turned and made for the exit. Behind him, Tiernon paused before saying, 'Leaving so soon, Mr Warlow?'

The DCI didn't bother turning around. 'I've found that there is only so much fun you can have in one day, Dr Tiernon. So, thank you for that.' He pushed open the door and strode out.

———

THE UNIVERSITY HOSPITAL OF WALES, also known colloquially as the Heath Hospital, was a warren. For a start, it was huge, with a thousand beds, and the car parks could only be described as woefully inadequate with no room to park a skateboard, let alone a car. But when Warlow asked at the neurosurgical ward about Daniel Clark, they redirected him to critical care. And though he'd hoped to see the wounded officer himself, he failed. Covid had spiked again and visiting had been restricted, particularly in an area with such severely ill patients. But the senior nurse he spoke to on reception, once she'd seen his badge, explained that Daniel was not available for visits as they'd induced a coma and he'd be kept that way while they tried to control his oedema.

Warlow nodded, filed away the word 'oedema', and wandered along to a family room. Everyone wore masks. Warlow being no exception, having carried one up from the mortuary. Half a dozen people sat in the room. All of them unsmiling, all of them carrying the weight of worry and concern that comes when a loved one is severely ill. They weren't all there for Daniel Clark, but in one corner sat a couple of about the right age to be Daniel's parents, five or six years younger than Warlow. He took a punt and introduced himself.

'Mr and Mrs Clark? DCI Evan Warlow. I'm a colleague of Daniel's.'

They looked up, fear sparking in their eyes, and he realised that everyone here was waiting desperately for news of the people they loved. People who were close by but might as well have been on a different planet. And that news could be good or bad. Warlow shook hands as they introduced themselves, then pulled up a chair and kept his voice low for privacy.

'They wouldn't let me see him. How is he?' Daniel's mother asked.

Neither of Daniel's parents' faces was visible under their masks, but he read the pain in their eyes. John Clark had been attempting a crossword. Only four words were pencilled in on the folded paper he'd put down on the chair. Beth Clark had been holding her phone. And it was this that she now turned so Warlow could see the screen image there. Just the one. A hospital bed and a patient surrounded by equipment and lines going into both arms from drips. The beard was the only thing that gave any inclination that the person in that bed was male because most of the head was swathed in bandages and a tube running into his mouth and down into his lungs had been taped over that mouth, linked up to a ventilator. But the thing that made Warlow wince was the swelling. The nurse had said oedema, but Clark's face looked grotesque. A Halloween mask swollen to the size of a football.

Beth Clark spoke. Her voice distant and emotionless.

'His Glasgow coma score is still five. They say that's okay after such an injury. Is it, you think?'

Warlow had no answers. All he could offer was a thin smile.

'The bullet is still in there,' John said. 'They don't take them out unless they have to. Removing it is too damaging.'

Warlow nodded. He hadn't known that, but it seemed best to simply agree.

'They've been marvellous here,' Beth added. 'Everyone is very kind. But they can't tell us anything. They say that it will be weeks before… before we know. All they can do now is hope he doesn't bleed again.'

'I'm sorry this has happened to Daniel, Beth,' Warlow said. 'Things like this should never happen.' He felt hopeless even saying these empty words, but they were all he had and so he said them, nevertheless. 'We're all thinking about you and Daniel.'

'Why has this happened, Evan?' Beth asked. She didn't cry. Warlow suspected her tear glands were bone dry by now.

'We're doing everything we can to find out, Beth.'

'Someone was killed, we heard,' John whispered.

'Someone was. Not a police officer.'

Both the Clarks wobbled their heads in pained disbelief.

'Was this one of these mass shootings you read about? Like in America?' John asked.

Warlow's turn to shake his head. Since yesterday, since they'd had to consider a spree killing, no reports of anything else had come in. 'We don't think so. But we can't be sure of anything at this stage.' The Clarks regarded him in bewilderment. He had to give them something. 'It's likely that Daniel and Leanne, the other officer shot, arrived on the scene as something else was about to take place. But of course, no one was expecting there to be firearms.'

'Leanne, how is she?' John asked.

'Her injuries were not—' Warlow caught himself just in time. Life threatening had been on the tip of his tongue. Those were not the words you wanted to utter here. 'Not as serious,' he finally said.

'Good,' Beth Clark said and glanced down at the image on her phone again. At the damaged, frail, helpless being in the bed, that would never be the Daniel she knew ever again. Though she didn't say it, Warlow read it in her eyes and in the ragged inhalation of breath that came with it.

He told them to contact him if there was anything that they needed. John explained that they already had the Assistant Chief Constable's number but took his card anyway. Then Warlow excused himself and went back to the mortuary.

Tiernon paused when Warlow entered long enough to ask pithily, 'Feeling better?'

Warlow suspected the man was playing to the gallery again, suggesting that Warlow had to leave because of a weak stomach.

'No, I'm not. But it isn't anything to do with you for once.'

Tiernon waited.

'I have an unrelated question,' Warlow continued. 'Gunshot wounds to the head. What are the relevant factors in determining survival?'

Tiernon wisely chose not to play silly buggers and answered swiftly, 'Outcomes are worse where the bullet tracts are extensive or may cross the midline and damage structures in both hemispheres. Right hemisphere injuries result in severe motor damage. Left side is sensory.'

'Time scale?'

'If the patient survives the initial trauma, once devitalised tissue and blood clots are removed, the first week or two is critical. The main issues are further bleeding and cerebral swelling.'

Warlow nodded.

'How is he, the constable?' Tiernon asked.

'Stable, so I've been told,' Warlow said. 'Do you know anything about the extent of his injuries?'

Tiernon hesitated, but then said, 'I heard that more than one lobe was involved.'

Warlow felt his lips compress under his mask, but he said nothing more about it. 'Okay. Do we have what we need here?' He turned to Rhys. But it was Tiernon who answered, again with no hint of the acerbic tone he usually adopted.

'My preliminary report will be available by this afternoon. I'll make sure of that.'

'Good. We appreciate it.' Warlow deliberately picked

the pronoun, avoiding the singular so that Tiernon remained aware of who his employer was here.

The journey home in the Jeep was a sombre one. Rhys didn't even ask to stop for something to eat. But Warlow pulled off for the Outlet Mall at Bridgend, anyway. He parked and gave Rhys a tenner for some coffee from a franchise of his own choosing, declining the offer of something to eat when asked. When Rhys came back with a Gregg's coffee and the one chicken bake for himself. It was a moment worthy of comment.

'What, no crisps? You on a diet, Rhys?'

'Season has started, sir. I'm still not a hundred percent fit after the summer. But Gina's had a look at my diet and,' he made a mortified face, 'she's right. I am eating too much crap. Her words, sir.'

Rhys still played rugby when weekends allowed. And so far, had avoided any trauma to his face, which, seven weeks into a season, was a first.

'She's right,' Warlow said. 'If there was a potato famine, you'd be the first to jump off a bridge.'

'Not that bad, sir.' Rhys looked genuinely offended.

'Believe me, I've had a hearing test and there is proven damage from listening to you crunch those bloody things for hours on end.'

Warlow slotted his coffee into a holder and set off for the M4 again while Rhys bit into his bake, but not before throwing out a conversation starter. 'Gina's acting as the liaison for Daniel's family, sir.'

'Good,' Warlow said.

'Did you have anything to do with that, sir?'

'I might have suggested something along those lines,' Warlow conceded. 'They'll need all the help they can get. But she can handle the hyenas.'

'Sir,' Rhys said. They were both aware of how capable

Gina was of fending off unwanted interest, press or otherwise.

'Is she there now?'

'Just texted me, sir. She's with Daniel's wife, Siwan. They're expecting DI Allanby.'

'I noticed she wasn't at the hospital,' Warlow said. 'Daniel's wife.'

'They're doing it in shifts, sir. Her and Daniel's parents. Though there isn't much they can do up there, is there?'

'Bugger all. They can't even sit next to him. Bloody virus.'

Warlow overtook a lorry and eased the Jeep up to seventy.

'So,' Warlow said, changing tack. 'All working out at the new place for you and Gina?'

Warlow had helped the couple move in a few weeks before. Rhys nodded quickly, his mouth full.

'And she has you eating properly at last.' Warlow assessed the chicken bake. 'Well, almost properly.'

'Normally, I'd have had at least two of these, sir.'

'Some improvement, then. Glad to hear it.'

'Good diet and early to bed, sir.'

Warlow sent him a side-eyed glance.

'I didn't mean it that way, sir.' Rhys blustered out the words, spraying crumbs over the dash and flushing a bright red.

Warlow gave him an open-mouthed stare of disbelief. 'Right, keep your mind on the task at hand. Which at this moment is not pebble-dashing my car with chicken bake. Got the post-mortem stuff sorted in your head?'

'I have, sir. I made notes.'

'I'm sure you did. Right, no more multi-tasking for you, that is eating and talking. Let's get back to HQ and see what progress the others are making.'

CHAPTER SEVENTEEN

GIL AND JESS sat in a small, well-appointed sitting room in a semi-detached property on a new estate to the west of Carmarthen. They were still building here, extending the housing north of the A40. At least these were proper houses and a move away from the bungalows that planners had favoured for years. Gina had made them all a cup of tea. Or rather, she'd made all the police officers, including herself, a cup. Siwan Clark, the woman they were all here to support, had declined. She preferred simply boiled water.

'Nice place you have here, Siwan,' Jess said. And it was; tasteful and uncluttered, with a nod to repurposed art. Jess had quizzed Gil about the correct pronunciation of her name on the way across from HQ.

'Sue-ann,' he'd explained. 'As always, ma'am, every letter is enunciated in Welsh.'

They'd gone at Jess's suggestion, as a courtesy, to reassure one of their own, or at least the partner of one of their own, that they were on the case.

'We've only been in a couple of months. They were late finishing it.' Siwan half smiled. A ghostly, insipid thing.

'Just as well we got the mortgage when we did, though. Now that interest rates have got bad.'

'Were they ever good?' Gina said and got a few nods for her effort.

'Any news of Daniel?' Gil asked.

'His mother texts me every hour. Just to check in. But you feel so useless. The doctors say all we can do is wait.'

Brave words. But she didn't appear brave, this slip of a woman, hunched forward, on the edge of a leather armchair, knees together, her hands clasped between her thighs. As if she was holding in all the emotion for fear of it spilling out and making a mess on the laminate flooring. Siwan was twenty-five, just eight years older than Molly. Her world had been shattered by a single bullet, but she was holding it together, and she'd made a big effort for the visit, Jess could see that, dressed in tan ankle-length trousers and a dark blouse with chunky white trainers on her feet. Not much makeup but enough to give the good cheekbones genetics had given her some colour.

Her gaze flicked from Gil to Jess and back. 'Do you have any idea what happened?'

Gil answered, 'Not yet. But we are going to find out, Siwan. Be sure of that.'

She smiled again at that. A brief ethereal thing. But Gil's words had the desired effect. She sat back, smoothing down her trousers with the palms of both hands.

'And Officer Mellings, Gina, will help with anything you need. She can deal with the press, or work,' Jess said.

Siwan shrugged. 'I'm between jobs with my acting, anyway.'

'Tough for actors. One of my girls used to go out with one,' Gil said. 'Flat out crazy for a while and then nothing.'

'At least I still have my vlog,' Siwan said. 'That keeps me busy.'

The perplexed expression on Gil's face was enough to

get Gina to explain. 'Video log, sarge. Siwan has quite a following. She's an influencer.'

'Micro-influencer,' Siwan said. 'I'm pretty niche.'

'Really?' Jess perked up. 'What kind of thing?'

'A bit of fashion, some lifestyle. I've been decorating the house with a low waste and recycling angle. People like that. But travel is what I love doing. Dan and me, we've done what-you-can-do-in-a-day vlogs all over Wales. Comment on the Airbnbs, pub food, the sights. The dream would be to do that all over the world. But now, I don't suppose that will ever happen.'

'She has twenty-five thousand followers,' Gina said in an attempt at buoying the conversation.

'*Arglwydd*, that's more than the Sgarlets,' Gil quipped. A rugby reference to the local team that anyone tuning in to TV coverage on a cold, wet Friday night would attest to.

'I thought I'd confront what's happened to Dan in my vlog. Get out in front of it. I haven't posted in two days and already people are asking why I'm not posting.'

'You're sure about that?' Jess asked. She wasn't a big fan of social media other than to keep in touch with her daughter's trends.

'It'll be much worse if I don't,' Siwan said.

'You want the world to know your business?' Gil asked.

'I want them to know the truth. Otherwise, there'll be all kinds of rumours.'

Jess pursed her lips. 'Everyone and their aunt will know after mid-day. There's a press conference and we will be releasing details since there appears to be no next of kin.'

'The deceased?' Siwan asked. 'You've identified who it is, then?'

'His name is Lee Barret. He's a local,' Jess explained.

'Any idea why he was shot?'

Gil swung his head back and forth in a no. 'But we are exploring some angles.'

Siwan eased out a breath and looked around the room. 'I'm aware how all of this must sound, vlogs and Instagram, but it's my living. These people, my followers, are my friends.'

Jess saw Gil's expression out of the corner of her eye, but she kept her gaze on Siwan. Gil might be sceptical of social media, but through Molly, Jess knew that both new and established companies relied heavily on all forms to sell products. Facebook, Twitter, Instagram, TikTok, these were the marketing platforms. Of course, they used celebrities, but ordinary social media content creators like Siwan were gold dust because they had already established trust between themselves and their followers. To companies, that trust was a marketable commodity and worth money. Sometimes, so Molly would say with an accompanying roll of her eyes at her mother's naivety, a shedload of money.

As they left, Jess glanced at Gil and smiled.

'What, ma'am?'

'Influencers and Vlogs. I see I am going to have to explain some of this to you, Sergeant. What do you know about Pinterest?'

'Pnot pmuch, ma'am.'

'Yes,' Jess muttered. 'It's going to be a long journey back to HQ.'

———

THE TEAM CONVENED at 1pm in the Incident Room. Warlow had missed the press conference, but there'd been no new information to impart as far as he was concerned. Two-Shoes had appealed for anyone near Telpyn Beach between the hours of six and eight last Sunday morning to come forward. She explained that their input, no matter how seemingly unimportant, could hold vital clues. As expected, Lee Barret was named as the dead man.

Now, armed with fresh tea, Warlow kicked off proceedings. Though a quick gander around the room demonstrated the distinct absence of one member.

'We still waiting for Catrin?'

'Running a bit late,' Jess said. 'Dental appointment.'

'Hmm,' Warlow grunted. 'Right, then we'll start without her. But before we begin, I'd like to introduce DS Wil Hopper who has joined us from Serious and Organised Crime to help in the hunt for Lee Barret's killer.'

A man in his early thirties pushed off from the desk he'd been leaning on. He stood at about average height with an angular frame and angular features that gave him an intense appearance. All augmented by a trimmed and dark beard. His features, combined with a mop of dark and long hair, leant him an energy that meant he would not have been out of place fronting a heavy metal band or riding a motorbike wearing a leather waistcoat. That this appearance had been cultured in order to make him look as unlike a police officer as was possible wasn't lost on the audience.

While Hopper retrieved a file from his backpack, Gil still felt the urge to lean into Rhys and whisper, 'Looks like that Dr Who bloke, don't you think?'

'The latest one, the girl?' Rhys whispered back.

'Don't be so soft, mun,' Gil rumbled dismissively. 'The Scottish one, you know? Him, but after an accident with a hair dryer.'

His accent, when he spoke, gave away Hopper's Cardiff upbringing as he responded to Warlow's introduction. 'Thanks, sir, glad to help.'

'Can you fill us in on what you know?' Warlow asked.

'More what we suspect at present, sir. We'd been surveilling Dunbar, Lee Barret's partner, for some time. He first became known to me by sheer chance in a pub in Liverpool. The man I was working with, in the organisation I'd infiltrated, met with Dunbar.'

Quickly, Hopper explained about the drugs find washed up on the beach at Abermawr and of how Dunbar was suspected of laundering money and handling the collection of drugs from Ireland. Barret's role, evident now by the appearance of those uncollected drugs, found, very probably, because of the harvester's death, was the part of the puzzle that Hopper had been waiting for. It didn't give them any direct information about who the likely killer might be, but the drugs link was an ominous development.

'Rival factions?' Jess asked.

'Possibly, ma'am. It's known that a Midlands-based syndicate has been making inroads into drug distribution in West Wales.'

'Not more Peaky bloody Blinders,' Gil growled. He didn't need to elaborate. The shadow of DI Caldwell still hung over them all.

Then it was Rhys's turn to tell them about the post-mortem. His double-tap theory was met by nods from Hopper. 'As you say, it isn't a taught technique these days. Now armed officers are taught to keep firing until the threat is neutralised. But double taps have a kind of gangster edge. It might be what a paid shooter for a gang might do.'

Then Warlow told them about Daniel Clark and his meeting with his parents.

'How is his wife?' Warlow asked when he'd finished.

'Coping,' Jess said. 'Just about.'

'Having Gina there helps,' Gil added.

'Anything else?' Warlow asked.

Hopper stepped forward again. 'Not much, sir, but this morning I spoke to a CHIS who tells me that Dunbar has made several trips to Wolverhampton over the last three months.'

Warlow still preferred the word informant, but Covert Human Intelligence Source had legislation wrapped around it since 2021, putting the authorisation of criminal activity in instances of CHIS on a statutory basis. Much as he hated the word, it was now in common use.

'You think he might be involved with this rival faction?' Gil asked.

Hopper shrugged. 'It's hearsay. But I believe my source.'

'Okay. Then it goes without saying that what we need to do is find Michael Dunbar.' Warlow glanced at his watch. 'But in the meantime, I have an appointment with Stacey Campbell at the house she shares with Dunbar. Rhys, Wil, you're with me.' He paused and glanced at the door. 'When Catrin comes, tell her to get the Gallery updated. Gil, see if we can get anything from Barret's phone. See if he'd been in contact with Dunbar.'

'You think he may be directly involved, sir?' Rhys asked.

'Let's put it this way. It would be useful to know he wasn't.'

CHAPTER EIGHTEEN

THEY TOOK a job car to Tenby. The Audi that Rhys loved so much. Warlow sat in the back, Rhys drove with Hopper in the front next to him. There was parking on both sides of the narrow street, and Rhys found a spot close by to await Stacey Campbell's arrival.

'Always fancied some undercover work me,' Rhys said to Hopper as they waited.

'Not a job for anyone in a relationship,' Hopper answered. 'Some guys I worked with were married. But once you're in, you bump up against all sorts. It isn't easy to keep things on the straight and narrow. And they play for keeps these people. When we did that last raid in the op I was involved in, we found twenty guns.'

'Christ,' muttered Warlow.

'Sounds interesting, though.' Rhys sounded keen.

'It can get pretty hairy,' Hopper said. 'Not for the faint-hearted, that's for certain. Plus, you need a thick skin. You see things, criminal stuff, that your gut tells you is so wrong, but you have to go with it. And it can get tough.'

'I don't think Gina would approve of you going under-cover, Rhys. All that temptation,' Warlow said from the back. 'Besides, who's going to make her tea in the mornings?'

'There is that, sir,' Rhys admitted.

Hopper's ears pricked up. 'Gina? That wouldn't be Gina Mellings, would it?'

'You remember Gina?' Rhys asked.

'Ye-ah.' He grinned. 'She was starting out as I was leaving to go to the Task Force. We overlapped by a couple of months while I was still in uniform. You're a lucky man, Rhys.'

'Thanks.' A smile split Rhys's face.

Warlow wondered where this conversation might go next. It had the promise of becoming an interesting one, but just then a bright-blue Merc pulled up opposite and Stacey Campbell emerged.

Warlow got out and crossed the road to greet her.

'Thanks for coming, Ms Campbell.'

'Got to be done, I suppose,' she said. She was in a different coloured tracksuit, hair still up, expensive trainers on her feet and a handbag that was all green leather and gold fittings. The little badge on the bag's front told Warlow it probably cost more than he would get for his Jeep if he ever sold it. Rhys and Hopper joined them. Warlow introduced the sergeant, and they stood on the pavement while Stacey fished keys out of her bag and stepped up to the front door.

It wasn't a big house from the front. The end of a small terrace of three, all painted subtle pastel shades. The interesting feature was that the terrace stood at right angles to the street and Warlow wondered if it had been, at one time, a mews ending in a stone wall with trees beyond. He could just see an orange Sainsbury's sign in a car park beyond the trees.

The house itself had been extended at the rear up to roof level. And, since it was only fifty yards at most from

Queens Parade and Tenby's South Beach, Warlow harboured no doubt that this kind of place would ask half a million on the market. Not as ostentatious as Barret's, that was certain, but more central and, some might argue, a better investment.

Stacey turned the key and stepped inside, holding the door open.

'Hang on, I'll sort out the alarm first,' she said and turned to a panel on the wall. She frowned, her finger hovering over the keypad. 'That's odd. It's usually lit up.'

Warlow joined her in the hallway. It was a bright, blustery day and, with the front door open, there was no need for artificial light in the hallway.

'That's weird.' Stacey took a hesitant step inside, past a narrow cupboard under a mirror, towards a set of open stairs leading up. Beyond the stairs, through an archway which might once have been a door, was the kitchen, on the right another doorway into a lounge. But Warlow was staring at the alarm and the cable beneath it linking the system to its power supply. Now severed.

'Wait!' Warlow ordered. He stepped past Campbell into the hall. He got as far as the door to the living room. There, he stopped and called back over his shoulder, 'We'll need gloves and overshoes.'

He half turned to stop Stacey Campbell from getting any further, but she moved too quickly. 'What's wrong?' she asked and bustled to Warlow's shoulder where she froze as a huge gasp of horror brought her up short and a hand flew up to cover her mouth.

She was seeing what Warlow had already seen. The living-cum-dining room was now upside down. The wicker chairs had been upended; a big dining table was on its side. Cushions from the settee were over the floor, all of them slashed open. Whatever had been on a corner shelving unit was now broken or smashed.

'What's happened?' Stacey bleated.

'My guess is that someone has been here looking for something,' Warlow answered. 'Did you keep anything valuable here, Stacey? Money, jewellery, drugs?'

'Drugs? No,' she whined out the protest. 'We keep nothing valuable here. A couple of hundred quid in cash for paying the gardener and the window cleaner. My jewellery, the good stuff. I didn't keep it here.' She turned and crossed to another door opposite the stairs. She opened it, Warlow on her heels.

'Oh, no,' Stacey wailed.

The mess was worse in this room.

Rhys appeared with some gloves and overshoes. Warlow slipped some on and turned to Stacey. 'Stay here. We can't let you go in because this is a crime scene.'

'But I need to get some things for Dion.' Her objections were half-hearted moans.

'Not now. It'll have to wait. We have no idea what else we might find here.'

'You don't mean Mike, do you? Don't tell me you mean that.' She turned and shouted up the stairs, 'Mike! Mike!'

'I don't think he's here, Stacey. He wouldn't cut the power to his own alarm system. We need to make sure this place is secure and allow no further contamination. You understand?' He turned to Rhys and Hopper. 'Check upstairs.'

'Then where am I supposed to go?' Stacey wailed.

'We'll get the forensic team in as soon as possible. Where's Dion?'

'Alex has him. Why?'

'I'm imagining what this might have looked like if you and Dion had been here whenever whoever did this called.'

The colour drained from Stacey's face.

Good. She needed to be aware of the seriousness.

'How do you feel about answering some more questions? We can do it at HQ. You'll be safe there.'

'What about Dion?'

'Probably best he stays where he is. Can you make that happen?'

She stuttered out, 'Y-yes.' Her eyes huge behind those mad eyelashes. She reached into her bag for her pink phone, ready to make a call. Warlow called to Rhys. 'DC Harries?'

No reply.

'Rhys? What's going on?'

The DC stepped onto the landing with a sheepish grin. 'I couldn't find the light switch for the kid's bedroom, sir. Curtains were drawn, and it's dim in there. It was hidden under a box thingy on the wall. The light switch, I mean. Wil found it straight away—'

The look on Warlow's face stopped Rhys in full flow.

'It's an ugly old switch in the middle of a wall,' Stacey explained with an apologetic shrug. 'God knows why an electrician would ever put it there.' The words rushed out of her. A silly, inconsequential explanation for a trifle when you considered what else was going on. But Warlow sensed she was near to the edge of a precipice here, and the banal words were giving her enough traction not to slide off.

'No one up there, I take it?' Warlow kept his voice even as the DC joined him at the bottom of the stairs.

Rhys shook his head.

'Okay. Me and Sergeant Hopper will finish here. You take Ms Campbell to HQ and wait there.'

They stood while Stacey spoke on the phone, her voice at breaking point.

'The place is completely trashed, Al. They say I can't go in and get any stuff. Not straight away. And there's no sign of Mike.'

A pause as Alex said something.

'Yeah, yeah, that would be great. Tell Dion I'll be back later. I'll take him and Star for a Happy Meal on me. You okay with that?... Thanks, babe... Yeah... I'll let you know.'

When she turned back to Warlow, her hands trembled as she dabbed the corners of her eyes with a tissue. Warlow put a hand on her arm. 'This is the last thing you need at this moment, Stacey, but we have to assume it has something to do with what's happened to Mr Barret. You understand that?'

Stacey nodded.

'The DI I work with, Jess Allanby, will look after you, and I'll get back to HQ as soon as I can.' Warlow stood in the doorway as Rhys led Stacey away towards her Merc. He called after the officer. 'You drive. She's in no fit state.'

Hopper came to the top of the stairs. 'Same up here, sir. Every room's been turned over.'

Warlow walked up and confirmed what he'd been told. The stairs turned on a landing that led to the extension at the rear of the house. He walked through an open door and into a child's room with planets and stars painted on a wall. He pulled back a curtain and looked down into the well-appointed garden. A flagstone patio with big expensive-looking pot plants led to a patch of lawn with a cut-down goalmouth complete with net.

Seeing the house turned over had cemented the idea in Warlow that Campbell and Dunbar were both involved in whatever this would be. Yet, the shock on Stacey Campbell's face had been genuine. This was a family home for them and their son.

Warlow turned to see Hopper standing there, waiting. 'Anything?'

The DS wrinkled his nose. 'They were thorough, I'll give them that. Every room as far as I can see. But the odd thing is that nothing much has been taken. I mean, there's a telly and a PlayStation up here. They're usually the first things to go.'

'They would be if this were a burglary. But it doesn't have the feel of one.'

Warlow walked past him and down into the kitchen. All the cupboard doors had been flung wide, little hills of cereal had spilled onto the floor. The fridge door hung open and already the smell of rotting food was oozing out. 'Whoever was here was looking for something. Not hoping to fence some cheap goods off for a few quid.'

Behind him, Hopper's phone buzzed, and he held it to his ear. 'CSI on their way, sir,' he said a moment later.

'Good. Then I suggest we knock on some doors, see if anyone saw or heard anything.'

'Will do, sir.'

CHAPTER NINETEEN

WARLOW'S ATTEMPTS at gleaning intelligence from neighbours around Dunbar's house proved fruitless. He and Hopper drew blanks, both in terms of stares and all other forms of information. According to the people who lived cheek by jowl in that part of Tenby, they had seen and heard nothing untoward.

He'd taken his customary stroll around the area of a crime scene, taking in the street names. Trafalgar Road, Picton Road, Queen's Parade, Battery Road. The town epitomised Southern Pembrokeshire's moniker of "Little England beyond Wales". He had no strong feelings about it, though it irked some people. It wasn't as if this represented a recent phenomenon; after all, the Flemish and Norman colonisers built fifty castles to keep the driven-out Welsh at bay to the north of the county a thousand years before. But it always triggered a rueful smile in Warlow whenever he heard the current generation's clarion call for reparation to post-colonial states. Was there a statute of limitations on these things? How many generations should you go back? More a question for academic historians and vote-hungry politicians than Detective Chief Inspectors.

But the one lesson he drew from seeing these imperialist street names, the direct consequence of a linguistic contempt begun in the eleventh century, was that cultural suppression could never be the purview of the last couple of centuries alone, much as the shouty voices wanted everyone to believe.

He'd lingered at Battery Gardens to take in the view before retracing his steps to pause at the rear of Dunbar's house, where it backed on to an area of construction work at the business end of the adjacent supermarket. Making more room for recycling, it looked like. But the machines and building materials provided excellent cover for anyone seeking entry to the garden.

Still, he'd returned via a response vehicle to his desk at HQ empty handed, opting instead to pore over Povey's report on the murder scene at Telpyn Beach before dealing with Stacey Campbell. After a fingertip search of the site, the crime scene investigation team had managed to find a bullet. Early testing confirmed that it had some human blood on it which matched Barret's type. DNA confirmation would no doubt follow. But Warlow zeroed in on the detail.

"The bullet found thirty metres away embedded in the earth is a 9mm flat-nosed projectile. You will see from the images that it is grossly distorted from contact with material it has passed through. It has a non-concave base. The grooving is traditional, not polygonal, and the twist is right-handed. This all points to a 9mm semi-automatic weapon. No cartridges were found at the site. Given the crude grooving and the type of ammunition, it is likely that the weapon could have been a modified blank-firing type."

He scrolled down to an image of a distorted brass-coloured bullet nestling in the right-angle crook of a ruler. It showed a length of approximately fourteen millimetres and a diameter of about nine. The tip was no longer bullet shaped but smashed flat at an angle. Faint longitudinal lines were visible along the length of the projectile, too.

Warlow picked up the phone and dialled Povey immediately.

'What does your bullet report actually mean, Alison?'

'How much do you know about gun use, Evan?'

'Little, thank God. But let me guess, favoured by drug traffickers?'

'Top marks. Believe it or not, it's still incredibly difficult to get hold of a handgun in this country. Sometimes they do come in, usually through the Low Countries from Eastern Europe. But a commoner approach is to buy blank-firing pistols and convert them into live weapons.'

'How the hell do you do that?'

'Most blank firing guns have weakened parts and the wrong calibre barrel linings. But the people who modify these things know what they're doing. Make no mistake, they can be lethal. Of course, I have no evidence that this is what's happened here, but chatting to a colleague in the Midlands, he tells me this is the trend. We're working on identifying the bullet manufacturer, but that, I suspect, will be academic.'

Warlow let out a deep sigh.

But Povey remained irrepressibly professional and thorough. That was the one thing about her that Warlow could find to criticise. Even when the news was bad, she never hesitated to deliver it. 'It gets even better. We found no useful evidence at Dunbar's property, either. Whoever broke in was very careful.'

'How did they get in?'

'No idea. There was a thirty-second delay in the alarm. Common enough to allow a passcode entry. But they cut the power. This system's battery backups had been removed, also by the intruder I expect.'

'But wouldn't the alarm have gone off before they took the backup batteries out?'

Povey huffed. 'Yes, unless they were flat or old. The batteries, I mean. People aren't very good at replacing them, even rechargeable ones.'

'Hmm,' Warlow said.

'I know that hmm,' Povey replied.

'I don't like conundrums. It's a "c" word.'

'Quite a few of those around in this case, I'm afraid.'

When Povey had gone, Warlow read the report again and then had a look at what Tiernon had to say. He'd been as good as his word. But all his preliminary report did was confirm everything said at that morning's post-mortem. Cause of death, gunshot wound with fatal injuries to the great vessels of the heart. Barret wasn't drunk, according to his blood alcohol levels, and there was nothing obvious in his stomach that might show he'd been high. Toxicology would follow. So far, the experts were not proving to be of much use.

He sat back in his chair and glanced at his watch.

Christ, was that the time already?

He got up and ambled out into the Incident Room. Most of the indexers and collators had gone, but Rhys and Gil were beavering away at their desks. Warlow walked over and leaned forward with his hands on the DC's desk.

'I'm hoping you're going to tell me you've made a star-tling breakthrough, Rhys.'

The young officer glanced up into Warlow's face with an expression that might have been a grimace. 'I am working on something that might be useful, sir.'

'The Halloween menu at McDonald's doesn't count,' Gil remarked.

'That was just a flyer someone dropped off.' Rhys sat up a bit straighter. 'Besides, Gina's staying with Siwan

Clark until Dan's parents get back from Cardiff. Might end up being a takeaway tonight.'

Gil looked up from his work. 'Were you planning on dressing up, then?'

'No, sarge. Maybe a spooky film, though. Gina has a thing about that one where the woman ends up being able to walk on the ceiling at the end. What's it called now?'

'A bloody good trick if you can pull it off,' Gil muttered.

'It'll come to me, sir. Gina's a lunatic when she watches a horror film, though. Once we were having this curry and something happened on screen.' He paused, cogs whirring until his eyes opened wide. 'Oh yeah, The Ring, when they show that girl's face after she's found locked in the cupboard. Gina jumped two feet in the air, grabbed hold of my arm and dug her nails in. My prawn bhuna went flying all over the carpet. She can be a real screamer when she's excited.'

Warlow resisted the urge to look at the smile that spread over Gil's face with great difficulty.

'Sounds more like Fifty Shades of Ghee to me, Rhys,' Gil said.

Rhys cocked his head, eyes up at an angle as he ran Gil's phrase around in his head, repeating it in silence. Neither of the senior officers had the heart to tell him his lips were moving as he did so. After a long fifteen seconds, a smile broke over the younger officer's face. 'Ghee, as in that butter stuff they use in curries, right, sarge?'

'I knew you'd get there in the end.' Gil sighed. 'It was only a keema mattar of time.'

'Stop with the food jokes,' Warlow warned. 'I'm too hungry to cope with lamb curry puns.'

Gil cleared his throat. 'Jokes aside, while Rhys has been fantasising over a hamburger, I got Barret's mobile provider to cough up some records. We've not got into his phone yet. That's with the techs and their grubby little fingers. But EE has this minute emailed a load of information through and I was about to go through them when you came out of the inner sanctum.' Gil held up a thick wodge of paper. 'The nice man at the end of the phone somehow misunderstood what I'd asked for and sent me last month's, instead of only last week's.' Gil made a sad face. 'And I'll need to get away by six-thirty. I have an under-eights Halloween party in Tumble to get to.'

'What you going as, sarge?' Rhys asked.

After the briefest millisecond of hesitation, during which Warlow made a mental bet with himself that Uncle Fester would remain under wraps, Gil answered, 'A responsible adult. The hall committee chairperson is an old fishing mate. I take the little ones as a treat, and it stops them roaming the streets looking for sweets. Whoever invented that idea needs to be seriously vetted.'

'Then I suggest Rhys give you a hand with the phone records while I see how DI Allanby is getting on with Stacey Campbell. Where's Hopper?'

'Already in the viewing gallery, sir,' Rhys said, one despondent eye on Gil's pile of papers.

CHAPTER TWENTY

'Would you like another cup of tea, Stacey?' Jess asked, with a concerned smile aimed squarely at the woman on the other side of the table.

'No, I'm fine, thanks. I just want to know when I can go back home.'

Jess nodded. 'Of course, you do.'

'Such a shock, seeing all that. Your chief inspector... what's his name again?'

'DCI Warlow,' Catrin answered.

'He said it was lucky I wasn't there when it happened.'

'He's right,' Jess said.

Stacey's leg wiggled, one hand fiddling with the junction between a false nail and the fleshy bed it rested against on the index finger of the other. Something she'd been doing for at least half an hour. A wonder there was any flesh left. Her discomfort at being in the interview room oozed out of every pore. Still, it had not been designed to be a relaxing environment. And this woman had been through a lot in a few hours, Jess was prepared to admit. Still, she looked... jumpy, to say the least.

'It's a nasty shock, seeing your own home violated,' Jess said.

Stacey looked down at her finger. 'Mike said I should never speak to the police without a solicitor.'

'If you want to contact one, feel free.' Jess was all smiles. 'I mean, you're not under arrest and you're here for your own protection while we investigate the burglary. Obviously, if anything you tell us proves useful, we could use it in court, but we're here to help you. We're hoping you can help us.'

'How?'

Catrin stood a little way back, leaning against the wall, a notebook in her hand, flipping through the pages. But she answered Stacey now, 'At the risk of stating the obvious, a man has been killed. Your partner's business partner. It's not difficult to join the dots here. There's a good chance the break-in might have something to do with that, wouldn't you agree?'

Stacey pursed her lips and blew out some air.

'Do you have any idea what they might have been after, Stacey?' Jess leaned forward.

Stacey's eyes drifted back up to Jess's. 'Like I've already said, no. We keep nothing valuable there. Personal, I mean. There's a TV and stuff but nothing of ours if you know what I mean.'

'Why is that?'

'Mike's paranoid. Always has been. Anything worth real money we keep in safe deposit boxes. There's a place in Swansea Mike uses.'

Catrin wrote something in her notebook. Stacey watched, like a kid seeing a dinner plate being loaded up with Brussel sprouts and broccoli.

'What about your partner's business?' Jess asked. 'Did Lee Barret ever call at your house?'

'Of course, he did. He loves Dion. They get on…'
Stacey flinched. 'Got on well.'

'Do you remember seeing Lee Barret bringing anything to the house? Something he might have left there?'

Stacey shook her head.

'Were you aware that Mr Barret might have been involved in any criminal activity?' Catrin's question, no frills attached, drew a look of horror from the already twitchy woman.

'Criminal activity? What kind of criminal activity?'

'It's been brought to our attention that Mr Barret has been under observation for some time regarding drug trafficking.'

Stacey jerked in her chair. 'Drugs? Is that what they were after at my house?'

'We can't be sure,' Catrin said. 'But it's a possibility.'

'I hate drugs,' Stacey said, spoken with the vehement disgust of someone who may well have had first-hand experience. She sat forward, her mouth now compressed into a bitter oval. 'I had no idea Lee was into that. They've known each other for years, Lee and Mike. They have a successful business—'

Catrin interjected. 'But lots of businesses have suffered over the last few years. Covid, inflation. Odd that, somehow, L&M Jet-Ski managed to thrive.'

Stacey's horror was now tinged with anger. 'What are you saying?'

'I'm saying that it's a remarkable feat of survival in an industry, and I'm talking about tourism here, that took a pummelling. And yet, it looks like Lee Barret bought and paid for a million-pound house, and your property in Tenby is worth how much?'

'I think I'd like a solicitor.'

'Someone's been murdered here, Stacey,' Catrin said.

'Do you know anything about that? Is that why you want a solicitor?'

'No. I don't know anything.'

'It must be very worrying, though,' Jess said.

That threw Stacey. She blinked in confusion. 'What do you mean?'

'Mr Dunbar hasn't contacted you, has he?'

She shook her head again.

Jess nodded. 'Then it must have occurred to you he could be in danger, Stacey. Because it's occurred to us.'

Having it all pointed out like this seemed to come as a hammer-blow. 'Oh, God,' Stacey whispered.

Jess leaned forward. 'If he has contacted you, we need to know. If you know where he is, we need to know.'

Stacey's breath heaved in and out of her chest. 'I need the loo. I feel like I'm going to throw up.'

Jess threw Catrin a glance. The sergeant put her notebook away. 'Follow me,' she said, and led the woman out.

———

STACEY LOCKED herself in the loo. She wasn't a prisoner, but that feeling of being trapped had not left her since she'd walked in through the doors of the building. Her head was most definitely in the shed after walking into the house and seeing the mess. But truth be told, it had been in the shed ever since she'd got the text that morning from Mike. She sat on the loo seat and rummaged in her bag for the phone to look at the text again.

> Shit hit Fan, Trace. Keep phone on. I need
> to keep low profile. DO NOT CALL ME.
> Cops listening.

Of course, she had called him, but he hadn't picked up, which made things a hundred times worse. What did it all mean? She knew that the business wasn't completely kosher, but she had not been lying when she'd told that red-head sergeant she didn't know about drugs. She didn't. She knew that both Mike and Lee had various deals going on. But that was the nature of business, wasn't it? At least, that was what Mike told her. She'd said she didn't want to know. Now she supposed that perhaps that wasn't strictly speaking the same as being completely ignorant, but she wasn't involved in any way, that bit was a hundred percent. And if she had suspected, then she'd buried all of that without losing a wink of sleep. Mike was a great provider. They'd had such a great time. Marbella, the Caribbean, skiing in the States, Dion. And why would you ask questions when someone was paying for it all? Paying for it and wanting you to be a part of it. You didn't ask who fed the goose, so long as the golden eggs kept coming.

She hadn't asked.

Six years they'd been together, and Mike said that he was going to sort things for the long term. Invest. Buy some properties and put some in her name.

Something cold seemed to close around her heart then. If this was a drugs thing... now that Dion was a part of the equation, the idea of getting wrapped up in something drug-related and what might happen if she ever went to prison filled her with dread. If the police wanted to implicate her... she let out a quiet, shuddering sigh. She'd never forgive herself if she lost Dion.

She sat on the loo and bent at the waist, both forearms over her head, wincing at the thought, wincing at the mess this had already become. A thin wail of frustration and despair leaked out of her mouth like air from a ruptured tyre. Yesterday, the worst thing she had to contend with was a hangover and now... and now what? She didn't have any answers for the cops. But she couldn't stay here in this place any longer. She got up, put her phone back in her bag, and pulled the chain. Outside, the red-head loitered.

'Okay?'

'Yes.'

The sergeant turned to take her back to where they'd left the other officer, but Stacey didn't move.

'It's this way,' Catrin said.

'I'm not going.'

Catrin cocked her head. 'What's happened, Stacey? Have your heard from Michael?'

'You can't keep me here.'

'No one's keeping you here.'

'Good. Then I'm leaving.'

Catrin didn't move from the doorway. 'We don't think that's a great idea. Not yet. Someone has been killed. Someone broke into your house. Where will you go? At least tell us that?'

'No. That's my business. If you want to speak to me again, it'll be with a solicitor.'

'Okay, but wait until I—'

'No!' It came out as a shouted protest. 'I want to leave now.'

Catrin held up her hands. Quietly, she said, 'This way.'

Five minutes later, Stacey Campbell walked outside into the late afternoon, reaching for her car keys as, behind her, the red-headed sergeant spoke to someone on her phone. But that didn't matter. All Stacey wanted to do at that moment was get away.

CHAPTER TWENTY-ONE

'WHAT DO YOU RECKON, SERGEANT?' Warlow asked Hopper when Stacey Campbell left the room having threatened to throw up. Both men had been observing the "chat" on a screen.

Hopper snorted. 'Do I buy into the "I'm-a-victim-here-too" routine, sir? Simple answer, no, I do not.'

Warlow raised one surprised eyebrow. 'You think she's neck deep in this?'

'I wouldn't say that, sir. But she knows more than she is letting on.'

Warlow wobbled his head in a half-nod, half-shake type motion, meaning to imply he only half agreed. 'There was no doubting her reaction when she saw the mess after the break-in,' he pointed out.

'Agreed, sir. But I'm not convinced that she hasn't heard from Dunbar. She's his long-term partner, and there's the kid.'

Hopper was making good points. Whatever Dunbar's reason for not being around −Warlow was reluctant to admit even to himself the possibility that he too might be a victim – he'd want to reassure his partner and child, unless he was incapacitated, or a very cold fish indeed.

The door to the obs room opened and Jess put her head in. 'Campbell has taken herself off, Evan. She came out of the loo and decided she'd had enough.'

Warlow sighed. He'd hoped that being here might encourage a little cooperation once they plugged in to her concern over Dunbar's whereabouts.

'Did she say where she was going?'

'No. Is Povey still at the house in Tenby?' Jess asked. 'In case she goes back there.'

'Could be,' Warlow replied. 'She's sent a prelim report which tells us sweet bugger all. Better warn her that Campbell may be on the way.'

They got no further with this discussion because Rhys appeared behind Jess, his head above hers, bobbing animatedly.

'Uh, sir, we've found something in Barret's phone records.'

Rhys led the way back to the Incident Room and to Gil standing next to the board known as the Job Centre. He'd pasted up some A4 paper containing a list of numbers, with half a dozen highlighted.

'Barret's phone records.' Gil tapped the paper. 'Half a dozen texts from this one number early Sunday morning.'

'Whose number?' Warlow asked.

'Dunbar's. We know that from his employees.'

'Do we know what was said?' Jess muttered.

Gil looked pleased with himself. 'They're texts. So, yes, we do.'

Everyone in the room was aware of what that meant. It became a lot more difficult and time consuming when encrypted messaging services like WhatsApp were used. But texts were open season as service providers kept copies.

For short periods of time, admittedly. But they still kept them as a closely guarded secret.

'Good work getting them this quickly, Gil,' Jess said.

'Surprising how much speed the word murder can generate in even the most unenthusiastic of phone companies.' He put a hand to his ear and listened. The loudest sound came from the click and whirr of a printer. 'Rhys, fetch those sheets, would you?'

Gil took more A4 copies from the DC and pinned them up. It didn't take a genius to work out who was texting who.

Lee You Up and about?

> Picking dog crap off the beach.

With the Mitcher?

> Y. Quick walk before business.

What beach?

> Telpyn. People swimming man, FFS

Need quick catch-up

> Supply probs

Give me a bell.

> Nah, No phones. Quick coffee at Nino's in 20?

Make it 30.

'That last text was sent at 7.11am,' Gil said.

'What about the complaint about Barret and his dog?' Hopper asked.

Gil already had that written up. 'That came through at 06.59.'

'So, Dunbar wanted to see Barret about supply problems,' Warlow said.

Hopper's lips formed a wry smile. 'That's assuming there was a supply problem.'

'What do you mean?' Jess asked. 'They're in business together. Isn't it possible that this had something to do with jet-skis or paddleboards?'

'It's possible,' Hopper agreed, but with a hefty dose of scepticism in his voice.

'If they were handling drugs, though, couldn't supply mean that, too?' Rhys asked.

'Good point,' Catrin said.

Hopper's little smile remained unmoving.

'You're not convinced, Sergeant?' Jess asked.

'We'll only know if this has to do with their business if we go through their records. But what I see is something else.'

Gil glanced at his watch pointedly, his patience already running thin by the look of things. 'Much as I enjoy a game of bloody Cluedo, if you've got something to say, we are all ears, Wil.'

That earned him a pained glance from Hopper, but it did the trick. 'Okay. All this tells us is that Dunbar was aware of where Barret was at 07.11.'

'How does that help?' Rhys said.

But Warlow had already walked closer to the board, his mental cogs meshing together. 'It tells us that Dunbar knew where Barret was at the time of the murder.'

'You think that Dunbar might have shot Barret?' Catrin asked.

'All I know for certain is that Michael Dunbar is now

even more of a person of interest in this case than he already was. In other words, I would like the bugger found sooner rather than later.'

They set to getting Dunbar's details out into the policing ether and setting up a search for his vehicle through the national advanced numberplate recognition network. But it was all going to take time. At six-thirty, Gil logged off his desktop and stretched. 'Anyone heard how Clark is doing?'

'Gina texted to say that his parents are back home and that his wife is up with him now,' Rhys replied. 'Stable, she said.'

Stable. Still not Warlow's favourite word.

Gil was already on his feet, coat on. 'Grandchildren are being dropped off at Cross Hands. I'm meeting the Lady Anwen there and off to Tumble we go.'

'Watch out for the ghoulies and ghosties,' Warlow said.

Hopper, who'd been helping Rhys, looked up. 'Off to a Halloween party, Gil?'

'I am.'

'Nice costume,' Hopper said.

That brought Gil up short since he wasn't wearing anything different from his normal attire. 'Normally, I like to know people for more than a day before I let them insult me with impunity.'

Rhys, sitting next to Hopper, said, 'My name's not impunity, but I think he's going as Uncle Fester.'

'I can see the family resemblance,' Hopper said.

Gil glared at Rhys. 'Stabbed in the back, eh? Sergeant Hopper is a very bad influence on you, Rhys. Tomorrow, peeps,' he said, already walking through the Incident Room door.

A long thirty minutes later, after Rhys had yawned three times in succession in the middle of Warlow's instruction to them all to read Povey's ballistics report, the DCI called it a day. 'We'll not get much further with all this tonight. I suggest we come back tomorrow with fresh eyes, ears, and brains.'

'Sorry, sir. It's my blood sugar,' Rhys apologised after another yawn.

'Of course, it is, Rhys. The struggle is real.'

'Good one, sir. On point.'

'I didn't know you could speak millennial, Evan,' Jess said.

'I have a tutor by the name of Molly, as you well know.'

Jess gave in on that one.

'But Rhys is right.' Warlow stretched his arms above his head. 'There comes a point when keeping going is counterproductive. Things that take ten minutes in the morning will take half an hour now. Let's park all this until tomorrow.'

Rhys and Hopper got up together. 'Fancy a quick drink, sir? Rhys here has spurned me because Gina is on the way home. Would a swift half interest you?'

Warlow thought about it, but Cadi was still with the Dawes, her adoring and wonderful dog sitters. And unless the job forced him to stay away overnight, he always attempted to get back in enough time to pick her up. And a Cadi welcome was the best antidote to a lousy day he'd ever come across. Better than a swift half with Hopper even.

'Not tonight—'

'Josephine,' Rhys interjected with a grin.

Warlow gazed at him askance. 'Do you even know what that means?'

Rhys's grin faltered. 'No idea, sir. It's something Sergeant Jones always says, though.'

'Right, well, next time, ask him to explain it. Good

history lesson for you.' He turned to Hopper. 'Live locally, Wil?'

'Nah. Up Cilgerran way, sir.'

'Not exactly around the corner, then.'

'No. But I fancied something to slake my thirst.'

'When we do go, it'll be my round, then,' Warlow said. Hopper and Rhys left, laughing together, Rhys a good six inches taller than the sergeant. Jess, her coat already on, studied Warlow appraisingly.

'What?' Warlow asked.

'You, turning down a drink. I almost fancied one myself, but Molly has the supper on.'

'Wow,' Warlow said with more sympathy than he'd intended.

'No, fair play. She is getting better. She has one eye on uni next year and when I won't be there to pick up or cook for her.'

'Ah, university cuisine. So, she can open a tin?'

'That's unfair. I've been getting her to cook some easy sauces for pasta and make casseroles.'

Warlow looked suitably impressed. 'Right, I look forward to testing her culinary skills.'

Catrin joined the senior officers, phone in hand.

'You didn't fancy a drink either, Catrin?' Warlow asked.

'Me, sir? I'm not drinking.' She registered Warlow's expression and qualified it quickly. 'No-vember sir.'

'But it's October.'

'Starting early, sir. Giving myself a run-up.'

'How are your teeth?'

'Teeth?' Catrin sent him a blank stare of abject bewilderment.

'Dentist? Teeth? This morning?'

'Oh, this morning. Oh, yes, sir, it's a plaque problem, all sorted. Endodontics stuff.'

'Good. Glad you're okay.' His knowledge of endodontics bordered on the sod-all, and he'd probably struggle to spell it at a push, so he buried the subject. It was also about the best conversation killer he'd come across in a long time.

Catrin slapped her coat pocket and muttered, 'Keys,' before striding over to her desk.

'Have I struck a nerve there?' Warlow asked Jess. 'Asking about her teeth?' He added a little smirk.

'Oh, don't. You're as bad as Gil. And please tell me you're heading home. You look as if you could do with an early night.'

'Not the best night's sleep last night, admittedly. The thought of Tiernon and seeing Daniel Clark.' Warlow waved off the idea. 'Plus, Tom had left half a bottle of excellent Sangiovese.'

'How the other half live, eh,' Jess said.

Warlow followed the women into the corridor to wave them off. As he turned back, he came face-to-face with an apparition that spoke his name.

'Evan, still here?'

'Jesus,' he breathed and felt his pulse surge.

Except it wasn't an apparition. What stood in front of him was the very real form of Superintendent Goodey dressed uber-appropriately for the outdoors in a black anorak, fishing hat, and with shiny black bootees on her feet.

'Sorry, ma'am. You startled me.'

'It is Halloween,' she said, smiling at her own little joke. Warlow resisted the urge to add that, with the hat on, she'd pass for Freddy Kruger in the right light. No trouble.

'How is it going, Evan? The case?'

'Progress, of sorts. The more we learn of Dunbar, Barret's partner, the more I'm convinced we need to talk to him. At the very least, we need to eliminate him as a suspect.'

Two-Shoes nodded her approval. 'And how is Sergeant Hopper fitting in?'

A loaded question if ever Warlow had heard one. Hopper had been an asset, Warlow had to admit. But he also detected an underlying need for validation in Two-Shoes' question. Any help Hopper provided would, of course, reflect well on her.

'Yes, ma'am. He's been invaluable.' Warlow surprised himself by how natural the words sounded, even through his gritted teeth.

Two-Shoes smiled. A toothy grin that made her look ridiculously pleased with herself. 'Knew he would be. He did some quite astonishing undercover work for us. So much so that Merseyside police wanted to nab him. But he'd burnt himself out after that op. He needs some time to recover. But he has ambition, that one.'

'I can see that, ma'am.'

The slight edge to his tone triggered an admonishment from Two-Shoes. 'Eventually, all of us oldies will need to make way for fresh meat, eh, Evan?'

Warlow didn't like the way this conversation was going. He waited. On one level, of course, he agreed with the sentiment; none of them were getting any younger. But he drew the line at giving her the satisfaction of hearing him say it.

'I mean, there is a very large elephant in the room here,' Two-Shoes went on. 'We both know that Sergeant Jones has a sell-by date.'

The elephant reference wasn't lost on Warlow. 'Gil? Why would you even consider moving—'

'His secondment was only ever a temporary measure following his involvement with Operation Alice. The Chief Superintendent considered a rapid response major crimes team a suitable distraction. Unfortunately, the poor man seems to have been busier than ever since joining you.'

Warlow ignored the jibe. 'And you've run all this past Gil, ma'am?'

'Not yet. That is a conversation for another day. And let's see how young Hopper gets on, shall we?'

'He'd have big boots to fill to replace Gil Jones, ma'am.'

'And big coats, trousers, and shirts. Right, I'm off to face the dark night.' With that, Two-Shoes rustled away in her rain gear, leaving Warlow… unsettled.

At the back of his mind sat the little imp of mischievousness that desperately wanted to bring up the last "good idea" Two-Shoes had as regards the team. DI Kelvin Fucking Caldwell (KFC to his acquaintances) had not covered himself, nor the department, in glory. In fact, he'd covered himself in stinking effluent once you wiped away the blood. And any combination of these words and ideas might have been a good rejoinder to throw at Two-Shoes' departing back.

But he didn't.

Thinking of Caldwell and the axe an unstable killer by the name of Meredith had planted in the poor bugger's head was not a thought you wanted to take with you out into the night. Especially not at Halloween. And as for Hopper and Gil? All he could do was hope that Buchannan didn't drown on his bloody cruise. There were words between Warlow and him that needed to be spoken.

And they would be choice indeed.

CHAPTER TWENTY-TWO

BUT THE NIGHT, one that the past people of Wales celebrated not only as Samhain, but as their own, *Nos Calan Gaeaf,* translated as the night before winter begins, had one more surprise for Warlow. It came as he headed out, bypassing Carmarthen town on the dual carriageway parallel to the river to the Pensarn roundabout; a labyrinthine piece of roadway dreamed up by someone in the highways department either after a night on the town, or as a deliberate exercise in lane jockeying that had most drivers flummoxed. Warlow hung back a little before entering the three-lane approach to allow those unfortunates who believed they were heading east, but ended up corralled into going west, to realign their trajectories. Many the time he'd sat in the passenger seat, with Rhys driving, listening to the DC cackle as wacky races took place all around them. When Catrin drove, her word choices were not of the kind Warlow expected to hear from a well-brought-up young woman. Always worth hearing, though. The sergeant could be inventive.

But this evening, Warlow only had to brake once to allow a confused driver to change lanes. He was approaching the second roundabout that would send him all points west and to home, with the blown-up ghost on a bike outside B&Q now glowing eerily in the dark, when the call came.

He registered the ID and pressed the phone icon on the dash screen, allowing access via the car's system.

'Alun? Everything alright?' Warlow's thoughts raced. 19.17 by the dashboard clock. That made it 03.17 in the morning in Perth.

'Not really, Dad. There's been some complications.'

Warlow's gut coiled inside him.

'Hang on, Al. I'm pulling over.' He negotiated the second roundabout and pulled in to the B&Q car park a hundred yards further on where he parked across two bays, letting the car idle. 'What kind of complications?'

'Reba went into labour three hours ago. They were monitoring the baby's heart.' Alun sounded like he'd been run over by a tank. His words emerged thick and dry, almost without emotion, as if he wanted them out of his mouth, but struggled to make them emerge coherently. 'It had all been going well, though she'd been in labour for a good three hours and was having a tougher time than with Leo. But then the shit hit the fan, Dad.'

'What's happened?'

'She had this pain. A different pain, a bad one. She threw up and the baby's heart rate went crazy. And there was blood, from where the baby should have been coming from. A lot of blood. They made me leave. People came from everywhere. All they've said is that her uterus has ruptured. She's in surgery now. An emergency caesarean.'

'They do caesareans all the time, don't they?' Warlow had no idea how often, but he was familiar enough with the term and he desperately needed to say something to ease his son's anxiety. As well as his own.

'Not like this, Dad. I've just been with the midwife.

She's been laying it on thick. It's a rare complication, a ruptured uterus. Less than one in every five thousand births. It's bad enough for the mother, but it increases the risk to the baby a lot more. Once the uterus ruptures, there's oxygen starvation… oh, shit, Dad.'

'Bloody hell, Al. Is there anyone there with you?'

'Who, Dad? My mates from the pub? I haven't called Reba's mum yet. You and Tom are the only ones, and you're half a bloody world away.'

Warlow sighed. A parental sigh full of a desperate desire to help but knowing it to be practically impossible. Alun wasn't trying to guilt trip him here. He was merely stating the facts. 'I wish I could be there, Al. Not that I could do anything.'

'There's nothing anyone can do except the docs. The midwife said lucky we were here. They have everything prepped for this.' Alun sucked in a breath. 'I'm sorry to ring you like this, Dad. I didn't know who else.'

The car's engine thrummed gently as Warlow turned off the heater fan to hear better. 'Why are you apologising? I'm here.'

'They said the maximum time the baby had to survive was thirty minutes unless they were able to get it—' Alun choked back a sob.

'Let me ring Tom. He'll know more about this stuff than me. But listen, Al, you were in the right place. If it was going to happen, better it happened there, right? These people know what they're doing.'

'Yeah.' He sounded drained. 'You're right. Thanks, Dad.'

'Ring me back once you hear something. Just ring, it doesn't matter what time.'

Silence crackled over the line.

'Alun?'

'Yeah, I'm still here.'

'I'll ring Tom now.'

When he got through to his younger son, Tom, just a few years away from becoming a consultant himself, slid into professional mode. He was much more used to hearing tales of medical disasters than Warlow was, even if his specialism was light years away from Obstetrics. There were plenty of ENT emergencies that were life threatening. Facial fractures, inhaled foreign bodies, anaphylaxis. These were all in Tom's playbook. He listened to Reba's predicament calmly but didn't pull any punches.

'I've read about it, but never seen it. It can be catastrophic. But they were in the hospital, so…'

'That's what I said.'

'I'll ring Al now,' Tom said. 'Where are you?'

'In a B&Q car park.'

'No point staying there. Go home, Dad. I'll ring you back once I've spoken to Al. I can contact a couple of mates who are doing Obs and Gynae. But the people on the ground will be best placed.'

He was right.

But after hanging up, Warlow didn't go anywhere. He sat in the car watching the traffic go by, the ghost on a bike wafting around maniacally his only companion. His gut churned. Much like it had when Denise had given birth to their boys. He didn't enjoy being out of control. And illness was the architect of chaos if ever there was one.

After fifteen minutes of trying to get his thoughts in order, and them taking no notice, Warlow took Tom's advice and drove on. But after ten more miles, his roiling gut and spinning mind got the better of him. He pulled into a lay-by and rang Tom again. He didn't trust himself to talk and drive. Not with this as a subject.

'Any news?'

'Not yet, Dad. Except… they named the baby. She's called Eva.'

Warlow squeezed his eyes shut.

Eva. A good name. A strong name. The closest thing to Evan they could come up with. He realised that was a bit of a leap, but he found himself choking up as he listened to Tom.

'Dad, you okay?'

'Yes, I'm fine.' He sniffed. 'Must be a cold coming on.'

'Go home, Dad. Al will text me. I've told him to use the WhatsApp group we set up for Mum. For the funeral and stuff. He should have done that to begin with, but he isn't thinking straight.'

'Course he isn't. None of us are.'

But the phone call had reassured Warlow enough to allow him to do the needful and pick Cadi up from the Dawes. Long experience had taught the couple that when the pickups were late, Warlow didn't do small talk. He was never impolite, but not a conversationalist after 8pm, usually. And tonight was one of those nights. After the usual reassurances that Cadi had been her beautiful self and a dream companion to their own Lab, Warlow thanked them and left with a brief, 'See you bright and early tomorrow.'

He had considered unburdening himself to these pleasant, loyal people, but had dismissed the idea almost immediately. He couldn't. Because they would invite him in and make him tea and… he simply couldn't.

But, as he drove away, the conviction, absorbed into his DNA after years of working in a team, that a problem shared was a problem halved, became all-consuming. He'd tried being the strong silent type when it came to his HIV status. Confident he could carry that burden alone for many months. Ironically, when he'd been forced to unburden himself because he had it in his head he'd risked someone else's health, it had lifted a psychological barrier and let in the light.

And now, with Cadi in the Jeep, he knew bottling up all this anxiety and fear for his granddaughter – Christ, he was going to have a granddaughter – would do no good. There were people who would listen and understand, but he trusted only two of them, and one was at this moment providing security at an under-eight Halloween disco. The other was but a phone call away.

Without stopping, Warlow found the number in his contacts and made the call.

Twenty minutes later, he sat in the kitchen of a house in the wonderfully named hamlet of Cold Blow murmuring, 'Thanks for this, Jess.'

'Don't be stupid, Evan. There is no point sitting alone and mithering.'

When he'd rung her from the car, he'd wanted only to chat. But after two sentences of explanation, Jess Allanby had ordered him to get over to her place immediately. He refused. But Jess was having none of that.

'Do I really need to tell you how this works, Evan? You are leading a major investigation into a murder and the shooting of two police officers. That does not leave much, if any, room for extra pressure. But when it's family, what choice do you have?'

She was right. And she, of all people, understood. She'd been through enough personal stress over the last couple of years thanks to tricky Ricky, her ex.

As soon as he'd walked through the door, seventeen-year-old Molly had walked up to him and grabbed him in a hug. She'd spoken no words, but that hug had contained a thousand of them, nonetheless. Now she'd taken Cadi off to play some game that both girl and dog enjoyed. She was a patient trainer, that girl.

'Have you eaten?' Jess asked.

'I'm not hungry.' The wine Jess handed him acted as a

balm, soothing enough for Warlow to sip again and quickly.

'Don't give me that. You know what a case like this takes out of you. And now this?' She walked to the fridge and took out an enamel tin covered in cling film. 'Lucky for you, this evening Molly made a sausage and fennel risotto.'

'I don't want to take your food.'

'Don't worry. She made enough for the whole county and it's actually not at all bad,' Jess said with a touch of pride.

And so Warlow ate and sipped the red he'd been given and told Jess about Reba's rupture. A telling that somehow morphed into something bigger. He ended up revealing more than he'd told another living soul – apart from Cadi – about Denise, his ex, and the alcoholism that killed her. About how he felt guilty for what his sons had to endure as a result and how Alun, his eldest, had not forgiven his parents for the mess they'd made.

Jess let out a small, sympathetic chuckle. 'I knew some of this, but… Denise sounds like she was a handful.'

Warlow nodded, remembering the kaleidoscope of catastrophes their lives had become. 'I've always thought that term, the demon drink, had a special meaning when it came to her. With a full load on board, she was a different person. Almost as if she was possessed. I know I should have done more. Forced her into rehab, or something.'

Jess's expression remained unmoved. 'You need to listen to Amy Winehouse, Evan. She didn't want to go either. And if you end up there not of your own one hundred percent accord, we know what happens.'

'Of course, but the boys… they didn't understand any of that. The joke is that because of this,' he held up his glass of red, 'I've never met my grandson. Denise made me promise not to go without her. And while she was in denial and swigging at the teat of the Grey Goose, Alun didn't want her anywhere near.'

'Families can be messy,' Jess said, dropping her eyes to her own glass, where her fingers played incessantly with the stem.

'Messy and complicated.' Molly's voice came to them from the doorway. 'But let's deal with the important stuff first. The nitty gritty. How did you like my risotto?'

'I'm still conscious,' Warlow said.

'That's offensive.' On hearing Molly's raised voice, Cadi ears went up, tail in overdrive. Molly knelt and put her head next to the dog's. 'Your daddy is a very ungrateful man, Cadi.'

At the table, Warlow tilted up his, apart from a few dregs, empty plate. 'What does that tell you?'

'Ooh, don't tell Jess, but I think that means there's a plate to lick, Cadi.'

Jess sighed as Molly took the plate over to the dish-washer, opened the swing-down door and put the plate down for the excited dog to clean off. At the same time, Warlow's phone buzzed.

He read the text, looked up into Jess and Molly's expectant faces and said, 'Will you excuse me? I need to take a call.' Without thinking, he opened the back door and stepped out into the night.

CHAPTER TWENTY-THREE

STACEY CAMPBELL HAD MORE or less put the kitchen of the house in Tenby back into some kind of order by mid-evening. The burglars had taken nothing, but she'd filled two rubbish sacks with the food they'd tampered with. Or at least touched, as far as she could tell. Just to be safe, she'd thrown everything that had been open away. Just in case. She'd need to do a big shop to get Dion's cereals and stock up. In the living room, she'd righted the table and chairs, and pushed the settee and the damaged cushions back against one wall. They would all go to recycling. She couldn't stand the thought of having them in the house now.

Alex had warned her about going back to the flat alone when Stacey brought it up. She'd suggested they go together at some point to 'get the place straight.' But when Stacey had said she was popping out to Tesco to get a few things that evening, what she'd really done was driven across to the house alone. And yes, of course the police had warned against it. She just needed some head space to understand what the bloody hell was going on with Mike. She'd looked at his text at least a dozen times since getting back to the house on Pondicherry Street, and each time it left her with the same question.

Why?

Shit hit Fan, Tracy. Keep phone on. I need to keep low profile. DO NOT CALL ME. Cops listening.

What had he and Lee been up to? More than anything, she felt cheated and stupid. She'd told the police that she didn't know what deals Lee and Mike had going on. There were "deals" she knew about. Of course, there were. They offered special discounts for groups in the hire business. For the paddleboards and such. But those weren't the deals the police had referred to.

Stacey stood in the kitchen, looking around. At the polished concrete floor and matching worktop, the hot tap for constant boiling water, the wine fridge. It had all cost an arm and a leg and Mike had given her carte blanche. She thought of the thousands of pounds they'd spent and felt suddenly crushed.

Of course, she'd asked if they could afford it. And Mike had laughed and said simply that business 'is good, babe. Really good.'

But what if it was all a result of something illegal? Ill-gotten gains. It did not bear thinking about.

She wouldn't contemplate bringing Dion back to the house yet. But if she could tidy it enough and tell him they were awaiting new furniture, at least they might get out of Alex's hair. Her place was way too small for them all.

The doorbell rang as she crossed into another room to fetch yet another black bin bag. She came to a halt and sighed. Kids trick or treating no doubt. She had Drumsticks, bite-size Chomps, flakes, and Crunchie at the ready. Bought long before things had gone crazy. The last thing she wanted to do was open the door again, but the local kids hadn't shot Lee. Nor was Mike playing silly buggers their fault.

DO NOT CALL ME.

Stacey reached for the bag of goodies she'd put on the hall table and opened the door with a resigned smile.

There was no one there. In fact, the street in its little mews lane looked remarkably empty. She stepped out and looked right and left. Could be that the kids were getting excited enough to try tricks. No one ever egged houses in this neighbourhood, but it was a night for pranks.

'You're missing out on sweets,' she said into the night.

No one answered.

Stacey turned and had one foot over the threshold when a sudden movement behind made her turn. At that point, her world exploded in a whirl of movement and pain as someone, a man, not a child, dressed in black with a long white face with black ovals for eyes, nostrils, and mouth bore down on her. As she fell backwards, she clutched at the wall to break her fall. But the smooth surface had no purchase, and she clattered down. The noise that came out of her mouth was not the scream she wanted it to be, but a constricted grunt as the air from her lungs exploded out. The door slammed shut and then he was upon her, a gloved hand clamping down on her mouth, his weight pinning her, his other hand grasping her wrists above her head. Through the Scream mask, she registered his eyes glittering.

'Where is he?' the voice sounded muffled, but there was no mistaking the seething anger underlying it. His knee was between her legs, pressing up, the pain harsh and deep.

'Where the fuck is he?'

She couldn't speak through the hands. All she could do was shake her head in terror.

'Where did he hide it? Is it here? Fucking tell me, you bitch.'

A thousand thoughts raced through Stacey's head. That she was so glad she'd left Dion with Alex. That she'd been stupid to open the door. That she might die here on this floor. That she couldn't answer because she didn't know. All she could do was shake her head and mumble through the pressure of that clamping hand.

'Don't fucking lie to me. Where is that shit, Dunbar?'

The doorbell rang. Young voices through the door. 'Trick or treat?'

Scream man pressed his hand down harder on Stacey's mouth. She tasted blood on her lips, twisting her head right and left.

The doorbell rang again. 'Trick or treat?'

Her assailant looked at the door. Stacey's face slid under his grasp, lubricated by spit and blood until her mouth finally came free. 'Help! Hel—'

The hand clamped down again, harder, shutting off her cry.

Above her, Scream man cursed and glared at the front door. When it rang a third time, panic seized him. He sprang up and ran through the house, leaving Stacey to struggle upright, her breath wheezing in and out, staring around for her phone, little mini howls of fright bleating from her throat. And even though she was terrified and panicking, a tiny little spark of cunning lit up in her head. She stumbled to the kitchen, grabbed her phone from the worktop and stuffed it into a pocket, reaching instead for the landline they kept for the business. Once she had it in her madly shaking hands, she dialled 999.

———

Rhys, unable to wait for Gina to come home, finished yesterday's leftovers and, once he had confirmation that she was on the way, suggested pizza for the both of them.

For once, Gina did not object, which told Rhys something about the day she'd had. One Texan barbecue and one meatball marinara duly arrived five minutes after Gina walked through the door. She'd end up eating two slices of hers and he'd finish the meatball marinara over the next two days. Three at a stretch. He'd eaten a slice for breakfast before now.

Despite his surprise at Gina agreeing to his dining suggestion, he was certain that a cosy night of dinner and Netflix was unlikely to transpire. When, after they'd eaten, and she'd showered and put on her favourite joggers and sweatshirt, she joined him on the sofa with a mug of tea, he muted the sound and paused the film. Maybe this evening was not the right one for The Babadook after all.

'How were the Clarks when you left them?' he asked.

'Dan's parents were back from Cardiff. They're worn-out, poor things. I don't think they've slept much these last couple of nights.'

'Must be bloody awful for them. What about Siwan?'

Gina had a couple of Hobnobs on a plate and offered one to Rhys. He took one. But she wrinkled her nose in response to his question. 'I realise we're all different. Daniel's parents can't settle to anything, but Siwan.' Gina shook her head. 'She's keeping herself busy with her vlogging. Have you seen any of her stuff?'

'Can't say I have.'

Gina reached for her phone and scrolled through her Instagram feed. 'Hers is a kind of lifestyle, travel, women's struggles niche. She's been making content for a while, but she's not shy in putting out her own story. She's put #sombremoods up on her last reel.'

Gina's screen filled with an image of a low-lit room with all the photo frames on the wall turned to show only their back surfaces. Several long seconds passed before a figure appeared out of the dim rear of the room to take up position in front of the camera.

'Is that…' Rhys had to ask because the figure's face was obscured by some kind of mask. Or a veil? Whatever it was, it hung down from a band that ran from one ear to the other over the tip of the nose so that everything below it was covered. Above, Siwan's eyes were made up with dark eyeshadow.

'What the hell is—'

'Wait,' Gina instructed.

The voice that emerged from behind the veil was Siwan Clark's. 'As you can see, today I'm wearing a Hanfu veil to conceal my sorrow. You may have read, or heard, about the terrible shooting of a police officer in Tenby, in Pembrokeshire. That officer is my Daniel. I can't share anything else with you, but I've made this space a place of refuge and rest in order to try to soothe my heart while I wait for more news. Thank you for all your messages and for your support. We love you all.'

'Bloody hell,' Rhys said. 'That's random.'

'A bit random, agreed, but it's gone viral.'

Rhys kept his eyes on the phone as the video ran, the camera panning around the room's cushion coverings, throws in autumnal browns and dark greens. 'Did she have to do that?'

'My thoughts exactly. I didn't quite ask her that way, but I asked her. She said she needed to explain it to all her followers. Why she'd gone dark.'

'Crikey, I don't know if I'd have done that. If it had happened to me, would you have wanted to go… viral?'

Gina reached out and grabbed Rhys's hand. 'Don't say that. Don't tempt fate.'

'I'm not. It's an honest question.'

'Then no, I would not go public like that. Never.'

'Nor me,' Rhys agreed. 'Funny, me and Wil talked

about this. About ending up in hospital for the job. He said he was a free bird and that no one would be bothered if he got shot.'

'Wil, as in Wil Hopper?' Gina asked. 'That's a horrible thing to say.'

'He's a laugh, alright. He's been around and I'm learning loads.'

'Yeah, well, I'd be very careful if Wil Hopper is offering lessons.'

An uncertain smile played over Rhys's lips. 'What does that mean?'

Gina picked up her mug of tea in both hands. If Rhys saw the way she clenched her jaw, he didn't comment. 'I wasn't sure I should tell you,' Gina began. 'Wil Hopper knows me.'

'Oh, yeah, he told me that.'

'Did he also tell you he chased me for six months?'

'Chased you?'

'I met him for a drink. Once, that's all. I knew after half an hour it wouldn't go anywhere, so I shut all that down. Politely. But he wouldn't take no. Texts, phone calls, accidental meetings when I was out with girlfriends.' Gina made quote marks in the air around the words "accidental meetings".

'When was this?' Rhys asked, amused perplexity written all over his face.

'At least three years ago. Before he went into the drug squad.'

'Shit.'

Gina's big eyes widened in apology. 'I'm sorry, Rhys. It's water under the bridge, but you need to know. In case it comes up. That's all.'

'Right,' Rhys said in an airy way that made Gina's brows furrow.

'It was nothing. At least it was on my part. But Wil didn't like it.'

'He didn't sound aggrieved or worried or anything. When your name came up, I mean.'

'I'm glad. I don't want it to sour anything between you two in the job. This job especially. Not now that he's Two-Shoes' golden boy. But I don't want any secrets between us either.'

Rhys smirked. 'In a way, I can understand him not wanting to give up. Chasing you, I mean. The boys at the rugby club all say I'm punching well above my weight.'

Gina grinned. 'Shut up and come here.' She snuggled up to him, draping his long arm around her shoulders.

Above her, out of her line of sight, Rhys smiled, but slowly and inexorably, his eyebrows crept together in troubled thought.

CHAPTER TWENTY-FOUR

JESS AND MOLLY'S faces held identical expressions of concern and trepidation when Warlow stepped back into the kitchen. Molly, however, did not share her mother's patience.

'Well? Are they okay?' she ventured.

'That was Tom on the phone. He's just spoken with Alun. Reba's lost a lot of blood, but she's stable.' He winced at his own words. 'The good news is that they didn't need to do a hysterectomy, which is sometimes necessary if the rupture is too bad.'

'Oh, my God,' Jess said through the palm that had sprung over her mouth.

'What about the baby?' Molly asked, eyes wide with concern.

'She's in PICU – paediatric intensive care. The good news is that they got her out in eleven minutes. Tom says that's miraculous.' Warlow paused for a beat while his head pounded to the drum of his heartbeat, trying to get his non-medical head around the idea that you could cut someone's belly open and take out a baby in the time it took to read a chapter in a book.

'Poor thing,' Jess said. The emotion in her voice triggered Cadi who padded over and nuzzled her head against Jess's thigh. She looked down and fondled the black ears. 'I swear this dog understands every word we speak.'

'But they're okay?' Molly hadn't moved from her chair and wanted more information.

'As far as I can tell, yes. They're going to monitor Eva. They won't really know if... oxygen deprivation can be...' Warlow couldn't find the words.

Molly turned her face up to the ceiling and heaved out a sigh before turning a sympathetic face towards Warlow. 'Shame you can't teleport out there.'

It was a silly remark, but it broke the tension. 'I wouldn't be much use, even if I could.'

'Who cares?' Molly said with feeling. 'You'd be there.'

'I think Evan feels guilty enough already, Mol,' Jess murmured.

'Sorry. If it was me, I'd want as much, you know, emotional support as I could get.'

'You want emotional support when you go to the dentist,' Jess said.

That earned a scathing look from her daughter. 'Thanks, Mum.'

Warlow smiled, feeling the tension break. More grateful than he could ever express to these two women for being... normal.

'But that they're both okay must be a huge relief, though,' Jess said.

Warlow nodded. At this point, you added a little empty platitude. Something like, 'might have been a lot worse.' But he held back because thinking of the worst-case scenario would tie him in knots. The possibility that they both might have died at the birth. He wanted to think about something else.

'You all set for your London trip, Molly?' he asked.

Molly hesitated and Warlow read the confusion in her face. Why was he asking about something so trivial? But she was an emotionally intelligent girl, and, in an instant, the penny dropped. 'Next week. I cannot wait,' Molly answered.

'She's got it all planned out. An actual itinerary. Self-ridges, Harrods, the Tate. Oh, and Bryn's Union bar that does karaoke nights.'

'You're underage,' Warlow said.

'By four weeks. Come on,' Molly protested. 'See you in court.' But the question had broken her mood and there was a light in her eyes now. 'Bryn's meeting me at Padding-ton. I'm offloading Gwennan's cousin's present at a Leon's in the station. That's my one chore done and then, I'm on the town.'

'Hasn't Gwennan missed her cousin's birthday by now?' Warlow asked.

'Yes, but I said I'd take it. She doesn't want to post it. Doesn't trust the Post Office, she said.' Molly shrugged. 'But you remembered I was meant to take it up last month. Well done, Evan. See, you do pay attention now and again. That's a good trait in a detective. Unlike my mother.' Molly took over fondling duties with Cadi.

Jess simply raised both eyebrows.

Warlow pocketed his phone. 'Right, I've taken up enough of your time and emotional support.' He threw that one at Molly, who returned it with an old-fashioned glare. 'I need to get this dog home. Thanks for giving me a couple of shoulders to lean on. Oh, and the food. Not bad, Molly. One day, you'll be good.'

Molly feigned offence. 'Honestly, don't know why I bother sweating over that hot stove.'

Warlow bundled Cadi into the car and waved goodbye, glad he'd come. Glad of the company. Halfway between

Cold Blow and Nevern, his phone rang, and Gil's number came up.

'Uncle Fester, what can I do for you?'

'Sounds like you're still in the car.'

'On my way home as we speak.'

'At least you're not in pyjamas and slippers yet.'

Warlow's pulse ticked up a notch. 'What's happened?'

'Stacey Campbell. She's been accosted at her house.'

'Christ. This bloody case. Who's there?'

'Uniforms. But I'm on the way. The Lady Anwen's taking the kids home.'

'Right. I'll drop the dog off with the sitter again. She'll think it's Christmas come early. I'll meet you there. Oh, and give Hopper a ring. Might as well make use of him while we can.'

Gil didn't answer.

'Gil?' Warlow prompted.

'He's the one that rang me.'

'Ah. Finger on the pulse. The ambitious ones always seem to be one step ahead.' Warlow remembered those days.

'Ambition, is that what you call it? I've got a different word.'

Warlow let out a hoarse grunt but remembered Two-Shoes' unwelcome hint from earlier. 'He's young, that's all. I'll see you there in half an hour.'

————

THE NARROW STREET where Stacey Campbell and Michael Dunbar had their home was now awash with blue lights from a couple of response vehicles and an ambulance. Warlow parked where he could, a good fifty yards away, and walked towards the blue lights, passing the odd zombie and one bloke with a hatchet through his head pretending that they were extras in The Walking Dead. The little kids had long gone. These were teenagers who saw the opportunity to frighten innocent passers-by under the guise of Halloween as an offer they couldn't refuse.

They got short shrift with Warlow, whose glare of disapproval quickly made them decide this was not someone to wave their hands menacingly at. As he got nearer to the address, more people appeared on the street, enjoying the spectacle and the light show. This was better than any trick or treat. Better than what was on the telly, too, no doubt.

Gil was standing in front of the house, which had the door wide open, talking to a Uniform. A paramedic walked past carrying a bag just as Warlow arrived.

'How is she?' Warlow asked.

The paramedic returned a zipped lip stare that eased only when the DCI produced his warrant card. 'Bruised, but nothing major. Bit shocked, but she doesn't need the hospital, if that's what you're wondering.'

It had been.

'There's a neighbour in there with her,' the paramedic added.

Warlow nodded and looked around. What he wanted to do was to get the Uniforms to shoo all these people back inside their houses. But they had every right to be standing here.

'Get someone to take the names and addresses of the clowns in the fancy dress,' he said to the female officer. 'That should make the little buggers disappear. We can canvass the neighbours tomorrow.' Warlow turned to Gil. 'Where's Hopper?'

'Around the back, checking out the exit route.'

'And where is Stacey?'

'Kitchen, sir,' said the Uniform.

Warlow walked into the house. A second paramedic

stood back to let him pass. 'Finished?' Warlow asked.

'Yeah. All yours.'

Warlow stood back to let the paramedic pass and then said to Gil, 'Let's shut the front door. It's like a bloody goldfish bowl in here.'

Gil spoke to the Uniform and then followed Warlow into the house and shut the door behind him.

Stacey Campbell sat at the kitchen table. A modern matt white thing with wooden legs and chairs to match. Warlow was struck by how un-homely all the shiny surfaces and chrome fittings looked. More like a clinic than a nest. At the end of the table sat another woman. A little older, larger, cornrow hair with the tips stained blond and an expression of unbridled suspicion on her face with the arrival of the two officers.

Stacey glanced up but didn't acknowledge Warlow. She looked battered, both in terms of the bruises on her lips and by the events of the evening.

'Who are these two, Stace?' asked the larger woman in the voice of a tobacco addict.

Stacey nodded. 'Cops.'

'I hope you're not going to be here long. She's been through enough.' She sent Gil and Warlow glares of equal intensity.

Warlow acknowledged the woman. She was trying to be protective. You picked your battles in situations like this.

'We'll be as quick as we can, Miss…'

'Mrs. Layla Atherton.'

'Good to meet you, Mrs Atherton.' Warlow nodded at the woman, but then turned his full attention on Stacey. 'Okay if we sit?'

Stacey nodded.

'I know you must have told several people all this, but if you wouldn't mind saying it again, for my sake.'

'Can't you ask the bloke in uniform she's spoken to already?' Layla objected.

'No. Because then it's hearsay and I need to hear it from Stacey.' Warlow didn't take his eyes off the woman in question.

Stacey sighed. 'I was only going to pick a few things up, but there was such a mess. Your people were just leaving when I arrived. But it's Halloween. Trick or treat. I'd answered the door four times already, so the kids, they were clued in I was home. Word gets around. Who's giving out stuff and who isn't. I'd already bought loads. I had it in the car, ready. You'd know.'

Warlow pretended he did. No one came to his cottage on Halloween.

'The doorbell rings and I answer the door. But there's no one there. Probably kids messing about was my thinking. I turn to go back in and… he comes in after me, pushes me down—'

'He,' Gil said. 'You're sure it was he?'

'Yeah. His voice, His size. Definitely a man.'

'It's always a bloody man, isn't it?' muttered Layla.

'I fell. He got on top of me,' Stacey continued.

'Did you get a good look?' Gil asked.

'He had a thingy on… a mask like in that film. Long white face, black open mouth. He had gloves too. All I could see were his eyes.' Stacey had her hands on the table, the fingers of the left rubbing constantly at those on the right with repetitive, soothing movements. 'Dark eyes. I couldn't tell you the colour. I didn't think to…'

'Take your time, Stacey,' Gil said.

There were two mugs on the table, half drunk.

'Any chance of a cup of tea, Layla?' Warlow asked.

'Jesus, you lot have got some cheek.'

'For Stacey.' Warlow qualified his request.

Layla frowned. 'Oh, okay, yeah. This one's stone cold, anyway. But I suppose you want one?'

'No,' Warlow said, breaking his usual rule. 'We won't be here that long. We just need to hear this from Stacey.'

Layla got up and moved across to where the kettle sat on a worktop.

'Can you remember any details, Stacey?' Warlow asked. 'What did he say?'

'He wanted to know where Mike was. He wanted to know if... he asked where Mike had hidden it.'

'Hidden what?'

Stacey slid her eyes down, focusing on a ring on one of her fingers. Not the fourth one on the left hand, Warlow noted. 'I have no idea. I honestly have no idea. If I knew, I would have told him.'

'So, this was all to do with Michael?' Gil asked.

'I'm telling you what he said. Where is he? Where did he hide it? That's what he asked me. But I couldn't tell him because I don't know where Mike is. I don't know if he's hidden anything. Or what he might have hidden. Do you know?' Her voice rose with each staccato sentence until she looked up into Warlow's eyes.

He did not look away. 'No. Not yet. But you would tell us if you knew, right, Stacey?'

'Oh my God, how many times? I don't know what Mike has done or where he is.'

'Then what happened, Stacey?' Gil steered her back to the narrative.

'The doorbell rang again. Kids this time, yelling trick or treat. They kept ringing. God bless those kids. It spooked him. He got up and ran.'

'To where?' Gil asked.

Stacey's shake of the head this time was an echo of her vagueness. 'Out, through the back. I mean, I didn't follow him. I came in here and rang the police.'

'And he took nothing.'

She blinked then. Several times. 'My phone. He took my phone.'

'Why?'

Another shrug. This time accompanied by a mournful expression. 'I have no idea.'

'It's locked, right?'

Stacey nodded. 'Probably thinks he can unlock it. Maybe he thinks I know where Mike is and there are messages…'

'Are there messages?' Warlow asked, following her lead.

'No,' she said vehemently. 'I told you already. How many times?' She sniffed and buried her face in a tissue.

'Why don't you leave her alone?' Layla's voice came from across the room.

'You're right,' Warlow said. 'We should. That's more than enough for now. Try to get some rest, Stacey. We will need to take a formal statement tomorrow. Probably best at the station again. We can send someone to pick you up.'

'No. No, I'll come in.'

'Great. We'll need to give the place the once over, too. In case the attacker left some clues.'

Stacey nodded.

'Okay,' Warlow said, not unkindly. 'Like I say, get some rest.'

Fat chance, thought Warlow. But it was worth a try.

CHAPTER TWENTY-FIVE

OUTSIDE, the ambulance had gone, and the Uniforms had at last turned off the blue lights, but the crowd had not dispersed. Hopper stood next to the Uniform that Warlow had spoken to earlier as the breeze began to spit rain.

'Where are you parked?' Warlow asked Hopper.

'Around the corner, sir.'

'Let's go to yours, then.'

They followed Hopper around to a dark three-door BMW. With a silent nod to Gil's size, Warlow suggested the sergeant get into the passenger seat while Hopper pulled his seat forward to allow access to the back. The car smelled of fresh linen.

'Nice,' Warlow said. 'How long have you had this?'

'Couple of years. I got a good deal.'

'My car used to smell like this,' Gil said. 'When I drove it out of the showroom. Lasted half an hour before one of the little ones spilled a milkshake.' He shook his head wistfully.

'Nice image, Uncle Fester.'

Gil gave Hopper a steely look. Hopper grinned.

'Find anything?' Warlow asked Hopper once the younger man had sat in the driver's seat.

'We're checking the back door for prints, but it looks like he let himself out and ran off. The door was open when the Uniforms got here.'

'Knew his way around, then?' Gil asked.

'Are you asking if I think it's the same bloke that turned the house over, then yes, I do. Stacey Campbell wasn't here when he called before. If they drew a blank then, it makes sense that they'd came back for her.'

Warlow sat hunched forward, the two sergeants half turned so they could speak.

'What did she actually say?' Hopper asked.

'That he was disturbed before he did much damage. She cut her lip, but it looks superficial.' Warlow turned to Gil. 'Impressions?'

'Genuine. She's had a scare. And they were after information, that's clear. Nothing taken this time or last time. They haven't found whatever it is they're after. But why the phone?'

'Phone?' Hopper asked.

'Stacey said he took her phone.'

Hopper looked genuinely perplexed. 'Why?'

'So, he can get into it.'

'But it's difficult even for us to access information from a locked device and we have a room full of nerds,' Hopper protested.

Warlow nodded. The phone was an odd little wrinkle. 'So, we think that probably the same people, or person, who ransacked the place before have waited for Stacey, or possibly Dunbar, to come back.'

'It's a good ruse, though, picking Halloween. I mean, she'd be expecting to have her doorbell rung more than once tonight,' Hopper observed.

'They're not idiots. That makes a change,' Warlow

muttered. 'But we're still none the wiser what it is they're after.'

Hopper had the roof light on. It threw a yellow glow on his fellow officers' faces. He flicked his gaze now between Gil and Warlow. 'What did she actually say he asked her, sir?'

'He wanted to know where Dunbar was. And where he'd hidden it, whatever it is,' Gil explained.

Hopper sat back. 'They're looking for product, sir. They must be. Dunbar disappears, Barret is dead. This all adds up to someone either having messed up or trying to be too smart. Whatever it is, the people who've done this, to the house and now to Stacey, they want their product.'

'Should we have her under some sort of protection, then?' Gil asked.

Hopper responded instantly. He'd clearly thought it through. 'I would, sir.'

'Okay. Find out where she's wanting to go. She can't stay here. Wherever it is, we'll get a Uniform to stay with her and the child.'

Hopper nodded.

'And we can get her in for a full statement tomorrow. There's something about this that doesn't add up yet. Right. No point hanging around here.' Warlow waited while Hopper exited and fiddled with the seat again to let the DCI out.

While the younger officer hurried off to set some protection in motion, Warlow and Gil walked back to their cars.

'Keen, isn't he?' Gil said.

'Mustard personified.'

'Do you have yours a la Français or the full English?'

Warlow answered without needing to think. 'I enjoy a bit of whole grain. You?'

'I find the English type can get right up my nose.'

Warlow's lips twisted into a half smile. 'Now, now, Sergeant. We were all young once. And Hopper's keen to do the running around.'

'I don't mind you calling me Uncle Fester, but I draw the line with people I hardly know.'

'Name calling? You've never struck me as being sensitive.'

'Ah, but with him, there's a snide edge. Plus, he didn't like it when I traded insults.'

'Why? What did you call him?'

'Not just him. Him and his car.'

Warlow waited, but when Gil still didn't speak, he stopped on the pavement and turned to the sergeant. 'Well?'

'Spur of the moment thing. I mean, he does look like Tennant, you must admit. And that bloody car of his looks like something from a sci-fi movie. And it's chocolate brown.'

'The name?' Warlow insisted.

'Dr Who and the Turdis.'

Warlow sighed. 'Was that the best you could do?'

'*Arglwydd Mawr*, it's late. I've had to listen to Halloween disco music half the night. What do you expect?'

Warlow turned and walked on. 'He does look a bit like Tennant, I agree.'

'Then I rest my case.' Gil pulled up the collar of his coat and started whistling the BBC radiophonic workshop theme tune to Dr Who as they hurried through the rain.

———

WARLOW'S NIGHT was fitful in the extreme. Sometimes cases bothered him enough to keep sleep at bay. But this night had more to do with images of his first and only granddaughter, just a few hours old, taken from her mother's womb, alone in a machine without the touch and comfort of a parent's skin, or a nipple to feed on.

He kept spooning in the bromides. That she was probably in the best place, that they'd acted quickly, that it was the best day and age for this sort of thing to happen because medicine was bloody amazing. But all he could think of was that she'd be tiny and alone.

Molly was right. The sooner they invented a teleportation device, the better. Perhaps he should have a chat with Hopper, see if anything might be arranged via the Turdis.

He hadn't bothered picking Cadi up from the Dawes the second time around. Too disruptive for the dog. He found himself alone at three in the morning, making a cup of tea and pondering the Barret case as a distraction from thoughts of down under. Which said a lot about his state of mind and the problems he was contending with. This case had many strands that he hadn't quite knitted into a whole woolly cardigan yet.

He tried composing his thoughts around all the information he'd gathered during the day. Was it truly less than twenty-four hours since he'd visited Daniel Clark and spoken to Tiernon? He needed a Gallery and Job Centre of his own. But he was aware of where all this was coming from. Something he'd seen or heard during this long day was, like a stone in a shoe, annoying him. Yet, every time he thought he might get the damn thing to the front of his head, it wafted away like a ribbon in the wind.

In the end, he sat in the chair in his sunroom with only a sidelight on, looking out across the dark estuary and its glittering lights with his notebook by his side, jotting down random thoughts as they occurred to him.

Stacey Campbell phone. Why?

Talk to Clark's force partner face-to-face now that she has had a day to recover.

Drugs. Is there a chain? Hopper would know.

He fell asleep contemplating all these enigmatic questions. His dreams were fragmented and strange. But when he came awake, it was to the sound of his phone messaging him. A WhatsApp at four-fifteen in the morning. A strange time, but not of course in Perth, where it was twelve-fifteen in the afternoon.

The image stayed blurred when he opened the app. At first, Warlow couldn't tell what he was looking at, but then the pixelations solidified and Warlow's throat constricted. A close up, taken not more than a few inches away from a see-through Perspex box with round holes where whoever needed to, could put their hands through. A pristine white sheet laced by wires running out of shot, and there, laying on the sheet, her eyes open as if looking at the camera, was a tiny child, a clip over her umbilical cord, a nappy that looked too big for her, leads clipped to her chest.

Under the photograph, Alun had added some text.

> Eva Iris Warlow. Off oxygen. Doing her
> thing. She looks like her mother,
> Thank God.

An insult masquerading as fatherly love. The way it had always been between him and his sons. And there was something wonderful about being able to do exactly that under what might well have been, but for the fickle finger of fate, bloody awful circumstances.

> Waiting for the docs again. Fingers crossed

> Reba?

> Doing okay.

> Keep me updated.

Warlow held the image in his head when he turned over, taking positives from what Alun had said. But all thoughts of Stacey Campbell had gone with that image of his granddaughter. For now, as he lay in his bed, he only had thoughts for Eva Iris Warlow.

CHAPTER TWENTY-SIX

AT 8AM THE FOLLOWING MORNING, Warlow sat with his team in a half circle at the front of the Incident Room. Everyone was keen to get the details nailed down. So much so that they'd even put tea on hold until they got the meat and potatoes done. But first, Warlow wanted an update on their fallen comrade.

Rhys came up with the goods. 'Gina's over with Siwan Clark now, sir. His parents have gone up again. Siwan is planning on going this afternoon.'

'Status? And don't say stable. I hate stable.'

'The hospital says he had an acceptable night. No sign of recovery of consciousness yet,' a nonplussed Rhys said.

'They won't let him wake until his brain has stopped swelling,' Warlow murmured. He'd chatted to Tom about it. As time scales went, you weren't looking at hours here. More like days, or weeks even. 'How are his family?'

'Parents are really torn up, sir. They hardly know what day it is,' Rhys explained. 'His wife is trying to be positive. She's baring her soul on social media.'

'How so?' Catrin asked.

Jess answered this one. 'Has anyone seen her Instagram account?'

Shakes of the head all round apart from Rhys. Jess continued, 'She's an influencer. I mean, that's how she makes her money. Putting up images, sometimes with sponsored products on show.'

'Isn't she an actress?' Catrin asked.

Rhys nodded. 'She's been in a couple of the Welsh language soaps, but not long-running parts. That's where the money is, apparently.'

Jess had picked up her phone and scrolled to a screen-shot of Siwan Clark's page showing photos of rooms deco-rated in various ways. 'This is @cylcheto. Molly says it's Welsh for circle again. It's all about sustainability. Recy-cling. Eco-friendliness. Clothes and furnishings, makeup, food. There's a YouTube channel, too. She also has an eco-traveller account she shares with Daniel. But this one is her main page.'

'Nearly forty thousand followers on Insta, now, ma'am,' Rhys explained.

Jess nodded. 'I bet. My point is this is her job. She can't afford not to post. So yes, it may seem crass to use her situ-ation, this situation, but she probably doesn't consider it in those terms. It's her truth, and she's not scared of sharing it.'

'I hate that term,' Gil muttered. 'With respect, ma'am. It's either the truth or not the truth. His or hers shouldn't come into it.'

'But she makes money from this?' Warlow asked. 'By posting photos and, what is it called, vlogging?'

'She does,' Jess said. 'A lot of people do. Get enough followers and manufacturers will give you their products to test. Or restaurants give you free meals for an honest review. Clothes to wear, et cetera.'

'Different bloody world,' Gil muttered.

'I have someone who lives in that world,' Jess explained. 'Or at least, at seventeen knows how to navigate it.' With Molly's help, Jess had done some digging. 'Before Siwan married Dan, she had a slightly angled take on things. The generational burden. How unfair it is to expect anyone born after 1995 to behave the same way as baby boomers or even Generation X.'

'Generation X?' Gil asked.

'People born between 1965 and 76,' Jess explained. 'But I'm talking about millennials. You surely all know the words of this song, don't you? Why they only want to work at jobs that make an impact. How unfair it is to expect them to save because there's no way they'll ever be able to afford a house? Forget the long term, just go on holiday.'

'Sounds like a rant,' Gil said.

'She's got a point,' Hopper said.

'But that sounds more like something an activist would say than an influencer,' Catrin pointed out.

'Good to hear from you there, Catrin.' Warlow said. 'Since you're representing the group we're discussing. Aren't you a millennial?'

'I am, sir. But I don't think anyone owes me anything. My parents taught me that just turning up is not enough for a medal.'

Warlow smiled at that one.

'The point is,' Hopper said. 'We shouldn't blame Siwan Clark for the way she's handling this.'

'Fair enough.' Jess held her hands up. 'It's a situation none of us ever would want to be in. We can't tell how we'd react.'

Hopper nodded. 'I know Dan, sir, and Siwan is a nice girl.'

Gil's lips flattened. 'Who says she isn't? Surely, DI Allanby's point is that it's a different way of dealing with things. And this forum is all about understanding.'

Hopper folded his arms. 'Well, I vote we give her some slack. Just because she's into something some people find difficult to understand.'

They were soft words, but the implication was clear, and you could hear the frost forming in the air.

'But is it relevant to the case?' Warlow posed the question without expecting an answer, more by way of drawing a line under the discussion. They were being side-tracked by social media here. 'Let's get back to facts rather than feelings.'

'That's not a very millennial approach,' Gil muttered. 'Not much emotional nurturing there, Mr Warlow.'

Catrin half smiled at her fellow sergeant, but Warlow ignored him and asked, 'What about the Barret property search?' He studied the surrounding faces, waiting for an answer.

'CID got the warrant yesterday, sir,' Catrin said. 'Squeaky clean apart from a large sum of cash. In the region of thirty-eight thousand pounds. Fresh notes, too.'

Rhys picked up the baton. 'We managed to get bank statements, too, sir. Murder cases always make them cooperative. He was with more than one High Street and Internet bank. Bottom line is that the jet-ski business is apparently thriving. We've passed it all on to economic crime for the forensic accountants to look through. But the guy I spoke to there had a quick peep and first impressions are that the numbers were way above what similar companies around the coast are turning over. Plus, there were statements from three other business accounts that Barret was the sole trader in. Two were online accounts offering virtual jet-ski lessons and business mentoring courses. He charged about £400 an hour for consultations. Oh, and he had a business offering payday loans.'

Hopper huffed out his derision.

'You don't like the sound of that, Sergeant Hopper?' Warlow asked.

'Classic laundering strategy, sir. These other businesses, even the jet-ski business, are fronts. Somewhere they can inflate income through a drip approach. The big one would be the payday loans. That's a money service business, and it's the easy way cash gets back into the system. You pretend to lend someone money, cash usually, and they pay it back using the cash that you've given them off the books, which they get a small cut of, and then the company can deposit the residual "loan" into a legitimate account. Difficult to police and monitor.'

When Hopper had finished, Gil sat up in his chair. 'Right, well, that explains what I've been seeing in Dunbar's accounts, too. We did a sweep of his study after the break-in and found a couple of files on his laptop. Different names and accounts, but probably the same kind of thing Barret was doing.'

Warlow ran three fingers up and down his forehead. 'Sounds more and more like Barret and Dunbar were not squeaky clean. If we accept Sergeant Hopper's theory about Barret also being involved in transporting drugs on the coast, we've got a ring operating here.'

'I have no direct evidence, sir,' Hopper said. 'I'm putting two and two together, that's all.'

Warlow considered this. 'Personally, I like your maths, Sergeant.'

Jess had a notebook out and looked up from where she'd been writing. 'So, it sounds complex, this operation. Organised.'

Warlow stood up and arched his back. Last night's broken sleep had left him stiff and sluggish. But Jess was absolutely right. This case now had the stench of organised crime about it. But a fresh thought creased the DCI's forehead. What about the other end of the funnel? The sharp end. 'If Barret and Dunbar are middlemen, there'd be people above and people below, wouldn't there?'

Hopper ran with this. 'We could certainly look at low-level distribution, sir. I have a handful of names.'

'Let me have them. See if we can link any of them to Barret and Dunbar directly. Perhaps someone got greedy.' Warlow walked across to the posted-up crime scene photos. 'And what about the 999 calls from the beach? Any further with that witness?'

Gil's turn to shake his head. 'Pay as you go. Unregistered.'

That was odd, but not unheard of. In the current economic downturn, expensive phone contracts were an easy and expensive luxury to cut back on.

Rhys jumped in, 'And the cell site analysis on Dunbar's phone should be back this morning, too, sir.'

'Good.' Another piece of the puzzle would come with that. Where Dunbar was at the time his partner got shot. 'So, that leaves us once again with Stacey Campbell and how little, or how much, she really knows.' He glanced at Hopper. 'What time is she due in?'

'Around ten, sir.'

Warlow turned to Jess. 'Fancy another chat with her? She's fed up with seeing my face staring at her across a kitchen table, that's for certain.'

'Have you upset her?' Jess asked, raising just the one eyebrow.

'No, but she associates me with every crap thing that's happened to her over the last seventy-two hours. A friendly face would do no harm.'

'Fair enough.' She glanced across the room. 'Catrin? You free?'

'Certainly, ma'am.'

Hopper looked crestfallen. 'I was hoping maybe I could have a crack, sir.'

'No. I want you to work the drugs angle. I need those names from you.' Warlow was unmoved.

It looked to the assembled team as though Hopper might object. His eyes strayed to the door where he knew his mentor, Superintendent Goodey, might well already be in her office. A cynical person might have interpreted that look like a micro-aggressive threat to tell the teacher. Wisely, Hopper swallowed his disappointment, and the meeting broke up as everyone went about their business. It was Rhys who, in passing, noticed the big grin on Gil's face.

'What's up with you, sarge?' he asked.

'Me? Looking forward to a day's work, that's all, detective constable.' But as he turned away, the strains of a hummed rendition of the Dr Who theme droned up from where Gil sat scrolling through the documents on his screen.

CHAPTER TWENTY-SEVEN

THEY KNUCKLED DOWN TO IT. Warlow remembered to send the image of incubating Eva to Jess and got an 'Aw, brilliant' in reply. He was on the point of picking up the phone to Leanne Abbot, the other shot officer whom he hadn't yet spoken to, when the door to the SIO room opened and Two-Shoes walked in. She didn't knock and that, Warlow assumed, was deliberate. Knocking might imply that she was acknowledging his status in the Incident Room and God forbid she do that. Warlow suspected that secretly, and on occasion overtly, Two-Shoes liked to think that she was in charge.

Of everything.

'So, Stacey Campbell's attacker. Any clue?'

'None yet,' Warlow answered.

'I'd suggest providing Campbell some protection.'

'Already done, ma'am.'

'Where is she staying?'

Warlow explained about her friend.

'And have you considered looking into Campbell's finances?'

'She's denying all knowledge.'

'Less easy to sit on that high horse if we find her bank account stuffed with money.'

It had, of course, crossed Warlow's mind, but you needed grounds to request a court order. And, as yet, they had not enough evidence to sway a magistrate, though they were getting closer. It annoyed him to be reminded of it. But then, Two-Shoes had skills when it came to getting Warlow's goat.

'We're working on it, ma'am,' he said with his best trawled up smile, resisting the urge to make the 'ma'am' sound like a bleating nanny. Bloody hell, he was turning into Gil. Yet all the while, his brain was asking tough questions. Such as who had put that idea of chasing the money into the superintendent's head? It suggested that someone was feeding her information that only a handful of people, prior to their recent catch-up, had been privy to. He'd been planning to fill her in – in the knowledge sense, as opposed to shovelling dirt over a casket in a six-foot-deep hole – but only after they'd spoken to Stacey Campbell again.

'Sergeant Hopper is pulling his weight?' Two-Shoes' voice brought him back into the room.

'Definitely another tool in the box, ma'am.'

Two-Shoes' lined forehead developed trenches. She sucked in air through dilated nostrils. 'Sharper than the blunt and rusting ones there now, I hope?'

'Don't Blunt and Rusting have a solicitor's office in Cardiff, ma'am?'

'Is that meant to be a joke, Evan?'

'Yes, ma'am. And a terrible one. But as for tools, you know how us working people are. We get used to the feel of those old favourites. They may be worn but sharpen up nicely with a bit of honing. Tools that are more than capable of doing the job.'

Two-Shoes straightened a back that was already doing

a bloody good impression of an ironing board. 'I'll expect you to keep me appraised, Evan. Developments as soon as they occur.'

She turned and walked away, leaving Warlow to pull his lips back over his teeth in a rictus grin.

———

'THIS IS GETTING to be a bit of a habit,' Jess said gently as Stacey and the legal representative she'd brought with her; a short, balding man in his late thirties wearing a crumpled, too-small suit, settled in. Jess knew him from past interactions. Huw Pearson was someone who liked the sound of his own voice.

'Can I remind everyone that my client is here of her own volition and is happy to help regarding the attack on her yesterday evening? I'd appreciate it if questions were kept pertinent,' Pearson said.

'Getting to be a habit not pertinent?' Catrin, who was less guarded in her dislike of Pearson, asked.

The solicitor looked pointedly at his chubby wrist. 'If we could stick to the script, we can get this done and move on. Ms Campbell is still traumatised by events. She has better places to be.'

Jess pulled a typed sheet of paper towards her. Stacey's written statement, penned under the watchful eye of Mr Pearson, no doubt. Today, the victim had dressed in figure-hugging leggings and a pair of white trainers under a leather bomber jacket. Even though she'd been generous in applying makeup, her already full lips showed an uneven swelling and a bruised lip.

'Couldn't have been pleasant,' Jess said, and meant it. She'd spent too many hours talking to women who'd been abused by male attackers to think otherwise.

'I was stupid to open that door,' Stacey said, her mouth tight.

'No, you weren't. Your assailant knew what he was doing. Halloween night, lots of kids knocking on doors. It implies he had some guile.'

'Guile,' Pearson said. 'Is that what you've told your people to look out for? Someone with guile? Bound to catch him, then.' He smirked.

Jess ignored him. 'Odd that the only thing he took was your phone, though?'

'It all happened so fast. My phone fell on the floor. When he got spooked by the doorbell, he grabbed for it and ran. My phone, I mean.'

'Probably thought he could get into it. But you locked it, right?' Catrin asked.

'Locks automatically. I had facial recognition on it. It'll only open for me.'

'And after a few goes and fails, it would revert to a numeric PIN?'

Stacey nodded.

'So, if he took your phone, he was after information,' Jess said.

'It's all in the statement. What he wanted. What he yelled at my client.' Pearson held his palm up and pointed towards the typed sheet.

Jess nodded slowly. 'I'm interested in the information aspect, though. We've been investigating Lee Barret's financial affairs and come up with several discrepancies—'

'Whoa,' Pearson put his hand up. 'I asked if we could stick to the case in hand.'

Jess turned her grey eyes on the man. 'This is the case in hand, Mr Pearson. Only an idiot would pretend otherwise. Everything that has happened to Ms Campbell here ties into the murder of a colleague of her partner's. And the shooting of two of our officers. Are you suggesting that last night's attack was an isolated incident? When Ms Campbell's statement clearly states that her assailant was after information?' Jess picked up the sheet and quoted the assailant's words. 'Where is he? Where has he hidden it?'

Pearson dropped his eyes and pretended to write something down.

Catrin leaned forward. 'This must feel very raw, Stacey. But this is the second time someone has been in your home. They're looking for something. You've thought this through. We consider that Mr Dunbar may be involved in certain activities related to the killing of Lee Barret. Someone is looking for Michael. That someone isn't scared of being violent. Your best chance of helping Michael is for us to find him before whoever else is looking for him does.'

Stacey looked up, lips trembling.

'Stacey,' Jess urged again. 'If you know anything about what business they were in, what they were doing, you need to tell us now.'

Stacey exhaled deeply. 'I swear Mike didn't tell me anything. He said it would be best if I didn't know. That's the God's honest truth. The money… sometimes he'd give me cash to get stuff. Shopping, things for Dion. We had a joint account, too. A credit card that he always paid off. But he didn't talk business. Nothing except L&M Jet-Ski. That was his work.'

Jess glanced at Catrin. This had the ring of truth to it.

'So, have you blocked your phone?' Catrin asked.

'What?'

'Blocked your phone. So that no one can access it even if they tried.'

Stacey shook her head. 'No, not yet. I haven't had time to think.'

'It's an iPhone, right?'

Stacey nodded.

'I'd advise you do that right away,' Jess said.

Catrin waded in. 'Did you have a cloud account set up? You can get most of your messages and photos back that way.'

'Yeah. I think so,' Stacey said, but with little conviction. 'Mike did all that stuff for me.'

'And if you do, would you mind giving us access?'

'To my phone?' Stacey looked appalled.

'Mr Barret was murdered, Stacey. Perhaps by the same man who attacked you last night. You tell us he took your phone. If we can access your records, perhaps we can find a link.'

Stacey nodded.

'She is under no obligation—' Pearson began.

'Of course, but it would help us enormously,' Catrin added. 'We can get a warrant for your phone records, too. But if you can access them and download your phone contents to a new one and let us look, there'd be no need for a warrant.'

'I'll try. I'm not that good with tech. I think I've got my password and stuff written down somewhere.'

'Great. You have my number,' Catrin said. 'I'll wait to hear from you.'

Pearson's frown was getting deeper. 'This is way beyond the brief.'

Jess ignored him. 'We appreciate your cooperation, Stacey. You've been really helpful. Our priority now is to find Mr Dunbar and make sure he is safe.'

That made Stacey blink. 'Safe?'

'Someone desperately wants to find him,' Catrin hammered home the reasoning. 'We doubt it's to invite him for a round of golf.'

'Oh, come on,' Pearson objected.

'Will you be staying with your friend?' Catrin said, once again ignoring the solicitor. 'We'll make sure there's a presence. Get a car to patrol nearby.'

Stacey nodded. 'I'm getting extra locks put on the Pondicherry Street house. Someone is fixing the alarm, too. But I don't think I'll go back there now. Not until I speak to Mike. So, yeah, I'm staying with Alex.'

'Wise move,' Jess said.

Stacey threw Jess a troubled glance. 'This stuff you say he's involved with. Is it bad?'

'Illegal, yes.'

'And that's why Lee was killed?'

'It's a line we're investigating.'

Stacey glared in disbelief. 'But they were doing well. There was always money. I thought… oh, God…' She shut her eyes. 'I've been so bloody stupid.'

'Naïve maybe. Not stupid.' Catrin's voice had softened.

'Right, well.' Pearson gathered up his things. 'If we've finished.'

'For now, yes,' Jess said, once again levelling her gaze on the man before turning pointedly to Stacey. 'Let us know about your phone. Once you get it sorted. It'll save us a bucket load of time.'

Stacey nodded, but kept her eyes down, worrying at a chipped nail.

————

As BEFORE, Warlow watched proceedings from the observation room and then joined Jess and Catrin as they returned to the Incident Room. This time, armed with a fresh Rhys Harries brew and a Gil biscuit display, they stood, or sat around, to discuss what they'd learnt.

'Where's Hopper?' Warlow asked.

'Shot off once Campbell left, sir. Said he had something to do,' Rhys explained.

Jess sipped at her tea and stared at the many images now adorning the Gallery.

'What are the chances of her being able to recover the data from her phone?' Warlow asked.

'It's why we have cloud storage, sir,' Catrin said. 'If you lose your phone and can remember your login details, it should all be backed up.'

'She seemed less than enthusiastic,' Warlow said.

'I don't know many people who'd be keen to let you have full access to their phone, sir,' Catrin said.

'Wonder why that is?' Gil said.

'I expect we've all sent messages, or received some, we regret.'

'Or searched for something iffy,' Rhys said over the rim of his mug.

'Some more than others.' Gil sent him a pointed look.

'So, how long should we give her?' Warlow asked, looking for a consensus.

'She'll need to buy a new phone. If I was generous, I'd say by tomorrow morning,' Catrin answered.

'I don't think there's any need for that, sir.' They all turned on hearing the voice as Hopper, breathing hard, walked through the door.

'Where have you been?' Catrin asked.

'Down to the car park. Once I heard you'd finished with Stacey Campbell, ma'am,' he nodded at Jess, 'I had a bit of a brainwave. I followed her and the solicitor out to the car park. They'd come separately. I wandered over to where she was parked, low profile and all that. And… well, you can see for yourselves.' He took out his phone and brought up a series of photographs. There was Stacey Campbell in the driving seat of her blue Merc with the familiar grounds of Dyfed Powys HQ in the background.

Rhys's phone rang. He glanced at the caller ID, frowned but then gave Warlow a look of apology, pointed one finger at the phone in his other hand and said, 'I should…'

Warlow waved him off.

'Great, so she's well enough to drive, then,' Catrin said.

'Wait for it,' Hopper said. He swiped along another two images until he found the one he wanted and deftly enlarged it so that Stacey Campbell's head filled the screen. And there, held firmly against the left ear of that head, was a pink phone.

'Christ,' Warlow hissed. The brightly coloured cover was unmistakable. Yes, perhaps she'd already bought a new phone, but a matching cover, too? In that short a time?

'She's been lying to us, sir,' Hopper said.

Catrin studied her fellow sergeant with a mixture of suspicion and admiration. 'What made you think up this little plan?'

Hopper slitted his lids. 'People love their phones, don't they? And she seemed so okay with it. Losing it, I mean.'

'Good thinking,' Warlow said. 'But I wonder why she felt the need to do that? Lie to us about the phone.'

Great question. One that everyone appeared, by their expressions, to have a theory on. But at that precise moment, the Incident Room door creaked open to reveal a very grey, distraught looking Rhys Harries, his phone hanging loose at his side.

'Christ, Rhys, what's happened?' Gil asked. 'Is it Gina?'

Rhys had eyes only for Warlow. 'That was Gina, sir. She's with Siwan Clark. They've just taken a call from Dan's father.'

Silence descended on the room. Like an impending car crash, Warlow didn't want to hear what was coming, but he was helpless to stop it.

'He's gone, sir. Dan's dead.' Rhys croaked out the sentence.

Catrin turned away and walked to her desk. She looked to be shaking gently. Jess looked suddenly angrier than Warlow had ever seen her before. Gil had the appearance of a man who wanted simply to hit someone, or something, very hard.

No one spoke. Hardly anyone breathed. But eventually, Warlow found some words.

'I'm going to find Superintendent Goodey. She'll need to be briefed. You all understand what this all means.'

They did. Now they were investigating a double murder.

CHAPTER TWENTY-EIGHT

WARLOW'S MEETING with Superintendent Goodey went as well as expected under the circumstances. On hearing of Daniel Clark's death, Two-Shoes' frame became very rigid. She sat with both hands palm down on her desk in silence, Well, almost silence. It took Warlow a while to realise that the faint sounds coming from her were the mineral grinding of her back teeth until, at last, she spoke.

'We lost someone when I was with Avon and Somerset. He was only a year or two older than Clark. Caught thieves in the middle of a carjacking. They were just kids themselves, but PC Lennon was struck and run over. I was at that funeral, and I am not a religious person, but I prayed in that church that I would never have to go through something like that again.'

'No one was listening, ma'am,' Warlow said.

'Are you an agnostic, DCI Warlow?'

'More of a pragmatist, ma'am.'

Two-Shoes nodded and then stood up. She reached for her uniform jacket. 'Now I need to speak to the ACC. Once I've broken the news, I'd like to tell him we are getting closer to finding out who did this.'

'You can tell him that no one in my team will sleep much until we arrest someone. It's barely been forty-eight hours yet. But here, we have rules.'

Two-Shoes nodded. What you learned within the first two days of a murder investigation shaped the way it would go. She knew that. 'Then that will have to do. If you need me to be my belligerent and irritating self, just say the word.'

'If any heads need banging together, ma'am, I will do the needful.'

Warlow got up and followed her to the door.

'I suppose the only consolation is that he never woke up.'

'Not much consolation to his parents or his wife, ma'am.'

'No. It's the people left behind who always suffer in cases like this.'

She was right. Cases like this, when one of their own became a victim of doing their job, had fallout. Like a chunk of mountain sliding into the sea, the waves built into a swell that could drown you if you weren't careful. But that swell could become a tsunami capable of causing a lot of damage far away from where the incident occurred. Laws had been passed because of coppers getting killed. And Warlow could feel the power of that force building already.

He walked back to the Incident Room through a building that echoed with his footfalls. Normally, they'd be lost in the background noise of banter, people talking, laughing.

But no longer. Not now.

Word spread like a mudslide, covering everyone in its path and choking out everything except thoughts of sympathy, and, yes, that there-but-for-the-grace-of-God smidgen of guilt-ridden fear. It was only natural. But his job was to help people through this paralysing loop of sorrow and disquiet so that they could get on with finding the sod, or sods, responsible.

When he got to the Incident Room, everyone was there, sitting at their desks, pretending to do things while their minds were full of smoke. Even the indexers and secretaries had somehow dampened down their actions. No one was on the phone and every single person in that room looked up when he walked through the door. He wanted to do nothing except stride straight through to the SIO office and sit there, alone, letting the enormity of what had happened sink in while trying to not let it over-whelm him. He read that exact same sentiment on all the faces. All bar Jess's. She'd been on this roundabout before. She'd be like him, assessing how best to deal with this while the investigation remained a priority. And the only reason she had not stood up and spoken was that this was his case.

With the weight of expectation heavy upon him, Warlow stood in the middle of the room and cleared his throat.

'I see that you're all shocked and horrified. Some of you knew Dan Clark personally. Even if you didn't, he was one of us. And there will be a time for grieving. There'll be time for us to sit and contemplate what all of this means as we sing hymns in a chapel, or raise a glass in a pub. But we can't do that now. Not yet. We can't even clock off early because that might be the kind, respectful, decent thing to do. I don't need to tell you that there isn't anything decent about this abysmal case. And so, we, his colleagues, will put all of that on hold and find out who did this to him. He'd do the same if it was one of us.'

Gil nodded.

Jess's eyes shone.

Warlow continued in a firm voice, 'Let's go back to work. And if anyone doesn't play ball with you, just keep

Dan Clark's name in your head and let the buggers have both barrels.'

He turned to the indexers and typists and CID who were sharing the room with them. 'I'm addressing my team, but take it as read that it's meant for you, too. I am not an unfeeling man. If any of you think you'd like some time to reflect, no one will hold it against you.' He left the implicit question hanging. No one in the room moved a muscle. 'Good,' he said, 'I'm certain Dan Clark's relatives appreciate it. I certainly do.'

More nods. A little smile from Jess that told him he'd struck the right note.

Warlow turned back to the team.

'Where's Hopper?'

'He seemed to take it quite hard, sir,' Catrin said. 'He looked bloody awful. I think he might be throwing up.'

Warlow looked at the Gallery. 'So, where were we?'

Rhys got up. 'A bit further on than we were, sir. I've got Dunbar's cell site analysis. I asked the network provider to copy in the nerds, sir. They say that at the time of the shooting, Michael Dunbar's phone was within a half-mile radius of Telpyn Beach.'

'Half a mile?' Catrin asked.

'It's a big area. Not that many cell sites, sarge. But there isn't anything else within half a mile. Could mean within three yards or eight hundred.'

Warlow crossed to the map. 'I'd put my money on three yards.'

'It puts him at the scene, regardless,' Jess said.

'And we know from Barret's phone that Dunbar texted him that morning,' Catrin reminded them.

'Dunbar knew where Barret was.' Warlow put the palms of his hands on either side of his head for a count of three, like a man trying to squeeze away a headache. 'Catrin, we need to get hold of Stacey Campbell's records.

And her phone. Let's get a warrant for the house she's staying in at Knowling Mead. Let's ruffle a few feathers. And I want an alert out for Dunbar at airports and ports. Talk to Border Control. See if he's flown. If he hasn't, I don't want this bugger absconding. Now I need to find Hopper.'

The drug squad sergeant was indeed where Catrin said he'd be, standing at a sink in the men's room, water running, his face low over the porcelain.

'Are you okay, Wil?' Warlow asked.

Hopper turned his head to regard the DCI. 'I've been better.'

'We all have. But we have work to do, and I want to speak to the denizens of the deep.'

'The who?' Hopper asked.

'The people at the sharp end. The dealers. You said you had some names.'

'I do, sir.'

'Right, get yourself together. Meet me in the car park in ten minutes. You and I are going on a road trip.'

───────

DYFED POWYS POLICE HQ was not the only house of mourning as morning became afternoon. Gina had been at Daniel's parents' house as the news broke. She'd listened, sympathised, and shed a little tear of her own in the kitchen when no one was looking. But as the hours dragged by, Siwan announced that she had to go back to her own house because there were things to do.

Outside, half a dozen reporters hovered, waiting for a soundbite or a photograph. The death of a police officer made big news. Still, they were not interested in a lowly Uniformed PC walking in and out of the property. Gina took Siwan's car keys and drove her Mini two hundred yards to a different street. She returned and told Siwan to leave via the back gate and walk to the Mini to avoid the hyenas – the term for the press she'd adopted from Rhys. Gina would then follow in her own car to make sure no unwelcome press surprises awaited Siwan at the other end of the journey. And to deal with them in no uncertain terms if they were.

Twenty minutes later, they were in Siwan's brand-new kitchen north of the A40 on the western edge of Carmarthen. There'd been no press presence, though Siwan's phone was buzzing with messages as soon as they walked through the door.

'I'd turned it off at John and Beth's. Can't believe how busy it is.'

Busy, Gina thought. An odd word to use. But then she'd concluded already that Siwan Clark was a slightly odd girl. Or at least different. Different but still newly widowed.

'Are you sure it's wise to be alone here, Siwan?'

'You're here.'

'Of course. But… have you rung your parents? Or your sister?'

Siwan regarded Gina with her usual unreadable expression. 'I don't talk to my parents or my sister. They don't approve of my choices. Leaving college, vlogging, being an influencer. They don't think it's very worthwhile. Acting, now that's fine because it's so important for the cultural needs of the community.' Siwan delivered this last sentence in a sing-song voice that suggested she was paraphrasing someone, and not very kindly into the bargain.

'But still, now that Dan's gone, surely—'

'Not going to happen,' Siwan said.

Gina couldn't help thinking this was a terrible idea. 'I'm sorry to hear that. Family can be—'

'A pain in the arse,' Siwan said, and with the words

came a flashing of her eyes that carried both warning and resentment.

Still Gina tried. 'Your sister is in one of the soaps, isn't she?'

But the can of worms that Siwan's family relations obviously was now open and squirming. 'Yes, good old Mererid. Pretending to be a single mother with a drug problem five times a week. And in Welsh. So worthy.'

Gina was no soap addict, but of course, she'd watched some of the channel's output over the years. Her parents watched it all the time, though these days, like all broadcasters, a desperate need to compete with subscription channels and appeal to a younger, tech-savvy audience meant an inevitable tilt towards reality shows and box-ticking drama. Mostly copied from successful English counterparts.

'My friends are my followers.' Siwan held up her buzzing phone. 'As you can hear.'

'You do have a lot of followers.'

Siwan snorted. 'Not enough. I'm still only a micro-influencer. But I'm getting there. Reinvesting into the business.' Her phone buzzed, and she glanced at it again and sniffed. 'Everyone is being so nice.'

'What can I do now that I'm here?'

Siwan shook her head. 'I've been preparing myself. They told me Dan's injuries were serious. Because they said he might be brain damaged if he lived, I'm working on a memorial room for Dan. They'll want to see it.'

'They?' Gina asked.

'My followers.'

'Isn't that a bit… personal?'

Siwan inclined her head. 'My life, my work, is on Insta. I made as much money as Dan did last year. I can charge £250 for featuring something in a post or testing it in a vlog. We were going to scale up now that I have room in the house for more design ideas. And Dan would have wanted me to do this. He was very supportive.'

'Can I see it? The memorial room?'

'Of course.'

Gina followed Siwan upstairs to a bedroom overlooking the garden. Blinds had been drawn and spotlights on stands had been placed to highlight sections where images of places and materials lay draped on chairs. Framed photographs of Siwan and Dan hung on the walls, each section carefully curated in terms of colour and styled with swatches of material or accessories.

'What is all this?'

'My life with Dan. Where we went, trips we did. What I wore and what I might wear if we did it again.'

Gina could only blink in dismay.

'What do you think?' Siwan asked.

'It's—'

'Morbid? Go on, say it. That's what other people will say. But I'll record this, and it'll be on my channel forever. It's how I'm coping.'

'But are some of these things… have they been sent to you?'

A little light went on in Siwan's eyes. This was solid ground for her. 'Some of the bags and scarves, yes. High-end clothing hire is really big right now. I usually have them for a month to feature them. I'll wear something appropriate for the vlog, so that will be sponsored too.'

'My God.'

'I'm not going to sit in a dark room and weep if that's what you're expecting. I have a living to earn, Gina.'

Gina blinked several times. 'Right, of course.'

Siwan tilted her head and narrowed her eyes, as if seeing Gina for the first time. 'Don't fancy appearing in the vlog, do you? The face of Dyfed Powys Police. You're pretty enough. And you'd be stunning out of uniform all in black. I'd be happy to do your makeup.'

'Uh, no. They'd never agree to that. Unprofessional.'

And the thought of it makes my skin crawl.

'Pity. I'd have paid you.'

'Oh well,' Gina said and left Siwan to it. 'I'd better check in so that everyone knows where I am.'

When she got downstairs, Gina walked out into the postage stamp garden and sucked in some cool November air, hoping it might dispel some of the nausea that had crept over her upstairs.

Something DCI Warlow had once said to her made her pause. *People are full of surprises, and surprises come in two types. There're the flowers left in the porch type, and there's the opening of the toilet seat to a no flush type. The only way to avoid the latter is to always try to go before you leave home. But then the sods will trap you by offering you a cup of tea, and you end up in the toilet anyway.*

Its bleakness had made her smile when she'd heard it. She wasn't smiling now.

'It takes all sorts, Mr Warlow. Never a truer word,' Gina murmured to the damp autumnal sky.

CHAPTER TWENTY-NINE

HAVERFORDWEST HIGH STREET had the dubious reputation of having been named as one of the ten worst in Britain in a study conducted by some retail consultants. Warlow had worked out of the Merlin's Hill Police Station here more than once and had always found the town and its people agreeable enough. But then, he wasn't looking to expand a retail outlet any time soon. Regenerative moves were afoot, stimulated by the local council, but for now, on this gloomy November afternoon, he had to admit that the town looked desolate.

They'd taken separate cars and parked at the Police Station. Hopper jumped into the Jeep and Warlow followed the sergeant's directions for the last half mile to park on a side street off Trafalgar Road.

'Have you been here before?' Warlow asked.

Hopper grinned a denial. 'The Menzies would not be on my list of casual acquaintances, sir.'

'I'm not suggesting you've been out to supper with them. I meant, have you had recourse to visit this property in pursuit of an investigation?'

'Not that either. I got the address from one of my lot.'

Warlow opened his door and stepped out. 'Right, well, come on. Sooner we do this, the better.'

The house was a semi-detached, pebble-dashed box. It had a name. One that had faded so badly on the wall next to the front door that it was now impossible to read in its entirety. But the number 27 was enough for Hopper to confirm they were in the right place.

When Warlow depressed the latch on the front gate leading to a three-yard-long path through an unkempt patch of garden with empty takeaway boxes spilling out of the wheelie bins, a curtain twitched in one of the first-floor bedrooms.

'At least someone's in,' Hopper noted, and then glanced at the red Hyundai Hatchback parked opposite. 'Nice wheels. I'd put money on that being Luke Menzies'.'

Warlow walked to a front door that had once been white, but now looked more a flaky, psoriatic-grey. The bell next to it had fallen away from its fixings and so Warlow knocked. Firmly. Three times.

They heard a dog bark. A yappy noise. Not a deep throated Cadi warning. Warlow waited.

From inside, noises of an exchange,

'Who is it?'

'How do I know?'

'Well, answer the fucking thing, then.'

Ten seconds later, the door opened to reveal a man in his twenties dressed in a new-looking black and red logo'd tracksuit, staring out through a curtain of lank hair with an expression only slightly less welcoming than that of a mother bear with piles.

'Wha'?'

'Mr Menzies,' Warlow held up his warrant card, 'my name is Detective Chief Inspector Warlow, and this is Detective Sergeant Hopper.'

'So?'

'We're investigating the murder of a man we think you, or other members of your family, might know.'

'We don't know anyone who's been murdered.'

'We haven't told you his name yet,' Hopper said.

'Who is it, Luke?' A man's voice from inside.

'It's the filth selling raffle tickets.' Luke grinned at his own joke.

'The filth?' the older voice called out. 'What the fuck do they want?'

The door opened wider and a man, late forties in a white T-shirt and a full sleeve of tattoos on one arm extending up over his neck, pulled Luke back to stand in his place.

'They say they're investigating a murder, Dad.'

'Murder? The fuck has that got to do with us?'

'We think the victim is known to you,' Warlow said. He quickly realised that this conversation would never take place inside the house. Allowing a member of the constabulary to cross the threshold here would be tantamount to inviting a vampire inside.

'I told him we don't know anyone murdered, Dad.'

Paul Menzies, the father, had an arrest sheet as long as his tattooed arm, though he'd been out of prison for at least three years. A long stretch for him. But now, Paul rounded on his son, 'Shut up, Luke, you bellend.'

Luke's smirk faded at this rebuke.

'Who is it?' Paul's feigned ignorance came wrapped in a sneer.

'Lee Barret,' Hopper said.

It had no effect. Menzies turned down his mouth. Barret's name was all over the news, but they were pretending this was the first they'd heard of it. Luke's exaggerated shrug, however, was a sure sign that at least one of the Menzies had made his acquaintance.

'What's that got to do with us?' Paul spat.

'Sergeant Hopper here is a drug squad officer, for want of a better term.'

Menzies tattooed arm was ropey with muscle and veins snaking along his sinewy forearms. Whether or not his eye-popping belligerence had come from something he'd injected into those veins, or from something he'd snorted up his hairy nose, was anyone's guess. Perhaps warm and welcoming was his default disposition, and they'd simply caught him on a bad day. 'I don't give a flying fuck if he's the king's arse-wiper. It doesn't give you the right to come to my house and accuse me and mine of murder.' He took a threatening step closer to the officers.

Warlow didn't move. 'You're dead right there, but since I haven't accused you of anything, and all of this conversation is being filmed by body cam, we both know your statement will not stand up to scrutiny.'

Menzies moved back a couple of inches.

Warlow continued, 'But if our interpretation of the situation is correct, Barret's death might explain your mood.'

'Mood?' Menzies said.

'Yes. You don't strike me as a man at peace with himself. In fact, you strike me as a man who finds his business a little light in stock this week.'

Menzies didn't reply. But his silence told Warlow his dart had hit a bullseye. Behind Paul, another younger member of the Menzies clan made his presence known.

'What's this, Dad?'

His father did not turn around. Warlow suspected he was too busy trying to work out just how much the DCI and Hopper knew.

The boy persisted. 'Who are you talking to—'

'Shut up, Zac,' Luke snapped. 'Let Dad handle this.'

Zac.

The name buzzed around Warlow's head until it

popped into a memory slot. He'd be about the right age for Molly's persistent Pembrokeshire College horsefly. The one she'd supposedly swatted away.

But now that he had everyone's attention, Warlow ploughed on. 'Let's say, for argument's sake, that you were in a business arrangement with Mr Barret. His death might have holed your boat there, Mr Menzies. But I have much worse news. The incident that led to Mr Barret's death also involved a fellow police officer who was shot. That officer died of his wounds this afternoon.'

'Fuck,' Luke whispered.

Paul bristled. 'Nothin' to do with—'

'And that,' Warlow said loudly, 'means a shit storm of enormous proportions is about to descend upon anyone and everyone involved in this case. I'm here to give you an opportunity to cooperate with us now before the solicitors and higher-ups get their teeth into you.'

'What do you mean, cooperate? You expect me to confess to this?'

'If you, or anyone else in this house, are aware of anyone involved, now is the time to tell me.'

Menzies half laughed, but there was no mirth in the noise. He turned to look at his two sons before swinging back. 'My son Zac here, he's in college. He's doing business studies. He talks to me about business models. So, let's explore the business model you're talking about. Let's say, for argument's sake, that we were in bed with Mr Barret. That he was supplying us with a product. It would be cata-fuckingstrophically stupid of us to do away with him because it would only annoy the people supplying the product who might depend on us to distribute it to the punters.'

Warlow nodded. 'But if there were rivals in this business model, do you think they might want to disrupt the supply chain?'

Paul grinned. 'Not if they enjoyed having their testicles attached to their bodies. And that isn't any way to do business, by the way. But it has been known to be used as an effective deterrent by the import/export business owners who might be running an operation like this.'

Warlow's turn to nod. He didn't like drug dealers. In fact, he disliked them with a vengeance. But what Menzies had said made sense. Barret's death, tied in with the discovery of the washed-up drugs on a beach, was going to annoy a great many people. He could see in Menzies face that his arrival on the doorstep with Hopper in tow might not be the last time he'd open the door to someone very interested in the events surrounding Lee Barret's death. And those people would not be holding warrant cards.

Warlow leaned to the left to address Zac. 'Pembrokeshire College?'

'Yeah,' Zac said.

'We have a mutual acquaintance. Molly Allanby.'

Zac's eyelids dropped to half-mast and his arrogant mouth shaped itself into a lascivious oval. 'Oh yeah, her mum's a cop, right?'

'She is a colleague of mine, yes,' Warlow said.

'She's fit, is Allanby. Bit stuck up, but I'm working on that. I'm pretty sure she'll come round. Got to get that old farmer boyfriend of hers out of her system, though, right?'

'She seems pretty stuck on him,' Warlow said. 'You'd be better off aiming a little lower. Someone of your own… calibre.'

Zac's supercilious smirk froze. 'Nah, I've got moves, me. We'll see how she feels when she comes back from London, eh? Maybe she'll have had enough of old farmer boy by then. Be fucking ace to have a cop's daughter as a scalp.' He stuffed his index finger into his mouth and took it out wet with saliva while he cupped his genitals with his other hand and smirked afresh.

A half a dozen people had emerged from their houses nearby to watch the exchange. Warlow saw no point in aggravating the situation. But Hopper turned and looked to be on the point of addressing the onlookers when Paul Menzies' voice boomed out.

'The fuck you lot looking at?'

Quickly, the onlookers decided they had better things to do.

At the gate, Warlow turned back. 'You should stand as a councillor, Paul. You obviously have a way with people.'

'Piss off, copper,' Menzies said.

Warlow nodded. 'More than happy to oblige.'

As they walked away, Hopper, with not a little relief, muttered, 'Nice touch with the body cam, sir.'

'I presume you had yours switched on?'

'I don't wear a body ca—' He stopped and cringed. 'Nice one, sir.'

'You have a lot to learn, Sergeant. A lot to learn.'

CHAPTER THIRTY

PC LEANNE ABBOT shared a house in Whitland with two other people. One a male teacher, the other a female secretary at Glangwili Hospital. She was alone when Warlow called; her left arm in a sling, dark rings under her red-rimmed eyes. It was clear she'd been crying as they sat in the lounge on a cheap sofa. She explained to Warlow how she'd taken the call from the ACC an hour ago to hear of Dan Clark's death. But she wasn't crying now. What Warlow read in her face was a grim anger. The same expression he'd seen in the faces of most of the officers he'd bumped into since they'd received the news.

Hopper had gone directly to visit Siwan Clark and Warlow knew that was another personal call he needed to make. Another face-to-face expression of inadequate sympathy. But since he was driving through Whitland, it made sense to stop here. Leanne had made them tea in two mugs. Warlow's had words on the side. Foxtrot, Foxtrot, Sierra.

FFS.

An acronym that did not mean Free For Shipping. Much as the internet generation might be forgiven for believing it might. On a police officer's mug, coyly hidden in the phonetic alphabet, it summed up a sentiment that got most of them through the working day. An expression of annoyance at the job, the paperwork, the people who did sometimes stupid, sometimes silly – but all too often terrible – things that meant they, the police, had to clear up the mess. Warlow sometimes wondered if it had a place – in small writing, of course – on the Force Badge, under the three feathers.

Foxtrot. Foxtrot. Sierra. FFS. For Fuck's Sake.

'How are you holding up, Leanne?' Warlow asked.

'Arm's fine, sir. It's a flesh wound. The bullet nicked the deltoid. No bones involved.'

'But painful.'

Leanne remained impassive.

'How long had you and Dan worked together?'

'Six months, sir, on and off. He was mentoring me. We'd done a three nights stint.'

'Do you have a partner?'

'Yeah. Chris.'

'In the job?'

Leanne shook her head. 'No, sir. Plumber.'

'Now there's a man with his head screwed on.'

'Torque wrenched on, sir.'

Warlow raised an eyebrow.

'Plumber joke, sir,' Leanne said with the tiniest of apologetic smiles. 'One of Dan's.'

Warlow nodded. The situation was an awful one. You took your relief where you could find it. In the memory of your partner's silly jokes, even. He hadn't met Leanne Abbot until he'd walked through the door, but already he felt an affinity. Her smile stayed thin and pitiable.

'Can I ask how it's going, sir? The investigation?'

'Slow, if I'm honest. We have someone we would like to find.' He hesitated, but then realised that if anyone outside the team deserved to be on the need-to-know list, this woman did. 'Michael Dunbar. Ring any bells?'

'No, sir.'

'Ran a jet-ski hire place with Barret. But the business is a front for drug running and money laundering.'

'Drugs,' Leanne said. She choked back a strangled sob and sent her eyes towards the ceiling, searching for answers that were never going to be there. 'It's all so bloody senseless.'

Warlow nodded in agreement. 'It must feel that way. Nothing justifies what's happened.' But drugs and the man-made poison that they were somehow made it a hundred times worse.

Leanne wiped her eyes and muttered a 'sorry.'

Warlow waved a finger. 'No apologies, Leanne. Not to me. I've been where you are now. I suppose if you stay in the job long enough, it's inevitable. But it doesn't get any bloody easier.'

Leanne nodded. 'I've taken half a dozen calls since the ACC rang. From mates in the job, commiserating.' And then another tiny smile appeared. 'No one seems to know what to say other than that they're sorry. Except you, sir.'

'Oh, I am sorry. But I'm a damn sight more angry than I am sorry.'

Leanne blinked. 'So am I. But it's the guilt I'm having trouble with. I'm here and Dan isn't.'

Warlow held her gaze and didn't let it go. 'Bury that, Leanne. Get a shovel and dig deep, throw the thing in, and cover it up. Six inches to the left and the bullet that nicked your shoulder would have gone through your chest. There's no room for guilt here. Save that for the courtroom when we hear it from the jury and get this bastard in a cell.'

The young PC, who'd looked pale and defeated when

Warlow had walked in, now had a spot of colour high on her cheeks. She sat up a little.

Warlow took it as a sign. 'You happy to answer some questions, constable?'

'I am, sir,' Leanne said.

'I've read the statement you gave DI Allanby.'

Leanne nodded. 'She was lovely. No flannel. A bit like you, sir.'

'After you got the call from dispatch, you drove directly to Telpyn Beach?'

'We did, sir. I drove. Dan had been texting Siwan even though it was early.' She smiled. 'He was always texting Siwan. They'd had a tiff, and she'd got up early and wanted to make him breakfast.'

'A tiff?'

'His word, sir. Siwan had big plans. Dan was worried they were overreaching themselves, what with the new house and all. Siwan was always wanting to go away to take photoshoots of herself in different places. He'd roll his eyes, but always give in.'

'This influencer thing she does?'

'Exactly, sir. Sounds glam, but Dan felt they needed to slow it down now that they had the house. Plus, he loved the job. None of that was any of my business, of course. Unless he was whining about it in the car.' She smiled. 'He didn't do that often, but when you're on the job together, sometimes you just offload.'

Warlow understood. You told your work partners things no one else would ever hear.

'Anyway, he said Siwan wanted to make it up to him. So, he wanted me to drive while he got all lovey-dovey by text with his wife.'

'And this was at seven in the morning?'

'Yes. We got to the beach, and we parked up. The caller had said that Barret, though we didn't know his name then, often parked over a cattle grid. So, I pulled in there to block any exit. Actually, that was Dan's idea. We saw Barret and his dog in the field next to his car. We saw no one else. Both of us got out. Barret was friendly enough. In fact, he was genuinely surprised. He said his dog had bothered no one, but when we said someone had reported him, he got angry. Obviously had a temper.' She swallowed. 'That was when the shooter appeared.'

'From behind you?'

'He, or she, must have been there already because we heard no other vehicle. There was plenty of cover. I saw Barret reacting, saw him look at something, and then I heard the shots. I'd half turned and ducked. Dan wasn't so lucky. Five shots in rapid succession. Two lots of twos and then the one that hit me. I felt the pain in my arm, and it knocked me back. Barret was down. So was Dan. I was on the ground, but I saw someone run away. And this is the bit I don't think I told DI Allanby. The view through the hedge was patchy but some leaves had fallen. The shooter ran over the road and through the gate that led to the beach path.'

Warlow made a mental note but said nothing.

'And you think it could be Dunbar?' Leanne continued.

'We've analysed his phone records. He was definitely in the vicinity. We suspect he might be in hiding.'

'Why would Dunbar kill Barret?'

Warlow sat back and exhaled. 'Barret was harvesting drugs off the coast using his jet-ski. You've seen the news of washed-up packages. We are talking about a great deal of money here. There's enough motive in one of those little black plastic packages to explain all of this, as disgusting as that might sound.'

Leanne nodded.

Warlow looked around at the quiet room. 'Why are you here alone, Leanne?'

'My housemates have jobs, sir. I came out of hospital last night, but my dad is coming to pick me up. My partner is self-employed, so I'm going to my parents for a week or so.'

'Good. Best not to be alone if you can help it.'

'What are your chances of catching Dunbar, sir?'

'If he is in the country, we'll find him, don't you worry.'

———

WARLOW GOT BACK to HQ late that afternoon. In stark contrast to earlier, the room buzzed with activity.

He found Gil. 'Is everyone here?'

'You missed DI Allanby by ten minutes. Catrin's shot off to see the magistrates about a warrant for Knowling Mead for the morning.'

Warlow grunted.

He glanced around. Rhys was at his desk, eyes flitting from the screen to his keyboard.

'Hopper not back yet?'

Gil shook his head. 'Any idea where he's gone?'

'Seeing Dan Clark's widow. That's on my list, too.'

'I'll come with you when you go,' Gil said. 'Poor kid.'

The opening chords of Led Zeppelin's "Heartbreaker" struck up from Warlow's pocket. He took out his phone.

'Warlow.'

'Chief Inspector, it's Colm Tiernon.'

Warlow waved to Gil and hurried through to the SIO room and a bit of quiet. 'What can I do for you?'

'It's what I can do for you, I'm afraid. I've had the dubious pleasure of performing a post-mortem examination of your fallen colleague, Daniel Clark, this afternoon.'

Warlow sat. The movement, heavier than he'd planned it to be, caused the chair to scrape across the floor.

'Is all well?' Tiernon asked.

But Warlow was in no mood for games. They'd had no one to spare for this post-mortem and no one had asked questions yet. 'Do you have anything of use for me?'

'Massive head trauma from a gunshot will be the cause of death on the certificate. Clark was otherwise an extremely healthy man.' Tiernon's words, as factual and cold as ever, made Warlow cringe.

'The last half of that statement does not help,' he growled.

'I am not being facetious. I am trying to be concise.'

'The bullet?'

'Identical calibre and, on preliminary examination, markings to the one that was found in the field at the scene. But then, I'm not a ballistics man.'

'You've sent it over to Povey?'

'It is with the courier as we speak.'

Warlow sat, absorbing the information as static crackled over the line.

'I am very sorry for your loss, Evan.'

Warlow squeezed his eyes shut. He realised that this was Tiernon being empathetic. Yet, his words sounded like afterthoughts. An image of the mug he'd drunk from at Leanne Abbot's house popped into his head. FFS. But Warlow crushed his irritation. He had no right to be churlish with Tiernon here. This was him trying to be… human.

'Thank you, Colm. I appreciate it. I'll pass your condolences on to the team.'

'Best of luck. I hope you catch this killer.'

For once, Warlow detected a smidgen of sincerity.

CHAPTER THIRTY-ONE

IT WAS APPROACHING 5PM as Rhys turned over yet another sheet of call data records and groaned.

'*Er mwyn yr Arglwydd*, Rhys. What is it now?' Gil beetled his brows.

Rhys glanced over with an expression the sergeant had last seen on his four-year-old granddaughter when he'd told her she had to eat at least two slices of carrot and some broccoli before any cake was allowed into the kitchen.

'First off, it's boring as. Second off, the numbers are swimming in front of my eyes.'

'Second off doesn't make any sense,' Gil said. 'You've already been "off" with the first. You can't be "off" with a second—'

Rhys ignored him and pressed on with his whine. 'Can't we ask someone to scan them all and input the data into a spreadsheet? We could use a search thingy then.'

'Who do you suggest as an inputter?'

'We could try Difat.'

'Who eh Givah?' Gil had placed the cap of a high-lighter between his teeth and pulled open the pen to mark something in yellow, making his pronunciation of all hard consonants impossible, such that Difat became… 'Givah'.

'Not a who, sarge. It's a website where you can hire people. Difat. Do It For A Tenner. Though these days, with inflation and stuff, you'd be lucky to get anyone to do much for under twelve quid.'

Gil snapped the highlighter back into the cap and took it out of his mouth. 'Shouldn't be called Difat then, should it?'

Rhys considered this and shrugged. 'But I got a photo of me and my mate Taran in Ibiza fixed so that it looked like I was hovering over a swimming pool on Difat. Brilliant it was. Someone from Hyderabad airbrushed the springboard I was standing on out and it looked perfect. And I mean perfect.'

Gil's steady gaze did not flinch from his younger colleague. 'If you so much as sent an empty envelope relevant to this case to anyone, either online or by Pony Express, DCI Warlow would have you airbrushed out permanently.'

Rhys opened his mouth, but Gil stopped him with a held up hand. 'Do not ask me what the Pony Express is. Difat *mynuffern'i*. Now eyes down, highlighter pen at the ready. Pretend you're playing bingo.'

'Never played bingo, sarge,' Rhys muttered.

Gil jutted out an exasperated chin. 'Well, when you do, you'll be streets ahead of the opposition once we've waded through this lot. Patterns, common numbers, that's what we're after.'

Rhys sighed. The god of ennui must have been listening as, at that precise moment, face down on the desk, his phone buzzed. He'd been forced to go to vibration only because Gil had threatened to confiscate the phone if he had to listen to Rhys's cowboy whistle ringtone one more time.

The DC snatched up the handset and glanced at the screen.

'Uh, it's Gina, sarge. I'd better take it. She's with Siwan Clark.'

Gil nodded, but with one sceptical eyebrow raised. He tapped his watch slowly. 'Of course. But no sexting talk.'

Rhys's face crumpled as the phone kept buzzing, 'No such thing as sexting talk, sarge, It's either sexting… or talk.'

'Answer the bloody thing,' Gil blurted out the order.

Rhys got up and stepped out of the Incident Room towards the stairwell of conversation.

———

GINA SAT in her car outside Siwan Clark's property. She'd had a sudden urge to get out of there and go for a walk, but the rain, at that moment, teemed down like something out of a Bollywood monsoon. So, she'd got into her car and phoned Rhys. He didn't pick up immediately. Probably in a meeting. But then he answered.

'Hey. You're not going to tell me someone else has died, are you?'

'No.' She tried to keep it light, but it came out laden with more angst than she'd planned for.

'What's wrong, Geen?'

'Nothing.' Gina sighed. 'Just wanted to hear your voice.'

'Yeah, I get that all the time.'

He was trying to be funny for her, but all she managed in reply was a brief snort.

'Wow, and that's one of my best lines,' Rhys said.

'Which makes it even more pathetic.' She paused. No point taking it out on Rhys. 'Sorry. It's me. Well, it's more me being here, I suppose.'

'Hey, this isn't like you.'

'Siwan, she's… I don't know what she is. I mean, I've seen people poleaxed by grief. Literally unable to move. I've seen others who can't stop fidgeting. Cleaning the house, emptying the fridge. But I've seen no one deal with grief by posting about it online with a veil on. It's… odd.'

'We're all different, Gina,' Rhys said, suddenly sounding like his mother.

'But some of us are more different than others, yeah, yeah. That's also one of your favourite lines and it still doesn't sound right somehow. She's told me to set time limits for visitors. Even the ACC could only stay for fifteen minutes. Otherwise, it drains all her energy, apparently. And to cap it all, Wil Hopper just called in.'

'Yeah, the Wolf said he was calling.'

Rhys's affectionate use of Warlow's nickname did make her smile. And that smile made the muttered, 'Shame the Wolf didn't warn me,' whinier than she meant it to be.

'Why?' Rhys laughed out the word. 'You bothered by Wil? I thought you said all that was ancient history stuff.'

'It is.' She almost added, *for me at least*, but held back. 'I'm thinking of asking the Wolf if I can come off this case. Bad chemistry.'

'Because of Wil Hopper?'

She sighed to suggest a vagueness in her thinking. 'It's just getting to me. Just too flaky for me. Maybe I should talk to DI Allanby. Is she there?'

'Nah. Her and Catrin have gone after Stacey Campbell.'

'Crap,' Gina said.

In the brief silence that followed, she toyed with telling him the real reason. That Hopper had been nice with Siwan. Gentle, caring, said all the right things, telling her that though it didn't feel like it now, all this pain would pass and that one day she'd be laughing again. Siwan had nodded and blinked those big cow eyes of hers when Hopper had squeezed her arm. Gina had been touched.

But as he was leaving, he'd motioned to Gina to follow him outside. She'd gone, expecting some order to be passed on from Warlow about the case.

'She's very vulnerable right now,' Hopper said. 'Put off random callers if you can.'

'Of course. I'm good at that,' Gina said.

He grinned. A big wide thing that reminded her of a cartoon shark. 'Do you ever think about what it might have been like between us? If you'd let it happen, I mean?'

Taken aback, she'd mumbled, 'No, not really.'

Hopper had stepped closer. 'Think about it now. How everything would be different. Like that butterfly stuff. One little change, one insignificant action, and there's a hurricane a thousand miles away. I might not have gone to Liverpool. Wales might have won the World Cup. Dan Clark might not have died, even.'

'What?' The word came out in the middle of a high-pitched laugh of incredulity.

'All I'm saying is that random crap happens all the time. The world is complicated. But in a way it's really simple, too. I mean, here we are. The exact same people, but different from who we might have been.'

'What are you talking about?'

'Alternative futures. For you and me.'

She stared at him in confusion.

'Have you told Rhys about us?' he asked.

'There wasn't any "us", Wil. Not for me. But yes, I have told him.'

Hopper was still smiling. 'Good. Because we wouldn't want him feeling jealous, would we?'

'Jealous? What is wrong with you?'

Hopper dropped his voice but kept his shark smile as

he mocked her. 'What is wrong with you, *Sergeant*, if you don't mind?'

Gina turned to go back into the house with a shake of her head.

'You're the reason I went to Liverpool, Gina. Why I went undercover.'

'I'm not listening to this.' Gina did not stop walking.

Hopper's voice had followed her. 'Water under the bridge, right? We both have other fish to fry now, right? Just be careful of all that hot oil.'

Gina hurried into the house and shut the door. Hopper was still there, standing in the road, his shape blurred through the frosted glass panel. Her heart pounded in her ears as she'd stood leaning with her back against the door.

'Gina, you still there?' Rhys's voice broke into her reverie.

'Of course, I'm still here.'

'You could try DI Allanby's mobile.'

'No. I'll wait and catch her later.'

'You sure you're okay?'

'I'm fine. Always am after talking to you.'

'I know, I get that all the time, too.'

This time, the snort she let out was longer and ended up in an indulgent little chortle.

CHAPTER THIRTY-TWO

AT 8.30 AM WEDNESDAY MORNING, Stacey Campbell sat in the bedroom she shared with Dion at Alex's house in Knowling Mead, her phone in her hand. She'd checked it at least a dozen times in the last fifteen minutes. All her attempts at phoning Mike had gone to answerphone, and he had not replied to any of her texts.

On the one hand, she was so glad she'd lied to the police about having her phone stolen. On the other, she knew it was likely to come back and bite her. Her heart raced every time she thought about that. The only trouble she'd ever had with the police was a drink-drive charge when she was eighteen. She'd taken her friend Sharon Sadler home from a party at two in the morning because the idiot had done half a dozen espresso martinis and then gone overboard with sambuca shots. She'd been punished for that good deed and lost her licence for six months.

'Come on, Mike,' she said, her breath churning out of her throat after the words. 'Where are you?'

But there was no answer. She scrolled to her texts and the exchange she'd had with him the previous day.

Hey, Stace.

Mike, where are you?

I can't say.

Let me ring you. Please.

NO. No way. Too risky.

Why Risky? You are scaring me.

I'm scared, too. Shit scared.

What is going on?

I been stupid. I took some stuff. I thought
they wouldn't notice.

Lee did. He was going to tell them so.

I had to stop him.

What you mean stop him?

Lee. I stopped Lee. Shot him.

Shit, Mike! This is doin my head in. What
about Dion?

I was doing all of this for you and Dion.
What about the cop? Is he okay.

She hadn't answered. She couldn't tell him the truth.

Bad. You've got to give yourself up, Mike.

Shit, what a mess. The people I work with.
They don't take any prisoners. If they find
me, I'm screwed, babe.

> Let me ring you, please.

No, they listen. I've seen it on TV.

> Where are you?

I'm going to try and sort something. For you and Dion. Put some cash where they can't find it. Then I will. I will talk to the Cops. I promise. Keep your phone with you.

> Where are you, Mike? Where are you?

She'd pressed the phone icon, desperate to continue the conversation. But it rang and segued into the automatic message.

… the person you are trying to contact is not available…

Stacey sat on the bed and let the tears come. Let the sobs come. They were still coming when she heard someone pound on the door and a loud voice yell:

'Police. Open the door.'

She opened the door at the third knock. Catrin stood on the threshold, holding an A4 sheet up at eye level. At the very top, and underlined, were the words {OCCU-PIERS'S} COPY.

'What's that?' Stacey asked.

'It is a warrant to enter and search premises,' Catrin said.

'I don't live here,' Stacey said.

'The warrant is for the property and, by extension, you,' Jess, standing next to Catrin, explained.

Behind the two detectives, uniformed officers, one holding the big red key – the battering ram used to break locks – stood on the path, waiting to force their way in if necessary.

Stacey looked confused. 'But all my stuff is in Pondecherry Road. You know that.'

'Really?' Jess held up her phone with the image Hopper had snapped of Stacey in her car in the car park of police HQ in Llangunnor, holding a phone to her ear.

Stacey's eyes flicked from the image to the faces of the two detectives.

'Okay, just so you know, this can go one of two ways,' Jess explained. 'We don't think your phone was stolen. We think you still have it—'

'I could have borrowed Alex's phone,' Stacey exclaimed.

'Yes, you could have,' Catrin said. 'Except we've contacted Alex. By phone. Which is a Samsung and is not encased in that neon-pink covering that you like so much.'

'So,' Jess continued. 'Either hand over the phone and your laptop, iPad, et cetera, or we'll search the premises and confiscate anything we think is relevant. All computers, all laptops, kids' electronic toys... whatever. Your choice, Stacey.'

'I want my solicitor.' Stacey's mouth became an ugly pucker.

'By all means,' Catrin answered with a sharp look in her eye. 'Why don't you give him a ring?'

'You should be on the telly,' Stacey said.

Jess sighed. 'None of this is funny, Stacey. Two people are dead. And we do not have to wait for a solicitor to be present to enter.' She turned and waved to a Uniform, who stepped forward.

'Wait,' Stacey said. 'Okay, okay, I'll get it.'

Jess and Catrin followed her in as she headed for the bathroom. The officers stood on the threshold as Stacey lifted the toilet lid, but suddenly she shot her hand out to behind some bubble bath and shampoo bottles on a shelf and brought out the pink phone, dangling it over the toilet bowl between thumb and forefinger, a new look of defiance in her face.

'I could drop it in here. Accidents happen. Tell me why I shouldn't.'

'It would be an idiotic thing to do, for a start,' Catrin said.

Stacey had begun to shake. 'I'm not stupid. Mike is in trouble, isn't he? Bad trouble.'

'So will you be if you drop that phone, Stacey.' Jess's voice remained calm. 'If you do, we'll arrest you for obstruction on the spot. And this is a murder case. Two people dead, shot in cold blood. One of them is a police officer. What do you think a magistrate, or a jury, is going to think about you deliberately making our life difficult? We're talking prison here. You will lose Dion. Be very sure of that.'

The words fell like blows on Stacey. She staggered back, colliding with the bathroom wall. Catrin stepped forward and took the phone from her hand. 'What's the code, Stacey.'

She looked up, those ridiculously full lips trembling again. 'It's my face.'

'There must be a code, too,' Catrin insisted. 'For when you switch the phone on.'

'Seventeen, eighteen, nineteen,' Stacey mumbled.

Catrin, like Jess, wore nitrile gloves. Touch phones relied on capacitance between a finger and the screen. Contrary to what many people thought, the gloves were thin enough to allow the charge to function, and the phone lit up when she punched in the numbers.

She scrolled to the messenger app, read the recent batch and, stern-faced, held the phone screen up for Jess to see. Both officers exchanged grim looks. Catrin tried ringing Dunbar's number with the speaker on. It rang ten times before going to the messenger service.

'Ring Rhys,' Jess ordered. 'Tell him Dunbar was texting yesterday. Tell him to get on to the phone company and the nerds. Let's see if we can pinpoint this.'

But Catrin had turned back to the phone. She looked up, her eyes alight. 'May not be necessary, ma'am. I want to try something.' She swiped through the screens and grinned. 'You share music with Michael Dunbar?'

Stacey nodded, looking perplexed.

'Have you ever lost your phone, Stacey?'

'Yeah. Not this one, but a couple of others—'

'Yes,' Catrin said in triumph, eyes on the screen. 'Family sharing is switched on.'

'In case the phone is lost,' Jess said with a smile. She knew all about it. Molly was great with tech, but she'd left her phone in changing rooms and buses before now. Jess had insisted that whenever she went out, she'd share location so that if the phone got lost, they'd find it again. If it was stolen, then turning up at a strange address with a detective inspector would ensure it would be returned.

'So, we can find his phone.' Jess nodded.

'We can try, ma'am.'

'Wait, so you know where he is?' Stacey wailed.

But Jess and Catrin had already turned to hurry out of the house and all she heard was the dark-haired inspector talking into her own phone. 'Evan, it's Jess. We may have a location for Dunbar.'

———

It had a name, as all the old Welsh properties did. Usually descriptive, pertaining to the landscape; a geographical feature, or the proximity of water. All vitally important in the days before electricity and reservoirs. On the Ordnance Survey map, the place was called Pantpriddog. The translation split the place name into two, *Pant,* meaning a hollow, *priddog,* meaning earthy.

'An earthy hollow,' Gil had translated when Rhys had pulled it up on an OS map. More research had revealed that it had been empty for forty years and for sale for all of that time. Five acres of land and stone outbuildings. But there'd been no takers.

'I wonder why,' Catrin had said as they'd stood around Rhys's desk studying the area where Dunbar's phone was showing up on Google Maps.

Now they were about to find out.

They'd gone in convoy. Warlow with Jess in the Jeep. Rhys, Catrin, and Gil in the Audi. They had not waited for Hopper, and he was making his way on his own. He'd texted Gil to say he'd caught up with them on the A40 at Nantgaredig and was right behind the response vehicle containing a couple of Uniforms that Warlow had brought along.

They turned off near Llanegwad and headed north to Llanfynydd, villages with names that started with the double 'L's that confused non-Welsh speakers so much. Once, in response to one of KFC's mildly racist remarks, Rhys had come up with a figure. Six hundred or more places in Wales began with the word Llan. Places where a church or a Christian settlement had put down roots a very long time ago. Not simply a plot to tongue-tie visitors, as KFC had suggested. But as the team headed further north, they left houses behind and wound onwards through nothing but sparsely populated, hilly farmland.

'According to Google, there's a pub in Cwmdu,' Jess said, 'which doubles as a shop and post office.'

'Out here they learn to multitask,' Warlow muttered.

'Quick pint as you post your parcels. Could be worse.'

But Warlow wasn't really listening. He was looking for the turnoff to Pantpriddog. But all he could find was a metal gate, loosely tied with sun-bleached baling twine, barring the entrance to what once was a lane and was now nothing but a vague ribbon of lesser growth in the greenery. At the height of summer, this entrance might not even have been visible. He stopped, wound his window down and stuck his head out to talk to Rhys, driving the Audi behind.

'Park up and get the others to come to the Jeep. I've got a 4-wheel drive. Looks like we may need it.'

Jess got in the back with Catrin and Gil joined Warlow in the front. Rhys opened the gate and then leant to talk to Warlow. 'What about Wil Hopper, sir?'

'Tell him to get into the response car with the Uniforms. You too.'

Warlow took it easy. Under the nettles and grass there was a track of sorts. The Jeep bounced and rocked as it negotiated the rutted road. 'Still got a signal on that phone, Catrin?'

'Yes, sir. His phone is still switched on.' She had Stacey Campbell's pink iPhone in her hands, the Find Me app open.

Warlow pushed the Jeep on along the overgrown lane as brambles scraped along the windows and the dipping branch of a young oak stroked the roof.

'Is the Temple of Doom up here somewhere?' Gil asked. 'You'll need a respray after this.'

'Least of my worries,' Warlow said.

The car lurched and tilted as it rounded a corner.

'Dare I say it. This would be on my list of a good place to hide out.' Catrin stared at the dense undergrowth on both sides which eased as they pulled into a tumbledown yard in front of a grey stone ruin with only half its roof intact and no glass in the windows. Off to the side, half hidden under the branches of an ancient oak, sat a silver Land Rover.

'That's Dunbar's,' Catrin said.

Behind them, the response vehicle pulled up and Rhys, Hopper, and the two Uniforms got out. The sun had already set, and the oppressive overcast afternoon was leeching colour from their surroundings as a gloomy reminder of how quickly night was approaching.

'I've been to nicer hotels,' Gil quipped.

Hopper appeared next to the driver's side window. Warlow wound it down. 'Uniforms will do the outbuildings, sir. Rhys and I will do the house.' He glanced at the two female officers in the back and then at Gil. 'No point us all going in. I'd stay in the warm if I were you.'

'No,' Warlow grunted. 'If he's here, we don't know what his state of mind will be.'

He exited, and Gil opened the passenger-side door at the same time.

'Where are you going?' Warlow asked.

'I'll be at the back, watching yours.' Gil grinned and pulled his anorak on. 'Let's not pretend he won't have heard us coming. I doubt he's put the kettle on.'

Everything looked sepia to Warlow, and he took off his glasses, varifocals he always wore for driving, to polish them quickly. It didn't help. Hopper and Rhys took the lead, both, like the DCI, wearing stab vests. Both holding torches. They stepped over the threshold of the empty doorway into a dark room with an earthen floor and rotting joists for a ceiling. The room had a pungent, stale odour. A heady combination of fungus and sheep faeces. But it wasn't the sheep who'd brought along four car batteries linked up to a lamp and a small heater stacked against a far wall.

'Police,' Hopper shouted. 'Michael Dunbar, we know you are here. Make yourself known.'

No answer came back to them. In the silence that

followed, all they heard was the rustling of the dying leaves on the trees.

Rhys and Hopper's torch beams picked out empty food packets, water bottles, and a rolled-up sleeping bag.

'Not my idea of five-star accommodation,' Gil muttered, peering over Warlow's shoulder.

'He must have been desperate to come here,' Warlow agreed.

'There's another doorway, sir.' Rhys stepped forward, careful to avoid the debris, and moved left into a smaller room.

'Looks like an old kitchen with a stove and a bathtu—oh shit.'

Warlow hurried after Hopper to join Rhys, who stood just inside the tiny kitchen with an open stone fireplace and a chimney breast. In front of that, most of the floor space was taken up by a metal bathtub. Curled up in that bathtub was a body. Male, naked, legs bent to fit the tub, arms tied with tape behind him. The victim's right forearm was tattooed in a pattern that was difficult to make out. The fingernails were broken and bloody. A testament to the scrabbling desperation that had accompanied this death. Warlow thought he glimpsed an inked serpent's tail where the arm lay free of the dirty water. Over the corpse's head was a cinched-tight plastic bag. Everyone there was glad it was opaque because it meant they didn't have to look at the face.

'Looks like we found Dunbar, sir,' Hopper said.

Warlow, his heart galloping, dismayed and disgusted by the squalid nature of this place and another murdered victim, could only grunt before breathing out the words, 'Someone better ring Povey.'

CHAPTER THIRTY-THREE

The day sped by. The team focused their activities on the scene and the surroundings. Late that afternoon a little after 5, they convened in a pub in Pontargothi on the way back, just half a dozen miles from Carmarthen. An easy turn off the A40. The Sal was a traditional pub and one of the few that survived the ravages of Covid. Warlow remembered it from years ago when you ate what fish was caught that day in the estuary, served up in huge portions by a larger-than-life landlord. These days, things were a little more refined; there were even nocellara olives as nibbles.

'Posh,' as Gil said when he'd glanced at the menu. One of his favourite pastimes when in a pub.

Warlow paid for a round, and they took their drinks to a snug. Only Gil ordered a full pint. Warlow stuck to a half, as did Jess. Catrin and Rhys opted for Coke, though Rhys, unlike the sergeant, went full fat. Hopper opted for a bottle of IPA.

'So, have we checked if Dunbar was tattooed?' Warlow asked.

Catrin cupped a hand around her glass as she

answered. Ice clinked as she played it back and forth. 'Rhys contacted one of his employees. Dunbar has a dragon wound around his forearm, sir. We thought it best not to ask Stacey Campbell yet.'

Warlow nodded and sipped at his half of lager. He liked sours when they were available. But for now, this was cold and smooth and ran down his parched throat like a silky balm.

They settled into a silence for a while, each with their thoughts, but Warlow didn't need to be a mind reader to understand that every one of them had that filthy, decrepit house between Llanfynydd and Cwmdu imprinted on their brains. But it was Gil who captured the moment.

'*Ych a fi.* A horrible way to go.'

Rhys, who'd been eyeing the selection of crisps in a little basket on the counter, turned back. 'They say suffocation is as bad as drowning. The victims fight for air.'

'It looked like an execution.' Catrin kept her gaze firmly on the drink she was yet to touch.

'It's a message,' Hopper said. 'Organised crime gangs use guns for efficiency when they need to eliminate people quickly. But if they want to send a message, they'll use suffocation. Often with mutilation.'

'*Moch,*' Gil muttered.

Catrin threw Jess a questioning glance, but the DI shook her head. 'I know what that means. And Gil's right. The people who did this are pigs.'

'So, that's our conclusion, then?' Warlow flicked his gaze around the team. 'That this has the mark of a gang-killing upon it?'

Hopper laid it out. 'They break into his place. Threaten his partner. We know he's stolen something from them, either money or product. That's in Campbell's phone texts. They'd have been looking for him, sir.'

'But how the hell did they find him out there?' Gil asked.

'Could it be that it was a place they'd used before?' Rhys asked.

Hopper nodded. 'Good point, Rhys. You're not a pretty face, are you?'

'You mean not just a pretty face,' Rhys corrected him.

'I know exactly what I mean,' Hopper said with a grin. 'But you're spot on. That farmhouse is exactly the sort of spot used for dropping off. Not overlooked. No passing traffic. What they'd do is park somewhere where there are other vehicles and then use a push-bike, or perhaps walk in and walk out. All kitted out like ramblers. One to drop off, and someone else to collect.'

'You mean drop off drugs?'

'Drugs, money, or both.'

Catrin took a sip of her Coke at last. 'At least we have him confessing to Barret's murder,' she said. They had that on Stacey Campbell's phone, but the Uniforms had also found Dunbar's phone in the undergrowth. Catrin rang his number and though it hadn't put out a ringtone, it buzzed enough for them to find it after a quick search. They'd concluded that perhaps, in a last act of defiance, Dunbar had thrown the phone before whoever killed him could get a hold of it. Otherwise, if the killers had taken his phone, Warlow thought it unlikely they'd have found the body for a very long time.

'There'll be no trial, then,' Rhys said.

He was right. Dunbar's death and his texts left many questions unanswered for Daniel Clark's parents and his widow. Knowing who did it was a start, but the senseless nature of such a crime would haunt them. Finding all this out was an empty resolution devoid of any real closure.

'If we accept Dunbar killed Barret and Daniel Clark, that still leaves us with finding Dunbar's killer.' Warlow

LINES OF INQUIRY   239

kept Hopper in his eyeline. 'I feel that ball is bouncing close to your court, Wil.'

'I'll put feelers out, sir. I'll speak to my CHIS again.'

'Meanwhile, we'll canvass the area,' Jess said. 'Call in on the farms. Check for deliveries. See if anyone saw any strange vehicles in the last twenty-four hours.'

A thankless task. They'd seen no traffic in the last two miles leading to the turnoff for Pantpriddog. But they were all aware of what needed to be done.

'Even though we've found Dan Clark's killer, it doesn't feel like a celebration, sir.' Catrin put down her glass.

'You'd need to be a hard-hearted bugger if it did, Catrin. No winners here. Not today.' Warlow downed his half. 'But you're right. Sorry to break up the party, but I have no stomach for this.'

They all nodded.

'I suggest we call it for today. Povey will get that plastic bag off and we can confirm Dunbar's ID. But now, let's get home and come back tomorrow to fight another day.'

'What about Stacey Campbell, sir?' Catrin asked.

Jess stood up. 'I'll call in on my way home. There are still Uniforms there if I'm right.'

'Why don't you let them do it, ma'am?' Hopper asked.

A fair enough question. They were all tired, but Warlow noted it was Hopper who suggested it, not one of his team.

'She's been stupid, but she deserves a bit of compassion,' Jess said.

'We do things properly on this team, Wil,' Warlow added.

Hopper raised a hand in acceptance. 'Fair enough, sir.'

POLICE CONSTABLE GINA MELLINGS took the call from Warlow. It was an opportunity to discuss her situation regarding Siwan Clark – she wouldn't mention Hopper – but the nature of the DCI's call and the task she was given made complaining sound way too churlish. She put all of that on the back burner as she stood in Daniel and Siwan Clark's shiny kitchen. Siwan was upstairs in the room that doubled as her studio. Gina considered texting her, asking her to come down, but that was pathetic. The widow had gone upstairs to do some "editing" and told Gina to help herself to tea, or coffee, or anything else she wanted. As if Gina had been some kind of errant houseguest. But then, that was why she was here. To provide support and to liaise. It was what FLO stood for.

And now Warlow had asked Gina to break the news that they'd found Dan's killer. Not a pleasant job, but one that the Wolf clearly thought Gina could handle. She should have been flattered by that.

So, why the procrastination?

Shaking her head at not having any answers, Gina left the kitchen and took the open tread stairs to the "studio" in the bedroom. She knocked softly and waited. Siwan opened the door, headphones displaced to around her neck.

'Sorry to disturb, Siwan, but there's been a development in the case and DCI Warlow wanted you to know.'

Behind Siwan, Gina clocked a desk with two monitors, one with a frozen image of the woman in front of her, full face, talking to camera. On the screen, she wore a dark Hanfu veil.

'Oh, okay.' Siwan made no move to leave her doorway.

Gina launched into it. 'They've found Dunbar. He confessed to shooting Dan.'

'Oh.' Just that. Flat as a pancake. 'Has he been arrested?'

Gina's brows knitted. 'No. He's dead.'

Siwan blinked rapidly. 'Shot, too?'

'No.' Gina toyed with saying more but held back. Warlow had filled her in, but those details were not important here.

Siwan seemed lost for words, confused, and struggling to assimilate what had been said.

'Come down to the kitchen. I could make us a cup of tea,' Gina suggested.

But Siwan did not move.

Gina's eyes strayed to the screens.

'I'm editing,' Siwan said, noting Gina's drifting gaze. 'Do you want to see?'

She stepped back from the doorway. Gina hesitated, but then took a step into the room. She reminded herself that this was how Siwan was coping with it all. She ought not to judge.

Siwan went to the keyboard, clicked a few keys, and the screen changed to a frame containing a video clip with all kinds of icons and a timer running across the bottom. But the second screen, which had been blank, flickered into life. On it was a What Cando page. Gina had seen the like before. She'd even contributed to some causes over the years. Floods in Asia, that awful thing where half a mountain had fallen on a village in Tibet. But this time, the fund had a photograph of Daniel Clark in uniform.

'That appeared yesterday. I have no idea who started it, but I got an email from the site. The money raised will come to me, apparently.'

'It's already up to eight and a half thousand?' Gina asked.

Siwan nodded. 'People are kind. But it's important I get my truth known, too. That's why I need to do the blog.' She turned her big eyes to Gina. 'You understand that, don't you?'

What Gina understood was that most YouTube blog-gers had very large egos and narcissistic streaks. At least that was how the cliché crumbled.

'I'm aware of what people think,' Siwan said. 'But I didn't ask for this. What happened to Dan, I mean. But I will not let it ruin our plans. There is so much rubbish out there.'

'On social media, you mean?'

Gina nodded with a little pout. 'I want to change that. I want to give people something meaningful.'

'What about companies using you to showcase their things?'

'It's a business, too, of course it is. But I want what I do to be a force for good. For change. I want Dan's death to mean something. Not the drugs thing. I don't know anything about that. What I want is to give people like me a voice.'

'Like you?' Gina asked. A perfectly innocent question but asked with a dollop of trepidation.

'I want to show my followers they can get what they want. Before we agreed to disagree on my lifestyle, my mother would tell me I could do and be whatever I wanted. That is so not true. I want to show people of my age that you can get to a point in life where you can do things. Be someone. And get there before you're too old to get off the couch.'

By wearing a veil dressed in a high-end coat and handbag?

Gina didn't respond. She'd heard this kind of thing delivered by a little bluebird in two-hundred-and-eighty characters all too often. All part of the great tapestry of 21st Century life. Before she'd closed her account, Twitter was full of the: I want it all and I want it now, crowd. And though not quite the same, as a police officer, she'd been on cordons facing off with groups who saw disruption to the normal fabric of society as the only way to invoke social justice, whatever the hell that was supposed to mean. She'd even had to drag protestors off roads. Of course, she'd been intrigued by it all, but hadn't bought into the package. Gina, like most other people her age, had suffered because of a lousy economy and a pandemic. Things were tough, what with the cost of every sodding thing. She hardly knew anyone her age who had not had their adult-hood and the independence that came with it slowed down or paralysed as a consequence. And added to that, she, and all her girlfriends with no children, had ovaries that kept on ticking like some awful Countdown challenge.

But entitlement was not the same as getting rewarded for hard work and graft. It wasn't a difficult equation. You should be able to reap what you sowed. Yet, some people seemed to want to use different maths to get the same answer. Gina, though, preferred the real world to the hand-wringing that came with waking up every morning wondering if her job was impactful enough.

She knew it was.

'And how do you get to that point?' Gina asked. 'Where you can get what you want?'

Siwan's smile was the kind that you gave to a foolish child who had asked a silly question. 'Aspiration has to be paid for. Otherwise, what is the point?'

So, nothing to do with ethics or morals or feelings. She bit her tongue. She wanted to ask why Siwan didn't do something else, something more… tangible. This business, the constant need to be relevant on social media, seemed so fickle and paper thin. But no matter how you painted it, or dressed it up in pretty clothes and drapery, it all boiled down to filthy lucre. And as everyone was aware, people would do some strange and incredible things in pursuit of that golden calf.

Yet, Siwan was now a widow and Gina was prepared to almost forgive her, though it came with all kinds of uncomfortable caveats. She was now a young woman alone in the world. You did what you had to do to survive. Even if that meant wearing a Hanfu veil and showing the world what colour your grief was.

But it still left a nasty smell in Gina's nose as she watched Siwan proudly run, with commentary, her latest vlog.

CHAPTER THIRTY-FOUR

WARLOW HAUNTED the Incident Room for an hour after he got back. After phoning Gina and giving her the responsibility of breaking the news of Dunbar's death to Siwan Clark, he sat gazing at his screen, scanning reports and waiting for Povey. He'd wrestled with the call to Gina. Under normal circumstances, he shied away from asking junior officers to do that kind of heavy lifting. But FLOs established links with the relatives. And Gina was a more than capable officer in Warlow's estimation.

Gil had offered Warlow a bed at his Llandeilo home, which would have meant half the commute time between HQ and Warlow's cottage overlooking the Pembrokeshire coast, but he'd politely declined. The need for his own bed this evening burned strongly within him.

Povey eventually rang just before seven.

'Definitely Dunbar,' she said as soon as he'd offered his hello.

'What else can you tell me?'

'Tiernon's been and gone. He'll do the post-mortem tomorrow.'

'Time of death?'

'Complicated by the body lying in cold water, but a rough estimate would be within the last eight to twelve hours.'

'He was texting his partner this morning after she'd left us and lied about having her phone stolen.'

'Well, that would be a more accurate timeline than we could provide. I'd say it's consistent, and that he died between then and you finding his body.'

The thoughts that ran around Warlow's head were a morbid brew cooked up via tiredness and frustration. If Stacey Campbell had cooperated earlier, they might have got to Dunbar before his killer did. As it was, Campbell might face a charge of perverting the course of justice. Yet, from what he'd assessed of her reaction to questioning, he sensed she had little knowledge of Dunbar and Barret's activities. The screen they'd used to hide their drug-related activities had been an effective one. Stacey was guilty of nothing but misguided loyalty. And though not punishable by law, she'd already been delivered a hefty sentence in the form of Dunbar's death.

'Are you lot clocking off for the night now? Or should I hang on until you find the next corpse?' Povey asked, with more than a hint of exasperation.

'I'll check the boot of my car when I leave the mother ship, but I think you're probably safe to head home yourself.'

'Ha, ha,' Povey mimicked a laugh. 'That would be funny coming from anyone but you.'

Ten minutes later, Gil put his head around the SIO office door. He wore a bright-blue puffer jacket in readiness for the cool night. Warlow thought of the giant marsh-mallow monster from Ghostbusters. Luckily, Hopper had long gone, or he'd have said as much. But Warlow had rules about commenting on people's appearance. Be it friend or foe. If you dished it out, you ought to be prepared to receive it in equal measure. Best therefore to remain thoughtfully silent.

Though it was a struggle.

'Offer still stands,' Gil said. 'The Lady Anwen would be more than delighted if you dossed down chez Jones.'

Gil's insistence on referring to his wife as the Lady Anwen might have begun life as an ironic tilt at her insistence on calling the house "The Jones residence" whenever anyone phoned. By now though, Warlow used it almost as often, and as affectionately.

'No, I need to get home. I need to see my dog.'

'Tidy. Cadi'll be forgetting what you look like. Any news from Australia?'

Warlow couldn't help the sigh that escaped his lips. 'No. A couple of texts. Of course it's morning there now…'

Gil nodded but didn't leave. 'By the way, Superintendent Goodey sent me a lovely memo.' The absence of her nickname made Warlow frown in wary expectation.

'Oh?'

'She says there's a vacancy in Evidential Retention. A supervisory role in disposal of crap from old cases. Something less demanding I might like to consider.'

Warlow winced. 'Those her actual words, were they?'

'As good as. That's the way I read it anyhow.'

Gil waited a beat, his eyebrows raised in expectation.

Warlow made a noncommittal gesture involving his hands and shoulders. 'I should have read the subtext. She's Wil Hopper's cheerleader, but I didn't think she'd make you an offer. Christ, Buchannan has been away for what, two days at the most and already she's meddling.'

'I get the impression she doesn't think I'm up to the job.' Gil's smile was half-baked.

'She hasn't got that from me, Gil.'

'I know.' Gil nodded and then slapped his ample

stomach under the zipped-up coat. 'Still, she may have a point.'

'Does she?'

The sergeant put down the backpack he always carried to work containing his sandwiches in Tupperware boxes. A bag that was much lighter leaving the building than arriving. 'When I came off Operation Alice, I was toying with jacking it all in. The Buccaneer convinced me you needed help, and that I was the man for the job.'

'He was right for once, then.'

The ghost of a smile reappeared on Gil's lips. 'I said I'd give it six months.'

'Obviously, if you want to go…'

Gil's bushy eyebrows danced. 'This job saved my career, Evan. I've never had much of an ambition for inspector. Too much bloody paperwork.'

'Amen to that.'

'I'll leave that to the youngsters like Catrin. But Two-Shoes has an eye on the future, I can tell. And I suspect she doesn't appreciate my sense of humour.'

'What makes you say that?' Warlow took a verbal step up the garden path.

'She ran a diversity course last year. Mandatory as per. She asked me how it went afterwards, all informal-like. And I said it had been worthwhile, and that I was more comfortable now working with colleagues of differing ethnicity. She nodded in that way she has that makes you feel like a fourth former and I should have shut up then. But I couldn't resist saying that I was already seeing Colin from Bradford and Eurig from North Wales in a totally different light.'

Warlow shut his eyes and winced. 'But can you see yourself sifting through old evidence bags?'

'Regular hours. Good for granddaughter-sitting duties.'

'And what about the hunt?'

Gil huffed out a wry exhalation. Since Warlow began taking Gil on the odd ramble, and they could be very odd rambles where Gil was involved, the sergeant had lost a few pounds. There was still some way to go, but a few pounds were better than none. The hunt was something the two senior officers sometimes talked about on these strolls.

Warlow and Gil still shared that rare, some might say precious, commodity that came with not having been brainwashed by post-modernism. It made life a lot easier if you still believed in the rule of law and that not everyone had the right to be offended by what other people thought. They were old enough and wise enough to understand the difference between a perceived ideological criminality that preoccupied so many people keen to pour vitriol into the world through their touchscreens, and what was simply a bad joke.

Neither man ever mentioned the term "evil" to one another. And yet they knew instinctively what it meant. To try to define it might sound affected, even grandiose. They defaulted to a simpler dichotomy. Right and wrong. And they both retained, with pride, a sense of privilege, which was nothing to do with colour or sex. Because for them, it meant simply that they'd attained a place of competence in the world. A commodity of experience that made them valuable cogs in the machinery that existed solely to try to keep society functioning against an ever-inventive antisocial element. The thieves, the fraudsters, the violent, the manipulators, the killers. The hunt was their opportunity to right some of those wrongs. It drove them, these middle-aged foot soldiers. It still did.

Or so Warlow thought.

'I'm still in the hunt. But maybe there are better hunters. Like Hopper, for example. He's definitely Two-Shoes' flavour of the month.'

'Perhaps. But do nothing rash,' Warlow said.

Gil swung the backpack onto his shoulder. 'Oh, you know me. *Araf deg mae mynd ymhell.* I don't rush anything.'

'Yeah,' Warlow said. 'That I had noticed.'

———

THREE HOURS LATER, Warlow sat in his home with his dog at his side. She had a scruffy teddy bear she carried around with her. Warlow had a theory that it might be a substitute for the pups she would never have. Sometimes he got a hold of it while she was otherwise occupied with a chew or sniffing about in the garden, and put it through the washing machine, but those opportunities were rare. Mostly, she transported it from room to room, a pacifier for her canine brain.

He'd poured himself half a glass of Primitivo, and, with one hand on Cadi's soft head, listened to the radio for the national news. The police presence at Pantpriddog had not gone unnoticed. No doubt the sight of forensic investigation unit vans and blue lights all over a part of the world where the most exciting thing to happen normally would be a few sheep out on the road had piqued the press's interest. And so Warlow listened to "unconfirmed reports" that a "body had been found", and that a "spokesperson for the police would not confirm whether the findings could be linked to the murders of Lee Barret and Daniel Clark".

There'd been no confirmation of Dunbar's identity officially yet. No doubt that dubious honour would rest with the ACC or Two-Shoes, and he suspected that would happen tomorrow now that Stacey Campbell had been informed. For now, the press was serving up their favourite food: conjecture on toast.

Cadi deposited "Arthur", the name Warlow had given

to the bear, in his lap. He threw it across the room for her to retrieve. He'd called it Arthur because it made sense to call an "*arth*", the Welsh word for bear, Arthur. It had a nice alliterative ring to it.

Cadi brought Arthur back for a rinse and repeat.

Warlow obliged.

Satisfied with those two affirmations of her role in the world, the dog took Arthur back to her basket and lay down.

The mobile rang from where it had been left on the table.

'Dad, it's Tom.'

Warlow's insides twisted as a spurt of adrenaline swished through his vitals. 'Hey, Tom. Any news?'

'Yeah, I dropped Al a text earlier. He's just got back to me. Reba had a bit of a rough night. She needed another transfusion.'

'Oh, Christ. Should I ring him?'

'No, he's going to talk to the PICU team again this morning. His morning, I mean. He'll ring when he can, I'm sure. This time difference is a real pain when something like this happens. Eva's had a stable night, though.'

Stable. How he hated that bloody word.

'This transfusion…'

'Doesn't mean she's losing any more blood, Dad. It just means they're adjusting. Replacing what she's lost.' Here was the son placating the father. The irony of it wasn't lost on Warlow.

'Okay.' The word emerged, buried in a sigh.

'How are you? I heard on the news that your officer died.'

'He did.'

'That must be hard for you.'

'Not just for me. Everyone is hurting.'

'Do you know who did it?'

'We have a working theory.' No escaping police protocol, not even with his son.

'Bloody hell, Dad.'

Warlow brought the conversation back to family. To safer ground, though for now just as troubled. 'You two okay?'

'We're fine. If I hear anymore, I'll let you know.'

'Yeah. Ring me any time. You know that.'

'How's Cadi?'

Warlow looked across to where the dog was laying in her bed, Arthur under her chin. 'Life of Riley, as per.'

'Good for her, I say.'

'Indeed.'

When Tom had gone, Warlow scrolled to his texts and the photograph Alun had sent of Eva in her incubator. He turned off the radio and sat in silence. Once more, Cadi, sensing his mood through some canine voodoo, came and nuzzled his hand.

'One day, you will meet this little girl, and she is going to love you,' he said to the dog. 'I promise you that.'

She looked up into his face, her brown eyes fixing on his, and wagged her tail.

CHAPTER THIRTY-FIVE

NEXT MORNING BROUGHT ANOTHER EARLY, before eight start. Catrin had added an extra whiteboard to the Gallery and Job Centre. At the very top of this one, Michael Dunbar's face stared out from an official-looking headshot taken for a brochure advertising L&M Jet-Ski Hire.

It made sense to have his image physically distanced from the details of the deaths populating the other boards. To emphasise that Dunbar's killing was a part of, but separate from, what had already happened.

Tea had been provided, and the team sat or leaned at desks while Warlow took the lead, the boards at his back.

'Let's take what we know at face value. We have Dunbar's text from his phone to Stacey Campbell. In that text, he confirms killing Barret. From Leanne Abbot's statement, the person who shot Barret also shot and killed Dan Clark and wounded Leanne.'

'And we have Dunbar's phone at the site where his body was found, sir,' Rhys said.

'Campbell claims he did not speak to her at all after the shooting. Only texted,' Gil said.

'Yes.' Warlow worried at a little patch of stubble on his chin that somehow escaped his razor before dawn that morning. 'Do we believe her?'

Jess took up this thread. 'She claims he was paranoid about being traced. Claimed that they, whether that was us or whoever he thought was after him, could listen in.'

Catrin weighed in. 'Or he didn't trust himself. If he was switching his phone on and off only to text, it would be a way of staying off the service provider's radar. Perhaps he didn't trust himself to remain brief in a call?' Catrin had her notebook open on her lap. She had the word "surveillance" underlined.

'Were we listening in on his conversations?' Warlow looked at Hopper.

'No record of police surveillance, sir, no. But given what's happened, he may have been more worried about his suppliers keeping tabs.'

Warlow frowned at that. 'Are you telling me they, whoever they are, can bug people's phones?'

Hopper's silence answered the question.

'What I don't understand is why Stacey didn't use the app that we used to trace him.' Rhys regarded the team's faces for answers.

Jess provided it. 'I asked her that. She says she forgot he'd put the thing on there. I mean, he wasn't lost exactly, was he?'

Warlow, Catrin, and Gil all turned bemused faces to her. 'You buy that?'

Jess's turn to shrug. 'I do. He wasn't lost. He told her he needed to stay off the radar. And unless you use that app, you forget it's there, especially if she didn't set it up.'

Warlow nodded. 'What about the Dunbar crime scene?'

'Povey's still up there. Her team is searching. So far

nothing,' Gil said. 'The plastic bag used for the suffocation is from a store in Tenby that Dunbar bought vaping materials at. My guess is he transported stuff from his house in it. Supplies maybe. And the batteries he used to power the heater and light are from jet-skis. Something he'd have easy access to.'

Warlow turned again to Hopper. 'Wil, anything at all for us on the organised crime angle?'

Hopper pushed off Rhys's desk where he'd been perching on one hip. 'I've put feelers out. Some new players are trying to grab a market share. There are Albanian gangs making inroads. They smell opportunity in rural areas. Especially tourist areas. Fresh meat.'

'Names?'

'None yet, sir.'

'Are we likely to get any?' Gil asked.

Hopper's response was an enigmatic smile and a couple of raised eyebrows.

Warlow turned to look at the boards. He paced up and down twice before muttering, 'I dislike loose ends.'

'We've noticed,' Gil said drily.

'So, help me tie some off.' Warlow stopped pacing and let his eyes roam over the photographs, timelines, and posted-up notes.

No one answered and so he growled, 'DC Harries, what are your thoughts?'

Rhys, who had been surreptitiously shunting the snap-on cover of a ballpoint pen around the edge of a sheet of paper like a toy train set, jerked upright, almost spilling the two inches of tea left in his mug all over the desk. 'Uh, everything checks out, sir. Phone records confirmed cell site analysis, they point to Dunbar holing up at the farmhouse. And previous analysis puts his phone near Telpyn Beach at the time of the shooting as we know. All fits with a drug-related killing, sir. I defer to Sergeant Hopper's expertise there.'

Warlow threw him an appraising, over-the-shoulder glance. 'Know your limitations. Good, Rhys. Catrin?'

Catrin consulted her notebook open on her lap. 'Farm to farm enquiries last night yielded nothing. But we found an Asda delivery driver who spotted a Lycra-clad cyclist near that stretch where the turnoff is.'

Warlow puffed out his cheeks.

'As for vehicles,' Catrin added, 'the same Asda man delivered to a farm on the edge of Cilycwm, and that's how we found him. He went up and down the stretch of road and was in the area for about twenty minutes in total. During that time, he passed two white vans, three SUVs, and four cars. Two silver, one black, and one red.'

'Does he have OCD?' Gil asked.

Catrin shrugged. 'Lucky for us, he gets bored and has an excellent memory.'

'Those are meagre pickings,' Warlow grumbled. 'Gil?'

'We've had some feedback from the forensic accountants, and it looks certain that Barret and Dunbar were washing money. The figures do not add up. But it's like we're staring into a deep well with no lights on our helmets. I think we need to get our hands on something tangible.'

'Such as?' Hopper asked.

'Such as the Menzies. I've had a chat with Dai Vetch.'

The muscles on Hopper's face tightened.

Gil was having none of his hubris. 'No offence, Wil, but I've known Dai for a long time, and I wanted his take on the Menzies. Paul, the father, has been a bit player for a long time. But his sons… Dai thinks they're champing at the bit and want more.'

'They were not happy chappies when we told them about Barret's death,' Warlow said.

'But they're the upside-down crucifixes at the end of this clanky chain,' Gil said. 'They're nasty pieces of work. Perhaps they know more than they're letting on.'

Jess turned to him. 'Worth us having a chat on our turf instead of theirs, then?'

'Won't do any harm, ma'am,' Gil said. 'Let's shake the tree and see what falls out.'

Hopper scoffed at this. 'They're hardly likely to mosey on up here for a voluntary interview.'

Gil had the bit between his teeth. 'Anything we could use? Parking tickets, speeding offence they haven't responded to?'

No one spoke until Gil addressed Catrin. 'Did the Asda man say a red car?'

She nodded. 'Yep.'

Gil nodded slowly. 'Doesn't one of the Menzies' boys drive a red car?'

'Hardly damning evidence,' Hopper said with a sceptical laugh.

Warlow smiled. 'Agreed, but we could use the "a car answering that description was seen in the area" approach.'

'Did the Asda driver mention a Hyundai i30, Rhys?' Hopper threw the DC a side-eyed look who responded with an airy grimace.

'I was thinking more in terms of it being red,' Warlow said.

Hopper let out a laugh. 'You can't be serious! Bring them in based on them driving a red car?'

'It'll do for what we need,' Warlow insisted. 'Let's get the buggers in for questioning under caution. We stay within PACE guidelines. If they refuse to come in voluntarily, we'll arrest them on suspicion. Nothing will stick, but it might put the willies up them for a while. Unless you have a better idea?' He looked pointedly at Hopper who shook a no, but with a face like a slapped arse.

Warlow glanced at his watch. At least this was something. 'Rhys, you're with me. We're off to another post-mortem.'

'Happy days,' Rhys said.

No one replied. Disturbingly, they realised he actually meant it.

————

GINA MELLINGS WALKED into the Incident Room, confident of not finding Rhys there. He wasn't because he'd texted her to tell her he was on the way to Cardiff for another appointment with the dead. A text with two tagged-on, open-mouthed, grinning, eyes shut in ecstasy with two bunched fists on either side of the face, emojis of excitement.

It wasn't Rhys she wanted today.

She'd texted Jess Allanby, and the DI had agreed to speak to her in private. The one person she hoped not to see was, mercifully, also not in the room when she walked through to the SIO office.

Hopper had gone with Catrin on urgent business to Haverfordwest.

At the door, Gina knocked.

'Come in.'

Jess got up as soon as the door opened, a big smile on her face.

'Thanks for seeing me, ma'am,' Gina said.

'Any time. Have a seat. I'd offer you tea, but our chief tea-maker is being Igor to DCI Warlow's Dr Frankenstein.'

Gina grinned. 'He enjoys being Igor, ma'am.'

'I'm sure that makes role play fun. Now, what is it you wanted to see me about?'

Gina sat. 'It's this case, ma'am. My part in it anyway. I probably should be speaking to DCI Warlow, but I wanted to run it past you first because... he might decide I'm being silly.'

'I doubt that.' Jess smiled and waited.

'I'm finding it difficult being at Siwan Clark's property, ma'am. It's probably me, but the way she's dealing with all of this is hard to handle. She's channelling her grief into her online presence.'

'Her influencing?'

Gina nodded. 'She's posting wearing a veil. It makes me very uncomfortable, commercialising it like this.' Gina shut her eyes and exhaled. 'And I hear how that sounds. So what if I'm uncomfortable? She's a widow at twenty-five. But I don't want to let my difficulty in accepting that affect my judgement.'

'Is it impacting your effectiveness in the job?'

'Yes, ma'am.' She'd hoped that by telling Jess this simple truth, that would be enough. She should have known better.

'And?'

'There isn't an and, ma'am.'

Jess sat back. 'I've worked with you on a handful of cases, Gina. DCI Warlow has asked for you to be the FLO in the last two cases where it's been at all possible for that to happen. Siwan Clark's appropriate, or inappropriate, response to the loss of her partner may be a hard pill to swallow, but it isn't the whole story here, is it?'

Gina shut her eyes, and the sigh that escaped her came from a deep drift mine of unspoken despondency. 'Sergeant Hopper is... he and I... we have a bit of history, ma'am. For me, it was a night out, a drink, and nothing more. I did not like what was on offer. Not enough to go any further than the door of the pub we were in. I got an Uber home, and that was it for me. Wil saw it differently.

He pursued me for several weeks afterwards.' She paused before adding, 'I've known other men to be persistent, but not like Wil.'

'Right,' Jess said, and a moment of understanding sparked between these two attractive women.

'It's just that I wasn't expecting to see him again. And to be in a situation… in a case like this… where he is involved with both me and Rhys professionally, it feels very awkward.'

'Has he been unprofessional?'

Gina paused, thinking through her exchanges with Hopper. They'd been awkward alright. But she hadn't felt threatened. Admittedly, his "different futures" riff had left her bemused, but she'd brushed all that aside. 'Bit of a power trip, him being a sergeant now and me just a PC. But then he's a bloke, and it could simply have been his testosterone fuelled idea of a joke.'

'Has Rhys said anything?'

'He thinks Wil is a rockstar. The undercover thing, the drugs raids.' She sighed.

'Some men find sailing close to the edge an adrenaline rush, don't they?'

Gina frowned. Something in the way the DI said this implied more than a basic understanding. 'Rhys I can be… easily led.'

Jess nodded. 'This will stay between the two of us. I'll see what I can do to get you moved. It might take a couple of days, so you need to stay put for now. I'll sort it out with DCI Warlow.'

'Does he need to know the details, ma'am?'

'No. Just enough detail. He's a very understanding man, Gina. Don't worry, we'll get you out of there.'

'You make me sound like a celebrity, ma'am.'

'You're almost a part of the team, Gina. That carries a lot more weight around here than celebrity.'

Gina sighed. 'Why does life have to be so complicated?'

'Nature of the beast. Now, how's living in the new place going?'

CHAPTER THIRTY-SIX

WARLOW AND RHYS travelled up to Cardiff in the Audi.
Warlow let Rhys drive both up, and now that the deed was
done, back. It meant less noise pollution from rustling crisp
packets and sweet wrappers, and it gave Warlow control of
the entertainment system. As a result, they'd been able to
listen to something decent both on the way up and on the
return journey, which was what they were nearing the end
of now. Warlow had playlists. Rhys listened appreciatively,
occasionally nodding along with an exalted, 'I know this,'
and a cheesy grin.

Sometimes he'd even guess the artist, though more
often than not this would be wrong and a decade or two
off, as many of Warlow's seventies and eighties favourites
had been sampled, if not butchered, for later releases
under the dubious label of "mixes". Warlow took pleasure
in correcting the young officer with facts. But what it also
meant was that they did not have to listen to the self-indul-
gent, auto-tuned, celebrity mumblings that seemed to have
taken over the airwaves and which Rhys's generation were
being subjected to.

Not that Warlow harboured any strong opinions about it. No siree.

'Ever listen to podcasts while you're driving, sir?' Rhys asked. An example of one of his less random non-sequiturs.

'Now and again. You?'

'I like ones about conspiracy theories. You know, did we really land on the moon, or how lizard people might be ruling the planet.'

'That's what I like,' Warlow said. 'Knowing my officers are grounded in reality.'

'Thank you, sir,' Rhys replied.

Warlow waited for however long it might take for a tumbleweed to roll by before adding, 'Remember those irony lessons we gave you when you first joined the team, Rhys?'

'I do, sir.'

'We need to send you on a refresher course.'

They drove on for a few miles, James Taylor being lyrical in the background until Rhys voiced another thought that, judging from the way he'd been frowning for the last two minutes, had been troubling him. 'Dr Tiernon said there wasn't any sign of torture, sir. So, I'm wondering if whoever found Dunbar got what they wanted.'

'Yes, well, I'd query the lack of torture. Tiernon meant lack of other torture. Having a plastic bag held over your head and then releasing it would, I'd hazard a guess, get you to say almost anything.'

Rhys winced. 'That's rough, sir.'

They were on the A48, having left the M4 behind them. Dunbar's post-mortem had yielded little in the way of new information other than to confirm the cause of death as suffocation and that his hands and feet had been taped as had his mouth for some period prior to his death.

They'd await the usual toxicology, but stomach contents revealed he'd eaten within three hours of his death. Rhys would explain all of this to the team before they all got access to Tiernon's full report. But as they approached the Llangunnor turnoff, Warlow felt a sudden urge to not take the turn.

'Keep going, Rhys.'

'Where to, sir?'

'To the beach. I need some fresh air.'

———

RHYS PARKED on the verge just north of the cattle grid where officers Abbot and Clark had parked their car on the day of the shooting. It was a little after one in the afternoon and traffic on the coast road was light. Rain was due in by late afternoon, but for now it was dry, and the day before's breeze kept it reasonably mud free underfoot.

Warlow crossed the road to the beach path.

'What we need is a dog, sir.'

'If only. Don't tell Cadi we've been here today. She'll never speak to me again.'

They took the path winding down through the trees to the beach, but Warlow stood at the junction, where the coastal path branching east met with the closed-off stretch to the west.

'Leanne Abbot said she saw Dunbar cross the road and head towards the path we've just walked along.'

Rhys looked around, studying the terrain. 'Are you suggesting he might have taken the closed-off route, sir?'

'I am, Rhys. And so are we. Get your Google Maps out.'

Warlow climbed over the stile with its pasted-up warning of "Path closed because of Landslip".

'Is it safe, sir?'

'Let's find out.'

Rhys's map showed the path angling back towards the road, which was also its narrowest point in terms of proximity to the cliff edge. This was where the landslip was. Not an unusual scenario for the coastal path. A stark reminder of the case that brought him out of retirement, where just such a landslip had revealed the corpses of two missing hikers.

On such a rugged coastline exposed to the battering south westerlies, erosion was an ever-encroaching problem. The path often required rerouting while new ways were found to avoid danger areas. After about six hundred yards, Warlow slowed and stared at the problem area. Where the cliff had fallen away, a long drop with no protection had been revealed. A clear danger to the public. Warlow climbed to some higher ground next to the hedge separating the path from the coast road. It was difficult and steep, but passable. He worked his way past the danger area with Rhys in tow. A few yards further on, they rejoined the path. It widened until it emerged just east of a private property that effectively cut off further access west and drove hikers onto the coastal road itself, heading down into the village of Amroth.

Both men stood at the wooden gate at the exit point.

'He could have come this way, sir. It is passable.'

'Yes. But from here down into the village, he'd be exposed. Traffic would have to slow to pass a lone walker. Unless he had transport.'

'You think he parked here?'

The access road down into the property that cut off the path had No Parking warnings everywhere. Warlow took in his surroundings. 'Not a car. Too risky. I was thinking more two wheels than four.'

Rhys turned to consider the way they'd come. As well as the narrow walkers' gate, next to it, a five-bar wooden gate led into a patch of open ground surrounded by gorse bushes. Easy enough to hide a cycle, even a scooter or motorbike.

'Let's get someone to look at this area for tyre tracks.'

Rhys had his notebook out and scribbled something down. 'Where to now, sir?'

'Back to HQ. You have lunch?'

'Leftovers from yesterday, sir. Gina packed it.'

Warlow stared into Rhys's face for signs of regret but saw none. 'Good, so you won't mind sharing with me, eh?'

Rhys's mouth drifted open as he struggled for a response.

Warlow turned away with a shake of his head, muttering into the breeze as he walked away. 'Irony *and* leg-pulling refresher course. Make a note.'

———

Luke Menzies had, of course, refused to answer questions or attend for a voluntary interview, so they'd arrested him on suspicion. Luke wore the never-cooperate-with-the-police-on-principle badge with pride.

Warlow asked Jess and Catrin to conduct the interview, and once again, Hopper could not hide his resentment. He and Warlow were in the observation room, waiting for the solicitor Luke Menzies had insisted upon, to get settled.

'But it was me who picked Luke up, sir,' Hopper said.

'You and Catrin,' Warlow pointed out.

Hopper shook his head. 'I know their type, sir.'

'And you think that DI Allanby and Sergeant Richards don't?'

'I'm not saying that, sir—'

'Good, then say nothing. Don't forget, you are new to

this team. And as far as I'm concerned, you need to earn your spurs. These two,' he nodded towards the screen where Jess and Catrin sat patiently waiting, or with Catrin, not so patiently, if her glare was anything to go by, 'already have theirs and they are very sharp. Now, let's let them do their thing, shall we?'

On screen, Catrin read out the usual caution, and got everyone to announce their presence. The solicitor had come up from Pembroke Dock and had a round sweaty face that he kept on dabbing with a tissue. He introduced himself as 'John Bailey'.

'Mr Menzies, you're here as part of our investigation into the unlawful killing of Mr Michael Dunbar,' Catrin said.

Luke, slumped in his chair with his feet crossed, legs angled out to the side and his arms folded across his chest, looked intrigued. 'Definitely dead, then, is he?'

'We're investigating reports of a vehicle seen in the area in which the crime was committed. A vehicle whose description matches that of your car.'

'So, a red Hyundai?'

Catrin did not confirm or deny this statement. 'Where were you between the hours of 9am and 5pm yesterday?'

Luke Menzies did not move. 'Want me to make you a list?'

'If you could, that would be useful.'

Luke made a show of trying to remember before he finally spoke. 'Uh, got up at about half-nine. Took my brother to college by half ten.' He grinned. 'School isn't like it was in my day.'

Catrin wrote it down and then looked up, waiting for Luke to continue.

'Then I went for a coffee.'

'Which café?'

'That cave place. Good there. Killer brownies, man.'
Luke appeared to be enjoying himself.

'Who were you with?'

'Jason Vine and uh, Laura. Don't know her second name. Stayed there for about an hour, then I went home and played some Duty and had some lunch.'

'What about the afternoon?'

'Worked with my dad.'

'You're unemployed, aren't you?' Jess asked.

'Officially, like. But I help my dad out if he needs me. He's a man with a van. Moves things about. Local deliveries and that.'

'Where were these deliveries?' Catrin asked.

'We was all over. Down the Dock, one over in Goodwick. All over.'

'What were you delivering?' Jess asked.

The grin had not yet left Luke's face. He turned to the solicitor, who seemed to take his cue. 'What relevance does that have to the reason for my client being here? Surely, it is enough to prove there was no possibility of Mr Menzies being wherever it is you think he might have been. Which is the purpose of this interview, am I correct?'

Catrin did not acknowledge the statement. Instead, she slid some pages out of a folder. 'When was the last time you saw Michael Dunbar, Luke?'

'Dunbar, Dunbar…' Luke frowned in mock concentration.

Catrin turned over the A4 sheet. A photocopy of an image which showed Luke Menzies, Paul Menzies, and Michael Dunbar outside a pub. When the weather was warmer, judging by the way they were dressed.

'Oh, wow, you've been watching us.' Luke stared closer. 'You mean Mikeski. We call him the Russian sometimes, Mike-ski, see? Yeah, I remember now. We did a bit of moving for him. Garden furniture. In my dad's van.'

'Garden furniture?' Jess asked.

'Yeah.'

'We know that Michael Dunbar was a drug trafficker,' Jess said.

'Oh, wow. Mikeski? A drug trafficker?' His acting was terrible.

'Did you know that, Luke?' Catrin asked.

Luke looked at the solicitor, who nodded in return. Then he turned back to Jess, all smiles, and delivered in a stage whisper, 'No comment.'

'Is that the business you and your father were discussing with Dunbar? Not garden furniture?' Jess asked.

'No comment.'

Catrin leaned in. 'Is it you who's done the dirty work here, Luke? Did he steal from you as well as the suppliers?'

'No comment.' Luke grinned.

In the observation room, Warlow fumed gently. 'That'll be it now. No comment all the way to Christmas. Where's the brother, Zac?'

'In a family room, sir,' Hopper said.

'Right.' Warlow went to the door. 'I'd better see if he's okay.'

Zac sat on furniture that was upholstered and therefore a site more comfortable than the interview room chairs. He looked up from his phone screen when Warlow entered the room.

'Anything we can get you?'

'Yeah, out of here. I should be in college.'

Warlow considered the boy. He was thin like his dad, wiry and on edge. Despite the bravado, he wasn't comfortable being here. 'What I hear is that our officers offered you a lift to college when they picked up your brother, but you declined.'

'This is harassment, this is.'

'No, this is me asking if you need anything. You can leave at any time.'

Zac drew his lips back. 'Good, cos my dad is on the way, and he is buzzing.'

Behind Warlow, the door slid open, and Jess looked in. 'Evan, a quick word.'

Her eyes made contact with Zac, whose own eyes widened above a salacious grin.

'You're Molly's mother, right?'

Jess tilted her head. 'You know Molly?'

'We're in college together. We are big pals.'

'Funny, she hasn't mentioned you.' Even though she had, Jess was not giving this twerp an inch of ground.

'Don't worry, she will. I've got moves, me.'

'You keep your moves to yourself,' Warlow said. Though this was all puffed-up showboating from the teenager, it left the DCI oddly unsettled.

Zac sensed that he was getting under their skin and continued to goad. Being an irritating little shit seemed to run in the family. 'Nah, I've got good feels, man.' He tapped his chest with the thumb side of his fist. 'Me and Molly the dolly.'

But Warlow had had enough. 'Stay here. When your father arrives, we'll bring him to you.'

'He's not very happy.'

'Neither am I, in case you haven't noticed.' Warlow closed the door behind him.

Outside, Jess walked on a few steps before saying, 'He's a charmer.'

'Runs in the family. But being an oily scrote is not a punishable offence, I'm sorry to say. At least not in the eyes of the law.'

Jess nodded. 'I see no point in keeping Luke, either. He's clammed up and we have zero leverage.'

'Agreed.' Warlow said. 'But I'm with Gil. It was worth a try.'

'Yeah. We've shaken the tree, but it's born no fruit.'

'Except a couple of very bad apples.'

Jess's long-suffering smile, though fleeting, was enough to brighten Warlow's day for a short while. You took your pleasures where you could at a time like this.

CHAPTER THIRTY-SEVEN

THE NEXT TWENTY-FOUR hours passed by with meetings and gathering evidence. And though Warlow's mind strayed intermittently to his son's family in Perth whenever a slack moment appeared, no change was the message he kept getting by text and a couple of downbeat phone calls. Eva remained in PICU, Reba, though no longer requiring transfusions, remained weak but recovering.

But the case, complex and consuming, kept his mind occupied most of the time. With what they had – Dunbar's confession and murder – the team spent a lot of time re-interviewing people they'd talked to only briefly before, in an attempt at nailing down details. People like Stacey Campbell's neighbours. But a dark figure walking around Tenby's streets on Halloween night had not raised many eyebrows. Whoever barged their way into Dunbar and Campbell's house had been canny.

Roadblocks were set up on the quiet stretch of road leading to Pantpriddog, Dunbar's hiding place and ulti-mate death chamber. They were looking for regular users. People commuting to Carmarthen from the hinterland.

But by mid-morning on Friday, they'd drawn a blank. As had Povey after her team looked carefully at the patch of ground inside the gate that led to the closed-off section of the coastal path at Telpyn. A place Warlow'd earmarked as a viable escape route for Dunbar after he'd shot Barret and Clark and Abbot. But the killer had covered his tracks exceptionally well. Still, they had his texts to Barret on the morning of the shooting. They also had his texts to Stacey Campbell. Both damning in their own ways.

But Warlow liked to be a hundred percent sure, and what they were missing was physical evidence. The weapon, for instance. And in that, he found an unlikely and vociferous ally in Stacey Campbell. The team worked through the weekend and, on Saturday morning, six days after Barret and Clark were shot, she turned up at police HQ demanding to see the DCI.

He went down to reception to meet her. She'd abandoned the gym wear for jeans and a blouse. Both black, as one might expect. Stacey had already been in to give a formal statement with a solicitor and had stuck to the story that she did not know that Dunbar and Barret were anything other than entrepreneurs in the adventure holiday business. She admitted not knowing how many pies they had their fingers in, but that did not make her an accessory. Today, despite the lips and the makeup, she looked like sleep had been a stranger these past nights. She looked, in fact, like someone who'd just lost a partner that had become, in the eyes of the world, a notorious murderer and drug lord. A fact she was not thrilled about. She voiced those misgivings to Warlow as they sat in a room he'd asked the duty sergeant to provide for him.

'I've come here to say two things,' Stacey said. 'First, I wanted to thank you for getting Mitch back. Dion loves that dog. She's a big softie. I heard you had a hand in that.'

'None of what's happened is the dog's fault,' Warlow said, knowing he sounded like a stuck record but that didn't change the facts. He wanted to add that canines had his every sympathy because they got no say in who their owners were. But of course, he kept quiet.

'And second, Mike isn't a murderer.' Her lip quivered as she said this. In fact, her whole body quivered. Once again, she appeared not to know what do to with her hands, settling, eventually, with them plonked in her lap, jewellery clanging every time she fidgeted.

'Stacey, I understand how you feel. But murderers don't wear labels. If they did, it would make my job a lot easier.'

Stacey persisted. 'But Mike wouldn't. He couldn't kill Lee. They were friends. If you'd seen them together, they were like a pair of those smart, naughty boys always trying it on at school. Cheeking the teachers, bunking off. You know the type. They never grew up. Mike would never…'

Warlow hadn't cautioned this woman. This was old ground they were going over and he had a mound of paperwork upstairs. 'He told you he did, though, Stacey. He confessed. We've seen the texts.'

'He wasn't himself when he sent those. He was scared. And Mike didn't scare easily.' Her hand jingled up from her lap and clutched at the open neck of her blouse.

Warlow compressed his lips. She could protest as much as she wanted to, but the texts were black-and-white evidence. 'Before all this happened, did you pick up on anything wrong?' Warlow asked, suspecting this was futile, but unable, out of common courtesy, to dismiss this grieving woman out of hand. 'Did you talk about money? Was he worried about anything?'

'What we talked about was buying a place in Spain. He'd always fancied moving out there. Once the summer ended here he always looked for a bit of winter sun. Why would he throw all that away? He had the money.'

That part at least was true. More bank accounts had come to light. Some, if not all of them, now inaccessible to Stacey because of confiscation of assets. That would take a while to sort out. With both Barret and Dunbar dead, there'd be no prosecution. That aspect of things, including assessing Stacey's involvement, ended up on the Crown Prosecution Service's desk. They'd need to weigh up the evidence. She'd need a good lawyer. And listening to her, Warlow could not help wondering if perhaps Dunbar had opted for that one big payday. Enough to buy a property in Spain and retire. But he would also know that stealing from a big supplier would have consequences. And that was what bothered Warlow the most about this case.

'Have you found who killed Mike, yet?' Stacey warbled out the question.

'No.' Warlow saw no point in lying, but he added some sugar to coat the bitter pill. 'Not yet.'

Stacey dropped her chin. 'A week ago, we were talking about going away in February. Get Christmas over. Take Dion somewhere warm.'

Warlow felt some sympathy for this woman. And especially for Dion, who was as much an innocent victim as Mitch the dog. But Dunbar was no angel.

'Michael was a criminal, Stacey. He may have hidden it from you, only you know the truth about that. But he was involved in a drugs ring as was Lee Barret. Whoever it is they were dealing with…' Warlow shook his head. 'It's clear they're capable of extreme violence.'

She looked at the bangles on her wrist before dragging her gaze back up to Warlow's face. 'Do we get protection?'

'For now, yes. And we are doing our absolute best to find out who killed Michael. You can be sure of that.'

'You promise?' Stacey's quivering lip was threatening to break into a full-blown blubber.

'I do,' Warlow said. 'One hundred percent.'

'When will we get his body back?'

'That's up to the coroner. It's out of my hands.'

'They haven't let me see him; you know that?'

Warlow had seen suffocation victims. More times than he cared to recall from suicides and hangings and one or two murders. 'You know what, Stacey? I'd try and remember him the last time you shared a joke. Honestly, it's the best way.'

She nodded and reached for a tissue from her expensive handbag. Warlow let her blow her nose and showed her out.

Not the most auspicious start to the day, listening to the objections of a grieving partner. But all part of a trend since he'd sensed the investigation slowly slipping from his grasp. Other agencies were now involved, and Hopper's role had slid into one of liaising between the various interested parties here.

After Stacey had gone, Warlow went back to the Incident Room. As he walked through the door, Jess, Rhys, and Gil all looked up without speaking. Catrin had yet to make an appearance and Warlow made a mental note to speak with her. But these silent stares from the three of them made his spine tingle.

'What?' he asked. 'Have I splashed water on my trouser front again?'

Jess inclined her head in silence towards the back of the room and the SIO office. Warlow saw the door was ajar and someone was moving about in there.

'Who?'

Gil shifted in his seat and lifted one foot off the floor, followed by the other.

Warlow squeezed his eyes shut.

'How long has she been here?'

Rhys held up five fingers.

'I could sneak out—'

'Ah, Evan, there you are.' Two-Shoes' voice sent a tentacle of acknowledgement across the room to slither around Warlow's neck and pull him in. She stood in the doorway, hands clasped behind her back in a trademark copper's stance.

'Morning, ma'am. I was just on my way to—'

'Good. I need just a quick word if I may.'

Jess muttered as he walked past, 'Good luck with that, then.'

Warlow glared at her.

'Has someone got you any refreshments, ma'am?' Warlow said as he followed her into the office.

'No. I had my elevenses at half ten. Sit.'

Warlow obliged, suddenly aware of how Cadi felt when he ordered her to sit on her haunches; hoping that he'd get thrown a bone here and not be shown the birch. Not that he'd ever shown Cadi any kind of stick-related threat, other than to take one off her when she became too exuberant and picked one up off the beach. Sticks were not good for dogs, contrary to common belief.

Two-Shoes put both hands on the desk, the fingers of one hand cupping the closed fist of the other as she regarded Warlow for several long seconds before breaking into a smile. 'Congratulations, Evan. We are impressed with how quickly you've sorted this one out.'

'I'd hardly say it's sorted out, ma'am. We're getting nowhere fast with finding Dunbar's killer.'

'But you have Dunbar as the shooter.'

'We have his confession in a text, ma'am. Plus, we have him pinged near the scene at the time of the shooting, as well as an increasing amount of evidence that he was involved, as was Barret, in drug trafficking and money laundering.'

'Like peeling an onion, then,' Two-Shoes said, her smile not slipping for an instant. 'And Wil Hopper in the thick of it.'

'He's been an asset.'

'Then you could see him as a part of the team?'

Warlow suspected that this was the reason for Two-Shoes' visit, though even he was surprised by how quickly they'd arrived at this point. 'Be happy to consider him once we have a vacancy, ma'am. As it is, we have a full complement.'

Two-Shoes nodded. 'I have made Sergeant Jones an offer that he is considering.'

'I hope you made it clear that the suggestion did not come from me, ma'am?'

The Superintendent doubled down on the smile. 'I prefer to think of it as an offer more than a suggestion.'

'Is there a difference?'

Her thumbs popped up from her clamped-together hands and began rotating around one another. 'I think there is. Sergeant Jones needs to consider his health and his pension.'

'I can't argue with that,' Warlow remarked.

'One more thing. The Menzies. I've been asked to let you know that any further involvement on your part needs to be run through me.'

'You, ma'am?'

Two-Shoes' face became stern. 'Hopper will have told you that the Menzies are under surveillance and have been for some time. Don't worry, you needed to involve them. No one was going to stand in your way about that. Not after what happened to Daniel Clark. But you've also let slip that surveillance.'

Warlow had wondered if showing Luke Menzies

images of him and his father rubbing shoulders with Dunbar might come back to haunt them. And here it was, in the form of a Two-Shoes' finger wagging. Or thumb wagging, to be accurate. Warlow dragged his gaze away from those fidgeting digits. He didn't blame Catrin one bit for showing Luke Menzies the image of him with his father and Dunbar outside the pub. He'd have done the same.

'Luckily, we've let it be known through Hopper's CHIS that it was Dunbar who had been surveilled,' Two-Shoes added. 'The point is that other departments have their remit. One of those is having eyes on the Menzies. Once the time is right we can pounce. Then we will follow the yellow brick road all the way to the wicked witch's house. The suppliers.'

As far as Warlow could remember, the yellow brick road led to the Emerald City, but that might be splitting hairs in the context of this conversation.

'As it is, they're keeping their heads down after you poked a stick at them,' Two-Shoes continued. 'But unless you have any hard evidence, we need to keep them at arm's length.'

'They're a slippery bunch, ma'am. I would not put it past them to have gone looking for their missing merchandise.'

'There is no evidence of that,' Two-Shoes said.

'No. There isn't.' He paused before putting a finishing touch on the sentence. 'Not yet.'

'Well, once evidence is found, if it is found, I want it run past me before any further action is taken. Are we clear?'

'We are, ma'am.'

'Good.' Two-Shoes got up, her smile back. 'Is Sergeant Hopper here? I'd like to say hello.'

'No, ma'am. He's with CID in Cardigan. Working with them on the washed-up drug haul. Seeing if there's anything that might help us with a lead on Dunbar's murder.'

Her smile eased in disappointment. 'Never mind. I'll catch him next time.' She walked to the door, turned and, like all good headteachers, gave Warlow that titbit of praise that made it all so worthwhile. 'And well done you and the rest of the team, Evan. Any issues, any issues at all, my door is always open.'

CHAPTER THIRTY-EIGHT

A BIT like you did with a bad smell in the toilet, Warlow gave the superintendent five minutes to vacate the Incident Room before venturing out himself. When he did, he wandered over to Jess's desk. She contemplated his approach with a knowing grin and a freshly steaming brew in her hands.

'What the hell do you call this?' Warlow demanded, raking his gaze over the surrounding desks whose occupants were all similarly tea'd up. 'Lolling around drinking tea while I'm neck deep in the investigation's weeds being grilled by a senior officer.'

'Went well, then, did it?' Jess held up her mug to cover her smirk. 'This one's yours.' She extended a finger towards a receptacle at the edge of the desk. One with "Coppers Do It With A Truncheon" as a logo.

Warlow, still feigning opprobrium, picked up the tea, sipped, and closed his eyes in ecstasy. 'Rhys, I have to say that your breakfast-blend-making skills have come on leaps and bounds since you first joined us as a child apprentice.'

The DC swung around to face his boss. 'Gina bought me a gizmo, sir.' He held up a tiny hourglass style sand-timer in a reenforced metal cylinder attached to his keys. 'Glow in the dark, sir. Never get the brew wrong with this.'

Warlow nodded his approval. 'She's a keeper, that one.'

'Actually, sir, she plays full back.'

Gil, who'd been arranging a plate of biscuits, stopped, and slowly turned his head to contemplate Rhys. '*Arglwydd*, be still my beating heart. Rhys has cracked a joke and by Grabjar's Hammer, it's one worthy of mirth.'

'Nice Galaxy Quest reference, sarge. Except it's not Grabjar's Hammer, it's—'

Gil steamrollered on. 'I comment only because your jokes are not usually funny, and when you are funny, you're not usually joking.'

Rhys pondered for a moment, but decided, wisely, to respond with nothing but a beatific smile.

Warlow sipped his tea. These were brief enough moments of levity in what had been, and still was, a dour few days. Three people had died, including one of their own. That fact still hovered over everyone, rendering smiles and laughter strained and self-conscious.

'Where's Catrin?' Warlow asked.

'She has an appointment,' Jess said, still with both hands around her mug.

'Another appointment? On a Saturday?' Warlow did not hold back his surprise. He stood with his back to the Incident Room door, which Two-Shoes had left ajar. 'Christ, it's a wonder she has any teeth left. That dentist must have used a bloody cement lorry's worth of fillings by now. Come to think of it, I did see one on the way in with its drum rolling—'

'Actually, sir, it wasn't the dentist.' Catrin's voice from the doorway stemmed Warlow's flow. 'And I have been meaning to talk to you about it. I have already spoken to DI Allanby.'

Jess's eyes never wavered from Catrin's face.

'It's alright, ma'am. I've decided.'

'Decided?' Warlow swung around to face her. 'Sounds ominous.'

Catrin walked across to Jess's desk and stood addressing the team, her coat still on. Gil, using his feet as propulsion, wheeled his chair over. Rhys stood up and strode over on long legs. Behind them, the Incident Room hummed with activity, but for all intents, the team were in their own little bubble. Warlow, though, was aware of how public this was.

'You prefer the office?'

Catrin shook her head. 'You should all be told. I mean, it's not as if my absence hasn't been noticed.' She side-eyed Warlow. 'It's not the dentist. Sir. I've been to the hospital. Me and Craig, we're going for IVF treatment.'

Rhys, frowning, mouthed towards Gil, 'IVF?'

'In vitro fertilisation,' Gil said. 'Tidy.'

'I've been through cycles of medical treatments, and they've not worked. So, they're going to harvest some eggs. That's why I've been away. Sorry, sir, but they had a couple of cancellations and I slotted in. It's the NHS.'

'I know it well,' Warlow said, hoping that his diatribe of earlier had not made him sound like too much of an arse. He also had an insider's view, via Tom, of an institution which, because of its free-at-the-point-of-contact nature, had the unique status of being both a national treasure and a national disgrace at the same time. Very British in that sense. But in need of an overhaul, on that most people agreed. Still, it would be a brave and suicidal politician who put his or her head above the parapet and administered the necessary blow.

Rhys grabbed a chair and put it behind Catrin.

She watched him with barely restrained amusement. 'I'm not ill, Rhys.'

'I know, but… I'll be back in a jiffy.' Rhys hurried out of the door.

'It's only fair you're all made aware,' Catrin continued. 'But, sir, I will not let it interfere with work. I'm booked in for egg retrieval next month. I won't be off for more than a couple of days.'

'You don't need to worry about that,' Jess said.

'They say that I might feel a bit bloated, and I'll get some cramps.' She looked up at Warlow. 'Sorry, sir.'

'No need to apologise, Catrin. On the one hand, I'm sorry you have to go through this. But on the other, I hope it works out. Sorry if I overdid the ogre boss, bit, too. You and Craig will be fantastic parents.'

Catrin beamed, and she dabbed away a little droplet of moisture gathered in the corner of her eye. 'Thank you, sir.'

Rhys came back with a mug of tea, tea bag still in. He fished out his key and placed the hourglass on the table. 'Four minutes to brew. Sorry that the bag and milk are in together, but…'

'It's still tea,' Catrin said.

'This IVF,' Rhys asked. 'Does Craig have to have anything done?'

'No, he only has to produce sperm.'

'He can do that alright—' Rhys caught Warlow's heavy-lidded glare and shut up.

'Lots of people need some help to conceive, mind.' Gil's statement drew everyone's eyes, many of them narrowed in suspicion. 'I read that near a third of couples trying to have children end up getting some sort of treatment. The Lady Anwen and I, in fact, wondered if we might be having some trouble before our first. Back then it was injections to help ovulate and monitoring temperature to work out the best time to bring sperm to egg. Many's the time I'd get a call on the job, to go home, and get… on with the job.'

Jess, smiling, shut her eyes.

Catrin simply stared.

Warlow could find nothing to say.

'No trouble with number two, I hasten to add. From then on, all channels of communication remained well and truly open, as they say.'

'They say nothing of the kind,' Warlow said. 'It's only you that says it.'

Gil, however, was on a roll. 'How about you, Rhys?'

'No, sarge. I haven't had any children yet, so I wouldn't know.'

Mugs froze on the way to lips.

'I meant, are you and Gina planning anything?'

'They've only just moved in together, man,' Warlow chided the sergeant.

'I thought we were having frank and open discussions like grown-ups?' Gil protested.

Warlow tutted, but Rhys seemed unfazed. 'Not sure about any of that, sarge. Gina hasn't been her usual self these last few days. Hasn't enjoyed this case much.'

'Is that why you've been moping about?' Gil asked.

'Moping she'll get over it once she leaves the Clarks', more like.'

Gil heaved out a Muttley laugh. '*Iesu post*, two jokes in ten minutes? Rhys, you're on a roll.'

Catrin turned to Jess. '*Iesu post* doesn't have much of a translation, ma'am. Jesus post, that's about it. Mild blasphemy only.'

'Never mind, Rhys.' Jess put down her mug. 'This is Gina's last day.'

'Yeah. She'll be fine by the weekend, I'm sure. Where's Sergeant Hopper, by the way? I've been digging out some stats for him. He wanted to find out if there'd been a surge in overdoses over the last six months.'

'Cardigan,' Warlow repeated what he'd told Two-Shoes.

'Is he likely to be helping us out with other cases, sir?' Rhys asked.

Warlow kept his eyes on the DC to avoid having to look at Gil. 'We'll wait and see. He's been very useful on the drugs front.'

'I've enjoyed working with him, sir. He knows loads about how drug rings work and county lines and he's done dozens of raids. He knows where people hide things in houses. Once he said someone had their toilet on wheels and a ramp. The whole thing slid out of the wall. There were floorboards in the room so you couldn't see the join in the floor and there was a stash of cocaine in the wall behind.'

Warlow grinned at the DC's enthusiasm.

'He was great when Stacey Campbell's place was burgled. Quick at searching too. He taught me to push a half-open door fully open in case someone was behind it. And he knew where the bedroom light switch was.'

'Difficult to find, was it?' Jess asked, equally amused by Rhys's gushing account.

'It was hidden under a photograph in the middle of the wall, ma'am. Gina says all light switches are ugly, anyway. But Stacey Campbell had hidden this one under a hinged box with a photo pasted on it. Brilliant. I said to Gina that when we get our fixer upper, that would be a good thing to do. I found a YouTube video of someone making them.'

'What did Gina say to that?' Catrin asked.

'She said, "What fixer upper?".'

Warlow cleared his throat. A signal for frivolity to end. Rhys got the message and shut up.

'What did Stacey Campbell want, Evan?' Jess asked.

'She's still protesting Dunbar's innocence. She asked when his body might be released by the coroner. She wants to see him one last time.'

'Not such a good idea.' Jess made a face.

'That's what I told her. Two-Shoes has also told me that the Menzies are off-limits. Ongoing ops, apparently.'

'You still think they could be involved, sir?' Catrin asked.

'In Dunbar's murder, no. The crime scene is too clean. But they know more than they're letting on. Albanian gangs or otherwise.'

'They're not likely to give any of that up,' Jess said. 'Not after what happened to Dunbar.'

Warlow nodded. Next to him, Gil sat unusually pensive.

'What's up with you, Gil?' Catrin asked.

He looked up, his eyes coming back into focus. 'What? Me? Oh, gathering wool as us old folks do.'

'What does that mean?' Catrin frowned.

'I need to let the dust settle a little. Plus, I am still reeling from DC Harries' attempts at humour.'

Rhys feigned dropping a microphone. 'I'm here until next Saturday, sarge.'

'Unfortunately, we both know that isn't true. You are here for the foreseeable.'

'Has anyone heard more about that fund they've set up for Daniel Clark?' Catrin scanned the faces.

'It's over forty thousand already,' Rhys said. He used his phone to call up the app.

Catrin scowled. 'I don't like funerals at the best of times, but that's one I am not looking forward to.'

'It'll be massive,' Rhys said.

Warlow replaced his now empty mug on the desk. 'Agreed. But Daniel Clark is not the only victim here. Catrin, since you're on half time—'

'That's not fair.'

'—get hold of the Asda van driver. He mentioned something about seeing a cyclist, didn't he? Let's see if he can be a bit more specific.'

'Right, sir.'

'And check with Stacey Campbell whether Dunbar had a bike.'

'You think the Asda man saw Dunbar on that road?' Jess asked, bemused.

'No. But I wonder if he saw someone else on his bike. It's possible Dunbar used a bike to get away from the scene when Clark and Barret were shot. He could easily have stashed it where the closed-off section of path was. If he took a bike to Pantpriddog, someone else might have stolen it to get away after Dunbar was killed.'

Nods all around.

Warlow sighed. 'Sadly, at the moment, that is all I can think of to do even though I can't help feeling there's a part of this picture that's missing.'

'I hate it when that happens,' Rhys said.

This time, they didn't think he was joking.

CHAPTER THIRTY-NINE

On Monday, Gina spent the morning with John and Beth Clark because she wanted to hand over personally to the colleague taking her place. In all honestly, she'd have been happy to stay with these traumatised people, but she couldn't pick and choose. The Clarks came as a package and included in that package was Siwan Clark, the widow. Still, Gina had done what she came to do and earned the Clarks' profuse thanks for her help.

'We don't know what we would have done without you, Gina,' Beth Clark said as the officer put on her coat to take her leave. There were hugs from John and Beth in the hallway and one final check that Gina had everything. It was then that she saw the mobile sitting on the hall table.

'Not mine.' She tapped her pocket to make sure hers was stowed. 'Better not take that by mistake.'

'Oh, no. That's Siwan's. She left it here this morning. She's never done that before. And we can't ring her to tell her it's here. She can't be thinking straight… not after…' Beth sniffed, on the verge of more tears.

'I can take it to her,' Gina offered without a second thought. The words slid out of her mouth before she could stop them. On the one hand, seeing Siwan Clark again was the very last thing she wanted to do. On the other hand, her guilt over abandoning these people weighed heavily on her heart, never mind her mind. Returning Siwan's phone felt like an appropriate act of contrition. 'I'll nip in. It's on my way.' She picked up the phone and turned one last time. 'Look after yourself, you two,' were her last words to this grieving couple who would never, in all probability, come to terms with losing their son.

The journey from Cynwyl Elfed, where the Clarks' lived, to Siwan's new build, west of Carmarthen, took only twenty minutes under blue skies. But pre-dawn rain meant damp roads and filthy spray-coated windscreens that required intermittent wipers and a squirt of screen wash every couple of miles. The ghostly bike rider outside B&Q flapping its arms had gone. No doubt it would be resurrected next Halloween. Gina took the Showground turnoff and doubled back to cross over the A40 towards where Siwan lived. But as she approached the newer roundabout which led to the university, she looked right and did a double take when she saw a surf-blue Mini Clubman. She recognised that car. She'd even driven the thing. Now Siwan was behind the wheel and just too far away for Gina to wave to her.

But it also meant that the woman she was visiting had left the building.

Gina groaned in frustration. What now? Quickly, she negotiated the roundabout and followed Siwan's Mini. Luckily, its colour made it an easy target. With a bit of luck, she'd be heading to the shops in town or back to the Clarks' for her phone. Either way, Gina would catch up.

The first part of that plan foundered the instant she exited the roundabout, expecting to see Siwan's car head left for Johnstown, but it crossed the A40, following the road that Gina had come in on. Okay, perhaps she'd decided to shop in the quieter village of St Clears. Less chance of being recognised or bumping into one of Dan's colleagues there.

Half a dozen cars stood between Gina's and Siwan's. But instead of heading west, the Mini turned left at a veterinary centre towards the village of Llanllwch, along the rather grandly, and ironically titled Manor Way, since the road was little more than a lane, narrowing at points to a single line of traffic. Only three cars separated the vehicles now. Gina thought about flashing her lights. But she was not in a police vehicle. All she'd do, if she started flashing, was incense those in front.

Her traffic colleagues would tell her that was too dangerous a way to stop anyone.

Best she follow until Siwan came to a halt.

There were no shops out here. Nothing but narrow lanes flanked by hedgerows and farmland. Gina glanced at her watch. She was on the clock. Still, no one would know that she'd left Beth and John Clark's. And something about this had begun to bother her a bit. This road led to Llansteffan. Another castle town on the western edge of the estuary with beaches and views across Carmarthen Bay to Worm's Head on the Gower. Perhaps Siwan wanted some fresh air.

It looked like the caravan that sat between her and Siwan shared the same idea. At the village of Llangain, at a T junction, the caravan turned right. When Gina looked left, she glimpsed the blue Mini disappearing around the bend on the B4312.

So, not Llansteffan, then, Siwan.

Gina followed. Now only half a mile of road stood between them. When she passed the brown sign showing Coed Green-Castle Woods 300 metres away, Siwan's brake lights remained visible on the right-hand bend ahead. When Gina got to that point, the road stretched straight and clear ahead for a mile with no sign of the Mini. The only turnoff was the left-hand turn into the parking for Green-Castle Woods. Gina indicated to turn in herself, waiting for oncoming traffic to pass. The parking here comprised two rectangles separated by a narrower strip of hedge. While she waited to drive in, Gina saw Siwan's Mini had pulled in on the left, hidden from the road by the low trees that hedged the car park.

Next to her car stood another vehicle. A BMW.

Gina knew it. Not many of that colour around.

And she recognised the figure leaning against that BMW too.

The road cleared, allowing Gina to turn. And she did. But instead of heading left to where Siwan had parked, Gina turned right and pulled in tight to the hedge. Just enough to be out of the eyeline of the person leaning against the BMW.

But Gina saw everything in her rear-view mirror. She observed Siwan get out of her Mini and greet the figure who pushed off from the BMW, all smiles. A hug ensued, followed by a brief discussion before Siwan Clark and DS Wil Hopper walked off to the left towards the woodland.

Gina sat in her car, paralysed, embarrassed, not quite knowing what to do or think. The obvious, the logical thing to do would be to get out, hail the two of them, hand over the phone and go.

But she didn't. She sat there, letting the spin dryer that whirled the thoughts around her head complete its cycle.

Siwan and Wil. It had a nice ring to it. But why on earth meet in this out of the way spot? There were only five other cars in the car park, and that included hers.

Don't be stupid, Gina.

You know why.

How would it look if they'd met in a public space? The

newly widowed partner of a police officer having a fling with another cop.

Fling.

That was stretching it a bit. What if they were simply out for a walk? What if Siwan fancied a stroll out of the glare and scrutiny of the public eye? And what if Wil had simply offered his support and a stroll in the woods?

On the surface, a more than plausible explanation.

No, not just on the surface. Surely, the only explanation.

Yet, she knew Wil Hopper from old. A charmer most definitely. But also a persistent bloody pest.

But a sex pest?

Gina let that thought soak in.

Now she was caught well and truly on the horns of a dilemma. She wouldn't follow them because she'd have to explain how she knew they were here. That meant admitting she'd followed one of them.

Not an option.

She decided to wait it out. She'd seen an entrance three hundred yards back where she might pull off. Park there and follow Siwan back home. Pretend the Green-Castle Woods episode had never happened, since it was none of her business. Yep, that would work. It would be fine.

Gina drove out and found the turnoff, wishing for somewhere nearby she could get a coffee. Instead, she made do with some tepid water from a plastic bottle as she waited for the flash of bright blue that would signal Siwan's Mini on the return journey. Meanwhile, there was always a bit of paperwork to do.

She'd been parked for fifteen minutes when a streak of common sense hit her. She'd arrived at this point via a circuitous route. But in fact, this spot was ten minutes from the centre of Carmarthen town on the other side of the woods. Instead of sitting here pondering, a quick Tesco's shop would kill an hour before she shot back to Siwan's and pretend nothing had happened. The distraction might even help calm her jitters.

Decision made; Gina began making a mental shopping list.

―――――

PAUL MENZIES HAD ALL the kit. Merino-base layer, lined-bib tights, a neck tube, waterproof jacket, and grip gloves. And that was before he'd even got on his bike, a Cannon-dale SuperSix he'd got off some twat who hadn't been able to pay his dues after a bad day at the races had sent him off the rails to double down on his coke habit.

That was not Paul's problem.

He'd always ridden bikes, but this one was as sweet as they came. And the thing about a bike was that the filth had no way of following him. In a car, they could track you. The bastards had their cars and cameras everywhere. But on a bike, you went places cars had no chance. In and out like a rodent up a sewer pipe. And he'd got into it. The biking. Once or twice he'd been followed by another biker, but you'd spot those a mile off. In fact, he was sure he'd seen that bloke Hopper on one once. He'd lost him easy enough. Fact was, most of the filth were too fat to get on a bike, never mind ride one.

And it meant he could do his rounds with no one knowing where he was. Nip to places on spec if he had to. Like now, in the college car park with Zac. The boy had found a buyer for some jellies. Easy enough to deliver a handful. Plus, he needed a photo of the girl. Zac had texted him to say she usually came in by half ten. They needed a photo of her for the pickup at Paddington. A recent one so there'd be no mistakes.

But Paul liked to do the details himself. Less room for error. Less chance of someone else fucking it up.

He stood with Zac in the car park astride his bike. With helmet, goggles, and in his kit, no one had a clue who he was.

'And here she is, regular as clockwork,' Zac muttered as a yellow VW Up pulled in.

Molly Allanby parked forty yards away. She slid out in baggy jeans and white trainers with a shaggy coat on top. But Zac walked across, phone out, full of himself as he strode up to her and pretended to show her something. Molly brushed him off with a shake of her head, and walked on, unaware that what Zac was really doing was videoing.

'She's a looker,' Paul said when Zac got back.

'You dirty old man,' Zac said.

'Statin' the obvious. And don't tell me that isn't why you picked her?'

'Dad, if we can get her, it'll be a way in, I'm telling you.'

Paul nodded. At first, he'd thrown the idea out as being completely fucked-up bad. How would muling up a DI's daughter be a good idea? But all they needed to do was set the hook. Other people would do the manipulating. Once they had this girl, others would work on the mother.

'Job done,' Zac said, as Molly, straight-backed, walked towards the building entrance without a backward glance.

'Send that to me. How quickly can you get rid of the stuff I gave you now?'

Zac nodded towards a couple of kids smoking at the end of the car park. 'They're waiting on me.'

'Okay. I'm off before some nosy teacher sticks an oar in.' Paul turned the bike and cycled away. Another job done.

CHAPTER FORTY

WHILE THE MENZIES took photographs of Molly Allanby, Warlow sat in the SIO office staring at the screen on the monitor in front of him and the satellite map imagery he had up there, trying to put together Dunbar's movements after he shot Barret and Clark. He still couldn't quite fathom why this aspect preoccupied him so much. After all, Dunbar was dead and so were Barret and Clark, but the logistics of it... mithered him. Even though Jess—or was it Molly—had only ever used this word a couple of times, it fitted, and Warlow latched on to it.

They had to assume that immediately after Dunbar got away, he'd got to his Land Rover and driven up to the Pantpriddog farmhouse to lie low. They'd searched the ANPR database for signs of the vehicle heading north but had found nothing. Canvassed the parking areas in Amroth, still nothing. The other option was more complicated. Dunbar had been on his own the day before, with Stacey out for the night and Dion staying with his friend. It remained possible that Dunbar might have taken the car up there prior to the shooting and travelled back down by some other route.

The Asda man's mention of seeing a cyclist should not be dismissed.

But that meant Dunbar would have had to cycle back up north to Pantpriddog from Telpyn Beach. And as yet, a search of CCTV in and around Amroth had not revealed many early morning cyclists that day. Those that had appeared had been in groups of two or three.

Not being able to tie off these loose ends kept nagging at Warlow and fed into the swell of disquiet rocking his mental boat over the murders, Eva and Reba's predicament, and Two-Shoes' meddling. Accepting those identifiable causes of his fluttery stomach was the easy part. The harder part, trying to put a finger on what else he wasn't seeing here, mithered him like an un-scratch-able itch.

And though lunchtime approached at a gallop, the flut-tering kept hunger at bay.

When Gil knocked on the door and put his head around, Warlow welcomed the interruption. What he didn't like was the serious expression on his colleague's face.

'Come in.'

'You look on top of the world,' Gil said.

'Back at you, as Rhys says so annoyingly.'

'Yes. You and I both may have overdone the fun and laughter these last few days.' Gil sat in the chair with the look of a man with something on his mind.

'Don't tell me this is about evidence recycling?'

'That? No, well, that lip-smacking offer of Two-Shoes is still simmering away but, no, that's not why I'm here.'

'One of the grandchildren ill? Last time you wore that expression, two of them had chicken pox.'

Gil snorted. 'No. Not them, either. This is much closer to home. And I am well aware of how this is going to sound coming from me under the circumstances. That's why I'm knocking on your door instead of sharing it with the team.'

Warlow sat up. The gnawing disquiet inside ratcheting up a notch. 'What is it?'

'Rhys.'

The DCI relaxed a little, though Gil wasn't usually this worried about their young DC. 'What's he done now?'

'It's that video he wanted to show us. The one about the DIY cover for an unsightly light switch.'

Warlow waited, anticipating more to come and letting Gil get there his own way.

'Fascinating stuff,' the sergeant added. 'You ought to have a gander at it. I've watched it twice.'

'Were there no cats playing a piano available?'

'It's worth a watch. That's all I'm saying.'

'You fancy having a go, then?' Warlow asked, attempting to lighten matters.

'No, I do not. But I've been running through what Rhys said about that light switch at Stacey Campbell's house. You were there, right?'

Warlow cast his mind back to the afternoon that Campbell met them at the house on Pondicherry Street. 'I was. I sent Rhys and Hopper upstairs to make sure no one was lurking up there.'

'And Rhys couldn't find the light switch to the bedroom.'

'No. Because it was an older part of the house and they'd plonked the switch in the middle of the wall—'

Gil ploughed on, cutting Warlow off. 'And Stacey Campbell had hidden it under the ingenious hinged light switch box masquerading as a photograph. Rhys has photos of that wall. It tickled him. He even sent them to me.' Gil showed Warlow a photograph of the landing wall and the images hanging there. The DCI peered at it.

'Can you see the odd man out?'

'No,' Warlow said.

'Neither could I.'

If there was a punchline here, it was a bloody long time in coming. 'Where's all this going, Gil?'

The big sergeant closed his eyes and inhaled. As if preparing to deliver something he'd wrestled with. Something unpleasant. His eyes snapped open. 'I'm speaking to you because to anyone else I might come across as a curmudgeonly, sulky old flatfoot with an axe to grind. But I want to state that I have no animosity towards the party involved. Truly. However, if it turns out I'm right, there'll be animosity aplenty.'

The sergeant had all Warlow's attention now.

'What if we've got this all wrong?' Gil asked, watching Warlow's face as he spoke, his own a serious mask of disquiet. 'What if Barret wasn't the target here?'

Warlow stared back at Gil, searching his expression, trying to work out what he was implying. 'That makes no sense at all.'

Gil kept his voice low. 'I've been asking myself all kinds of questions since I saw that video of Rhys's. Why haven't we been able to trace the 999 caller who reported Barret and his dog? Why were there no sightings of Dunbar's great big Range Rover that morning? And how would you know that a hinged box could cover an unsightly light switch if you weren't a DIY expert yourself?'

'This is worse than being in the bloody car with Rhys,' Warlow said. He had some answers and laid them out. 'The 999 caller was a pay as you go. I've been pondering the travel, too, and perhaps Dunbar went up to Pant-priddog the day before and came down some other way.'

'By bike?'

Warlow nodded.

'It's a bloody long way,' Gil pointed out.

'Great minds,' Warlow muttered. Not impossible, but

still a bloody long way there and back on the open road if you were fleeing a murder and trying not to be seen. 'And as for the light switch. No, I do not know anyone who's an expert in craft or DIY, so—' Warlow paused there as the metaphorical light switch flicked on in his head and the full weight of Gil's words cascaded over him like a ton of very hard and pointy bricks. 'Oh Christ, no. Gil, no…'

'Evan, I hope I'm wrong. I truly do.'

But Warlow wasn't listening. The patterns had all shifted inside his head.

What if we are getting this all wrong?

Warlow stood up. 'Get the rest of the team in here.'

'What if I *am* wrong?' Gil asked again.

'That's not the right question to ask, Gil. It's what if you're right.'

The look the men exchanged then contained a hundred caveats. 'Only one way to find out, then,' Gil said.

'Exactly. But I'll do the digging. Softly, softly.'

Gil nodded. 'Then I'll make sure the cavalry is standing by.'

For once, The DCI did not object.

CHAPTER FORTY-ONE

WARLOW PULLED up outside Siwan Clark's house. He got out of the car just as a Citroen pulled up behind him. His heart sank as Gina Mellings got out, bright and smiling as usual.

'Hello, sir. What are you doing here?'

'I could ask you the same thing. I thought you were off this case.' The smile on his face belied the challenge in his voice.

Gina, taken aback by Warlow's abrupt tone, spluttered out an explanation, 'I am. Siwan left her phone at her in-laws and I'm dropping it off.' She looked at the cars parked in the driveway, one of them a familiar BMW. 'That's Wil Hopper's car.'

'I hope so,' Warlow said. 'I'm meeting him here.'

'Sergeant Hopper is having a busy morning.'

Warlow frowned. 'What do you mean?'

'Nothing, sir… he's been with Siwan most of today.'

Warlow ran a hand over the back of his neck, his lips drawn back in a forced smile. 'Okay, well, now that you're here, you'd better come in with me.'

'Sorry?'

Warlow half turned so that his back was to the house. 'If you leave, it'll look strange. Listen to me, Gina. Get Siwan Clark to leave with you. Make an excuse to get out of the house. Take her for a coffee or something.'

Gina knew better than to ask questions. 'Okay… I can try.'

'I'll explain everything later.'

Warlow turned his face to the house, grinned again as if this was all the biggest joke in the world, and walked to the front door. Hopper opened it without the DCI needing to knock. 'Saw you arrive, sir. And you, Gina. Must be my lucky day.'

He let them in.

'Where's Siwan?' Gina asked.

'Upstairs.' Hopper led the way into the living room. 'I've been helping her with funeral arrangements.'

'Has she heard when they're releasing the body?' Warlow asked.

'Not yet. And any mention of funerals when she's with Dan's parents cause the floodgates to open.' Hopper shut the front door.

From above, Siwan's voice called down. 'Is that DCI Warlow? I'll be down in five minutes.'

Gina answered, 'Siwan, it's Gina, too. I have your phone.'

'Oh, thank God. I had no idea where I'd left it.' Siwan appeared on the landing, earphones once more around her neck.

'Shall I come up?' Gina asked.

'Yeah, fine.' Siwan backed into her bedroom.

Gina headed for the stairs but hesitated as a thought struck her. 'I still haven't bought you that coffee,' she said with one foot on the bottom step. 'There's that place at the bottom of Job's Well Road that does a lovely flat white with coconut milk if you're up for it. DCI Warlow says he wants one. Be good to get away from all of this for ten minutes.'

'Coffee sounds like a great idea,' Warlow said. 'I can catch-up with Sergeant Hopper if you two want to get some. I'm not going anywhere.'

'We can bring you back one, sir,' Gina said.

'I'll have one of those flat whites.' Warlow turned to Hopper. 'Wil?'

'I'm fine,' Hopper said.

'Fine,' Siwan called down. 'Just give me two minutes to answer some emails.'

Gina disappeared up the stairs to find Siwan.

Warlow turned to Hopper, who hadn't moved from the living room door. 'Do we have much to catch-up on, sir?'

'I hope so,' Warlow said. 'We've not seen much of you these last couple of days and we've had some significant developments on our end. Let the girls get the coffees and I can fill you in. Then I'll talk to Siwan and tell her what I can. It's remiss of me not to have done that yet.'

'I've been keeping her well informed, sir.'

'Even so. It's my case. I feel it's my duty.'

'Fair enough, sir,' Hopper smiled broadly. 'For a moment there, I wondered if you wanted to get the women out of the house so that we could be alone.'

'Why would I want to do that, Wil?'

'Could be that you wanted to talk to me about Sergeant Jones, sir. We both know he's getting a bit long in the tooth.'

'You need long teeth in this job sometimes.' Warlow found a comfortable chair and adjusted the scatter cushions before sitting, pulling two away and putting one on a side table, the other at his side. 'Long teeth help chew through the wrapping paper to get to the good stuff underneath.'

'Really?' Hopper said, grinning.

'Dog analogy,' Warlow said.

'Oh, that reminds me, sir.' Hopper walked out into the kitchen and grabbed his backpack. 'There was something I wanted to show you.'

Warlow watched as the sergeant returned with his bag reached in, rummaged a little and pulled out a heavy dark object.

Warlow started, staring at the barrel of the pistol in Hopper's hand. 'Where did you get—'

Hopper put his finger over his lips and pointed the gun at Warlow. Then he mouthed the word "phone" and made a gimme movement with his hand. Warlow half stood, reached into his pocket and took out his phone. The movement woke the screen to show the voice memo app running. Hopper pointed to the table. Warlow put the phone down. Still with the gun trained on the older man, Hopper picked up the phone and turned off the power.

'Nice try. I wondered why you wanted me here and not the station. Why was that? Keep me off guard? More chance of me incriminating myself?'

'Something like that.'

'Didn't work, did it?'

Warlow looked away before turning back, his eyebrows much closer together than they were. 'Tell me why?'

'God, how much time do we have?' Hopper pretended to look at his watch. 'All you need to know is that this was a fucking genius plan. A plan that had no right to work the way it did. But then, that's the way genius stuff is, right?'

'Is that what you are? A genius?' Warlow asked, his eyes flicking from the gun barrel to Hopper's face.

Hopper's lips drew back. 'What I definitely am is a rich copper now. And that is a bloody rare commodity.'

'Is that what this is about, Wil?' Warlow sounded incredulous. 'Money?'

'Money and a different life. I've lived that different life, don't forget. I've been there and seen the way these gangs operate. They have the best of everything. I've tasted that. It's like a ring of power. Once it's on, it's bloody hard to take off. I got the gun from a raid up in Merseyside. No one missed it. Easy as that.'

'You stole Dunbar's drugs.'

'No need. I got to the floating shipment before they were found on the beach. Dunbar told me where they were, attached to a buoy ready for pickup. You tend to cooperate with a plastic bag over your head, or the threat of it being put on again. You talk. Scream sometimes but talk too. There were a dozen wrapped parcels found. There should have been fourteen. I have the other two. The big guys think they've been lost at sea. No one misses it that way. They're worth two million each, by the way. Two little parcels worth four million quid. And I know how to sell it. There's a gigantic market out there.' Hopper grinned again. 'Just doesn't make sense, does it? Them getting all that money and us putting ourselves in harm's way for a few thousand quid a year.'

'You killed Daniel Clark.'

Hopper nodded. 'Yeah, well, multi-tasking was always my strong point.'

Warlow dropped his head. 'Why? Because you fancied his wife?'

'Right place, right time on that one. Money makes money. Everyone thinks Dunbar killed Barret and someone else killed Dunbar. The mystery man, aka me. Happiness all around.'

'We know, Wil.'

'You think you do, but you don't.' Hopper tapped the side of his head. 'This is how it goes from here. You and Gina turn up here, and what you don't realise is that the real killer is waiting. The same man who broke into Dunbar's and turned it upside down, the same man who threatened Stacey Campbell. All bullshit. All me. But also, the same man who made Dunbar drive up to an empty farmhouse through the night and kept him there, used his phone to communicate with Barret and Campbell. That part is all true. But he's desperate now, this man. He kills you and Gina and injures me. There's a struggle. I get the gun. I shoot at him, but he gets away. That'll explain the residue on my hands. I give chase through the rear of the houses, but I don't get far because of my injuries. The killer, in the meantime, gets away.'

Warlow nodded. He thought of Eva and Reba. Of the women upstairs.

'Nice idea about the phone recording. Shame.' Hopper smiled and tutted. 'You need to start thinking outside the box, sir.'

'In that case.' Warlow reached for the cushion he'd moved. He did it slowly. A tiny movement so that Hopper could see the other phone he'd secreted underneath it. This phone, DI Allanby's phone, was on and transmitting every word.

Something passed over Hopper's face then. An expression somewhere between disgust and shock and barely restrained rage.

'Who's at the end of this?' Hopper hissed out the words. And though he tried to give an impression of control, his voice faltered over the second word as a spasmodic swallow caught in his throat. He picked up the phone. 'Who's there?' He ground out the words again.

No one answered. Warlow had issued strict instructions that no one should engage. So far, everything was going as planned. But he should have known better. Hopper was on the edge, his world crumbling around him. He needed a way out.

'We know, Wil,' Warlow repeated softly. 'The world knows.'

'How did you—?'

'What does it matter?'

'It matters to fucking ME!' Hopper ground out the words through a clamped-up jaw.

Warlow knew better than to procrastinate. 'The light switch in Dunbar's house. Only someone with a home decorating craft fetish would have any idea about that. Or someone who'd been there before, searched for it and found it. You showed Rhys the switch because you knew where it was. Because you'd broken in and found it once already.'

Hopper's rueful laugh of understanding held not one iota of mirth in it. 'You worked that out, did you?'

'Not me. Gil.'

'That fat bastard?'

'We prefer clever bastard.'

'I should fucking shoot you now.'

Warlow nodded. 'There are half a dozen armed police officers in the street outside, Wil.'

'You're lying.'

'I'm not. You know how this goes when a firearm is involved. The Tactical Firearms Commander insisted.'

Hopper crossed the room to the window, fingered open the slats of the blinds and looked out. 'There's no one there.'

'Oh, there is.'

'Why should I believe you?'

'Because I'm here in front of you. I didn't want to believe Gil. I wanted you to explain it all away as us letting our imaginations run riot.' Warlow gave a disapproving shake. 'Did Dunbar give you the code for the house alarm in Tenby, too? Cutting the power cord was a neat bit of deflection.'

Hopper's eyes stared right through Warlow. 'You know

I can't go to prison.' He choked out the words. 'You know what they'll do to me.'

There it was. That little ember of doubt. The moment Warlow had been waiting for. 'These are special circumstances, Wil. If you give up now and cooperate—'

'Sir?' Gina's voice came from the door to Warlow's left. A question full of confusion and horror. Hopper moved the gun towards her, his eyes widening, the trigger hand wavering. The fluttering in Warlow's stomach that had been there for days exploded into a Catherine Wheel of sparks.

In one movement, Warlow grabbed the cushion at his side and lobbed it at the gunman.

Not the most damaging of weapons, a cushion. But it was solid and Warlow's aim was true as it flew towards Hopper's head. The gun went off, but by then Warlow was moving out of the chair, towards the open doorway where Gina stood, paralysed. He grabbed her, pulling her into the hallway, falling to the ground as he screamed out a word for whoever was listening on Jess's phone.

'Mayday. Mayday.'

A booming noise at the front and rear of the house filled his ears followed instantly by the sound of wood splintering. Warlow was on top of Gina and flat on the floor. Armed officers burst in from the front and rear. Warlow knew better than to move. Except to look back over his shoulder and see Hopper emerge through the living room doorway, rage distorting his face as he brought the gun down towards where Warlow and Gina lay.

A hard and loud voice boomed out. 'Drop the weapon or we will shoot! Drop the fucking weapon!'

A shot. Next to Warlow's head, a skirting board shattered. Splinters of wood flew up to pepper Warlow's face. Then four shots, louder, rapid, a different calibre.

'Man down! Man down!'

More shouts. More screams. A cacophony of chaotic noise. Warlow had to show his hands, put them behind his back. Then they were pulling him off Gina, dragging her out. Someone yelled Warlow's name. He looked up into the barrel of an automatic rifle before Jess came through the door and helped him up.

'Ours. He's ours!' Jess's voice sounded muffled through the ringing in Warlow's ears as he staggered outside into the garden, Jess supporting him on one side, Catrin on the other. He took in the surreal sight of a birdbath and a bird table, a little fountain sprinkling water at the edge of a lawn. But then he caught sight of Gina. Upright, pale as milk, but safe in Rhys's arms.

Warlow crossed to her and put his hands on her shoulders.

'You okay?'

Gina nodded.

'Jesus, when I saw you in that doorway.' Warlow let out a long swoosh of air.

Gina blinked, her eyes wide, the shock clear. 'I was only going to ask you how many sugars, sir. For the coffee.'

'One. Always one.'

A burly armed response officer walked out of the door and addressed Jess. 'Secure, ma'am.'

'Is he dead?' Warlow asked.

The officer hesitated, glanced at Warlow and the other officers, but saw the nod from Jess. 'Suspect is dead, ma'am. Took four rounds, all direct hits.'

In his head, Warlow heard an echo of one of Gil's favourite words. *'Tidy.'*

CHAPTER FORTY-TWO

AN ALMOST HYSTERICAL Siwan Clark emerged from the house a few minutes later. She'd heard the gunshots only through the muffling effect of earphones and had assumed they were a car backfiring. Her trauma came from two big armed cops bursting in, yelling, making her lie face down on the floor. She looked so awful the crime scene manager suggested that the paramedics take her to A&E.

'That'll be her out of commission for a good six hours, then,' Gil said.

Jess watched the ambulance drive away. 'Doesn't matter. We'll need her statement in due course, but not now. Best we get our own sorted first.'

Later, while Povey did what needed to be done at the Clark house, the team upped sticks for HQ. Warlow had to give a statement to include all the events leading up to what had taken place in the house. Jess assumed control, and he was more than delighted to let her continue. When he was done, the indexers and secretaries had all gone home and just five officers sat waiting for him when he arrived at the Incident Room. Gil's first comment on seeing Warlow walk in did little to dissuade him that the team was better off at that moment with Jess in charge. '*Iesu*, you look like Cadi dragged you through a hedge.'

'Thank you for that, Sergeant.'

'Backwards,' Jess added.

'Alright,' Warlow protested, but half-heartedly. He had felt better. 'Still, if none of you object, I'd like to get some of this straight in my head.'

'Thought you already had, sir. The way you set Hopper up.' Rhys sat next to Gina, holding her hand. Having given a much-abbreviated statement compared to Warlow's, she was now reaping the benefit of two cups of tea and a couple of biscuits.

Jess took the reins. 'The short version, then. Hopper was corrupted, and I mean morally, by his time under-cover. A touch of Stockholm syndrome, perhaps? But whatever the psychopathy, he became resentful and greedy for the traffickers' lifestyle and money. Having tasted it, he let it get under his skin. Gina tells us he's a narcissist. But as part of the job after his undercover stint, he surveilled Barret and Dunbar. He was aware of their operation, perhaps didn't share all that intel but instead, waited for the right moment. He steals a part of the consignment that Barret was supposed to pick up, letting the rest be found. Then sets Dunbar up as the killer, making it look like Dunbar took a cut somewhere along the line. My feeling is that when he saw Clark at Telpyn Beach, he shot him and Leanne Abbot to make it even more believable. After all, if he'd been a paid killer, he would not have been able to let police officers give chase.'

'Oh, God.' Catrin dropped her head in disgust.

'Does that tick all the boxes?' Jess asked Warlow.

'Almost.' Jess's words were like heavy hailstones beating down on his head. 'There are a few things that Hopper let slip that still don't quite fit. He wanted money and a different life, that I get, but the rest is hard to reconcile.'

'You mean, he could have wounded Clark? Like he did Leanne Abbot. Instead, he shot him in the head.' Gil's words were icy reminders of where Warlow was going with this.

But when Catrin elaborated, her voice rang with disbelief. 'You aren't trying to say that he killed Clark so that he could get close to his wife, are you, sir?'

Warlow shrugged. 'I'm considering all avenues here.'

Gina spoke up, 'I wouldn't put it past him, sir. He was a creep.'

But the team was spared further conjecture by a cursory knock on the door. It opened to reveal Two-Shoes with her pasted-on smile.

'I believe congratulations are in order.' She beamed at them. 'Though I don't remember being consulted about armed response.'

'You were in a meeting, ma'am, and the ACC was available. I had little time to consult,' Warlow said. Two-Shoes' nostrils flared. Warlow had sailed straight over her head for this one and he'd do it again in a millisecond. Having opted to challenge Hopper and knowing there was a firearm involved, he'd wanted armed officers on standby, not thinking for one moment they'd be needed. But Gina and Siwan Clark had been a complication. He'd tried to get them out of the building before confronting Hopper but had miscalculated. He'd have to live with that and looked forward to it revisiting him in the early hours of the morning along with all the other demons that chose that hour to call. Still, considering what transpired, Two-Shoes had not a leg, or even a shoe, to stand on here. Instead, like the ethical chameleon she was, she doubled down on the gushing praise.

'Never mind. All's well, et cetera,' she announced, not meaning a single syllable of it, then dropped her voice to show her earnestness. 'And especially well done for seeing through Sergeant Hopper, Evan. Genius.'

Of course, all wasn't well, except in Two-Shoes' squaring-away-the-case mind. Someone else had died today and Warlow couldn't simply shrug that off.

'I'd prefer not to hear that word, genius, ma'am. It's one Hopper used to describe himself. Besides, you are congratulating the wrong man. It wasn't me that worked all this out and put Hopper in the frame. It was Sergeant Jones.'

For the briefest of seconds, Two-Shoes looked like someone who'd accidentally ingested a fly, and who, knowing that no amount of coughing would bring it back up, took the only sensible option and swallowed it. She didn't dare regard Gil immediately, but eventually, her grin widened, and she swivelled first her eyes, and then her entire head over to where he sat. 'Well done, Sergeant'.

'All in a day's, ma'am. I put it down to experience.'

Warlow coughed. Or at least made a noise like coughing, which was better than the wheezy giggle that threatened.

'I am sure it is,' Two-Shoes said. 'Once again, first-class work. I shall leave you all to your celebrations.'

When she'd gone, Catrin, straight as a die as always, was the first to voice the group think. 'Anyone else fancy a big runny slice of humble pie with their lukewarm tea?'

Jess looked at her watch. 'It's well after six. And despite the superintendent's suggestion, I suspect that none of you feel like celebrating. We've all got homes to go to. I have a teenager's packing to check and Evan – you look bloody awful. You need to go straight home.'

'I'm going, don't you worry. But first I wanted a private word with Gina. That okay, Officer Mellings?'

Gina, surprised, nodded. Warlow walked her to the SIO room but didn't go in. He kept his voice low and asked her only a few pertinent questions before smiling broadly and giving her a quick hug. Rhys, waiting patiently, put his arm around her as they left the Incident Room, leaving Jess and Warlow alone.

'What was all that about?' Jess asked.

'An apology,' Warlow muttered. 'I should never have put her in that situation. But if I'd sent her away outside the Clark property when she pitched up, Hopper would have seen it as odd.'

'Has she forgiven you?'

'She said she'd do it all again in a heartbeat.'

Jess grinned. 'See what effect you have on these young-sters?' She studied his face and put a finger up to his fore-head. 'You have a cut there.'

'I know. Wooden shrapnel from the skirting board.'

Jess sighed. 'We need to get you some armour. Like a knight.'

'My joints make enough noise as it is. No need for any extra clanking.'

'Are you okay, though, really?'

'I am. Too tired to think properly.'

'What's there to think about. Job done.'

'Hmm.'

Jess frowned. 'Oh, God. Don't tell me there's more?'

Warlow thought there might be. Something about this whole business and the people involved kept gnawing at him. But he was too drained from events. The adrenaline rush of Hopper pointing the gun. Gina appearing in that doorway. He squeezed his eyes shut to try and banish the images. 'I need to let the dust settle,' he muttered.

Jess regarded him from three feet away with an unfor-giving look in her eye. 'You're not driving home, are you? You're staying at Gil's?'

'I am. He's gone to fetch the car.'

Jess nodded. 'They may give you a bit of tin to hang on your jacket for this.'

Warlow snorted. 'I think I twinged a rib when I fell on that floor. Hurts when I laugh, so don't. Please.'

Jess smiled. 'We're in tomorrow. You don't need to be.'

Warlow gave her a look.

Jess smiled. 'Alright. I'll see you then.'

CHAPTER FORTY-THREE

FOUR DAYS after Wil Hopper was shot by armed police in Daniel and Siwan Clark's house, the press coverage remained incessant. Though he'd been asked for a statement on more than one occasion, Warlow let Two-Shoes do the heavy lifting. Something she seemed to revel in, which made her even more of an odd fish in his mind. He'd said nothing to her about her misreading of Hopper, concluding that though efficient, she was about as emotionally intelligent as a slug. They both knew she'd been grooming Hopper for a role in Warlow's team. A gaffe of stupendous proportions whichever way you looked at it. And not her first when DI Caldwell came to mind. Another example of a corrupt copper who'd wanted it all, including Warlow's scalp. He'd told no one about these thoughts except Buchannan, who'd rung him from the port of Queen Elizabeth in Sri Lanka to congratulate him and commiserate with the loss of two colleagues. But Buchannan needed to be updated, even if everyone else in the hierarchy turned a blind eye.

Mid-morning on that Thursday, Warlow sat in the SIO

office sifting through reports that Hopper had written on his undercover work which made for a fascinating read. Jess had mentioned Stockholm syndrome, and here, with the benefit of hindsight, even Warlow could find hints that Hopper had been drifting too close to the dark side.

The psychologists would have a field day.

Jess had sent him a link to Siwan Clark's latest vlog. She'd been dressed in funereal black, with words flowing across the screen that meant nothing to Warlow, but which were, he was told, lyrics from one of Dan's favourite songs. All this while Siwan walked alone on a windswept beach, sporting a coat which, Jess had assured him, was from a designer who'd empathised with Siwan's plight and lent her the coat for the shoot.

The video had so far accumulated sixty-five thousand views, and it had only been up for a day.

Catrin appeared at the door with Rhys at her elbow and above her head.

'Got a minute, sir?' Catrin asked.

'Always,' Warlow replied.

They came in and sat down, leaving no room for anyone or anything else. They both wore serious, unhappy expressions. Catrin got straight to it. 'I've emailed you a copy of what I just received from digital forensics, sir. They found something on a flash drive on Hopper's keyring. They missed it first time around because it looks like a key.'

Warlow nodded, He'd seen the type of thing. Key shaped with gold contacts at one end.

'You need to listen, sir,' Catrin continued, emphasising the verb.

'Listen?' Warlow cocked an eye.

Catrin nodded and watched the DCI find his emails and open the audio file. The tech who'd found it had labelled it Telpyn/created 15/09/22.

Warlow clicked open the file and listened. A woman's voice came over the speaker. Clearing her throat and then speaking in a northern accent.

There's a man on the beach. He has this dog, a big dog. Looks like a Rottweiler or a pit bull. One of those dangerous dogs. It went for mine. I'm on Telpyn Beach.

After a ten-second gap, the words were repeated. This time in a different, more local accent. Then again, after another ten-second gap, the words were repeated in a softer, neutral English accent.

'Now listen to the other file I sent, sir. The one recorded by the dispatcher the day Barret and Clark were killed.'

'Police, what's your emergency?'

'There's a man on the beach. He has this dog, a big dog.'

'He has a big dog?'

'Looks like a Rottweiler or a pit bull. One of those dangerous dogs. It went for mine.'

'Where are you, madam?'

'Telpyn Beach.'

'It's the same,' Warlow said, his voice dry. 'The last one of the three from the hard drive. It's the same voice and accent.'

Catrin nodded, her mouth tight. 'We agree, sir.'

'We think this is Siwan Clark, sir. We believe she'd been practising those words in different accents months before that call. Two months before Daniel Clark was shot,' Rhys said.

Warlow's scalp contracted as a tingle spread down into the nape of his neck. 'Gina was right,' he said.

'Gina, sir?' Rhys looked confused.

'She saw Hopper and Siwan Clark the afternoon he was killed going for a stroll in the woods. And Siwan Clark had conveniently left her phone at her in-laws.'

'So that it couldn't be placed with Hopper,' Catrin filled in the blanks.

'Looked to Gina like they'd done that sort of thing before.' He threw the young DC opposite him a flinty glance. 'Did I tell you she was a keeper, Rhys?'

'You did, sir. Lots of times. But, this recording, does it mean Siwan Clark and Hopper…' Rhys struggled to articulate his thoughts. 'Were they… did they do this together? Why?' His incredulity was a testament to his good nature. But there was no room for any forgiveness in this case, which seemed to have something ever more rotten and harrowing waiting for them around every bend.

'Hopper's drugs haul, which we still haven't found, runs into the millions. There's half a million in insurance money coming Siwan Clark's way, too. Not such an unusual sum these days for a young couple with a mortgage on a new property. Lenders insist on it,' Warlow said. 'How much is the online fund up to?'

'A hundred k, the last time I looked,' Catrin said.

'That all adds up to a lot of money.' Warlow muttered.

'It's hard to believe all this is because of money, sir.' Rhys shifted in his seat uncomfortable with the concept.

'I'm not a big believer in the scriptures, Rhys. But if you're referencing the seven deadly sins, I'd say envy more than greed, has a lot to answer for. It's been making a comeback ever since phones became supposedly smart and we opened the Pandora's box that is social media. I'm not an expert, but I've sat in courts with people a lot more clued up about this stuff than I am. Fact is there is an epidemic of envy. A bloody pandemic. What do you see when you look at your feeds? You compare your humdrum life with celebrities with money. Or your friends on holiday, their new car, a new suit, that handbag you'd always wanted. The people posting are hungry for validation, so they post more vapid nonsense that'll make you feel even more inadequate. I'd even suggest tha some probably even seek to create that jealousy and envy. It's a toxic mix.'

Rhys still seemed reluctant to take it all in. 'Hopper and Siwan Clark, though?'

'She's an actress, Rhys. Used to doing different voices. Playing different parts.' Warlow's mind was filling in the blanks that, even ten minutes ago, looked as though they'd remain empty. 'Leanne Abbot told me Daniel Clark had been texting Siwan the morning they called at Telpyn Beach. So, Siwan knew where they were. Knew they'd been called to Amroth on a bogus domestic shout—' He stopped then as another appalling thought struck him. 'We need to get hold of that call, too. The one that took them to Amroth on a bogus domestic. I wouldn't be surprised if it's her using one of her accents. I bet that call came from an untraceable SIM, too.'

Rhys, as if he'd been punched in the stomach, could only blow out air.

'So, Hopper and Siwan Clark knew Daniel and Leanne Abbot would be the closest to Telpyn when the call about Barret and his big bad dog came in.' Warlow swallowed loudly as the pieces kept falling in place. 'She and Hopper must have planned it out. He'd watched Barret, was aware he liked Telpyn Beach. He'd texted him using Dunbar's phone to confirm his presence there, and to make sure that when we pinged that phone later, it would place Dunbar in the area, though he was miles away trussed up at Pant-priddog farm. That's the trouble with all this tech. Not too hard to manipulate if you're savvy enough.'

'My God,' Catrin muttered as if the room had filled with some awful stench.

'I doubt he, she or it was around that morning, Catrin.' Warlow heaved out a sigh. 'Hopper and Siwan Clark must have waited for exactly the right circumstances to put this in play. Barret already on the beach, Daniel Clark driven there by a siren call from his own wife.'

Both the young officers had lost their colour. 'It's hardly credible, sir,' Catrin said.

'Occam's razor, Sergeant. And that's exactly what Hopper said, remember? "It had no right to work as well as it did". They had time on their side. They may have waited months for the perfect set up.'

No one spoke for a beat until Catrin said, 'That's sickening, sir.'

'What if she says it isn't her, sir?' Rhys asked.

Warlow nodded. 'Voice identification evidence can be difficult. And she can say what she likes. But I've worked with a couple of experts. There's such a thing as a voice spectrogram. Doesn't matter what accent you use; your voice is unique when it comes to this stuff. Bit like a fingerprint.'

'That sounds good, sir.'

Warlow nodded. 'So, let's get her in for questioning.' Both junior officers stood up, their chairs scraping in unison across the floor. 'And Rhys,' Warlow added, 'get hold of Gina and ask if she'd like to sit in the observation room and watch us interview Siwan Clark. She deserves that.'

'I will, sir.'

Rhys disappeared to make a call. Catrin turned at the door. 'Who do you think is the bad influence here, sir, Hopper or her?'

'If it was her, she'd be a bad influencer, wouldn't she?'

Catrin's smile was as thin as a razor.

'She'll say she was coerced into it. We'll say it's conspiracy to commit murder, at the very least. But it's not our job to make judgements. Let the jury do that. We need to make sure there'll be no doubt left in their minds when they do. Have you told Gil and Jess?'

'Not yet, sir.'

'Right, time for a pow-wow, and I don't give a stuff if, according to some, that's a culturally inappropriate term, I've used it for years and I'm not going to change now. And as far as I know, you can't be arrested for that. It's your chance to shine, Sergeant. Let's not let this evil little sod wriggle off the hook. We need another warrant for her house. It's already been a crime scene, but we're extending the remit here. Oh, and tell Rhys to get that kettle on and Gil to get that Transplant box open. I feel a sudden urge for baked goods.'

They wouldn't rush into it. They'd set it up with all the right paperwork. Warlow fancied something early in the morning. Dawn raids always seemed to catch criminals on the hop. And if they were right, he had no sympathy for Siwan Clark. That well had run dry.

Much later, with the afternoon sliding into evening, when they'd agreed on a plan and Warlow was back in the SIO room, Rhys's head popped back around the door. 'Forgot to tell you, sir, Superintendent Goodey called in earlier, but you weren't here. She wanted an update.'

'Did someone fill her in?'

'DS Jones, sir.'

Warlow smiled at that. 'What did she say?'

'Nothing much. Except that at least it meant we could take the Menzies off our wanted list for now. She seemed pleased about that.'

Warlow was on the point of thanking the DC when it struck him. That final loose thread that had irritated him so much wafted in front of his inner eye and began to unravel in his head.

'You okay, sir?' Rhys asked when Warlow's silence became long enough to warrant the enquiry.

Warlow refocused on the young officer. 'I am, Rhys.

Never better. Now, find DI Allanby and tell her I want to see her, will you?'

Two minutes later, Jess stood on the threshold.

'We're arranging it for early tomorrow morning. Half a dozen Uniforms for the search and to carry out whatever we need into the vans. I don't expect much resistance but—'

Something in Warlow's face brought Jess to a halt. 'What?' she asked.

'You know what they say, that old cliché about all your life flashing in front of you at the moment of your demise. While I was lying there on the floor with Gina waiting for a bullet in my back, none of that stuff happened. But my brain seemed to go into overdrive. I saw things... differently. But it's only now I'm understanding all that.'

'What are you talking about?'

'Molly goes to London tomorrow, am I right? The much-vaunted long weekend?'

'She does.'

'Then I won't be with you to execute the warrant on Siwan Clark.'

'What?' Jess sounded incredulous.

'Give me five minutes to explain.'

'I'm all ears. I can't wait to find out what could be more important than conspiracy to murder a police officer?'

'Molly, and London, and Zac Menzies and his smug innuendos could be.'

'What the hell are you talking about?' Jess had the look of someone suddenly confronted by a lunatic.

But it was Warlow's turn to glance at his watch. 'Just listen to me for ten minutes, and then I'll give you the spare key to Ffau'r Blaidd, and we can both get on with what we need to do.'

'Why would I need a spare key to your place, Evan?'

'That's all a part of the bargain.'

Jess flicked up an eyebrow, but to be fair to her, all she said was, 'I'm listening.'

'Good. Then I suggest you take a seat for this.'

Slowly, Jess pulled out a chair and, with her eyes getting bigger by the second, sat and listened.

CHAPTER FORTY-FOUR

WARLOW GOT up at 5am the next morning. His phone dinged a message notification almost immediately. From Alun in Australia.

'Can we speak?'

His phone rang a minute later. A video call.

A face swam into view. Then a hospital room and bed. 'Hi, Dad. Oh, you're in your PJ's. Nice dressing gown, though. I know it's early, but Reba insisted. Ring your dad, ring your dad.'

'I'm up.'

Reba's voice came over off-screen. The image lurched as Alun swung the camera until his daughter-in-law appeared, sitting propped up, looking tired but smiling. And she had enough reason to smile, too, because there in Reba's arms, and with Alun's brawny hand resting on her tiny, swaddled body, was the most recent member of the Warlow clan.

Eva had her eyes shut, a wisp of dark hair on her head, and the puffy featureless face of a newborn.

But she looked… normal. Beautiful, complete, and normal.

'Sorry, Evan,' Reba said. 'It's been an eventful few days.'

'You're telling me. You lot don't mess about, I'll give you that. But she's there with you. And looking amazing and well. You both do.'

The camera settled on the baby. 'Yes, they said her sats were normal, and she wanted food. So, here she is. She's her father's daughter there alright, wanting food.' Reba's face again, this time with a ready grin.

'I am so glad that you two are alright,' Warlow said, shocked by the emotion in his voice.

'They've been brilliant here, Dad,' Alun this time. 'Bloody amazing.'

'That's good to hear. You spoke to Tom?'

'He's next on the list.'

'He'll be up.'

'He will be. Been texting me every couple of hours.'

Warlow nodded. 'So, you'll be staying in a few days longer?'

'Yeah, Reba's uterus is a concern.'

'Don't say it like that,' Reba protested. 'There is a lot more to me than my uterus.'

'I don't know about that. I only married you for your uterus.'

Reba thumped her husband one in the shoulder. None too gently either.

'Good to see you two looking so well,' Warlow said, unable to stop grinning.

'As you can probably tell,' Alun replied with a coy look and a rub of his arm. 'Reba's on some good meds.'

Warlow laughed. 'Let me see the princess again.'

The camera panned down to his granddaughter, eyes

shut, swaddled tight. 'You ought to give her a proper middle name,' Warlow said.

'Like what?' Reba asked.

'Macduff. He was untimely ripped from his mother's womb, too.'

'Hah, a Macbeth reference,' Reba said with a delighted giggle. 'Now that's worth considering.'

'Hang on,' Alun protested.

'Well, it'll be my nickname for her, regardless,' Warlow said.

'Bloody hell, Dad,' Alun muttered. 'Shakespeare at five in the morning?'

'Indeed. And this time, not a tragedy either. So, why the hell not, I say? Now tell me when they think you'll be able to take her home.'

———

THE 08.22 GREAT WESTERN RAILWAY SWANSEA to London service arrived a minute late at 11.12. Molly Allanby had all her stuff ready and on the airline-style window seat next to her as the train rolled smoothly into Paddington Station. She'd packed everything into her Osprey rucksack, much to her mother's disgust. Jess suggested taking one of those pull-along suitcases, but Molly was having none of that.

'I'm not fifty years old, Mum.'

And anyway, all she needed were three T-shirts, under-wear, two pairs of jeans and a dress/shoe combo in case she and Bryn ended up going out-out somewhere.

She'd done a bit of science revision on the way up, but the bloke in front viewing an Avengers movie on his phone distracted her. As did the people at each of the seven stations the train stopped at on the way. Molly'd grown up in Manchester with police officer parents, so she was no shrinking violet, but living in Pembrokeshire had sheltered her from the joys of people-watching. And doing it on a train was even more fun. It astounded her how so many people of all ages liked to get dressed in the dark. What were they thinking? That and the tingly excitement of seeing Bryn after a long couple of weeks put paid to all thoughts of revision after Swindon.

Some people had already made their way along the aisle to the doors at the end of the carriage, but Molly waited for the train to stop and for people to get off. She wanted Bryn to be on his toes on the other side of the ticket barrier, searching for her when she arrived. She liked the idea of being the last off, just to keep him guessing. Adding that extra bit of drama to the occasion made her smile.

And then there was her friend Gwennan's cousin. She was supposed to be in Leon, waiting for the blasted present. But that would only take a minute or two. After that, there was the complete city to get stuck into.

Molly took her earbuds out and stashed them away. She had her ticket in her jacket pocket and was good to go. She'd opted for the quiet carriage at the farthest end. It meant a long walk up the platform.

She noticed the police presence immediately. This was a busy station in one of the world's biggest cities and two armed officers loitered near an exit. A sign of the times. She took in a couple more ahead wearing yellow waistcoats stuffed with accoutrements, and one, all in black wearing a British Transport Police cap, had a spaniel on a lead. A spaniel wagging its tail maniacally as it sniffed at trundling bags and the odd passenger.

Molly grinned as the dog came up to her, lifted its nose and promptly sat down. The two yellow jackets officers a few yards behind looked over. She looked back at them, confused.

'Could you take your rucksack off, miss?' asked the dog handler.

'What?'

'The rucksack.'

Molly slid off the bag. Only now did she realise the handler was a woman.

'Go, Jasper,' said the officer. Jasper did his tail-wagging thing again and once more sat down.

'Do you have any drugs in the bag, miss?' asked the handler.

'Drugs? No, God, no,' Molly protested with a shake of her head.

The yellow waistcoats approached. The three officers made a semicircle around Molly.

'I do not have any drugs, I swear—'

The dog handler leant down to fondle Jasper and give him a treat. She kept her head down so that Molly, and anyone else watching, would not see her face.

'Molly,' said the officer, still looking at the dog, 'we're going to let you put the rucksack back on, and we're going to walk, with no fuss, away from the main concourse to the stairs behind us.'

'What?' A flustered Molly took a step back. 'How do you know my name? I'm meeting someone.'

'You are. And that's fine, but you have to trust us here. Bryn, isn't it? That's who you're meeting?'

Molly stared in bewilderment at the officer. 'How do you know Bryn?'

'Just walk with us, Molly,' urged the bigger of the two officers in yellow waistcoats. 'Less drama, the better.'

'I want to see your warrant cards.'

One of the yellow waistcoats grinned briefly. 'Good girl. Always ask for ID.' He pulled out a British Transport Police wallet with a warrant card on display and spoke into his radio. Molly heard the reply on the officer's speaker, confirming the name on the card.

The dog handler stood up. She wasn't grinning, but the encouraging tone of her voice jarred in Molly's confused head. 'Just walk with us, Molly. Everything is going to be okay.'

'How is this okay?' Molly protested. But she shouldered the backpack and turned towards the stairs behind her, a little way past the carriage she'd exited from, glancing anxiously back towards the ticket barrier.

They walked quickly, Jasper and the handler behind, the two officers either side of her, escorting her up the stairs and across the bridge towards platform one.

They walked past the statue of the Unknown Soldier and, just before the clock, stopped at a glass-fronted arched doorway, with the words MacMillan House in black letters on the curved pane above. Just inside the door was a desk with a doorway behind. To the left, a set of scuffed stairs led up. One of the yellow waistcoated officers opened the door for her and she stepped in. Another uniformed police officer came out from a room behind the desk and nodded at the little entourage.

'Up the stairs, Molly,' said Jasper's handler.

Molly decided she would not cry. But as the stairs turned and the door to platform one closed behind her, it was all she could do to hold tears back. 'Can I at least phone my mum?'

'Of course you can, Molly.'

She swung her gaze up to the voice on the stairs above her. 'Evan?' She croaked out the word.

Warlow walked down towards her and held her in a hug. 'You're okay, Molly. This is all okay. There's nothing to worry about.'

She pulled back, flustered, red in the face and more

than a little angry, the tears flowing now. 'If this is a prank, I'm going to seriously kill someone.'

But Warlow didn't smile. 'No prank, Mol. Jasper is the real deal. He's sniffed something in your backpack. But then, we thought he would.'

'What?' It was more a screech than a question.

'You're carrying a parcel for your friend, aren't you?' Warlow asked.

'For Gwennan, yeah, I'm supposed to be meeting her cousin here.'

Warlow led the way towards a suite of rooms and entered the first one.

'Can we see it?' the handler asked. 'I'm Jane, by the way.' She held out her hand and smiled. Molly, still bewildered, shook it before removing the cheaply wrapped parcel. Once more Jasper went into overdrive and did his sitting-down routine. 'We need to take this,' Jane said. 'Be back in a few minutes, right?'

Molly nodded and turned again to Warlow. 'Am I being arrested?'

'Absolutely not,' Warlow said with a smile. 'But you need to listen to me carefully. Come over here and sit down.' There were seats lining the edge of the room. Cheap, plastic things that felt cold on the flesh, even through layers of clothes. Warlow sat with a befuddled Molly next to him. 'That present you're carrying from Gwennan to her cousin isn't a present. Zac Menzies gave it to Gwennan to give to you. We think they're drugs, Molly.'

'Oh, my God. Why would Gwennan do something like that?' Molly asked, distraught. 'Is her cousin a part of this?'

'She doesn't have a cousin in London, Mol. That's all made up. This whole little charade with you and Jasper had to happen because they'll be watching you getting off the train. Watching you until they got their stuff. Then they'd film you handing it over. And when, in a month or two's time, Zac asks you to do something else, you'd refuse, and he'd show you the video of you handing the parcel over and tell you what was really in it. And you'd be horrified and disgusted, but you'd think you might just do what he asked to save you having to tell your mum. Save her career and all the shame that went with it. They might ask you to do worse things. Trap you in a spiral. That's what county lines are all about. Manipulation and coercion. But this way, it looks like you've been caught out in a random search. Nothing they can do about that. And you're a copper's daughter. So, maybe your mum might have a bit of influence so that the charges might be dropped or not even happen. Let them think that because there won't be any charges. Let whoever wanted the drugs stew. The key thing is, they've seen Jasper doing his thing through no fault of yours.'

'But Gwennan…'

'We have someone who will speak to her. She's a victim, too, Molly. But I suspect she won't be much of a friend to you anymore.'

Molly took all of this in and nodded. 'What about Bryn?'

'He's fine. I've spoken to him. He's waiting for you on Eastbourne Terrace.'

Jane came back in with the contents of the parcel on a tray. 'Three rolled-up bundles of money. Half a kilo of cocaine. Jasper's favourite, right, Jasp?' The spaniel wagged its tail.

'I had no idea,' Molly said, her eyes huge.

Jane's smile was apologetic. 'I'm sorry we had to frighten you. But DCI Warlow was insistent.'

'Can I speak to Mum?'

'She's waiting for your call.'

'She knew?'

Warlow nodded.

'My God, she is such a witch.'

'That's why you two make a great team.'

Molly had her phone out. And all Warlow heard next was, 'Mum, yes, of course it's me. I'm in Paddington Station with Evan, pretending to be a drug mule. As you know.'

Warlow grinned and gave Jane and Jasper the thumbs up.

CHAPTER FORTY-FIVE

SEVERAL HOURS, and a long return train journey and car ride later, on what had become a cold and wet West Wales November evening, Warlow parked outside Jess Allanby's rented property in Cold Blow. The front door opened just as Warlow exited the Jeep and he braced himself for the onslaught of a black furry bundle of energy. He let Cadi's attack run its course amidst a barrage of wagging tail, wet nose, and wriggling torso. Jess, who'd picked the dog up from Warlow's house on her return from getting Molly to Swansea train station that morning, had walked and fed her. She looked on from the open doorway in amusement.

'Tea is brewing. Or do you want something stronger?'

'Tea will be fine.'

Two minutes later, Jess, Warlow, and Cadi, who, commensurate with her greeting ritual, was parading around carrying Arthur in her mouth, were all in the kitchen. Warlow sat clutching a steaming mug of warm brown liquid.

'Molly calmed down, yet?' he asked.

Jess laughed. 'That's a work in progress. Though she is

now the hero of her own narrative. It's given her and Bryn something to talk about. Though he is sworn to secrecy.'

'Will he keep quiet?'

'You're kidding. He'd do anything for Molly. But what about poor Gwennan?'

Warlow marvelled at her ability to be sympathetic when her own daughter had almost been sold up the river. It said a lot about her, all of it good. She considered Gwennan as much a victim as Molly, too.

'I've got Dai Vetch on the case. He's a good man. It'll be an intervention, of course. The parents will need to be involved.'

'They're nice people.' Jess shivered. 'That could have been me and Molly Dai Vetch was talking to, though.'

'How did it go with the warrant at Siwan Clark's?'

'No resistance, but she isn't saying anything. My guess is she'll play the coercion card. But for now, she's no commenting her way to a court case.'

Warlow nodded and a little sigh escaped his lips.

'Thanks again for today,' Jess said. 'What time was your train… 6.30 this morning, was it? You must be exhausted.'

'I was knackered on this last leg from Neath to here. But I woke up when I got a text from Australia. I had to stop and read it. Look.' He picked up his phone and scrolled through the messages until he found the last one sent. An image accompanied it and it was this he showed Jess. There stood a beaming Alun and a much healthier looking – almost blooming –Reba in a wheelchair outside in the hospital grounds. And in her mother's arms was Eva Warlow.

'They're all okay?' Jess squealed.

Warlow nodded, knowing his grin must have been gormless. 'Take a look.'

'Oh my God, she looks like you.'

'Don't say that. She's had enough to contend with already.'

'God, Evan. That must be such a relief.' Jess couldn't stop smiling.

'Let's put it this way, laying there waiting to be shot by Hopper was a walk in the bloody park compared to wondering how this lot were doing every second of the day.'

Jess nodded. 'Never goes away, that worry, does it?'

'No, it doesn't.'

She handed back the phone and pushed a tin towards him. 'There are biscuits if you're hungry. I'm not a heathen.'

'I'm fine. I grabbed a sandwich at Paddington. And I need to eat something decent tonight.'

'Good,' Jess said. 'Because I have a proposal. I've booked a table for two. Early supper at the pub Molly and I default to when we're celebrating. It's more than half decent.'

'What are we celebrating?'

'Eva Warlow?'

That brought a spontaneous smile to Warlow's face. A rare event over these last days. 'Sounds good to me. What about Cadi?'

'No dogs after six, I'm afraid. But she'll be fine here for a couple of hours. You can pick her up when we come back.'

So, they'd be coming back.

But Warlow said nothing about that. He'd cross that bridge when he came to it. Though it was a bridge he'd almost crossed a few times already since Jess Allanby had come into his life. And somehow, he didn't think he'd cross it completely just yet. But a quiet meal and a tête-à-tête sounded like an acceptable first step. A tenuous one, yes, because it felt like he was learning to walk all over again when it came to this sort of thing.

This sort of thing? You make it sound like it's difficult, Evan. When it's the most natural bloody thing in the world.

He batted that thought away.

For now, in this quiet, fenced-off moment of time, he sipped his tea, fondled his dog, grinned at a good-looking woman, and dared to believe that all was well with the world for once.

———

A FREE BOOK FOR YOU

Visit my website and join up to the Rhys Dylan VIP
Reader's Club and get a FREE novella, *The Wolf Hunts
Alone*, by visiting: **https://rhysdylan.com**

The Wolf Hunts Alone.

One man and his dog... will track you down.

DCI Evan Warlow is at a crossroads in his life. Living
alone, contending with the bad hand fate has dealt him, he
finds solace in simple things like walking his neighbour's
dog.

But even that is not as safe as it was. Dogs are going
missing from a country park. And not only one, now three
have disappeared. When he takes it upon himself to root
out the cause of the lost animals, Warlow faces ridicule and
a thuggish enemy.

But are these simply dog thefts? Or is there a more sinister malevolence at work? One with its sights on bigger, two legged prey.

Only one thing is for certain; Warlow will not rest until he finds out.

———

By joining the club, you will also be the first to hear about new releases via the few but fun emails I'll send you. This includes a no spam promise from me, and you can unsubscribe at any time.

ACKNOWLEDGMENTS

As with all writing endeavours, the existence of this novel depends upon me, the author, and a small army of 'others' who turn an idea into a reality. My wife, Eleri, who gives me the space to indulge my imagination and picks out my stupid mistakes. Others who help with making the book what it is like Sian Phillips, Tim Barber and of course, proofers and ARC readers. Thank you all for your help. Special mention goes to Ela the dog who drags me away from the writing cave and the computer for walks, rain or shine. Actually, she's a bit of a princess so the rain is a no-no. Good dog!

But my biggest thanks goes to you, lovely reader, for being there and actually reading this. It's great to have you along and I do appreciate you spending your time in joining me on this roller-coaster ride with Evan and the rest of the team.

CAN YOU HELP?

With that in mind, and if you enjoyed it, I do have a favour to ask. Could you spare a moment to **leave a review or a rating**? A few words will do, but it's really the only way to help others like you discover the books. Probably the best way to help authors you like. Just visit the book's page on Amazon and leave a few words, or a rating, if you have the time. I've made it easy with country specific links which will take you to the page. Tidy!

AUTHOR'S NOTE

Lines of Inquiry: Welcome, dear readers, to the sun-kissed world of South Pembrokeshire, where the warmth of the coastal breeze envelops you, and the tranquil beaches beckon with their allure. It is within this idyllic setting that Evan finds himself entangled in a web of intrigue and danger. Of course, as with all of these stories, the truth is never far away. Tales of drug hauls washing up on remote west Wales beaches are, unfortunately, not the product of fevered imaginations, but all too true. Dial in the risks that go with infiltrating organised crime and we have our story. We also have memories of day trips to Tenby. There were indeed trampolines at one time. Before Health and Safety identified them as far too dangerous. It remains an amazing seaside town. And remember, these are only stories...

Those of you who've read *The Wolf Hunts Alone* will know how much Warlow loves his dogs. And who knows what and who he is going to come up against next! So once again, thank you for sparing your precious time on this new endeavour. I hope I'll get the chance to show you more of this part of the world and that it'll give you the urge to visit.

Not everyone here is a murderer. Not everyone… Cue tense music!

By they way, there is a map and a glossary on the website to help you with all those pesky Welsh words. All the best, and see you all soon, Rhys.

READY FOR MORE?
DCI Evan Warlow and the team are back in…

No One Near

Amidst the tranquility of the Welsh hills, a honeymoon retreat turns into a nightmare when a dead body is found decomposing in the bedroom. DCI Evan Warlow and his team brave the bleak December weather to investigate the chilling case.

As they peel back the layers of the victim's life, it becomes evident that innocence might be an illusion, and the rural community is far from what it seems. With another victim attacked and a third disappearing, Evan races against time to catch a merciless killer who's checking off names from a deadly Christmas list.

Can he unmask the culprit before the season's festivities turn into a bloodbath?

Tick-Tock — December 2023

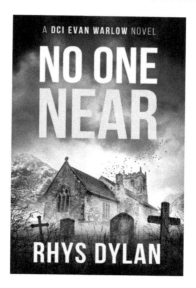

Printed in the USA
CPSIA information can be obtained
at www.ICGtesting.com
LVHW041400170124
769161LV00037B/746

9 781915 185174